PRAISE FOR
MIRRORLAND

"This ambitious blend of psychological suspense and horror casts a powerful light on the liberating power of imagination."
—*Publishers Weekly*

"Johnstone pulls out all the stops in creating an atmospheric mystery."
—*The Big Thrill*

"An inherently riveting and compulsive page-turning suspense thriller about the power of imagination and the price of freedom."
—*Midwest Book Review*

"Thrilling, dark, and propulsive, *Mirrorland* is an unsettling shape-shifter of a novel. This is a story about a mysterious death and a long-buried secret, but it's also a fascinating, terrifying portrait of how we seek refuge in our imaginations—and how easily imagination can be confused with reality."
—Anna Pitoniak,
author of *Necessary People*

"A dark and twisty thriller told with thumping heart and extraordinary tenderness—*Mirrorland* is as much a celebration of imagination and its escapism as an examination of trauma and its echoes."
—Kiran Millwood Hargrave,
author of *The Mercies*

"A sinister study in estranged sisterhood and the shape-shifting powers of repression and denial. Thick with propulsive twists and immensely readable."
—Sue Rainsford,
author of *Follow Me to Ground*

"Past and present collide in this vivid, ingenious, and totally absorbing thriller. *Mirrorland* is an amazing debut."
—T. M. Logan,
author of *The Holiday* and *The Catch*

MIRRORLAND

A NOVEL

CAROLE JOHNSTONE

SCRIBNER

New York London Toronto Sydney New Delhi

Scribner

An Imprint of Simon & Schuster, Inc.

1230 Avenue of the Americas

New York, NY 10020

First Scribner trade paperback edition January 2022

SCRIBNER and design are registered trademarks of The Gale Group, Inc.,
used under license by Simon & Schuster, Inc., the publisher of this work.

For information about special discounts for bulk purchases,
please contact Simon & Schuster Special Sales at 1-866-506-1949
or business@simonandschuster.com.

The Simon & Schuster Speakers Bureau can bring authors to your live event.
For more information or to book an event, contact the Simon & Schuster Speakers Bureau
at 1-866-248-3049 or visit our website at www.simonspeakers.com.

Manufactured in the United States of America

1   3   5   7   9   10   8   6   4   2

Library of Congress Cataloging-in-Publication Data is available.

ISBN 978-1-9821-3635-2
ISBN 978-1-9821-3636-9 (pbk)
ISBN 978-1-9821-3608-6 (ebook)

For Lorna

When you compare the sorrows of real life to the pleasures
of the imaginary one, you will never want to live again,
only to dream for ever.

The Count of Monte Cristo
Alexandre Dumas

*It always comes down to just two choices.
Get busy living or get busy dying.*

Rita Hayworth and Shawshank Redemption
Stephen King

PROLOGUE

September 5, 1998

The sky was pink. Which was better than red, El said, when we started to get scared again. Grandpa had always told us, *Red sky at night, sailor's delight; red sky in the morning, sailor's warning.* And he used to be one. The wind was cold, getting colder. El's face was still streaked with tears, and her fingers twitched. I couldn't stop shaking.

We held hands and followed our noses, until every street of high, crowded tenements and terraces blurred into one looming dark house where the murderers of children lived and lurked and watched. But we saw no one. Heard no one. As if we were in Mirrorland again. Safe and scared. All that changed was the smell of the firth, getting stronger, nearer.

The harbor was grease and oil and metal and salt. Seagulls were waking up, crowing like cockerels. We stopped next to a wooden warehouse, stripped and wet-dark. In front of it, a crane that dangled a hook on the end of rusty chains and a stony slope that soon disappeared underwater.

High tide. The only time to set sail for the high seas.

El gripped my hand tighter as we looked out at all the bobbing round buoys, the long pontoons. We saw sailboats, white and smooth with rattling metal masts. And out beyond the estuary, a tanker on the horizon. None were what we wanted. None were why we were there.

I searched through my rucksack until I found Mum's powder compact. Started to press its pad against El's cheeks.

"Your eyes are all red inside," I whispered, as she pretended it didn't hurt.

1

"You're still bleeding," she whispered back, hoarser than I was even though I had done more screaming.

"What are you two lassies doing out at this time of night, eh?"

His flashlight made me blink, but when I could look, he was just like Mum said he'd be: leathery and gap-toothed, a white and bushy beard. An Old Salty Dog.

"I'm Ellice," El said. I felt the points of her nails against my fingers, but her voice was still like the harbor water. "And this is my twin sister, Catriona."

"Aye?"

He came closer then, and when he staggered, I could smell rum. My heart beat faster. I squared my shoulders. "We want to join a pirate ship."

The light from his flashlight bounced dizzy white circles that made my eyes squint and water. And then he said a curse word— one of Grandpa's, but not one of his favorites—and began backing away from us, eyes wide like the Grebo masks of Côte d'Ivoire in Grandpa's encyclopedias.

"Stay right there, all right? Don't be going nowhere. All right?"

"But is there a ship due soon?" El tried to shout, as he disappeared back into the shadow of the warehouse. We heard its door creak open and bang shut, and El turned to me, made a choked sound, let me go. "Oh no! Your sweater. We forgot to take off your sweater!"

I suddenly felt something worse than just scared. As if I'd been swimming deep down in the cold and black and someone had reached in and pulled me out, and I couldn't remember how to breathe again. I dropped my rucksack, pulled off my coat, and even though I hurt all over, even though El's fingers pinched and scratched, I got my sweater off over my head, and dropped it on the stony ground as if it were crawling with spiders. I could smell it then, sour and warm.

"What'll we do with it?" El said, and her voice wasn't still or calm anymore. "He'll come back. He'll come back!"

She ran around the warehouse, picked up a broken mooring ring flaked with rust. We tied the sweater's arms around it in fisherman's knots, our hands cold, teeth chattering, and then we ran back to the choppy water beyond the harbor, threw it as far in as we could. The splash was loud. By the time we'd run back to the stony slip, we were out of breath, both trying so hard not to cry it sounded like we were choking.

When the wind suddenly turned, pushing us back from the edge, I thought I could smell the blood again: sour and dark. But the briny sea, like the squeeze of El's hand, was stronger.

"A wise sailor never leaves port on a Friday," I whispered.

El's fingers started to hurt mine. "It's Saturday now, you idiot."

But I knew she was just as scared. I knew she was wondering if it was too late to go back. "Will we be all right, El?"

We looked out across the firth, past the small green islet of Inchkeith and that faraway tanker. Shivering, still holding hands, close enough to feel each other's heartbeat as that red sky moved in from the North Sea, spreading like a bruise. El didn't look at me again until we could see it creeping over the breakwater.

And then she smiled. The wide, terrible smile that I knew she'd wanted to smile even along all those endless empty streets. She didn't stop, even when we heard the first engine, the first siren. Or when the warehouse door creaked open and slammed shut again.

She smiled, smiled, smiled. "We will not leave each other. Say it."

Footsteps crunching towards us. Another, louder curse. Enough lights to blind us so that we could no longer see the firth at all. Only each other.

"We will not leave each other," I whispered.

She gripped my hand even tighter, and I swallowed, watched her smile get sharper, darker, watched it disappear. "Never so long as we live."

"You'll be okay," a man who wasn't the Old Salty Dog said.

And a woman with kind eyes and a softer light stepped between us, held out her other hand. "Everything will be all right now."

*

And that was the day our second life began.

PART ONE

CHAPTER 1

I wasn't there when my sister died.

Ross called me; left close to a dozen voice mail messages before I checked any of them, each one more desperate than the last. And I'm ashamed to say that it was always his voice I heard first—familiar and forgotten, hardly changed at all—rather than his words.

I watch the news reports in Terminal 4 of JFK, during a seven-hour layover that eats away at my sanity until I have to turn on my laptop and look. Sitting on a stool in a noisy, too-bright Shake Shack, ignoring my cheeseburger as I scroll through the first of three reports on the BBC News webpage for Edinburgh, Fife & East. I should probably be just as ashamed that he is what I see first too. Even before the black headline: **Fears Grow for Missing Leith Woman.**

The first photo is subtitled DAY ONE, 3 APRIL, but it's already night. Ross is pacing a low stone wall next to the firth, caught between two silver lampposts that cast round, flat light. Though his face is turned away from the camera, no one could mistake his agitation for anything else: his shoulders are high, his hands fists. The photographer has caught the bright spotlights of a returning orange-and-blue lifeboat, and Ross's face is turned towards both it and the frozen fury of a wave breaking over the end of the pier. There was a storm soon after she went missing, he said in more than one message, as if it were my not knowing that extra terrible detail that had stopped me from replying.

It takes nearly two glasses of merlot in a darker, more subdued bar, well out of earshot of Shake Shack, before I'm able to play the first video. DAY TWO, 4 APRIL. And even then, when El's photo flashes up on the screen—laughing, head thrown back in what she always called her "Like a Fucking Virgin" pose, her silk blouse transparent, hair bobbed and silver-blond—I flinch and press pause, close my eyes.

Run self-conscious fingers through my tangled, too-long hair. I finish the wine, order a third, and the waiter who brings it to me stares so long and hard at my laptop screen, I wonder if he's having a stroke. Before I realize, of course. Amazing what you forget; facts of life that were once as natural as breathing. He thinks he's looking at a picture of me. Below the words: Is ELLICE MACAULEY ALIVE OR DEAD?

I pluck the buds out of my ears. "My twin sister."

"Sorry, ma'am," he says with a megawatt smile, managing to sound like he's never been sorry a day in his life. The constant smiling and *ma'aming* wears me out, makes me feel irrationally furious. That this is the only thing about America that I won't miss makes me feel more tired, more pissed off. I think of my condo on Pacific Avenue. The hot crazy circus of the boardwalk and Muscle Beach. The hot crazy nights of dancing in basement clubs where the walls run with sweat. The cool turquoise calm of the ocean. An ocean that I love.

I take another big swallow of wine, put my earbuds back in, press play. The photo of El cuts to a reporter: young and earnest, probably still in her twenties, her hair whipping viciously around her head.

"On the morning of April the third, Leith resident Ellice MacAuley, thirty-one, sailed from this yacht club in Granton Harbour on the Firth of Forth, and has not been seen or heard from since."

I start as the camera zooms out from the yacht club to show the distant rail and road bridges at Queensferry in the west, before panning back east towards the outcrops of Earlsferry and North Berwick. Between them, the gray firth and the low rolling hills of Kinghorn and Burntisland on the opposite shore. Then back to the harbor, its bobbing round buoys and long pontoons and white sailboats with rattling masts. A low stone slope into the water. A different crane. No warehouse.

How could I not have realized before that it's the same harbor—a place I haven't thought about in decades, and yet there it is, almost unchanged. A shiver cricks my neck. A dread that I don't want to examine any more than anything else that's gone through my mind since all those voice mail messages began filling up my inbox. I reach for my wine again, relieved when the camera cuts away from the harbor to archive footage of lifeboats and helicopters.

"The alarm was raised when Ms. MacAuley failed to return to the Royal Forth Yacht Club, and it was further determined that she had not reached her intended destination in Anstruther earlier in the day. The Coastguard and RNLI have been involved in the search, but continuing bad weather has significantly hampered their efforts."

A man: jowly, mostly bald, solemn like the reporter, but with a glint in his eye like he's faking it, stares into the camera, arms folded. Underneath his too-large belly: JAMES PATON, HM COASTGUARD SAR MISSION CO-ORDINATOR, ABERDEEN. "We know that Ms. MacAuley was a competent sailor—"

Do we? I think.

"—but, looking at the prevailing wind speed through the firth on the morning of the third, we estimate that she had already been missing for approximately six hours by the time the alarm was raised." He pauses, and even though he's only being filmed from the waist up, I can tell he's widening his stance, like a gunslinger. He only just manages not to shrug. "Over the past seventy-two hours, the temperature of the firth has been no more than seven degrees Celsius. In those conditions, a person could be expected to survive no more than three hours in the water."

Arsehole, I think. In El's voice.

The camera cuts back to the reporter, still pretending not to be bothered by her ruined hair. "Now, at the end of day two of the search, and in worsening conditions," she says, "hope is fading fast for the safe return of Ellice MacAuley."

A picture of El and Ross on holiday somewhere fills the screen— all tan and white teeth; his arm flung around her shoulders as she leans in, tips up her chin to laugh. I can see why the coverage is so eager and extensive. They're beautiful. They look at each other like they're both starving and satisfied. The intimacy of it makes me feel uncomfortable; it sours the wine in my stomach.

I pick up my phone, check the weather app. Edinburgh is still the second location after Venice Beach; I've never dwelled too long upon why. Six degrees and heavy rain. I look out the window at the dark, the long white lines of runway lights.

It's barely six a.m. in the UK, but there's already a new video:

9

DAY THREE, 5 APRIL. I don't watch it. I already know that nothing's changed. I know she still hasn't been found. I know that now, even more than yesterday, they don't expect her to be. There's another image below it, time-stamped less than two hours ago. DOCTOR HUSBAND OF MISSING LEITH WOMAN LOSES HOPE. The picture catches my breath. It hurts to look at him. It would hurt *anyone* to look at him. Ross is hunkered down next to a low wall, knees high and close to his chin, his hands clasped around the back of his neck, pressing his elbows tight together in front of himself like a shield. A man in a long anorak is standing next to him, looking down and obviously speaking, but Ross isn't paying attention. Instead, he's looking out at the firth, his mouth open and teeth bared in a wail of despair and horrified grief that I can almost hear.

I close the laptop with a too-loud slam. Drain my wine as people turn to look. My hand is shaking, eyes stinging. The hours between New York and Edinburgh loom and at the same time aren't enough. I don't want to go back. I'd give anything—*anything*—to never, ever, go back.

I get up to move on to another bar; I can't bear to face the *ma'am* waiter again. I grab my laptop, my bag, toss a twenty on the table. I'm more than a little unsteady as I weave between tables. I should probably have eaten that burger. But it doesn't matter. *None* of it matters. People are still looking at me, and I wonder if I've said it aloud, until I realize I'm shaking my head instead. Because I have to believe it. I have to believe that nothing has changed. That all this fear and quickening dread doesn't mean anything at all. I think of Edinburgh, of Leith, of that gray flat-stoned house with Georgian-bar windows in Westeryk Road. I think of Grandpa's gap-toothed grin, and it soothes the worst of my panic. *Nane ae it amounts tae a pun ae mince, hen.*

I wasn't in Edinburgh when my sister died. I wasn't in LAX or JFK. I wasn't even on the wrought-iron balcony of my California condo, looking out at the Pacific and drinking zinfandel and pretending I was exactly where I've always wanted to be.

I wasn't anywhere when my sister died.

Because she isn't dead.

CHAPTER 2

I stand on the sidewalk until the bus has lumbered out of sight. Either the weather app on my phone has broken or the weather finally has: it's cold and sunny in a cloudless sky. The wind from the city—smoke and double-deckers and breweries and coal fires—is thin and biting. I can smell the sea. Everything and nothing is the same. The houses are the same houses, the road is the same road, there's still a ground-floor mini-market just where it always was: Colquhoun's of Westeryk. A sudden, colder breeze lifts the hair from my neck, bringing with it another salt-sour taste of the sea. It must be cold too. I try not to think about that smug gunslinger. A lot colder than this.

I look at 36 Westeryk Road in increments. The metal gate is the same. The squared-off high hedges with patches of yellow and the path bisecting the flat lawn. I don't need to look up to know that the solemn symmetry of gray ashlar bricks and tall narrow-paned windows is the same. The two flanking stone walls with white fireclay balusters and red wooden doors leading to alleyways alongside the house.

I falter suddenly and swing around. There's no one there. But the sense that there had been is strong enough that I step forwards, my heart beating too fast. I look across the road at the red sandstone terrace El and I used to call the Gingerbread Coop. Its narrow houses and neat white lintels and window boxes full of pansies and petunias, so at odds with the looming gray house it has always faced. That sense of being watched—*examined*—intensifies; the hairs on the back of my neck shiver. *Stop it.*

I turn back to number 36, open the gate, walk the path, climb the four stone steps, and there is the red metal boot scraper, the red last step, the huge red front door. It's ajar. I once asked Mum why it wasn't called the Red House, and she blinked, gave me the *stupid girl* look that is sometimes all I can remember now when I think of her.

It's the Mirror House. Just like you and Ellice. Just like Mirrorland.

Perhaps El and I once had the same obdurate symmetry as this house—no perhaps about it, I know we did—but nothing can stay the same forever. I push open the door, step up into the entrance hall. Black and white checkered tiles. Dark oak wainscoting and crimson-red walls. As if to prove me straightaway wrong. I close my eyes, and at once I hear the heavy turn and clunk of a dead bolt. A flash of black dark. *Run.* But when I spin around, the door is still open, still warm with sunlight. *Stop it.*

I turn the brass handle of the second door, catch a glimpse of my big-eyed reflection inside it before the door opens onto the hallway proper, the curving shadow of the staircase. The old carpet is gone, in its place shiny parquet. The sun pierces the fanlight above the door, and at once I see myself sitting cross-legged inside that spear of light, reading Grandpa's encyclopedias, the carpet scratching my skin like pricking pins.

The hallway walls are crowded with familiar mounted plates, small and large, scalloped- and gilt-edged: finches, swallows, robins perching on leafy branches, bare branches, snowy branches. The tall oak telephone table and grandfather clock are exactly where they used to be as well, flanking the drawing room door. And even if that seems too unlikely—too bizarre, almost twenty years later—there they stand sentinel nonetheless. The smell is exactly the same, utterly unchanged: old wood and old age and old memory. My incredulity is tempered with a relief I hadn't been expecting, and an unease that I had. And when I take a long, deep inhale, something inside me loosens and breaks free. It's still a little like fear—it's brittle and has sharp edges. But it's warm too. Deep like the ocean. It has expectations. Too big a part of me is glad that I'm back here after all. Glad that all is exactly, incredibly, inexplicably the same as it ever was.

I turn into the kitchen as if this still really is my house, and there is Ross, on his hands and knees on the blue and white tiles. He looks up. Blinks. Flinches.

And I'm too busy thinking of all the things I can't say to him to come up with anything better than "I'm flattered. Most folk just say hi."

⋆

"Cat." His voice breaks as though my name has two syllables. When he stands up, I realize that there are slivers and chunks of smashed white china scattered all over the tiles between us.

"Can I help?"

"I'll sort it later." He steps over the broken china and stops a foot short of me. His smile is as tight as mine feels. "How's LA?"

"Hot."

His knuckles are white. "How was the journey?"

"All right. Long." I don't know why I can't speak. I don't know why we're trying to have this ridiculous conversation. Ross looks the same but different, just like the house. His face is pale, the skin beneath his eyes heavier than in those news reports, no longer purple but black. His stubble is dark, his hair messy as if he's run his fingers through it too many times. Underneath all that he looks older, I suppose, but it hasn't done him any harm. Not the way El going missing has. There are more wrinkles around those peat-brown, silver-flecked eyes; his face is leaner. I wonder if his smile is still crooked, if his left canine still slightly overlaps his front incisor. Immediately, I look away.

"They say it's always hardest coming back," he says.

"Yeah."

He clears his throat. "I mean, traveling west to east."

"I know," I say. "I know what you mean."

His T-shirt is wrinkled, his arms are goose-bumped. He steps forwards. Stops again. Rubs his hands against his face.

"God, how many years has it been?"

"Twelve?" I whisper, as though I don't know, and my throat closes up and my eyes start to burn. Suddenly all of it—El, him, this house—is too much. I'm tired and I'm sad and I'm scared, and most of all I'm so fucking angry—angry that I've had to come back here, angry that even one part of me *wants* to be back here. It's been less than twenty-four hours, but when I think of my beautiful Pacific Avenue condo now, it has the texture of glossy paper. Just some place I visited a long time ago.

Maybe that's why I don't step away from his embrace. Why I let him put his arms around me and pull me so tight against him that I can feel the scratch of his stubble against my neck, the warmth of his breath against my skin, the vibration of his voice—familiar and forgotten. Utterly unchanged.

"Thank God you've come back, Cat."

*

I try not to look at anything else as we climb the stairs, but it's impossible. The oak banister, curving and smooth under my palm, the spill of green and gold light from the stained-glass window onto the mosaic stair tiles. The second-floor landing squeaks underfoot exactly where I'm expecting it to, and I've already begun walking towards Bedroom 1 before I catch myself. Ross is standing inside the door opposite, with my suitcase in his hand and an embarrassed half-smile.

"That's our room," he says.

"Sorry," I say, walking back across the landing too quickly. "Of course it is." I can't help wondering what it looks like now. When El and I shared it, the bedspread was golden yellow, the wallpaper a rain-forest explosion of green and brown and gold. At night, we'd close the big wooden shutters over the window and pretend we were Victorian explorers in the Kakadu Jungle in Northern Australia.

I follow Ross into Bedroom 2. The guest room. Familiar neat pine furniture and a tall window looking out onto the back garden. There's a paint-spattered easel and pallet in one corner, two canvases leaning against the wall. Angry oceans, green and foaming white, under dark and thunderous skies. El could draw and paint before she could read.

"Is this okay?" Ross asks.

I recognize the cupboard alongside the wardrobe with a jolt; wonder in the same moment if it's still full of face paints, orange wigs, multicolored nylon jumpsuits, and false red noses. But its hinges and seams are painted shut. I look around the room again, at the wallpaper striped white and red and pink, and I start to smile. Of course. I'm in the Clown Café.

"Cat?"

"Sorry. Yes, this is fine. Great."

"You must find it weird being back here, I guess."

I can't quite meet his gaze. I still remember the day he told me they'd bought the house. I was sitting outside a loud and overcrowded bar on Lincoln Boulevard, feeling hungover and ridiculously hot. I'd been in Southern California for a few years by then, but still hadn't acclimatized to relentlessly sunny. The first thing I felt was shock. Everything else came after the call was over and I was left alone to imagine them curled up in the drawing room in front of the fire and its bottle-green tiles, drinking champagne and talking about the future. Although it wasn't the last time he called me, it was the last time I answered.

"I just can't understand how everything can still be here, after all this time. I mean, other people must have lived here since—"

"An older couple were here for years. The MacDonalds," Ross says. "They must have got most of the original furniture in the sale and didn't change much. When we bought it, we replaced most of what was missing."

I look at him. "Replaced?"

"Yeah. I mean, they left the big stuff: the kitchen cabinets and table, the range, the chesterfield. The dining room furniture. But most everything else is new. Well, not *new*—you know what I mean." His smile is strained and unhappy, but there's anger in it too. "Felt like every weekend, El wanted to drag me to antique shops or fairs."

I flinch at her name—I can't help it—and Ross looks at me carefully, holds my gaze too long.

"You never asked me why," he says. "Back then. Why we bought this place."

I turn away from him. Look towards the window and that painted-over cupboard door.

"It came up for auction. El saw the notice in the paper." He sits heavily down on the bed. "I thought it was unhealthy to dwell on the past. I mean . . . you know what I mean . . ."

And I do. I was happy here. Mostly. And I've been so unhappy since. But I still know it's true: you can never go back.

"I got the deposit together, helped her buy it." He shrugs. "You know what El was like when she wanted something."

My face heats, my skin prickles. He's talking about her in the past tense, I realize. I wonder if it's because he thinks she's dead, or because she and I don't have any kind of a present anymore.

He clears his throat. Reaches into his pocket. "I figured while you were here you'd need these. So that you can come and go when you want." He holds out two Yale keys. "This is for the hallway door, but I usually leave it unlocked, and this is the night latch for the front door. There's a dead bolt too, but there's only one key, so I'll stop locking it."

I take the keys, squash flat the memory of black dark. *Run.* "Thanks."

He rocks forwards onto his feet as if yanked by strings. He starts to pace, running his hands through his hair, seizing big fistfuls. "God, Cat, I need to be doing something, but I don't know what. I don't know what!"

He wheels on one foot and lunges towards me, eyes wide enough that I can see the red threads around each iris. "They think she's dead. They keep skirting around it, saying it without saying it, but it's obvious that's what they think. Tomorrow, she'll have been missing for four days. And how long do you reckon they'll keep looking before all their muttering about weather and time and resources becomes *I'm very sorry, Dr. MacAuley, but there's nothing more we can do?*" He throws up his hands. His T-shirt is stained dark at the armpits. "I mean, it's not just her that's disappeared, it's a twenty-foot boat with a twenty-two-foot mast! How can *that* just vanish? And she was a good sailor," he says, still pacing. I'm pretty sure this isn't the first time he's said all this to someone. "She knew I hated it when she went out alone on that bloody boat." He drops back down onto the bed, strings cut. "I always told her something like this could happen."

"I didn't even know she could sail," I say. "Never mind owned a boat." Moored at Granton Harbour. I suffer an image of us standing at the bowsprit of the *Satisfaction* instead—laughing, shouting, the hot tropical wind tangling in our hair—and I feel a stab of something between longing and fury.

"She bought it online a couple of years ago." Another flash of anger. "Binding contract, nonrefundable deposit. She was making

16

good money from commissions, the occasional art show, but not enough. So I had to pay the balance. And she got what she wanted. Before she even knew how to bloody sail the thing. God, I wish I'd never—" He draws his hands down his face, dragging at his skin. "It's my fault. All of it."

I sit down next to him, even though I don't want to. I want to tell him that she's not dead, but I can't. He isn't ready to hear it yet. "How can it be your fault?"

He was away: some last-minute psychopharmacology conference in London. An annual requirement for all practicing clinical psychologists. "'The Efficacy of Psychoactive Therapies versus Safe Ratios,'" he says. As if that's important. As if I have a clue what that is. He blames himself for not being here, for not stopping her going out, even though we both know it wouldn't have made a difference. But that isn't all of it. There's something else, I can tell. Something he isn't saying.

"By the time I got back, she'd already been missing for at least five hours, probably more, and that storm had come in from nowhere."

I think of that Day One photo of him caught in the shadows between two round, flat spotlights.

"Yesterday, they widened the search to the North Sea. All the fishing boats and tankers out there are looking for her too, but . . ." He shakes his head, stands up again. "I know they're going to stop looking for her soon. I *know* they are. The police are coming round tomorrow morning. No one wants me down at the harbor anymore, doing fucking nothing but getting in the way." He snorts. "The wailing widower."

He seems so angry, so bitterly resigned.

"You must be knackered. Why don't you try to get some sleep?"

He immediately starts to protest.

"I can't sleep until tonight anyway," I say. "If anything happens, I'll wake you up, okay? I promise."

His shoulders sag. His smile is so wretched, I have to look away from it. I look out instead at the green windy sway of the orchard beyond the window.

"Okay," he says, reaching out to squeeze my hand once. "Thank you." At the door, he turns briefly back, his smile more like his own. "I meant what I said, you know. I'm really glad you're back."

I root about in my suitcase until I find one of the vodka miniatures I bought on the flight. Sit down on the bed in the warm space where Ross was, and drink it. On the bedside table, there's a framed photo of a very young El and Ross grinning next to the floral clock in Princes Street Gardens. His fingers are inside the waistband of her denim shorts; hers are splayed across his stomach. Had I gone by then? Had I already been forgotten? I look at El's big happy grin, and know the answer.

I turn away, look around at the room again instead. The Clown Café was solely El's invention: a richly imagined roadside American diner, with walls of red and white and glass tubes of pink neon. An old record player was a jukebox playing fifties Elvis. The pine sideboard was our table; two high stools, our chairs. The bed was a long serving counter, and the cupboard, the john.

I wasn't keen on Clowns; back then, we both believed absolutely that they were a species entirely separate from people. I felt as much pity for them as queasy mistrust: it seemed to me that they had few opportunities in life other than those allotted to them, and even at eight years old, I could relate to that. El thought traveling with a circus would be just about the best job in the world, of course.

But the Tooth Fairy was afraid of Clowns. And we were afraid of the Tooth Fairy. So we'd hide out here in the Clown Café—our skin itching under face paints and plastic noses, nylon wigs and jumpsuits—drinking coffee and eating fried doughnuts with two Clown veterans called Dicky Grock and Pogo. Dicky Grock was the Clown Café's cook: mute and sad-faced, an ex-juggler who'd hated the big top and had retired early. And Pogo was small-boned and large-toothed, king of the short gag, with a particular propensity for sneaking up behind you with a bullhorn. I was as terrified of him as I was of the Tooth Fairy.

But it was always worth it. The discomfort, the fear, the queasy unease. Because the Clown Café was ours. It was important. It was one of the best hiding places in the world.

I swallow. I haven't thought about the Clown Café in years. I haven't thought about *us* in years. Suddenly desperate to breathe fresh air, I go to the window, pull up hard on the bottom sash. When it doesn't budge, I look down. There are maybe a dozen long crooked nails hammered into the sill through the window frame. And there's no reason for that to scare me, but it does. It scares me as much as that split second in LA when I thought El might actually be dead. Or that part of me that's glad I'm here. In this place where my first life ended and was never ever supposed to restart.

"Oh, El," I whisper, pressing my fingers against the cold glass. "What the fuck have you done?"

CHAPTER 3

The house is both too quiet and too loud.

I stand on the landing at the top of the stairs and take a breath. The carpet is gone from here too, but the glass globe that hangs from the ceiling rose and the gold light from Westeryk Road that floods through the open bathroom door straight ahead are the same. I look around at all of the closed doors—Bedrooms 1, 2, 4, and 5—and remember the names we gave them: the Kakadu Jungle, opposite the Clown Café; the Princess Tower, opposite the Donkshop. My heart, too, remembers to beat a warning close to the mouth of the dark corridor between the Clown Café and the Princess Tower, but I ignore it, turn and walk quickly towards the room at its gloomy end. Bedroom 3. It must have had a name too, but I can't remember it. When I reach the door, its matte-black panels thick with dust, I realize that I've wrapped my arms tight around my torso to avoid touching the narrow corridor walls. I shake them out and take another breath. *Jesus, come on.* But when I close my fingers over the handle, I hear El shriek in my ear, *Don't go in! We can't ever go in!* and then Mum's voice—higher, sharper, never inviting opinion or dissent—*You ever go in there, and I'll have both your guts for garters, you hear me?*

I do.

I let go, step quickly backwards, unwilling to turn my back on that door until I'm on the landing again, standing inside warm gold light. I'm shuddering hard and long with no idea why. The why itches under my skin; I can feel it, but not enough to want to scratch.

Stop. Just ghosts. That's all.

I slow my breathing down. Cross over to Bedroom 5, push open its door. Grandpa called it the Donkshop because that was the boat's engine room; it was its power, its beating heart. The solid oak dou-

20

ble bed and wardrobe are there, and the big ugly desk where he would work. I remember the loud hiss of radio static; even with his hearing aids, Grandpa was deaf enough that the whole house knew every single football result by the end of a Saturday afternoon. But the radio is gone. There are no mountains of screws and bolts and springs, mutilated machines and motors. There is no smell of oil and warm metal. The Donkshop's heart stopped beating a long time ago.

The Princess Tower was Mum's bedroom. A lump rises in my throat as soon as I open its door, see the small single bed against the wall, the pink pillow and eiderdown, the white dressing table with pink frilly skirt and padded stool. A shiver runs through me, because despite what Ross said, it all feels so *real*, so unchanged, as if frozen in time for two decades. As if Mum has only just left the room. She let us in here only rarely, I remember, mostly to read to us, and even as a child I was struck by how at odds all those pink and lacy frills were with our stern and decidedly unfrilly mother. How fit instead for a princess.

She was from one of Mum's favorite bedtime stories: a fairy princess called Iona, because it meant "beautiful," and she was the most beautiful princess in the world. I sit down on the bed, look out of the big window towards Westeryk Road, remember the slow, soothing warmth of Mum's palm against my hair. One terrible day, the fairy princess was stolen from her mother by an evil hag. The hag cut off her wings and imprisoned her in a tower so high that no one even knew she was there. But the princess was never sad or afraid. Because she knew that one day she would escape. One day, her golden hair would grow long enough that she could tie it to her bedpost and use it as a rope to climb all the way down to the bottom.

But how will she untie her hair? El asked once.

And Mum stopped stroking ours. *She'll cut it off.*

There was never a TV in the house. And the only radio— Grandpa's transistor—was sacrosanct. Our whole lives were about stories. Mum had many rules, but that we should read, that we could learn everything we ever needed to know in life from books, was absolute and never wavered. Some stories, like the Princess Tower, were strange amalgams of those collected in *The Arabian Nights* or by the Brothers Grimm; some she read from books: the fantasylands

21

of Narnia and Middle-Earth, Treasure Island and Neverland; most were entirely homemade tales about pirates and princesses, heroines and monsters. All were terrifying—exciting, cautionary tales for the unwise, the naive, the cowardly, and the foolish.

Snow-white is quiet and gentle. She sits at home, helping with the housework or reading to her mother. Rose-red is wild. She likes to run and laugh and catch butterflies. The tickle of her breath against our skin. *You must always hold on to each other's hand.* The slow tightening of her fingers. *Rely on no one else. Trust no one else.* The pull and twist of our hair until our eyes watered. *All you will ever have is each other.*

I get up fast, rub the goose bumps on my arms. But I don't leave. I go to the white-painted cupboard next to the window where Mum used to keep all of our books, pull open its door. Between towering stacks of paperbacks, El stares out at me with her gray-blue eyes, and I stagger backwards against the wall. Her face is pale, ashy. There are new wrinkles around her eyes and her mouth that match mine. The paint is thick and careless as if spread by a knife. The backdrop is a vast mirror; reflections within reflections, her dark, tired face reaching smaller and smaller into infinity. Too many Els to count.

Looking at her has always been like looking in a mirror, of course. Twins run in our family, Mum said, but we were different. *Special, rare like owlet-nightjars or California condors. More than one hundred thousand other children have to be born before a mum gets to have children as special as you.* She had a book with complicated diagrams, curled up fetuses holding hands inside the womb. The egg that made us split late, more than a week after fertilization, and that meant we were more than just two halves of the same whole. We were Mirror Twins. Mum would dress us in identical clothes: childish homemade pinafores and white, high-necked blouses; gingham dresses that reached long past our knees. She would sit us on her pink stool, stare with bright eyes at our reflections inside the dressing table mirror as she twisted our long blond hair into pigtails.

A few days later and you would have been fused together into someone else, like sand and limestone into glass.

The idea had frightened me. As if we had only narrowly escaped becoming a monster.

I stare at El's self-portrait. She's angry—*seething*—I can see the hate in her eyes, the press of her lips over teeth that I know are gritted. But under all that anger there is fear. I still know her enough to see that. I wonder who put it there. And why she felt the need to paint it. I look down at my wrists, reluctantly remember the bite of her fingers. Deep enough to leave red marks that would later bloom purple and yellow.

I hate you. Go. All I want is for you to be gone. The snarl in her voice, the cold victory in her eyes. *To never have to think about you again.*

I close the cupboard door, lean hard against it, my head throbbing. How can I tell Ross that she's not dead? How can I explain? Because even back then when she'd hurt me so badly, I knew what she said wasn't true; I knew her enough to see the hurt under all that rage. I felt it. In too many ways we *were* like sand and limestone. When we were six, El fell out of Old Fred. I was in bed with the flu, my head and chest full with the hot suffocation of it, my mind with the worry of wondering if you could die from it, but I still felt her screams as if they'd come from my own throat. I still felt the stomach-twisting terror of falling through the branches, the shock of hitting the ground, the agony that burned up through my ankle and into my knee. Grandpa said it was just a sprain, and sure enough within a week El was more recovered than I was. She brought me hot lemon water and handfuls of daisies from the garden so that we could make chains while I lay in bed, still wheezy and feverish. The first time she was allowed to visit, her eyes went round and wide when I told her how much it had hurt when she fell.

I got dizzy, she said. *My chest and head filled up and I couldn't breathe. That's why I fell.*

Afterwards, she was always trying to prove what I considered already proven. It became like a game to her: she'd think nothing of throwing herself out of trees or down stairs, not if she could share the pain, the fear, the danger with me. Her arms and legs were constantly covered in scratches and bruised pinches. It didn't matter how much I begged, how much my life began to feel like walking through a minefield on someone else's legs. How paralyzed I became by all heights—that dizzying terror of always waiting to fall—a vertigo that left me only when I left this house. El would just laugh, deep and long, and she'd hug me tight until that hurt too.

On April 3, I slept until ten because I'd stayed up late to finish an overdue think piece for a lifestyle magazine: "Ten Body Language Signals That Could Mean He's Cheating." After a breakfast of coffee, I walked along Venice Beach's boardwalk, wandering among the stalls and tourists and Bob Marley flags; the skaters, performers, psychics, and artists. When the day got too hot, I sat on a bench in the shade of palm trees, and I watched all that life pass me by instead, breathed it in as if I were part of it. Wondered idly which nightclub I would go to later, what outfit I would wear, whose hands would touch me.

I walked back to the condo around five, slept for an hour, showered, put on a little black dress and too-high heels. I missed the step down onto the balcony, nearly dropped my opened bottle of wine. It slipped wet and cold between my fingers, and it was just about the fastest my heart had beaten all day. I sat on the balcony, rubbed my toe, drank my wine, and watched the sun go down over the horizon, spilling red across the Pacific. I felt nothing. Same as any other day. Same as any other night. And I've felt nothing since. No terror, no shock, no agony. No excited flutter in my belly, no foreign, fathomless fear. Nothing has been ripped from me, nothing has ended. Everything is exactly the same. El is not lying somewhere in the dark and in pain. And she's not dead. I would have felt it. I would have known it. No matter how estranged we are. I'd know it.

*

I go into the kitchen. Better to get all of it over with at once. Mum's old Kitchener range—vast and ugly and cast-iron black—looks like it's still in use: there's a kettle on its hot plate and a pile of ash in the coal grate. I can see the curls at the nape of Mum's neck, the slumped slope of her shoulders as she stirs and tuts, the tight knot of apron around her waist, the scuffed heels of her shoes. Condensation growing downwards from the top of the window, hiding the back garden. Bleach and lavender, sharp scotch broth and the sweet lemon cakes we sometimes baked after school. The large wooden table and its old scratches, dents, and stains still takes up the lion's share of the space. I can see Grandpa sitting with his bad leg up on a neighboring chair, shiny smooth head and vast sideburns, throwing back his heart meds the same way he did orange Tic Tacs, banging his big fists on the wood whether happy, angry, or sad.

I can see Mum turning away from the range, the skin around her eyes pinched like dried wet newspaper, soup splattering onto the floor from her ladle, her voice high so Grandpa could hear her. *Someone gets stabbed in Edinburgh three times a day.* El and me—maybe eight, nine, probably no more, because Mum's hair is still mostly fair, nearly blond like ours—looking at Grandpa with wide, alarmed eyes until he grins, flashing white teeth. *Poor bastard, eh?*

He was from the East End of Glasgow, although he'd been an engineer on North Sea fishing boats since he'd turned sixteen. Gran had died of cancer when Mum was still a teenager. Every year on the date of her death, Mum would shut herself in her bedroom and not come out until the next day. But not Grandpa. He was ferociously stoic. He was like a caricature in one of Mum's stories: a hard life forged into a hard man, whose world had neither changed nor grown, no matter how many boats he'd sailed on, how many places and people he'd seen. But he'd also spend whole summers in the back garden with only El and me for company, picnicking and laughing and joining in our endless treasure hunts; on rainy days, building ever more elaborate blanket forts and castles indoors. When he went to Leith's weekend market, we'd sit at the kitchen table for hours, waiting for the "Bluebell Polka" or "Lily of Laguna" whistled off-key and his distinctive limping silhouette through the glass hallway door, the canvas bag full of tablet and toffee swinging from his elbow. He'd been the salve for Mum's indiscriminate terrors and omens. Always sitting still except for his hands, pretending to listen as she talked in low, urgent whispers, rolling his eyes as she fluttered and flapped.

Worry gies wee things big shadows, hen. Jist chuck it in the fuck-it bucket.

This was where we lived. El, Mum, Grandpa, and I. In this cozy, ugly room. I'm smiling as I look around at the wonky beige wood units. At the old boiler, its silver flue plugged into a hidden chimney that was forever trapping birds. I used to listen to them, scratching and flapping, the sounds muffled as if they were underwater. Beneath the old hanging clothes rack, there's a new Smeg fridge-freezer, an incongruent sapphire blue. And beyond the towering Georgian window, with its many small glass panels framed with hardwood glazing bars, the old apple trees sit and sway.

I turn back towards the open door into the hallway and the grandfather clock, the telephone table, all those china bird plates. There's a hollow space inside my stomach. It's easy, I know, to be tricked—fooled into believing something is real when it's not. Especially if you want to believe it. But this house is more than old memories. It's like a museum, a mausoleum. Or a moment of catastrophe, preserved like a body trapped under pumice and ash. Was that why El had needed to buy it, to fill it back up with all that was lost? Did she see that auction notice in the paper, and arrange a viewing out of little more than curiosity, hardly expecting that it would be like stepping back into her childhood? It would have been hard, I suppose, to come and then go, to resist its pull. Although I was always the more sentimental one. El mastered the art of chucking it in the fuck-it bucket before we'd even reached puberty.

I retrieve the dustpan and brush Ross has left on the floor, sweep up all the broken china I can find. As I'm crossing the kitchen to the scullery, I come to an abrupt halt close to the Kitchener. I stare down at the long join between two tiles, its grout cracked, stained dark. My heart skips a beat. I feel suddenly sick, look quickly away. A bell rings—loud and sudden and close. My heart skips another beat and then starts to gallop. I turn around, stomach squeezing, fingers and toes tingling, and my eyes go straight to the wooden bell board just inside the kitchen door:

Dining Rm Drawing Rm Pantry Bath Rm
Bedrooms
1 2 3 4 5

Every spring-mounted copper and tin bell below each room has a star-shaped pendulum hanging from its clapper. And every room in the house apart from the kitchen has a bell pull: a brass-and-ceramic lever connected to long copper wires hidden inside the walls, along cornices and behind plaster. Whenever a lever was pulled, those wires tightened around pivots and cranks, shuddering through rooms and floors and corridors until they reached the kitchen, where they would shake the coiled spring of a bell mount, ringing its bell loud and long. I remember that those pendulums would swing for minutes after the ringing had stopped, and so whenever El or I wanted to guess which room's bell pull had been pulled by the other, we would stand inside the entrance hall instead. A rudimentary telepathy test that convinced no one because each bell also had a distinctive peal. We had swiftly grown bored with the game; only Mum seemed to love it, clapping her hands or giving us one of her rarely delighted smiles every time we got it right.

The ringing comes again, louder, shriller, and I jump. I'm staring at the bell below Bedroom 3 when something whispers very close to my ear:

There's a monster in this house.

I shiver, bite down on my tongue. None of the bells or pendulums are moving. But it takes far too long for me to realize that the ringing is the doorbell. *Christ.* I go back into the hallway, take long, slow breaths. It's just jet lag. That's all. The glass door is open. The big red door is shut. When I go up on tiptoes to look out through the peephole, all I can see is the path, the gate, the squared-off high hedges. No one is there.

My toes touch against something smooth and cool. An envelope sitting on the hessian doormat. CATRIONA in black block capitals across the front. No stamp or postmark. I'm reluctant to pick it up, but of course I do. My fingers are clumsy as I tear through the envelope, pull out the card inside. It's a sympathy card: a narrow-neck vase spilling with creamy lilies and tied with a bow. A debossed gold cursive font: *Thinking of You.*

I go back into the hallway and close the door. Snib the lock. Open the card.

LEAVE

27

CHAPTER 4

Detective Inspector Rafiq is one of those women you wish you were but are glad you're not. She's slim and small, but her voice is a loud and impatient Glaswegian that overrules everyone else with little effort. Her hair is black, her clothes are black, her grip is surprisingly warm.

"Please, Miss Morgan, take a seat," is the first thing she says to me, as if this is her house.

We're in the Throne Room. I have no idea why. It, too, is frozen in time: gold filigree wallpaper, gold-and-black swirling carpet. The dining table is covered with a linen tablecloth, but the chairs are the same huge and heavy mahogany thrones that christened the room, their backs upright and ornate, carved deep with the same swirls as the carpet. When I sit down and DI Rafiq sits opposite me, I immediately feel like we're in an interview room. Perhaps that's why we're in here.

"It's Cat. Short for Catriona." I have the sympathy card in my jeans pocket. Having slept on it—or more accurately, tossed and turned on it—I've decided that it has to be from El. She'd know that I would come back. And no one else, other than Ross or the police, even knows I'm here.

"I'm Kate." A smile reveals two neat rows of teeth.

Ross is in the kitchen banging cups. Kate Rafiq's colleague, a young, smiling guy called Logan, sits on my right. I think she introduced him as a detective sergeant, and I've watched enough crappy cop shows to know that means she's in charge. He has dark ridiculous hair: floppy and gelled on top, shaved at the sides and back. His stubble is very carefully careless. He looks like an overpaid footballer. And he's too close; I can hear the soft, slow inhales and exhales of his breath. With him beside me and Rafiq in front, I feel penned in. And resentful, because I also feel like shit, hungover without having earned it, and this is just another ordeal that El is forcing me to go through. I don't care if the police, like Ross, believe something's happened to her—believe even that she's dead. Because she fucking isn't.

"The resemblance is uncanny," Rafiq says, shaking her head, swinging her sleek ponytail.

"We're identical twins," I say.

"Aye, right enough." She's interested in my hostility, leaning forwards, pushing her elbows into the tablecloth. And I suddenly regret the good jeans I've put on, the sheer silk blouse. It's too contrived. Too much not me. Too much, I suddenly realize, like El.

"You've come from LA, that right?"

"Venice Beach. It's just south of Santa Monica."

An arch of her eyebrows. "How long you lived there?"

"Twelve years." I look out the window as a red double-decker groans past, rattling the glass.

"And what is it that you do, Catriona?"

"*Cat*. I'm a freelance writer, magazines mostly, some digital media. Lifestyle articles, opinion pieces. I've got a blog, a website, a verified Twitter account with over sixteen thousand followers." I stop talking, look down at the table. Even to my ears, I sound ridiculous.

"LA's a long way from Leith. You mind me asking what prompted you to leave Scotland in the first place?"

I shift forwards in my seat. "What does that—any of that—have to do with El going missing?"

Another flash of neat teeth. "I'm just trying to get a picture of El in my head, that's all. Every wee bit of information helps. And it seems strange to me that identical twins would live so far apart. In the last twelve years, how often have you come back?"

"I haven't."

"Ross says you and El had a falling-out just before you left."

"We just stopped being close. People do. And then I left. That's it."

"So, there was no specific reason behind the move? Or the staying away?" A pause. "For twelve years?"

I fight against the urge to stand up; it would give her too many wrong ideas. "I got sick of Edinburgh and I left. I stayed sick of it, so I didn't come back. *That's it.*"

She leaves a silence that I too quickly fall into.

"Are you trying to suggest I've got something to do with this shit-storm?" And I realize that despite myself, I am standing, the throne wobbling behind me, balancing precariously on its back legs. "That El and I had a big fight, and I stropped off to America to plot her death for twelve years?"

"So you think your sister's dead?" Rafiq asks. I don't miss the quick look she shoots towards Logan.

"The opposite," Ross says, elbowing his way into the room, and then setting a tray down on the table. His smile is tight as he presses down on the cafetière. "She thinks El's engineered the whole thing for attention." He looks better for his sleep, but his eyes are still red and swollen. And his voice is raw, stripped too thin. "Don't you?"

I sit back down with a sigh. Obviously, I haven't hidden my feelings as well as I thought. Logan goes on breathing soft and slow next to me like he's sleeping.

"It's what she does," I say. "This is exactly the kind of thing she'd do. Give it a few more days and she'll come waltzing back through the door, demanding a weekend break in Paris and an apology," I glance at Ross, "for whatever it was you did." Beside me, Logan takes another ponderous breath, and I round on him, face hot. "Do you *speak?*"

Logan blinks, and then grins, revealing good teeth and better dimples. "Aye."

"Okay," Rafiq says. "You're right, Catriona, we don't know El as well as you do, but we have to treat her as a missing person till we know otherwise, that's just our job. Let's start all of this over again, eh?" Her smile is warmer, but I know that I should have kept my mouth shut. Said nothing at all.

"I'm the SIO on El's missing-person case. That means, to all intents and purposes, I'm in charge of it." She turns her head. "Logan, why don't you prove you're not actually mute, and give us a quick recap before we go through any updates?"

Ross finishes pouring the coffee and sits heavily down as Logan nods, takes out a tiny notebook, flips its pages.

"Okay. Ellice MacAuley was first reported missing by the Royal Forth Yacht Club's boatman at approximately six thirty p.m. on April the third. He took her out to her swing mooring in the East Harbour at eight a.m., about quarter of an hour after high tide."

The only time to set sail for the high seas. I think of darkness and a cold red sky, the wide and choppy firth and the smell of blood: sour and dark.

"CCTV saw her arrive at Lochinvar Drive on foot. Examination of her laptop shows that she accessed AIS that morning to check shipping positions in the Firth of Forth." Logan looks up. "Apparently that's normal procedure before going recreational sailing. She told the boatman that her plans were to sail to Anstruther, have lunch, and then sail back. She left in her daysailer, *The Redemption*—alone—about ten minutes later."

He licks his right index finger, turns over the page without looking up. This irritates me too, seems like a ridiculous affectation. Don't they have smartphones or tablets for that kind of thing these days?

"One Robert McLelland, the skipper of an inshore fishing vessel called *Sea Spray*, later reported having seen the boat one nautical mile northeast of Inchkeith at eight fifty a.m. According to the Coastguard, the conditions, specifically wind speed, were such that she should have arrived in Anstruther around eleven a.m., noon at the latest. When she had not returned to Granton Harbour by six p.m., the boatman contacted Anstruther, who had no record of her arrival. It was then that the yacht club reported a Concern for Person to police and HM Coastguard.

"Following initial witness statements and risk assessment, the attending officer reclassified Ellice MacAuley as a high-risk Missing Person. Her husband, Dr. Ross MacAuley, was contacted, and he communicated that he was on his way back from a conference in London. Sorry," Logan says, glancing up, briefly flashing his dimples again. "Bit clunky, that bit."

Rafiq rolls her eyes.

"Em, okay. The MRCC—that's the Maritime Rescue Co-ordination Centre—in Aberdeen appointed James Paton as search-and-rescue mission coordinator."

The fat, smug, jowly gunslinger. *In those conditions, a person could be expected to survive no more than three hours in the water.*

"Local Coastguard units and rescue teams were deployed to search the coastline. Two RNLI lifeboats were launched, from South Queensferry and Kinghorn, and a SAR helicopter was sent from Prestwick to cover that last known sighting near Inchkeith in the north, and Anstruther Harbour in the northeast."

Logan's careful, nitpicky delivery is beginning to drive me to distraction. Despite myself—and all that resentment and certainty—I'm beginning to feel uneasy. Queasy. I have another sudden and unwelcome flashback to El clinging to a rattling mast and wildly flapping mainsail; shouting, laughing, baring her teeth to the wind and swinging lanternlight—and I want to stand up again. I clasp my hands together instead, stare hard at the drips of condensation inside the empty cafetière.

"By eight p.m., there had been no confirmed sightings of either the sailboat or Ellice MacAuley, and the MRCC were advised that bad weather was moving in from the North Sea. Hang on . . ." More flipping of tiny pages. "I've got the Shipping Forecast somewhere . . ."

Ross's head drops lower, his hands moving to clasp behind his neck. I swallow.

"Skip it," Rafiq says.

"Right. Okay, so, the case was then reported to the UK Missing Persons Bureau, with CID taking over, DI Kate Rafiq as SIO. Upon the arrival of Ross MacAuley at his address in Leith at approximately eleven p.m., I carried out a review of the initial MPI form and drove him, at his request, to Granton Harbour."

I suddenly realize that it was Logan who had been standing next to Ross in that second terrible photo of him staring out to sea, arms held in front of him like a shield as he screamed.

"The search was suspended at eleven forty-five p.m. because of the rapidly deteriorating conditions, and resumed at nine a.m. on April fourth. It was hampered by continuing poor visibility and considerable media interference. By the afternoon, the search area was widened to the North Sea. All commercial craft within the area were alerted and issued with a description of both *The Redemption* and

Ellice MacAuley. As of now, there have been no reported sightings of either."

Logan clears his throat, turns another tiny page. I realize that I'm holding my breath and force myself to let it go.

"It's the opinion of the MRCC that if the boat got into difficulty on its outward voyage to Anstruther, there is a high probability that this would have been witnessed, either by other vessels or from the coast. Also, the dimensions of the mainmast are such that it would be highly unlikely that it could have sunk without subsequently being visible above water. If Ellice MacAuley got into difficulty, such as falling overboard, the current water temperature is such that she would have become unconscious within an hour, and couldn't be expected to survive more than three. And the boat would either have run aground, or been spotted on the outward tide.

"*The Redemption* was fitted with an ISO 9650 life raft, and Ellice MacAuley also had an inflatable Gumotex kayak, which she often used to get herself to and from shore. We have circulated descriptions of both. There has been no mayday, and nothing from her GPS unit. The EPIRB—the boat's emergency beacon—hasn't transmitted any location either. If not manually activated, it would have automatically turned on when it came into contact with water."

Ross stands up. His hands are shaking. "You're here to tell us you're giving up. All of you: the Coastguard, the lifeboats, *you*. Right?"

Kate Rafiq stands up too, puts a hand around his wrist, and surprisingly he lets her, even though he's still vibrating with rage, grief, maybe fear, I don't know. I only know it's misplaced. A waste of his energy.

"Ross," she says. "I promise you we'll not stop looking for her, okay?"

"*But?*"

"The MRCC will almost certainly start scaling back their search; if not today, then tomorrow." I see her slim fingers tighten on Ross's wrist when he immediately starts to protest. "But that doesn't mean we've given up, all right? What it does mean is that we have to carry out our own review. We may have to start thinking of El's case as a long-term missing investigation. We have to consider whether or not she is still high-risk."

"Of course she is!" Ross shouts, wrenching his arm free, staggering back from the table, rattling crockery. His bloodshot eyes find mine. "I told you, didn't I? They're fucking giving up!" Before he frowns and looks away, presumably remembering that I'm about as unhelpful an ally as he could find.

"We're not giving up," Logan says, and I realize that everyone's standing now. Everyone except me.

"Ross, what I said to you that first night is still true," Rafiq says. "Missing folk are always one of four things. They're lost; they've suffered an accident, injury, or sudden illness; they're voluntarily missing; or they're under the influence of a third party, as in an abduction." Here, she finally struggles to hold Ross's furious gaze. "And right now, we haven't the evidence to determine which applies to your wife, okay? So we have to cover every base until we do. That's all this is."

"Now," she says, sitting back down, nodding at Ross and Logan to do the same. I have the absurd urge to laugh when they obey straightaway. "We have some more questions to ask, Ross. Personal questions. Would you prefer it if Catriona left the room?"

"No," Ross says, sullen now. The wind's gone out of his sails. I immediately want to laugh again, and I take a too-hot swallow of coffee instead. "Ask what you like."

"You told Logan that El had been depressed and distant before she went missing, that right?"

I sit up straighter, shooting Ross a glance that he doesn't see because his eyes are closed.

"That you were having trouble as a couple—"

"I didn't say that," Ross snaps. "We were just . . . I was working away a lot." He shakes his head. "I was *working* a lot. El and I, we hardly saw each other. When she wasn't painting, she was out on that damn boat."

"And you never accompanied her?"

Ross glares at Rafiq. "I've never sailed. I can't swim, don't like the water. I've said this already."

34

"El's state of mind," Rafiq persists. "Would you say that her depression had worsened in the days or weeks leading up to her disappearance?"

"No. Look, I treat people with serious depression. That's my *job*. El was mildly depressed. That's all. For Christ's sake, I know what you're trying to suggest now, and you're—"

"What *are* you trying to suggest?" I say. Though I know, of course.

Rafiq looks at me. "I understand that El tried to kill herself once before?"

"Oh, fuck off," I say, turning on Ross. "Did you tell her that?"

Before I can stop it, I suffer a flashback of El lying in a hospital bed. Dark-ringed eyes in a talc-white face—everything with El has always been black or white. The swing of an IV. A drip stand, a heavy saline bag. Layers of tight bandage stained with blood pulling at the cannula in the back of her hand. Her smile. Tired and trembling but filled with so much joy. So much hate.

"She didn't try to kill herself then, and she hasn't now," I say through gritted teeth.

"You're saying that her overdose at the age of . . ." Rafiq looks down at her phone ". . . nineteen, was what? A cry for help?"

I can't help the snort that escapes. "Something like that."

Rafiq shares a none-too-subtle look with Logan. "El hasn't accessed either of her bank accounts since she disappeared. She hasn't contacted anyone. She hasn't turned on her phone. Nobody matching her description has been admitted to any hospitals in the area. There have been no reported sightings of either her or her boat since eight fifty a.m. on April the third. Ross found her passport exactly where it always is. *Why* are you so sure your sister's all right?"

"I told you," I say. "Because this is what she does." Because it's what I would never do. Because we are not the same. Have never been the same. Because she is my exact opposite. My reflection. My Mirror Twin.

"Pretending you've drowned is a pretty extreme thing to do, would you not agree?"

The phrase *she always goes overboard* flashes through my mind, and I straightaway squash it just as fast and hard as the inappropriate giggle that tries to follow it. "Yeah, well. Like you said—you don't know her."

I watch Rafiq and Logan exchange another look, and I know what they're thinking, because part of me has started thinking the same thing. I sound like someone trying very hard to convince herself that what she thinks, what she's been thinking ever since she got on a plane at LAX, is still the only possible truth. That queasiness has returned to squeeze at my stomach. The smell of coffee makes it worse.

Rafiq leans forwards. "Something bad has happened to your sister. Whether you believe that or not is irrelevant to this investigation, but I must admit, I find it awful curious that the twin sister of a high-risk missing person doesn't seem even a wee bit bothered about her." She cocks her head, reminding me of the tiny-boned birds on all of Mum's mounted china plates. "I've worked in this job long enough to know when something's off, or when someone's not telling me the whole truth."

We're going down a bad path here, and I can only think of one way to turn us back. "This was delivered yesterday," I say, putting the sympathy card on the table.

Ross snatches it up. He looks at my name on the envelope, takes out the card, and opens it without a word. His shoulders sag, and he grips the card so tightly between thumb and forefinger it starts to crumple.

"Hey, no, it's all right," I say, reaching out to touch him before thinking better of it. "This is a good thing. It's El. It has to be." I frown when he still says nothing. "It's hand-delivered, Ross! That means she has to be nearby. It means she—"

"El got these," he says, in that raw stripped voice. "She got dozens of these."

"Oh." Something like a chill runs up my back.

"Right up until she disappeared."

Rafiq carefully takes the card from Ross, reads it, and then puts it back inside the envelope to give to Logan. I watch him put it inside a clear plastic bag, imagine a scenario where El didn't send it, and feel alternately hot and cold. It suddenly occurs to me that it surely can't be routine for CID to be involved in missing-person cases. I look at

Rafiq. "Is that why you're investigating? Because of the cards? Do you know who—"

"We'd already opened an investigation into similar threats against your sister, aye. Was it you who found it?"

"Yes. Someone rang the doorbell." *There's a monster in this house.* I rub my arms. "The card was lying on the mat."

"Maybe now you'll start taking them fucking seriously," Ross growls.

Rafiq stands up. "Ross, I can assure you that we're taking everything very seriously. We'll run forensics on this one, just like we did the others."

"But why would someone send me the same threatening cards as my sister? It doesn't make sense. No one knows I'm here except Ross and you." And El.

Rafiq frowns. "They may be related to El's disappearance, and they may not. Right now, finding El is our utmost priority. The cards have never escalated in threat, and we've found no evidence that El was being stalked or threatened in any other way. And the fact you're now the target makes me suspect a nosy neighbor with a grudge and too much time on their hands, rather than anything more sinister." When Ross starts to object again, she holds up a hand. "Which is not to say that we won't continue to investigate them as part of this case. Or that you shouldn't get in touch straightaway if you receive any more."

She steps back, looks at us both. "We came here to reassure you both that as of now, nothing has changed. We and the Coastguard are still using all available resources to look for El. But it would be a good idea for you to start preparing yourselves for the likelihood of that changing if there are no new developments in the next twenty-four hours. Okay? Has Shona been in touch with you today?"

Ross nods.

"Shona is your family liaison officer, Catriona. She'll keep you updated with any new developments. Meantime, Logan here is still your first single point of contact. And get in touch with the Missing People folk again, Ross—El's entry still hasn't gone live. You've still got all the other helpline numbers, aye?"

"I don't need a counselor," Ross says. "I just need my wife."

Rafiq gets up close to him, and still manages to look him in the eye even though he must be close to a foot taller. "We'll find her, Ross."

And I've watched enough crappy cop shows to know they're pretty much never supposed to say that.

I walk them out into the hallway, and Logan stops, smiles, hands me his card. "If you need anything, want to know anything," he says.

Rafiq opens the door, and I watch them go down the steps into the sun. At the gate, Rafiq stops to let Logan out before turning around and beckoning me like I'm a cocker spaniel. I go down into the cold bright garden reluctantly, folding my arms over my chest.

"Where would she go? If she chose to leave, where would she go?"

I blink. "I have no idea."

"What about her husband?"

"What about him?"

"Is there anything you want to tell me about him—about them—that maybe you weren't comfortable saying while he was in the room?" When I don't reply, she can't hide her irritation. "We've spoken to Southwark University, confirmed that he was there when he said he was. I'm just asking you, as a close member of the family, if we should have any reason at all to be concerned about him?"

Her eyes flicker beyond my shoulder, and when I turn around, I see Ross's silhouette watching us from the window. I go cold. "No. Of course not. This isn't his fault. I told you, all of it's El. It has to be." And I resist adding that it's been a very long time since I was a close member of any family.

Rafiq studies me too long, too closely. "You really do think she's all right."

When I don't answer, she walks down the path and opens the gate without another word.

I watch them leave, listen to the BMW's engine until it's swallowed up by the city. When I look back at the window, Ross is gone. But I still feel like I'm being watched. I walk to the gate, look up and down the empty street. Stand in the sun until I feel warm again.

"Maybe she just doesn't know how to undo it," I whisper. Because buried under twelve years of anger and hurt and resentment is the memory of all the times we'd lie in the Kakadu Jungle holding hands, fighting to stay awake so we wouldn't be the first to let go. "Maybe she just doesn't know how to come back."

CHAPTER 5

I wake early and lie in bed, staring up at the Clown Café ceiling, trying not to hear the house. El and I would lie for hours inside our forts and castles, listening to it groan and shudder all around us, and she would hiss hot against my ear: *The house is full of ghosts.* We both believed it. But ghosts were never as scary as monsters. You just pretended you couldn't hear them.

I get dressed and creep downstairs, uncertain why I'm creeping, why I'm frightened. Because I am. I'm gripping the banister too hard. My heart is jumpy and too fast, too erratic, but at the same time I feel weary, spaced out, as if I've broken through the surface of a deep cold lake and swapped drowning for slow hypothermia instead. Bad things happened in this house, as well as good. But that was a lot easier to forget when I was an ocean away from its walls.

I run my fingers against the stairwell's wallpaper of Grecian urns and thorny vines, think of all the long wires, pulleys, and cranks winding around the house behind plaster and cornices like a hidden city of spiderwebs. Spun threads of copper, patiently waiting to shorten, to shake, to awaken those silent bells below.

The kitchen is empty, but there's evidence Ross was here: a used coffee cup, cereal bowl filled with water in the sink. A note on the table:

No news. Couldn't sleep. Gone for walk to clear my head. Police station after prob. Help yourself to whatever you want x

Ravenous, I stand at a counter and chew my way through two bowls of corn flakes, milk running down my chin. Mum turns around from the ugly range, pats the crown of her head, drives her wrinkles deeper. *Don't slitter, Catriona.* Grandpa looks up from his *Daily Record. Ye're bein' a stander, lassie. Sit the shit doon.* Today, I miss them both so badly it hurts.

After two strong coffees, I go upstairs, fetch my laptop. I check my email at the kitchen table, hoping that this will somehow bring me back to that safe and glossy life in California. Instead, I work my way through three form rejections for on-spec pitches, and a final eviction notice from the owner of the Pacific Avenue condo: a bikini model called Irena, who spends her winters in Palm Beach, and promised me she wouldn't be back until June.

I close my eyes. Rub the heel of my palm against my breastbone. I have almost no money. I have no career. I live hand to mouth, lurching from one flat-fee gig to another. No awards, no recognition, no Pulitzer, no great publishing deal. Nothing has panned out the way it was supposed to. The way—after running away from Scotland—I imagined I deserved it to. And now I have no home to go back to. It's all slipping away from me. Slowly but surely. And I blame El. For all of it. Then and now. I blame only her.

I'm on the verge of shutting the laptop when I see the subject line of the last unread email. I stop, my fingers hovering over the keyboard.

DON'T TELL ANYONE

Who would I tell? is my first stupid thought. I look at the sender's address: john.smith120594@gmail.com. It doesn't mean anything to me. More American marketing probably, they're pretty ingenious at dodging spam filters. But something in me already knows it isn't. Something that feels new and familiar at the same time. Indifferent and afraid. The Wi-Fi is slow. As the email downloads, I hold my breath hard inside my throat, and that same something in me says delete it. Delete it now.

The body of the email, when it finally appears on the screen, is only two words.

HE KNOWS

I push my chair away from the table. And then I'm standing at the window, looking out at the apple trees swaying in the breeze, their big branches and heavy leaves moving, restless. I look down at the sill and the half-dozen nails that have been hammered into it, just like in the Clown Café. My fingers bump over them. Back and forth until it starts to hurt. Because I don't know why they're there. I can't think of any good reason at all. And even though I'm inside a swath of trapped and glass-warmed sun, I'm cold enough that my teeth chatter, that I can feel goose bumps through the sleeves of my shirt.

The beep of a new message makes me jump. I step back into the shadows of the kitchen, eye the laptop screen with distrust.

It's john.smith120594 again. No subject line this time. Just one sentence.

CLUE 1. WHERE OUR TREASURE HUNTS ALWAYS STARTED

I close my eyes. *El.* Of course it is.

The comically huge mortice key is in the scullery back door just like it always was, and when I turn it, it's just as stiff. The old gravel yard is gone, replaced by flat paving and ugly concrete plinths supporting uglier concrete urns. I stand on top of the high staircase leading down from the scullery to the back garden, and I can see El and me marching around and around that gravel yard, kicking up its silver and gray chuckies, trying not to skid around its corners.

The greenhouse is gone too. But the old stone washhouse, with its red-framed window and small slate roof, still stands dwarfed by the corner of the house. Rusty padlocked chains are strung across its red wooden door. It was always locked up like that, I remember, as if condemned. The garden walls still tower, covering its borders in shade, but now trellises of lilac and clematis and trumpet vine hide the dark, wide stones and their seams of moss. My gaze slides to the expanse of high wall alongside the washhouse. No lilac and clematis there, not even the strangle of ivy. A flash of red. An itch. *Red.* A whisper of silvery, shivery dread.

I ignore it. Go down the steps and into the garden. Through the orchard, dense and rustling. Past a shed I don't recognize. Khaki-green-painted wood and a black tarred roof.

And then I'm standing in front of Old Fred. Where our treasure hunts always started.

El hid the clues, and I followed them. Tiny little squares of paper scrawled with cryptic messages only I had a hope of understanding. She'd hide them anywhere and everywhere, each little square of paper leading to the next, and only at the last one would there be a prize instead. Almost always a drawing or painting of us that I'd pin to the walls of the Kakadu Jungle like a totem.

Old Fred looks the same. Squat and wide and appleless, his branches low and inviting. I walk around him to where El carved our names into his trunk, and breathe in cold, sharp air when I see they're still there, scored deep into the brittle bark. Hardly faded. Not inside a heart, but a circle. I reach out to touch them, and then snatch my hand back when I see what's been carved beneath.

DIG

I stand for a moment, glance up at the house's empty windows. And then something halfway between hope and frustration makes me obey.

It doesn't take much digging around the roots to find something. A deep hole covered over with leaves and loose earth. When my fingers touch something solid, I pull it out. A shoebox. I lift up its lid slowly.

I see the empty bottle first: a pirate grinning at me, standing with one foot on a barrel, one hand on his cutlass. Captain Morgan Spiced Gold Rum. Next to it are unopened tins of food, careful neat stacks of them: tomatoes, baked beans, sweet corn. Immediately, I think of Mum supervising the six-monthly restocking of the Survival Packs stored under our bed—black canvas rucksacks stuffed with nonperishable food and bottles of water. I think of her forcing us to run through the house on endless fire drills, intruder drills, nuclear war drills; refueling our panic, that ever-present hum of doom.

There's also a tin of paint. A tester pot. I pick it up, turn it round. *Blood Red*. I drop it back into the box as if it's hot. It lands on a tiny square of folded paper. My heart is beating fast when I take it out, open it up.

12 November 1993 AGE = 7+a bit!
Theres a monster in our house at night.
Not evry night, but lots of them. He has a blue beerd and is so very frightfull and ugly that all ladys should hide from him and never venchure to go into his company.

Thats what Mum says. Its from a book.
She says Bluebeerd and Blackbeerd are brothers. She says Bluebeerd lives on land and Blackbeerd lives on sea and Bluebeerd is worse but I'm more scayerd of Blackbeerd coz hes a pirate and Bluebeerd is just a man.

I hear a sound like a bird cry—press my hand against my mouth when I realize it's me. My fingers are shaking. My breath feels hot. I can see El, half-slumped over her desk, diary open, elbows wide, brow furrowed in concentration as she writes slowly in that same careful cursive.

I get up quickly, start carrying the shoebox back towards the house. My heartbeat is inside my throat and temples. I slow when I reach the paving, glance across at the washhouse and its chained door. Stop when I see another flash of red in the corner of my eye. Turn back to face that flanking high wall seamed with moss and lichen instead of clematis or ivy. Nothing. But when I close my eyes, I imagine the words splashed across that naked old stone in blood:

HE KNOWS

Moonlight, I think. *There should be moonlight.*
And then I'm running up the stairs and back into the scullery, turning that huge rusty key behind me before shoving the shoebox into the nearest cupboard. I go back into the kitchen. Look up at the bell board, at the bell and pendulum below the number *3*. Imagine that gloomy thin corridor above my head, the dusty dark panels of the door at its end. Mum's sour breath on our skin, the snap of her teeth. *You ever go in there, and I'll have both your guts for garters.* Because Bedroom 3 was

44

Bluebeard's Room. Because the bodies of his wives hung on hooks from the walls, and it was filled with blood. Because at night, when he was hungry, he prowled corridors and rooms looking for more. I go suddenly cold. The thought—memory—is as certain as it is obscure. The why that itches under my skin. And in the wake of that memory comes another. I look back at the bell board, the faded *Pantry*. El and I hid from most of the house's ghosts and monsters inside the Clown Café. But we always—*always*—hid from Bluebeard inside Mirrorland.

The pantry is at the very rear of the hallway, crouching in the shadows opposite the stairwell's flank, and hidden from view by a black velveteen curtain. I pull it open. It's heavy, dusty. The rattle of metal rings against its rail makes me want to cringe, and fills me with a sense of unwelcome longing. The pantry is smaller than I remember, long and narrow and cool. The wallpaper is still messy daffodils, their orange and yellow now faded into shades of gray. There's a wooden table against the window looking out into the back garden; when I lean against it to squeeze past, I run the pads of my fingers across scores and scuffs warmed by the morning sun. The cupboard is still there too. It takes up the entire southern end of the room. The latch lifts up as smoothly as if I'd last done it yesterday instead of nearly twenty years ago.

The smell hits me first. It's entirely wrong. Gluey instead of musty. When my eyes adjust, I realize why. The whole of the vast cupboard's interior has been covered in cheap beige wallpaper. I drag over a stool, climb up into the cupboard, and with only the shortest of hesitations, start to smooth my palms over the paper. I half expect to find nothing at all, but when I feel the outline of something hard and metal, my heart skips a beat. I dig in my nails and rip the wallpaper away. *Please be here. Please still be here.* By the time I've torn most of the paper from the wall, I'm sweating, breathing too heavily. But there it is. As if it had never been hidden at all. A full-size, quarter-paneled door with rusting hinges and two heavy slide bolts.

The door to Mirrorland.

*

I look at the door for a long time. There used to be something pinned to its surface. One of El's paintings: an early effort focused more on color than form. Blues and yellows and greens. I close my eyes. The Island. Of course, The Island. A rough coastline of rocks and beach, an interior of forest and flatland. A tropical paradise instead of a snowy wonderland, since Mirrorland was our Narnia. Of sorts. Though it had more color, more ambiguity. More terrors. More fun.

I'm holding my breath. I draw back the bolts. I pull open the door.

It's the cold I feel first; the cold that I've forgotten. When I let my breath go, it fogs white in the dark space ahead of me. My fingers grip the door. There was a treasure map on this side of it. Black roads and green spaces. Long blue water. A volcano. The memory sharpens and then loses focus. I'm procrastinating, I realize—hesitating, even though that thick sense of longing is back, that urgent need to step down into the darkness, to step out of this house and into another world. I felt it just the same the first time Mum showed us this hidden door, this secret space. Fear, deep and brittle and delicious.

I step out of the cupboard, out of the house, and down onto the first wooden tread. I shiver as I look up at the low wooden roof and narrow wooden walls that enclose the staircase. As the creak of that old wood settles and suffocates, I wonder if my nervous excitement is merely the ghost of the child I once was. Creeping down here in the dark, in the night, so many, many times with El, it seems impossible that our sticky, hot hands haven't left behind some residue on the walls and banisters; our flashlights, no shadows of dancing, jagged light; our terrorized giggles and whispered *shoosh!*es, no echoes.

This time, I only have the light on my phone. It casts an ugly white glow that creates more shadows. The old vertigo—that dizzying terror of always waiting to fall—seizes sudden hold of me, and I find that I can't move. I close my eyes, breathe slowly until it passes. Because I'm no longer a child. My fantasies can no longer ride roughshod over logic, over reality. There is nothing to be afraid of down here. Two hundred years ago, when Westeryk was still a village and this the largest, grandest house within it, before this door was hidden behind a cupboard, it was nothing more than a convenience, a contrivance. Access to the kitchen was possible only from the back garden or the front door. This pantry, this door, this staircase, and the alleyway beneath are nothing more than a tradesman's entrance.

The rear of the house sits on far lower ground than the front, its rooms elevated ten feet or more above the back garden. This covered steep staircase serves the same ordinary purpose as the scullery stairs: access to ground level.

And yet my light still shakes as I descend, as the staircase's walls and roof open up into drafty space, and at the bottom of the stairs, I hesitate again. The darkness has more dominion here, my memories more power. Anticipation, sharp and bitter, like lemon juice rubbed into a cut.

I step down onto stone. Down into Mirrorland.

My phone judders frantic light across brick and wood and cobwebs, and I grasp it in both hands. *Stop.* I'm only in an alleyway. A ten-foot-wide, stone-paved corridor between the exterior southern flank of the house and the boundary wall, sheltered from the weather by a low wooden roof like a medieval hoarding over battlements. Stretching from the now bricked-over door to the front garden in the west and the stone washhouse in the east. The latter sits squat at the end of the alleyway like a sentinel, a gatehouse, blocking the exit into the back garden, save for a small door set into its only exposed side.

I turn through one more circle, my frozen breath spinning a wreath of fog around me. The morning sun is still low enough that it breaks through the cracks in the wooden roof as tiny shafts of bright white. I look up, see the bare bulb hanging down from the hoarding's ridge board in just the instant I remember it. When I pull on its string, I'm rewarded—incredibly—by immediate and strong light, as if I wasn't already struggling to believe that time here hasn't stood stock still, that everything I'm seeing and feeling is only that old ghost and echo of me, of us.

Of a magic place. Because, whatever else, I can't deny that. This might once have only been a tradesman's entrance, a means to a supercilious end; it might now be forgotten—only empty, drafty space and stone—but in between it was something else. Once upon a time, it was rich and full and alive. Gloriously frightening and steadfastly safe. Exciting beyond measure. Hidden. Special. Ours.

I turn back to look at the bricked-up door. The larger part of Mirrorland, stretching along the alleyway from the bottom of the stairs to that door was once Boomtown: a dusty boardwalk of fruit crates and wooden planks six or more feet across, staging a post office and a marshal's office, furnished with cardboard-box counters and tables, seats of cushions and blankets and pillows. The Three-Fingered-Joe Saloon was in the southwest corner against the boundary wall; in the northwest was a cluster of Lakota Sioux teepees and a training arena delineated by sticks laid end to end in a square.

Later, Boomtown became a prison; the Three-Fingered-Joe Saloon, a rather less exotic Recreational Dayroom; the wooden crates, the doors and walls of Cellblock 5; and us, its prisoners. *The Shank*. In its heyday, El used to make me sit beside her for hours, fashioning the bloody things out of sharpened toothbrushes and Grandpa's old razor blades.

I turn east, walk down towards the washhouse, running the palm of my right hand against the rough brick of the boundary wall. On its other side, I know, is another long alleyway and green garden, another cavernous house—a newer Victorian villa with bay windows and painted bricks and bargeboards. The alleyway narrows around a large locked armoire that I remember was once full of games and books. Beside it is a wide blue pram, with three rusted big wheels and a shopping tray, a white faded label in the corner of its moldy hood: "Silver Cross."

The washhouse door is unlocked; it was always unlocked—hence the padlock and all those rusty chains strung across its other exit into the back garden. The washhouse was the most important part of Mirrorland. Warmer and better built, better *felt*, once as vital as breathing. And yet less than half an hour ago, I stood outside on the scullery steps and saw only an old stone building with a red-framed window and small slate roof.

I open the door, step up onto floorboards speckled with old paint and dust. They groan and give underfoot, enough to make me want to test each step first. The washhouse smells of mildew and damp, and something sour and green like compost. It has me remembering all sorts of other things I've forgotten even before I turn into its biggest space, illuminated by daylight from the window. Boxes and crates are stacked high in every corner; wooden poles are balanced on piles of dirty sheets; there are two free-standing fans, their cords curled black.

"My God."

My voice echoes, hoarse and weak. I fold my arms tightly around myself as I stare at the washhouse walls. Sky blue and ocean green, white puffs of cloud and white frills of wave, the old brushstrokes messy and impatient. I look down at the floorboards, and under all the dust and dirt are the old charcoal lines of the *Satisfaction*.

Bowsprit. Jib. Forecastle. Foresail. I whisper the words under my breath as I walk over them. Main Deck and Gun Deck, El's black scrawls of *Rum and Water Stores HERE!! Magazine HERE!!* I walk from one end of the washhouse to the other: Crew's Quarters, Cargo Hold, Mainsail, Crow's Nest, Navigation Room, Captain's Quarters, Stern. A moss-covered hose is coiled around two taps, its nozzle—still set to spray—lying inside the old butler sink. I look at the Jolly Roger above it, its painted skull and crossbones stretched flat, fixed to the stone with black electrical tape. And then I look across at that little window, a porthole through which we bathed in moonlight and navigated by the stars. Because while Boomtown and the Shank were only for the day, the *Satisfaction* was mostly for the night.

The stern lantern still hangs on a hook screwed into the eastern stone wall, dusty, smaller than I remember, the candle inside foggy windows of glass long burned to the bottom of its wick. I reach out fingers to touch it, and then stop, pull them back with a sudden shudder that cricks my neck with an audible snap. I look up at the large hulking specter of Blackbeard's ship painted on the wall above it. Always in our wake. Always getting that bit closer.

Some things are gone. The big wooden treasure chest, bound with bands of black leather and a padlock gold with rust, where we'd hoard our booty from raids on Puerto Principe or the Spanish Main: silver cutlery sets, candlesticks, and trinket boxes that we borrowed from the kitchen and Throne Room. The water-filled umbrella bases that used to anchor our masts and sails are gone too. But everything else looks like we left only yesterday: giggling and creeping back up the stairs onto dry land, our lights dancing in the dark. Even the ship's wheel—stolen from the pram—is propped up against our wooden mast poles.

I walk slowly back across the chalk lines of the main deck. Stop and close my eyes. My lips feel tight, and I realize it's because I'm properly smiling for the first time in days. The *Satisfaction* was the first thing we made in Mirrorland. A two-hundred-ton, three-masted, fully rigged pirate flagship with powder chests, chase guns, and forty cannons loaded with hailshot. The *Satisfaction* was Mirrorland. We lived and breathed the magic of her. She was the fire that kept us warm, and then the fuse that set light to everything else. I can feel the give of the soft, rotting wood as I shift my weight from left foot to right foot, back and forth. I can feel the mist of warm rain against my face, the hose wrapped around the mainmast like a snake; the hard flap of the sheet sails as the fans whir and blow—sometimes a tropical ten-knot southeasterly, sometimes a forty-knot squall from the North Atlantic. I can feel the burn of old rope running through my fingers as I hoist, trim, and furl. El behind me at the helm, whisper-shouting her orders: *Come about! Heave to! All hands hoay!*

God, I miss her. It comes out of nowhere, but hurts enough that I can no longer deny it. Pretend it's not true. I miss her.

El is older than me by four minutes. We knew this because Mum mentioned it every day. It usually prefaced one of the stories that she told us almost as often: a depressing tale about the poison taster of an old Persian dynasty. The poison taster was a princess; always the eldest sister of the king. Every day, the heroic poison taster would take the first bite or sip of the king's food or drink, and every night she would swallow a pearl touched by all the king's subjects, and all of their murderous thoughts and plans and words would sink black and boiling into her flesh and bones, where they would fester and rot and burn. And although her life was full of pain and suffering and poor reward, her king's was not, and that was enough to sustain her, to every day set her to her task. To Mum, this meant that the eldest must always look after the youngest, but to El, it meant that she was in charge, she had the divine right to always, always go first.

So I insisted that we have a crew. Because if El allowed me a rare turn at the wheel as captain, it wouldn't happen again for weeks, and as first mate, I wanted to be the boss of someone too. They were an ever-changing crew of Old Salty Dogs, whichever historical pirates were in favor, the odd cowboy or Indian from Boomtown, and Clowns on sabbatical. Only three members of the crew were constant. Annie, our second mate and chief navigator: a tall, perpetually aggressive red-haired Irishwoman, named after the Caribbean pirate Anne Bonny. Belle, our gunner: young and loud with fearless fun; she wore dresses instead of breeches, hid knives in her ebony hair, and wore lipstick the color of blood. And Mouse, timid and obedient enough that she offset the worst of El's bossiness and spared me the worst of it too. Small and silent and pale, dressed always in black, she'd scurry fore and aft, port and starboard: our cabin girl, powder monkey, and skivvy.

Some nights, we only sailed. Searching for The Island and trying to keep ahead of the chasing specter of Blackbeard's *Queen Anne's Revenge*. Some nights, we dropped anchor to raid for booty or look for hidden treasure. Some nights, we battled a mutinous crew, devised complicated punishments for their insurrection: keelhauling bow to stern with ropes, or walking a plank greased with lard. More often subjecting them to ever more impossible challenges in order that their lives might be spared: we believed in cruel second chances. And some nights, we battled storms and other ships: naval frigates and merchant convoys, other pirate brigantines. Our ears would ring with the screams of splintering wood and dying men, the bellows of cannon and musketoons, the roar of the squall.

Ahoy, let's get 'em, sons of biscuit eaters!

Give no quarter! No prey, no pay!

Always, Blackbeard stayed on our tail. And always, *always*, we waited for Captain Henry to appear over that next horizon. To come to our aid and save the day. We knew that he would. We always knew absolutely that one day he'd come back again. For us.

I open my eyes, blink. Walk back across the deck of the *Satisfaction*, out the washhouse door, and back into the long narrow alleyway as if in a dream. I stop suddenly, turn to face the boundary wall. A shiver runs through me as I press my numb fingers against its rough stone. A big portrait of Captain Henry—painted by El—had once hung somewhere along it. Stern and unsmiling, the blues and yellows and greens of The Island behind him. I think of that empty rum bottle in the shoebox. Captain Henry had been our hero: the bravest and best of all pirates. The pirate king of the world.

I lean hard against the wall. So many things I've forgotten, which are still there—still here—in dusty, dark corners. I'm suddenly eager to leave, to feel warm, to breathe fresh air that doesn't smell of damp and moss. At the bottom of the staircase, I pause again. Look up, without knowing why—until I see the white card taped to the underside of the wooden roof with black electrical tape:

SNOW-WHITE SAID: "WE WILL NOT LEAVE EACH OTHER."
ROSE-RED ANSWERED: "NEVER SO LONG AS WE LIVE."

All pirates needed to have a code, Mum said, and that was ours. And although it is—was—as much a part of Mirrorland as everything else down here, something sets it apart. This card is new.

I see red—quite literally. *Blood Red*. HE KNOWS. I feel it, *hear* it, in a hot urgent whisper in my ear, and bat at it like a mosquito, panicked now, as if there are fingers around my throat that have begun squeezing. I hear a sound, upstairs yet close; alien yet familiar: a loud metallic echoing thud. An icy draft pulls at my hair, scratches my skin. The bare hanging bulb winks suddenly out, and when I lurch away from the wall, I feel a rush of cold air, hear a voice that might be familiar if it wasn't screaming.

"RUN!"

I do. I grab hold of the banister and start to climb, hands clammy, heartbeat erratic, the dark and freezing expanse of the alleyway behind me like a chasing monster, a roaring, building wave thick with seaweed and chitinous bones. The stairs are too steep. My knuckles scrape against stone. The hackles on the back of my neck send shudders down my spine, and those slices of daylight through the wooden roof are like cracks of lightning over my head. *Deadlights*, I think. *They're deadlights.*

I miss a step close to the summit and nearly take a header back down to the bottom. And then I'm inside the cupboard, slamming Mirrorland's door behind me, pulling across its bolts, and stumbling back into the bright of the pantry.

*

I'm not mad. I'm not the deluded, heartless bitch that DI Kate Rafiq probably thinks I am. My instincts, my certainties, are bang on. El is alive. Because she can't be dead if she's sending me emails. Burying shoeboxes in the garden and leaving coded warnings taped to ceilings. Churning up our past—a past I've chosen never to think of again—like a blunt plow. Playing her power games. *That's* fucking madness.

I know how this goes. How it's always gone.

This is a treasure hunt. She has the map. And I have no other choice but to wait until she gives me the next clue.

CHAPTER 6

The Kakadu Jungle shrieks and squawks into life all around us: owlet-nightjars, California condors, giant ibises, kakapos. The paperbarks and ironwoods and banyans roar with hot wind, the wetlands and rivers and falls roar with fast water. The birds rise with screams up into the canopy, the sky grows dark and squally, forks of lightning cracking through green and brown and gold, tearing through wood and iron and stone. And the shadows of bad men crouch in the darkness, bristling with rage and sharp teeth. Because all men are pirates, Mum says. Even Prince Charming is just like Blackbeard: sly and handsome, never ever to be trusted. We have to save ourselves.

And so El and I run. Our light flinching from yawning mouths of teeth. A towering wave of water and wind and flesh and lanternlight. High and wide and freezing bright. Rolling through the jungle like an explosion, an earthquake. Rolling towards us and our golden bedspread like a landslide of mud and stone and deadlights.

RUN!

It feels like I scream myself awake. Maybe I do, because when I open my eyes, Ross's face is frozen somewhere between alarm and concern, and his hand is gripping my right arm just above the elbow. I'm lying on the chesterfield in the drawing room. Next to a mahogany lowboy with claw-and-ball feet that Grandpa always swore was a Chippendale. And opposite a yellow brocade rocking chair and a leather recliner that look so exactly like the originals, too, I can almost see Mum and Grandpa sitting facing one another across the bottle-green fireplace. I look away, towards the turquoise-tiled Art Deco bar that Mum used to call the Poirot.

"You were screaming," Ross says with a frown.

"Jet lag," I say. I get up on unsteady legs, try to smile. "Think I need some fresh air."

In the entrance hall, I hesitate at the coatrack, and instead of my anorak, I choose a gray cashmere wrap coat that can only belong to El. I glance at the label before I put it on and belt it tight. Vivienne Westwood. We used to wear the same clothes, I reason, as I unlock the door. Although that's not really true. The minute we left this house, we abandoned almost everything that we had shared; everything that had forced us to always be the same.

Outside, the air is fresh enough, but it does me little good. As children, El and I also always shared the same dreams, the same nightmares. We dreamed of the Kakadu Jungle most often because we fell asleep every night holding hands under our golden bedspread, surrounded by rain-forest wallpaper and the residual echo of those bedtime games spent playing Victorian explorers. I haven't thought about—never mind dreamed about—the Kakadu Jungle in years. And I haven't missed it.

I open the front gate, and it squeals loudly. I step out onto the sidewalk, feeling bizarrely exposed. Why the hell did I put on this coat? And then my sense of anxiety changes, heightens. My skin prickles. When I spin around, I see a figure standing on the corner of the opposite sidewalk, watching me. A man. He's wearing a dark coat, and his face is obscured inside its drawstring hood. Deadlights, I suddenly remember, were a pirate's eyes in the dark. A low-beam flashlight, or a lantern shuttered dull against the wind. But deadlights were also the eyes of others. Others who looked for you—came for you—in the night. I'm breathing a little too hard, but I take a step towards him nonetheless. My "Hey" sounds more like a gasp. And by the time I manage a better one, he's turned and disappeared around the corner towards Lochend.

I don't follow. Instead, I turn in the opposite direction, and almost run to the entrance of Colquhoun's of Westeryk. The shop is quiet, almost empty. I quickly fill a basket with fusilli, red pesto, and focaccia before heading straight for the booze. My breath is still fast, still shaky. Maybe he's just a reporter. A nosy neighbor. Or maybe he's the creep who's been sending—

"Oh! Dieu merci! J'y crois pas—"

I rear back from both the voice and the sudden heavy hand on my forearm, knocking my basket against a shelf full of beer. By the time I've recovered my balance, the woman's hand is clapped hard over her mouth instead, and I know immediately what's happened, amazed that this possibility—this inevitability—has not occurred to me before now. Or at least before I put on the bloody coat. Nor how much more awkward it would be here than in a wine bar in JFK. She thinks I'm El.

"*Excusez-moi*—I am so sorry. I didn't . . ." She's tall, slim, in her forties, and her clothes are expensive, as is her makeup. Her black hair has been pulled back into a chignon. She has an air of effortlessness that probably requires a lot of effort. A lot more than I've ever been able to find.

"I'm Marie Bernard. And you are Catriona—Cat—from America." Her long fingers reach for mine and squeeze. Her smile is too bright. "Ellice told me all about you, of course."

I find the thought that El told her *anything* about me—*of course*—a lot more disconcerting than maybe I should. She smiles again, but I can see that her eyes are tired, red-rimmed. I think of the shouted relief in her *"Dieu merci!"*

"You look so like her." She leans closer—I smell Chanel No. 5—and then she shakes herself. Steps back.

"You're friends with El?"

"*Oui*." Something flashes dark in her eyes before it's gone. "We both are. This is Anna."

I follow her nod towards the only cashier. Who turns, looks me up and down once, then twice. She doesn't smile. "You do look exactly the same." She has an accent. Eastern European, I've already guessed, from her high blond ponytail and cheekbones.

I finger the lapel of El's coat self-consciously.

"I moved from Belleville, Paris, many years ago," Marie says. "El and I first met here, in fact. When the shop was quiet, the three of us would sneak into the back room and drink bad cocktails out of cans."

"Old stock," Anna says, looking at Marie. "Really bad."

Marie laughs, but her voice catches. "We are very good friends. We have good times together."

"El is a *good* person," Anna says. I'm a little taken aback at the sudden tears in her eyes.

Marie nods, turns to me. "There is still no news?"

"No, I'm sorry," I say. "Nothing yet."

There follows another awkward silence that I'm not very inclined to fill. El has never been a joiner. What few friends she had as a teenager, she knew only through me. Ross and I were the only people she ever let close, and yet these two women don't just know her, they seem to genuinely care for her. "And Ross?" Marie eventually says. "How is he?"

"As fine as he can be." I pick two bottles of wine, start inching towards the till. "I should . . ."

"*Bien sûr. Pardon.*" Marie's too-bright smile falters. "You must visit. For tea, *apéritif*, anything at all. I am just over there. The end house." She points at the Gingerbread Coop, and I notice a long keloid scar—stark against her dark skin—running from her wrist to her elbow. When she sees me looking, she snatches her sleeve back down. "And perhaps you could let me know if you hear anything?"

"Of course," I say.

She nods, presses her hand to the emerald-green scarf around her neck, and I realize there are scars on her knuckles too. And under all that immaculate makeup, the skin of one cheek is raised, rough like damaged plaster. The silence between us lengthens. And then she's waving, leaving in a cool jangling breeze and another waft of Chanel No. 5.

I immediately turn towards the till, feeling both guilty and relieved.

"Do you want a bag?" Anna says. Her expression is stony again, and when I nod, she snatches one from under the counter and tosses it at me. Begins scanning and discarding my shopping with brutal efficiency.

I clear my throat. "Are you all right?"

She thrusts a bottle of wine at me without looking up, although her cheeks have flushed pink. "I don't understand why you're here."

"I'm sorry?"

"El told us what happened between you." Her eyes flare, defiant again. "Why you left."

I can only imagine what she said. El can twist truth into the kind of knot that will never be undone. "What happened between us is *none* of your business."

57

Anna visibly swallows. Squares her shoulders. "You should leave. She wouldn't want you here."

I press my card against the chip-and-PIN machine. Snatch up my bag and march fast towards the door and the street. I'm too jet-lagged and already angry to trust myself to speak.

"You should be careful," Anna calls after me.

And although it sounds like a threat, the sudden lack of ice in her voice makes it seem like a warning.

*

Ross isn't downstairs when I return. That's probably just as well. I feel unsettled. The dream and the conversation with Anna have kept me on the same edge as El's email, the page from her diary, the rediscovery of Mirrorland. I knew that coming back here after all this time would feel strange, but I wasn't prepared for uneasy. Uncertain. Afraid.

I stand at the Kitchener. Overcook the pasta to the point of dis-integration, dump it all, start again. I watch the water bubble and churn, and remember Mum stroking my cheek, her nails scratching. *Don't be like me, Catriona. See the good instead of only the bad.* So I think of El and me sitting at the kitchen table, sneaking too-sweet bites of Grandpa's coconut toffee when Mum wasn't looking. Tossing loose socks up towards the hanging clothes rack we'd christened Morag. One point for landing over a wooden slat; ten for one of the cast-iron ends. My phone vibrates, and I jump, fumble it out of my pocket.

The email is from john.smith120594. Its subject line is HE KNOWS.

And its message:

CLUE 2. WHERE GRANDPA'S FIRST MATE IRVINE DIED

The anger is almost a relief. Less welcome is the sudden rush of recognition. I turn away from the range and sit down at the table, where Grandpa first told us about the fate of doomed Irvine. In 1974, Grandpa almost lost his leg—and his life—during a two-day fishing trip in the North Sea, aboard a stern trawler called *The Relict*. He told us the story so often, we sometimes dreamed of it: the snowstorm,

58

the shrieks of the gulls and gannets, the smells of the seabed as the floats and warps emerged from the Devil's Hole, a hundred and thirty fathoms down—salt and oil and earth. The drum stalling, the hydraulics screaming as the net snagged on the bottom and the boat tipped stern, and Grandpa and his oldest mate, Irvine, slid down the deck towards the jammed trawl doors and the sea. Grandpa's leg snapped in two between ramp gears, but still he threw Irvine a net hook, still he held on to his friend for dear life until his friend finally let go.

Every surviving deckhand on *The Relict* got something, but Grandpa got more, because he was the one who'd filed report after report about those faulty trawl doors; he was the one whose friend had died and whose leg no longer worked. In the end, he got enough compensation to comfortably retire and buy this house. *Folk have allus underestimated me, hen*, he'd say. *Ah wis that skipper's worst fuckin' nightmare.* Unlike Mum, Grandpa had only one rule, though it was as oft repeated as it was absolute: *There's an arsehole on every boat, and if there's no, it's prob'ly you.*

I get up, march across to the wonky beige units. I crouch down and start opening the doors, moving aside bowls and Tupperware until I find it. In the corner of the back wall of the last cupboard. A tiny swirling pool of charcoal and black Biro. The Devil's Hole. El was fond of vandalizing the insides of cupboards and drawers, small and sly, where no one was ever likely to look unless they knew it was there. She drew the Devil's Hole here a few days after Grandpa first told us the story. I have to get down on my knees to reach in for the folded square of paper beneath it. And just as I realize that there are two squares of paper this time, someone—something—hisses:

You're a disgusting wee bitch!

I rear back. I think I shriek. I know I snatch my hand out of the cupboard and frantically kick backwards with my feet until I'm on the other side of the kitchen again. I swallow. There's no one here. But I can still feel that voice. The venom in it, the spite. The fury. And in some far corner of my mind, I see a woman: tall with brittle black hair. *The Witch.*

"What are you doing?" Ross says, from the kitchen doorway.

"Slipped," I manage to say, affecting a laugh, rubbing my arm as

I shove the two squares of paper into my pocket, let him help me back onto my feet.

I know this woman—at least, I feel like I do. The vague recollections those hissed words have provoked are more like impressions, curls of smoke. Her voice, thin and high and cruel. Brows low, eyes narrow, staring down at me like I'm just about the worst thing she's ever had to look at. Grandpa finding me crying at the kitchen table. A wink, the cool, heavy pat of his hand. *Ye're a long time dead, lassie. Nothin' else ever worth greetin' over.*

I go back to the Kitchener, look down at the two tiles close to my feet, the dark rusty stain running through the cracked grout between them. I shiver. Shake it off. Glance at the pasta, bendy and well on its way to inedible again. "I think it's ready."

We both eat like machines: slow, steady, efficient. Afterwards, neither of us looks any better for it. I get up, open the Smeg door, take out a bottle of wine.

"The bottom drawer of the old fridge-freezer used to be crammed full of M and S sausage rolls, with 'FOR MY FUNERAL—DO *NOT* TOUCH' printed on big ugly labels," I say, trying to ease the tension. "Grandpa called them his *fancy horse doovers.*" I think of his easy, quick grins. *Good spread at a funeral's rare as rockin' horse shite these days, hen.*

When I turn around, Ross's frown is sharp, his eyes angry. And then his face relaxes, goes blank so quickly that I shiver, wonder if I imagined it.

"Are you okay, Ross?"

I'm almost relieved when that ugly sneer returns. "Why *wouldn't* I be okay, Cat?"

"I'm sorry. Of course, you're not okay. I didn't mean—"

"Shit. *I'm* sorry. Ignore me." He rubs a hand over his eyes, gives me a wan smile. "I'm just knackered. Really fucking knackered."

I open the wine, pour it into our glasses. "I met Anna today. Is she always such a bitch?"

"Anna?"

"In Colquhoun's. Blond, beautiful, Russian."

"Yeah, Anna. Not Russian, she's Slovakian. She can be . . ." He waves a hand. "I dunno, nippy."

I take a sip of wine. "El thinks Anna fancies you, doesn't she?" Because El has always been jealous. Possessive. Of Ross, at least.

When he doesn't answer, I seek safer ground. "I met Marie too. She was asking if there was any news and—"

Ross gets abruptly up from the table. "I don't know who that is."

"Well, she seemed to know you. Said she and El were friends. She lives in the Gingerbread Coop."

"The what?"

"Across the road. The terrace across the road."

He shakes his head, but his back is turned to me and I can't see his expression. "I have no idea who she is."

And what does it matter anyway? El always had secrets. She liked to keep everything—everyone—separate, apart. Even as kids, she couldn't stand it if different foods were mixed; she'd painstakingly push them to the opposite sides of her plate, leaving only empty space in between.

"I didn't know El was depressed," I finally say, to break the silence.

Ross turns around. "I'm a fucking clinical psychologist," he says, and there's no longer any anger in him, just a palpable exhaustion. "I see a dozen clients every day who have chronic depression, bipolar, PTSD." He sits heavily back down, rests his head in his hands. "And I couldn't even help my own wife."

"But you said it was mild. You told Rafiq El's depression was—"

"I know what I said. But Rafiq is looking for any excuse to get me off her back. You saw what she was like about the cards. She thinks I'm a pain in the arse."

"I'm sure that's not—"

"She probably thinks I left you that card myself," he says. "To keep them interested, keep the investigation *active*."

I want to talk to him about the cards, but his slumped shoulders stop me. I long to make him feel better, but how can I? He already knows that I don't believe El's dead. Or even truly missing. If I tell him about the email *clues*, I instinctively know he'll reject the idea that they're from El, even though it's the most logical explanation. And besides, no matter how much I might want to, I can't forget that DON'T TELL ANYONE. So, I nod, even though I know that I'm doing exactly what El wants me to: keeping Ross and me separate, pushing us to opposite sides of the plate. "Yeah, I can believe that. Bet she has every episode of *Prime Suspect* on her TiVo."

When Ross doesn't reply, I look out the window. The grass is turning golden as the sun sinks down behind the garden's back wall.

"Why are all the windows nailed shut?"

He blinks. Looks at the windowsill. "We assumed the MacDonalds did it for security—I mean, they were ancient." His smile lasts little more than a second. "I got a restorations guy round after we moved in, who told us we'd have to replace every bottom frame. Would have cost thousands." This time his smile is bitter. "I didn't mind them too much, to be honest. Thought they would help keep El safe when I wasn't here."

We sit for a long while, neither of us speaking, drinking until the wine is finished. Finally, Ross gets up, puts his glass in the sink. "I'm going to try and get some sleep."

"Okay."

He stops at the kitchen door. "Tell me why, Cat. Why you're so sure she's not dead."

"I'd feel it," I say. "If she died, I would have felt it. I'd *know*."

I can see his knuckles go white as he grips the doorknob. "You think *I* wouldn't feel it? You're the one who doesn't know her. You haven't known her for twelve fucking years, Cat! She wouldn't fake her own disappearance or death any more than she'd send threatening cards to herself. We were *together*. We loved each other."

I don't know who he's trying to convince, himself or me, but his words, his quick anger hurt me badly all the same, feel as sharp as a slap. They burn inside my throat and behind my eyes. Because he *wants* to hurt me, I realize. Even if it's only because he can't hurt El. Or because she is all he sees whenever he looks at me.

"She was different," he says. "After you left, she changed. She wouldn't do this. Never."

"People don't change that much," I say. Because I can't help it. Because I believe it.

His lips curve up into a humorless smile. "She always said denial was your superpower." And then he opens the door and leaves without once looking back at me.

I sit at the kitchen table. Look back out the window. I feel clammy, sweaty. Exhausted and awake. I pull out the first folded piece of paper from my pocket and open it.

JANUARY 10TH 1995 = 8 + A HALF
Mum says at night Bluebeerd hunts for another wife to lock up and hang on a hook when he gets angry. Bluebeerd is A COWARD OF THE TALLEST ORDER.

She says when we are on the Satisfaction looking for Captin Henry and The Ileland we have to BEHAVE and not FIGHT or Blackbeerd will get us. Coz Blackbeerd is the WORST PIRATE OF ALL. Hes sly and mean and all he does is lie. All he wants to do is catch us and trick us and throw us to the sharks. But he never does.

Shes just trying to scare us Ross says.

CHAPTER 7

August 23rd 1995 = 9 + 2 months (NEERLY!)
Its good when its just me and Cat but I like it when Ross is there
too even tho we have to play the things he wants to like spagetti
westerns.

Today we were deputys in Boomtown, holding off the
Oklahomebrays (not how you spell it I do'nt think!) We had to
defend the town on our own coz Marshal Hank was in Deadwood
and we did'nt know when he was coming back. I hid behind the
wall of THE THREE-FINGERED-JOE SALOON and had a COLT
45. (Ross banned the Clowns from playing—he's not scayerd of
Clowns like Mum or Cat, but he does'nt like them much.) Belle and
Mouse got shot in the CROSSFIRE coz Ross says they ca'nt shoot
for shit.
We're SHARP SHOOTERS like Annie. I'm better than Cat though.

Mum ALLWAYS says theres no such thing as a good PRINCE
CHARMING like in Cinderella or Sleeping Beauty.
BUT if theres pirates and princesses and fairys and Clowns and
mermaids and poison tasters and MIRRORLAND there MUST be
good prince charmings too.
Today Ross held my hand for nearly ten minutes. And smiled at me
when he climbed back up out of MIRRORLAND when we had to go
in for tea. I did'nt tell Cat.

I remember El's smile, on the midsummer afternoon when Ross
and his mother moved into the old McKenzie house next door. The

house had lain empty for months; boarded up with wood and later steel, the FOR SALE sign in the garden slowly strangled by weeds. When El turned back from the window, she was nearly breathless with joy and grinning wide. *It's a boy!* We were seven. The first time he stuck his head out of his bedroom window above our garden wall to ask her name, her excitement was so urgent, so contagious, that it instantly infected me, sitting cross-legged on our golden yellow bedspread and reading *Peter Pan*. It burned through me like lightning; made my heart thunder.

There was an old skylight set into the washhouse's slate roof. Black with dead leaves and dirt. The garden walls were too high to climb, and we knew exactly what Grandpa would say—worse, what Mum would say—if they caught us playing with a boy, so from the very start Ross was our secret, and we were his. The only time we ever visited Mirrorland during the day was on Saturday afternoons, while Mum hoovered and cleaned the house and Grandpa shut himself in the Donkshop, football results reverberating throughout the house. Ross would climb down onto the washhouse roof from his bedroom window, jimmy open the skylight, and then drop down into Mirrorland.

The first time he did, I could barely look at him. I remember that my hands were clammy when he blinked at us both with those peat-brown eyes, when he grinned his crooked grin. "You look the same."

El didn't suffer from the same chronic shyness as me. Within minutes, Ross knew our age, shoe size, likes and dislikes; that we were Mirror Twins: rare, special, two in one hundred thousand. And it's true that I was jealous then. Jealous of her confidence. Jealous that she got more of his attention.

We spent most of that first day with the cowboys. Saturday afternoons were for fighting or target practice. Mum said we had to be able to protect ourselves from the bad men and outlaws that hid behind doors and inside shadows. El was always a far better shot than me, and I was relieved when practice ended early so that we could help Ross make his own slingshot out of twigs and rubber bands.

Afterwards, I slunk off to hide inside the biggest teepee, a precarious frame of old scaffolding poles under a sheet. Chief Red Cloud, sitting cross-legged in breechcloths and feather warbonnet, barely spared me a glance. The Lakota Sioux taught us how to make war clubs and tomahawks out of gardening tools and feathers, or how to defend ourselves with blocks and strikes, holds and rolls. But never on days when they'd seen us hanging out with cowboys.

I said hello, sat down, pretended I wasn't hiding. Across from the chief, Belle reclined on cushions like an Arabian princess, rubies and long silver blades glinting in her hair. She smiled and winked at me. Of everyone in Mirrorland, Belle was who I longed to be the most: beautiful and wild, impossibly cool. Beside her, Annie snorted. She could never care less about any predicament of mine. I wonder now if she was some kind of extension of our absolute belief that all adult women were like Mum: stern, angry, often frightening. Annie had two Irish pistols, a long, jagged scar from temple to ear, and more courage than any other pirate on the *Satisfaction*. Standing tall in her high buckled boots, alligator-skin belt, and cowhide jacket with buttons made from whalebone, it was impossible *not* to be afraid of her. And she knew it. She grinned at me and lunged close. "You're a grand wee coward, so you are."

Mouse nudged my elbow, gave me a tremulous smile. She'd tied a piece of rope tight around the waist of her black sack dress, had drawn clumsy white chalk lines to match the stripes of the gingham dresses El and I wore. Mouse always tried to look like us and act like us, but she was too submissive, too skinny, her hair hacked short and dark like all the other deckhands. She smeared her skin white with clown face paint, stained her cheeks and lips rosy red like Belle's. A manifestation of our fears and uncertainties, we could tell her all our secrets, our terrors, and watch her absorb them like a sponge. And then we could punish her for them: ignoring her, mocking her, making her walk the plank or take a bullet in Boomtown. Mirrorland made our imaginations fierce and mostly unforgiving. And Mouse was by far our favorite piñata. But that day, she sat quietly beside me in Chief Red Cloud's teepee, patting my hand like Grandpa, eyes big and blue and full of the best kind of sympathy. "It'll be okay, Cat. *I* love you."

When Ross poked his head and shoulders through the entrance, I stopped breathing. "Cool teepee," he said. "How did you build it?"

And better than his obvious certainty that I *had* built it was the realization that he'd come to me, he was talking to me, in that moment he was ignoring everyone else *but* me. Of course, he hadn't been in Mirrorland long enough to know or see any of its characters yet, but he *could* see El over his shoulder in Boomtown, he could hear the impatient stamp of her feet.

El was still mad when Ross swung back up through the skylight a few hours later.

"Cat's afraid of heights, you know." She smirked. "Sometimes she can't even go down stairs."

"Shut up!" I cried.

But he only smiled at both of us. "I'll come back next Saturday," he said. "Don't tell your mum about me. She'll ruin it."

I fold up the second diary page, push it inside my pocket with the other. My back aches and my feet are numb. I've no idea what time it is, but I know it's been hours since Ross went upstairs to sleep and somehow I'm still here, sitting at the kitchen table, staring into old memories. Why does she want me to do that? *What* does she want me to remember? Is that even the point of this at all? I have no idea why this treasure hunt is so different than those of our childhood. Why she's emailing me clues that lead to shoeboxes full of junk or the hidden pages of a diary she wrote more than twenty years ago. While she's disappeared to God knows where.

Control has to be the most of it. El's need for control has always been as necessary to her—as vital—as oxygen. That can't have changed. She's emailing me clues instead of leaving them with the diary pages, because she wants to be in control of when I look. What I find. That makes perfect sense. Even if nothing else does. But it doesn't mean I have to play along.

I open my laptop. Click reply before I can think myself out of it.

Who is this? My sister is missing. If you don't tell me who you are NOW, I'm going to the police.

The beep of an answer comes so quickly, it makes me jump.

DON'T

This time, I reply with no hesitation at all. *What do you want?*

I KNOW THINGS. THINGS YOU'VE MADE YOURSELF
FORGET
THINGS HE DOESN'T WANT YOU TO KNOW
DON'T TELL THE POLICE. DON'T TELL ANYONE
YOU'RE IN DANGER
I CAN HELP YOU

*Fuck off, El. I know it's you. You need to stop. You need to come
back. Stop it. And come back.*

She doesn't reply. I sit at the kitchen table for a long time, no
longer numb and stiff, but hot and angry. Until I hear a sound in
the hallway. I get up and move slowly to the door, open it as if I
expect to see something crouched and waiting to pounce on the
other side.

The hallway is empty. The stained-glass window is black dark.
There's a light on: a Victorian oil lamp on the old telephone table
that casts a red milky glow across the parquet. The house clanks and
clunks and groans as if it's a sleeping machine, as if the walls are
breathing in and out, in and out.

I catch sight of my face in the mirror over the telephone table,
the glass speckled with age and curled dark at its corners; my face
clown-white and pulled ugly by shadows. Another noise makes me
freeze. It's low and keening, trapped like the howl of wind inside a
narrow space. And it's coming from the drawing room.

I tiptoe across the parquet. Turn the handle and open the door.
It gives a ludicrously loud creak, but Ross doesn't even look up.
He's sitting on the rug in front of the fire, turning the pages of a
photograph album. Their wedding album. The wedding I wasn't
invited to.

The room is warm, lit golden by two large Tiffany lamps. I
remember Grandpa used to always bring home a real Fraser fir from

Craigie's Farm every year, and for the whole of December it would sit in the front corner between fireplace and window, glittering and twinkling and shedding its needles, making the whole room smell like a winter forest. Every Christmas Eve, El and I would listen to the grandfather clock ticking ponderously down to midnight, excitedly watching the four crystal glasses full of sherry that sat waiting on the turquoise tiles of the Poirot.

Ross finally looks up at me. His face is wet, eyes red. There's an empty whisky tumbler next to his knee, a half-full bottle. He holds it out to me. I take it and retreat a few feet, sit on the old leather recliner. The whisky is pretty disgusting, something muddy brown and far too strong, but the burn is familiar, and the warm buzz reward enough.

Ross looks down at an enlarged glossy print of him and El standing in front of a grand sandstone building with Greek columns. He's wearing what must be the MacAuley tartan, and El is painfully stylish in a short white satin dress and red heels, her hair wound up high but loose. It's obviously raining and windy; Ross is battling to one-handedly hold a large golf umbrella over both of their heads, and they're leaning together, El's hand on his waistcoat, his around her waist, laughing so hard it's like I can hear them. It's a beautiful picture, and when Ross goes to turn the page over, his fingers are shaking. I don't go to him. I can't. But something in me—warm and familiar and unwanted—hurts for him. Not the pain I felt when he told me about El going missing—fast and hot and fleeting—but deep down, like an ache. Melancholy, old. Indulgent. Like rediscovering the door to Mirrorland. And all I want is for it to go away.

Ross makes another of those terrible sounds, and then he starts to cry, great ragged sobs that make my own throat hurt, my own eyes sting. When he finally looks at me, I nearly flinch from the desperation in his eyes. "Christ, Cat. What am I going to do without her?"

I'm suddenly furious with El. Not pissed off, not angry, not resentful. Violently furious. I KNOW THINGS. THINGS HE DOESN'T WANT YOU TO KNOW. Because who else can she mean but Ross? Who else can she expect me to think she means but Ross?

"I just don't . . ." He's still crying hard, wiping his cheeks with the heels of his hands. "I'm just so scared, Cat. I don't know what to do. I don't know how to go on without her. I don't know if I *can* go on with—"

"Hey. Don't talk like that. Don't ever, *ever* talk like that, okay?"

I abruptly remember another Saturday inside Chief Red Cloud's teepee, a couple of years after the first. The two of us sitting cross-legged, close enough to touch. A game of hide-and-seek maybe, or a rare occasion when El was speaking to neither one of us.

Ross was scowling. "I hate her."

"Who?"

"My mum."

"Why?" I tried to hide my excitement; the growing certainty that what he was telling me, what he was *about* to tell me, was something that he'd never told El.

He tried to shrug, bowed his head. "She hates me. And she hates my dad."

"*Why?*"

Ross was quiet for a long time, and then I heard him swallow. "One day after he went to work, she packed two bags and told me we had to leave. We moved here. I moved to a different school. She said I'd see Dad and my friends again. But we're still here."

He looked at me then, and his eyes burned with an intensity that was not quite rage, not quite pain. His whole body vibrated with it, and I was deliciously afraid. When I felt brave enough to reach out and touch his hand, I was thrilled when he gripped mine back tightly enough to hurt.

"Today's his birthday. I don't even know where we used to live. She won't tell me, and I don't remember." A tear splashed against his forearm, ran down to his wrist. "I *hate* her."

And while he still twisted my fingers hard enough to make my eyes water, he laid his head on my shoulder and sobbed so hard that he lost his voice.

El knows how much Ross loves her. And she knows *how* Ross loves. Completely. Absolutely. To the exclusion of all else. Is this how

70

she wants him to suffer? Is this what she wants to reduce him to—considering suicide, however seriously, because of what she's done? But I can't believe that. I won't. El is selfish and thoughtless, sometimes she's cruel. But she loves Ross, I know that. And she would never wish death on anyone, no matter how angry she is, no matter how much she might want to punish them. I stop short, heart skipping, anger draining away. Because that's not true. Once upon a time she *did* wish someone dead. We both did.

"I'm sorry." Ross looks at me, presses his lips together in imitation of a smile. "And I'm so sorry about tonight. Everything I said. I didn't mean that either. I was a shithead to you, and I'm sorry."

"It's okay."

His smile freezes and then falters, stops being a smile at all. "I just love her so much. I can't—oh, for fuck's sake." He starts wiping so furiously at his face and eyes, I want to wince. And it's his embarrassment, his frustration at his own grief that finally makes me get up and go to him. She doesn't deserve his tears, his despair. Much less anything else.

"Ross, stop." I kneel down next to him and the photo album, cup his face in both of my hands. His eyes are worse than bloodshot, no longer white at all. His cheeks are rough with stubble, wet and red raw. I wipe them gently with the cool palms of my hands, my fingers, and he closes his eyes, goes limp. I think of his crooked smiles. The excited twist of my stomach whenever he dropped down from that skylight and into our world.

And I do it without thinking, even though I know I was planning on doing it all along. Even before I felt that old, indulgent ache. I lean closer and press my lips against his.

For a moment, he freezes, and I think about drawing back, pretending it was just a peck that landed badly, but I can't, because I want—need—more. His smell, as unique and inimitable as that of this house, is not enough; the feel of his skin, his stubble, his tears under my fingers is not enough. I need more.

And then I get it. His hands come up to touch my face, my hair. When I press deeper, he lets me, and our kiss goes from chaste to something else in seconds. His mouth is hot, wet. I can feel the thunder of my heartbeat even in my toes. He makes a sound somewhere between a sigh and a groan, and I think, *Yes.* Yes.

Because it's just the same. The same rush. The same madness. Sweeping everything else away, including sense.

Ross is the one to recover his first. And I can see straightaway that it's not the same for him. Not anymore. He scrambles to his feet, but not before I see the horror on his face. He nearly tips over the whisky glass in his rush to get up and away from me. And it's only when he has, when I realize that I'm looking at a closed door and kneeling on the floor of an empty room, that I remember to be horrified too.

CHAPTER 8

john.smith120594@gmail.com   8 April 2018 at 08:45

Re: HE KNOWS   Inbox

To: Me

CLUE 3. DRAW A CLOWN TO WARN THE TOOTH FAIRY

Sent from my iPhone

*

El can go screw herself. I'm not going to do it. I'm not going to get up, I'm not going to go into the bathroom, and I'm not going to look. My head is pounding in twin spots right behind my eyes. My stomach gurgles and heaves, and my breath is hot and whisky sour. I've no idea how much of it I drank. Too much.

I lurch out of bed, stagger to the bathroom, and make it just in time, my retches loud and humiliating. I stay on my knees for a long while, and then I get up slowly, stagger to the sink. The tap water is warm, metallic, but I glug it down nonetheless, barely stopping to draw breath. When I can avoid it no longer, I look at the mirror.

There's nothing there. No round clown face painted carefully in El's acrylics. It was the only warning we ever gave the Tooth Fairy whenever she was on the prowl. A little clown face in the corner of a mirror that we hoped would frighten her back into hiding before we had to resort to painting our faces and putting on our wigs and noses and jumpsuits in the Clown Café. Because everyone—everything—is terrified of something. And for the Tooth Fairy, it wasn't just Clowns, it was the very idea of them.

I open the mirror, start searching through the cabinet for another diary page. I reach behind some pill bottles, and one teeters and falls, crashing and rattling around the porcelain until I manage to catch hold of it. It feels mostly empty, and I'm already putting it back when I see El's name.

PROZAC (Fluoxetine) 60 mg tabs
ONCE DAILY
WITH OR WITHOUT FOOD

If it were possible to feel any lower, I would. I pick up the neighboring pill bottle. Diazepam. Prozac *and* Valium. A folded-up square of paper—the next clue—is sitting in the space where they were. I pick it up, put back the bottles. Look at myself in the mirror. My gray face, limp hair, black-shadowed puffy eyes. I think of Grandpa's *There's an arsehole on every boat, and if there's no, it's prob'ly you.*

What the fuck am I doing? But I know. I know how I feel about him. I've always known. And I know that even if El was still here, I would feel the same: a hostage to memories—truths—that I've spent years trying to ignore. I'm appalled by how easily they've come back, as if they've only been treading water when I'd imagined them long drowned.

I sit on the toilet lid, open the diary page, catch a glimpse of its very last line, *I HATE CAT*, and then I let it drop to the floor to nurse my aching head in my hands. She is my sister. And once upon a time, before she decided that she hated me, El loved me. And I loved her. Nothing and no one existed but us. Ross is her husband. I kissed him; he didn't kiss me. He had every right to look horrified. And if his horror seems worse than his guilt, then that's probably because I'm an arsehole. A selfish, husband-snogging cow.

A coil of *what if?* is unraveling in my belly. What if those pills mean she *has* had some kind of breakdown? Wouldn't that better explain this bizarre treasure hunt? What if I'm wrong about her being okay? What if she really is in trouble? What if she's having the same sort of desperate thoughts as Ross? What if she's already—

I get up too quickly. Strip off my T-shirt and turn on the shower while still dizzy. Let the scalding water beat against my skin and my skull until its steam is all I see and the pain is all I feel.

Only once I'm dry and warm and dressed do I pick up that diary page again and start reading.

November 30th, 1996 = 10+1/2 (IN 1 MONTH!!!)
Cat's not speaking to me but I don't care. Its not my fault. Mum says even PIRATES have to have RULES. We're aloud to give someone the BLACK SPOT if we want. And anyway it was Ross's idea/fault. He told me it would be fun and it was till Cat started to cry. I tried to stop him. I felt bad so I helped her even tho I'm NOT supposed to. I used our SECRET PIRATE CODE which is only supposed to be used in DIRE EMERGENCYS. I'm not writing it here just incase—I know you want to know it but TOUGH LUCK!!! Only me and Cat know it and thats the way it's going to stay!! But she didn't care anyway and she didn't say thankyou!!! She just CRIED!!!

I think she's just mad coz Ross said my painting of DAD was BRILLYANT. She's always jellous and then pretends she isn't. She's just mad coz she knows Ross likes me better than her even tho we look the same.
Sometimes I HATE CAT.

I think of that portrait of the pirate Captain Henry taped to the southern boundary wall in Mirrorland. The painstaking hours it took El to paint it, making Mum describe him over and over again. He'd once been respectable, Mum said, had worked for the government for years before he'd had to leave us for a long life at sea.

Did I ever really believe that our father was a pirate king? I know I did. So much of Mirrorland began as Mum's invention before El and I turned it into something else, something more than alive. We were so proud of him. *That's our dad,* El told Ross that first day he swung down through the skylight. *He's called Captain Henry, and one day he's coming back for us. He's going to take us to The Island.* Our belief was unshakable, unbreakable. Through almost everything, that never changed. We believed it absolutely. Even though we were wrong.

Ours was never a religious home. Grandpa, in particular, was scathing of anyone who showed even the slightest hint of being a *holy wullie*. Nevertheless, El and I prayed every night on our knees next to our bed. An antidote against the sometimes dark of Mirrorland perhaps. Or an insurance policy. A just-in-case. We were good at those. We would ask God how he was, if he'd had a nice day. And then we'd ask him to bless us and Grandpa and Mum and Dad, later Ross too. We never dared mention the pirates, the Clowns, the Indians, or the cowboys. Different worlds, we considered, were best kept separate.

And then one morning, El woke up and announced, "God doesn't exist. We're not going to waste time praying to him anymore." The end of her nose was bright pink. Her eyes flashed in a bad imitation of Mum. "You don't believe in him anyway."

She was mostly right, but it was hardly the point. If anything, what I liked was the ritual of praying, the kneeling side by side and knowing we were the only ones in the house who did it, night after night, week after week, building up credit. Once upon a time, I derived great pleasure in being virtuous.

And we were deep in Ross and El versus me territory by then. I was mad. Sad. Some nights I'd lie awake in bed for hours trying to come up with something—anything—that El would object to, be horrified by, *notice*, but I never could.

"No," I said. "I'm not going to do what you say."

El wasted no time in paying me back. Within the week, she had turned everyone against me. Grandpa by telling him I prayed to a nonexistent God; Mum because I'd pissed off Grandpa; everyone else, because everyone else—except perhaps Mouse, who clung to her neutrality like a life raft—had already been on El's side anyway. Even the Clowns.

I dug in. I've always been stubborn if rarely brave. In this instance, it only served to escalate our impasse, until I was formally summoned to a parley on the *Satisfaction*. The Witch was in the kitchen that day, I suddenly remember. Sitting at the table, while Mum stirred a pot on the stove. The Witch lunged into the hallway as I came down the stairs, her brittle black hair coiled on her head like a snake, a long bony finger pointing at my chest, eyes narrowed in suspicion.

"What are you doing, you little horror?" Her glare was icy. She breathed through her nose like a bull.

I ran around the bottom of the banister and barged through the pantry's black curtain without answering her. But I crept down to Mirrorland with a heavy heart. Being shouted at by the Witch seemed like a very bad omen indeed.

El and Ross were sitting cross-legged in the Captain's Quarters. In the stern stood Annie, Mouse, Belle, and Old Joe Johnson, the barkeep of the Three-Fingered-Joe Saloon. The Clown representative, to my dismay, was not Dicky Grock, but Pogo. He squatted—grinning—next to the stern lantern, his long, white-gloved fingers clasped loosely between his legs.

"We've called this parley to give the first mate the opportunity to take back what she said about God or face the consequences," El said. "What do you have to say, First Mate?"

"I'm not taking anything back."

"Just say you take it back."

"No."

El gave a long sigh. "Let's vote. Annie?"

"Punishment," Annie said, tossing her red hair and grinning with sharp teeth. When she growled at me, I blanched.

"Punishment," Belle said, twisting a gold ribbon between her fingers, her expression sorrowful. "I'm so sorry, Cat, but you can't believe in us *and* God—you have to pick."

Old Joe voted the same, although he also looked sorry to have to do it. He'd lost a daughter my age in the last big Boomtown shoot-out. Pogo giggled loud and long before shouting "Punishment!" louder and longer through his bullhorn. When they were in the Clown Café, the Clowns were passive, quiet, often afraid. But never in Mirrorland.

"Quartermaster, how do you vote?"

Ross was only ever allowed on the *Satisfaction* during day voyages. It seemed to me hugely unfair that he be allowed an equal vote during parleys. He looked at me, and I saw that he was smiling. "Punishment."

I stared at him until his smirk disappeared, his face flushed red, and he looked away. But inside, my hurt eclipsed even my dread.

"Mouse?"

Mouse glanced left at El and Ross. "Forgiveness," she whispered.

"Big surprise," El said. "So. Looks like the decision is punishment, First Mate." Something crept into her eyes then; it gleamed. And I became cold all over when I realized that it was fear.

"What are you going to do?"

She marched towards me, one hand behind her back, and when she was close enough to touch, she wheeled her arm around and opened her fist.

I shrank from the small piece of black paper sitting in her palm.

"You have to take it."

"I don't want to."

We had never used the Black Spot before. Its possibility was an ever-present threat, but until then that's all it had been. It meant expulsion from Mirrorland. Permanent exile. I couldn't believe that my going against El on this one thing—a thing I barely cared about—deserved such awfulness. I was horrified, paralyzed with shock.

"Take it," El said.

And so I did. Holding it between thumb and forefinger as if it burned.

"We've decided you should be given one last chance to survive," El said, but that gleam told me I wouldn't like it. "You've one minute to find a hiding place inside Mirrorland, but it has to be a good one. If we find you before one hour is up, you have to leave Mirrorland and you'll never get to come back. Okay?"

I nodded. Even though it only felt like a stay of execution.

"Go!" Annie shouted.

"Go!" Pogo shouted. Black panda eyes in a chalk-white face; his bright red grin sealed around the bullhorn.

Ross laughed, Mouse cowered, and El's eyes shone like silver marbles.

I turned and ran towards Boomtown, my fingers catching against the walls. The post office was too small. The teepees too obvious—and the Lakota Sioux too uncertain an ally. I began to slow, panicky and indecisive, heart hammering in my chest, rejecting any and all hiding places, until I'd run out of time, until I could hear my jubilantly furious punishers stampeding down the alleyway towards me. I ran along the boardwalk, barged through the marshal's office door, and dove down behind the booking desk made out of old sofa cushions.

I was too frightened, too filled up with dread and inevitable doom, to do much more than cower when, seconds later, someone's shadow loomed over mine. Mouse's eyes were big and black and round in her white-painted face.

"I knew you'd come here," she whispered. "I knew I'd find you here."

I thought I could hear a smile in her voice, and I didn't like it. I thought of all the times I'd been mean to her after El had been mean to me, and wondered if here, now, was where she'd decided to get revenge.

"Don't be scared," Mouse whispered, and now I could see her smile. Her teeth. "I'll help you, Cat. I'll save you."

"How?" Because I could hear giggling getting louder, the scratching of Clown feet on stone. I could hear El's "Let's split up," Ross's low and excited laugh.

Mouse scowled. "Ross is mean."

"No, he's not. He's—"

Her shadow put its hands on its hips. "Do you *want* me to help you?"

My nod was frantic. But she didn't move, didn't speak.

I swallowed. Felt the sting of more tears. "Ross is mean," I whispered.

Mouse dropped down onto her knees beside me. "I'll help you."

"*How?*"

Her smile was back. Ruby-red and wide. "You can be me. And I'll be you."

I shook my head, retreated farther behind the booking desk.

"It's easy!" she said, eyes glittering as she stood again, spun around in a circle. "Look!" And I saw that her baggy sack dress had been painted with clumsy red splodges to imitate the roses on the matching pinafores El and I wore. That she'd plaited her short hair into stumpy pigtails tied with string instead of ribbon. I saw, too, that she was excited. My predicament made her happy. And that made me shiver. There was a darkness to everyone and everything in Mirrorland. But Mouse had always been the exception.

She crawled behind the desk on her hands and knees. "Go and hide!"

When I didn't, she loomed even closer.

"You have to hide!" I could still see the shine of her teeth, like the Cheshire Cat in *Alice's Adventures in Wonderland*. "It's easy, Cat! If you're quiet and small and scared in the dark, no one will ever see you. Go!"

I went. Back on the boardwalk, I could see big laughing shadows against the bricked-over door and the teepees, I could smell sweat and sugar and smoke. I could hear Ross's laughter again, the joy in it. Frightened tears were running down my face as I ran into the Three-Fingered-Joe Saloon. The bar was an old TV box reinforced with bricks and broken wood covered with a tartan blanket. When I heard El shout my name, I jerked open the lid and climbed inside, crouched down on my knees, and buried my face in the blanket's scratchy warmth.

The dark was nearly suffocating. *Please, please*, I thought, squeezing my eyes shut. *Please don't let them find me. Please.*

Because what would I do without Mirrorland? Without Ross, Annie, Belle, and Mouse? The pirates, the cowboys, the Indians, and the Clowns? What would I do without Captain Henry? What would I do without El? I would be alone. I would be stuck inside a cold, gray, empty, frightening world.

An hour is an eternity if you spend it hiding in a box waiting for the very worst to happen. When the adrenaline started to wear off, it was replaced with a kind of weary doomed acceptance that returned as quickly to horror when I heard loud footsteps on the saloon's floor.

Please. Please.

I heard the bony thud of knees. The shuffle of someone moving closer. Opening the lid.

It was El.

"Please don't tell," I whispered. "Please don't make me leave Mirrorland and never ever come back. Please!"

Her expression was in shadow. "You're crying."

And I realized that I hadn't stopped. The realization made my tears come faster; made the pain bigger, scarier. I gripped her wrist. "Please don't tell!"

"Stop it!" El hissed. "Let me go."

"You'll say you found me."

"No, I won't."

"Yes, you will."

"No, I won't, dummy. You're my sister. Why would I want you out of Mirrorland?"

So you can have it—and Ross—all to yourself, was what I thought and didn't dare say.

"We will not leave each other," she whispered. "Come on! Say it."

I swallowed. Let go of her wrist. "We will not leave each other."

She nodded. "Never so long as we live."

Every pirate code was in code. And ours meant *Trust me. Trust me and no one else.*

"It's just fifteen more minutes," she said.

And then she closed the lid, leaving me in darkness.

It wasn't fifteen minutes. Endless leg cramps fed my panic, my claustrophobia, my uncertainty. When the lid was finally opened again, I no longer cared about consequences or banishment or being alone in a cold, gray, empty, frightening world.

I got up on legs that were numb and prickling, the Black Spot still crushed inside my palm. El stood inside the saloon, and everyone else stood behind her. She didn't look relieved so much as triumphant. "You did really great. We've all agreed that you're forgiven."

I never thought the Black Spot was Ross's idea. I never blamed him at all. Maybe El's diary was wrong. Maybe her version of that day is no truer than mine. Because a memory, after all, just like a belief, can still be a lie.

But she was right about me being jealous. Of course she was, because who wouldn't be? She and Ross conspired to exclude me in the only way children can: with looks and laughs and whispered conversations that ceased whenever I got within earshot. They were both cruel, there's no denying that. I can still remember that feeling, and far too readily: the heartbreaking agony of being discarded by both of them. The endless worrying about what I had done wrong, what I was doing wrong, and never knowing it was nothing at all. Is *that* what I'm supposed to be understanding from these email clues, these diary extracts, these unwelcome reminders of our past seeping back in like damp through a badly proofed wall? That Ross was always hers, even in the beginning? Or that she always kept secrets from me—that, pirate code or no, she had never trusted me? Or does she just want me to know that I'm wrong? That something else I believe in doesn't exist? That she won't ever be coming back?

★

Ross has gone out. I'm both relieved and worried. And embarrassed. This time he hasn't left me a note. I sit at the kitchen table, google "how to track the original location of an email," and trawl through the results until I find one that doesn't make me want to frisbee the laptop across the kitchen. My first attempt turns up Private IP Address—No Info. My second, the address of the Google mail server in Kansas. Two coffees later, I've managed to install a mail tracker add-on, but if I want it to trace an address, I need to send El a new email.

After typing "EL" in the subject line followed by ten minutes of staring at the screen, I take DS Logan's card out of my wallet and pick up my phone.

"DS Logan."

"Hi, this is Cat. Catriona Morgan. Em, Ellice MacAuley's—"

"Cat. Hi." His voice changes, and I immediately want to hang up. "Is everything okay?"

"Yes, it's fine. I mean, I—I just wanted to ask you a question."

"Sure. Fire away."

"I was just wondering . . . did you ever suspect that El was sending herself those cards?"

For a moment, he doesn't reply, and I realize that I'm holding my breath, without actually knowing what I want him to say. When I find my gaze wandering to those tiles in front of the Kitchener again, I screw my eyes shut.

"No," is what he does say. "We never did."

When I end the call and start typing, I realize that my hands are shaking. They won't stop.

If you're in trouble, please just tell me. Please.
I'll believe you.

And then I wait.

CHAPTER 9

It's not until I'm halfway across the grassy Links that I realize where I'm going. The afternoon is cold and dry, but the clouds on the horizon are slate gray and growing darker. I walk briskly through the parkland, looking around at the old sycamores and elms pushed and pulled by the wind. Remembering how much bigger, denser, more threatening their specters had been inside that silent, gray-pink dawn.

The ruined plague kiln squats on the ground like a stone turret cut down from its castle, and I can't help thinking of all the bodies buried on top of one another underneath this grass more than four hundred years ago. Or of their swollen black and tormented ghosts, eternally searching the Links for their burned possessions. Grandpa's stories were always very different from Mum's: deliciously gruesome and lacking in any kind of lesson or moral at all. The back of my neck prickles, and I swing around, thrust out my hands as if to stop what—or who—I'm suddenly certain is behind me. But there is no one. The few other inhabitants of the park are nowhere near me, nor are they looking my way. *Stop.*

I leave the Links, walk along street after street—some cobbled, some paved—old Georgian terraces opposite modern glass-walled, metal-framed apartment blocks; cozy bistros alongside grubby newsagents with window bars. The air is heavy with fried food, cigarette smoke, the exhausts of slow-moving school buses. But what I see are old gothic houses where the murderers of children live and lurk and haunt; what I smell is the sharp brine of the sea, of safety, of escape.

The ten-story apartment blocks on the corner of Lochinvar Drive are new. They hide the firth from view for just that little bit longer, and I pass them slowly, heading down the drive and past a weather-beaten sign: "WELCOME TO GRANTON HARBOUR." Halfway along the drive, the heavens finally open, and I pull up the hood of my anorak, yank its drawstring tight. I left El's cashmere coat at home, partly because of the weather, and mostly because this is one of the last places anyone reported seeing her. It feels strange to be here, makes me feel oddly self-conscious, as if I'm doing something wrong. I could well be. Nothing, I suppose, has the potential to fuck up a missing-person investigation like an identical twin wandering about unchecked.

The Royal Forth Yacht Club is a low brown building with small windows. I can hear the yachts before I get close enough to the water to see them: that familiar jostle and rattle of wind, water, and metal. The harbor pontoon is busy, packed full of boats attached to bobbing buoys.

The wind and rain have woven together a gray-white shifting mist that has obscured visibility in the west nearly entirely, but to the north, I can just about make out the volcanic rise of the Binn and the rocky coastline of Kinghorn. The low stone slip that I remember so well is still here beyond the harbor wall, still mostly submerged. Now, where the warehouse stood, there is only a car park and boatyard, full of forlorn-looking sailboats sitting up on blocks.

Too many years in LA have stripped me of any immunity against relentless wind and rain, and so I stop to take a breather, squint along the harbor wall and out to the wild and dark firth. It feels like El is still here. *Why here?* That's what I can't work out. Because it can't—it *can't*—be a coincidence that the place we ran to all those years ago is the place El has disappeared from now. That here, where our second life began, is where everyone believes El's has ended. I feel a ghost of that silvery, shivery dread. That unraveling coil of *what if?*

I hear the startled "Shit!" before I see the owner of it: a young man, hunkered down against the pier wall. He's looking at me, one hand clutching at the lapel of his very obviously not waterproof jacket. His second "Shit" lacks the shock of the first, and of course, I realize what's happened. Again.

"I'm not—"

"I know." He gets up with a grimace that suggests he's been there for a while. "You're Cat, El's twin sister. I'm Sathvik Brijesh. Vik."

He's younger than I first thought. Not handsome, not in the conventional sense that Ross is anyway. His face is kind rather than arresting. He clears his throat and nods once, stares at me in a way that should be unnerving but isn't. I know it's only because he's seeing El. His shoulders sag. "I'm an artist. El and I met at a portrait exhibition that was showing our work: 'Blank Masks, Hidden Faces.'"

When he smiles, I realize that he is handsome after all. The skin around his eyes crinkles. "By day, I'm a lot less interesting: an underwriter for LMI. I share an open-plan office with ninety-nine other people. It won an award." He makes quote marks with his fingers. "'Most efficient use of people-space.' Sexy, right?"

He shakes his head, turns back to look out at the firth. "I've been coming here . . . I don't know why. To feel closer to her, I suppose." He closes his eyes. "And I enjoy being battered to bits by the weather, it calms me down."

I like him. El probably liked him too. I bend down to pick up a small stone. When I throw it into the water, it leaves behind a slowly widening circle pricked by raindrops. "'I tried to drown my sorrows, but the bastards learned how to swim.'"

"She said you were funny."

"She did?" This seems as likely as Marie's *Ellice told me all about you, of course.*

"She talked about you a lot."

We're talking about her in the past tense, I realize. Just like Ross.

"Did you ever go out on her boat?"

Vik looks at me quickly, sharply, as if surprised by the question. "No. I get seasick watching *The Blue Planet*." He looks over at all the neon buoys in the water. "It was a good-looking sailboat, though," he says. "All shiny mahogany and chrome fittings." He smiles again. "When she bought it, it was called *Dock Holiday*."

"D'you know which mooring was hers?"

He frowns, points to a yellow buoy close to the eastern breakwater wall. "I think that one, but I'm not sure. Around there anyway. She needed to motor out."

"She doesn't like yellow."

"What?"

"Yellow. She hates it. I always hated red and she always hated yellow." I stare at the buoy. "I forgot that."

"Are you okay?"

"Sorry. Ever since I've come back it's like I've only just remembered that there's so *much* I've forgotten." I pause, look at Vik. "I suppose you think she's dead too?"

He looks at me. "Yes." He says it carefully, like I'm a bomb that might otherwise go off.

"Did she tell you she was getting threatening letters?"

"Cards, not letters," he replies. Nods.

I take in a breath, hold it, let it go. "She's sending me emails."

"She sent you emails?"

"No. She's *sending* me emails. Today. Yesterday. Since she's gone missing."

"What do they say?" he says, in that same careful voice.

"Nothing important. But I know they're from her."

"Do they say they're from her?"

I grit my teeth, suddenly angry. "That doesn't mean that they're not. They are."

"And these emails, they say that she's alive?" There's nothing at all in his expression that says he believes this for a minute.

I shake my head, force myself to say nothing more. To tamp down my frustrations and doubts and *what if*s until they're flat and quiet again.

"Look," Vik finally says. "Could we swap numbers? I just . . . it's hard only getting information from news reports. I thought maybe you could let me know if anything . . ."

"Fine."

I give him my number, and he texts me his, and then we fall silent again, while the rain comes down harder, bounces up from the asphalt.

"She was terrified of him."

I turn my head so fast, my hair whips against my face, stinging my skin. "What?"

Vik's eyes are wet, and he's looking anywhere, everywhere, but at me. "She was terrified. In the last few months, she changed." His voice is lower, harder. "She'd lost weight, she wasn't sleeping. She had bruises."

"Who is *him?*"

"Cat. Maybe you should—"

"*Who?*"

But, of course, I already know what he's going to say before he says it. I watch the up-and-down bob of his Adam's apple as he swallows. When he finally looks at me, his expression is as sorrowful as it is certain.

"Her husband."

*

I go back to Westeryk Road because there's nowhere else I can go. And there's some defiance in it too, I suppose. I might be starting to believe that El could be in trouble—or worse—but I don't believe even for one moment that Ross has done away with her. Any more than I believe that she was terrified of him.

The house is in darkness. There's another envelope on the hessian doormat. The late afternoon light bisects my name, exposing only CAT.

I pick it up, rip it open. A picture of a teddy bear sitting in a hospital bed with a thermometer in his sad mouth, another teddy bear standing anxiously alongside. *Get Well Soon.*

And inside: YOU'LL DIE TOO

I turn around, run back down the path, through the gate, and onto the street. I look left and right, but there's no one there. The card could have sat on that mat for hours. It starts to rain again: fat cold splashes against my skin, my hair. I screw the card inside my fist.

"Fuck off!"

It hurts my throat, but I don't care. A double-decker goes past, and heads swivel towards me in bored interest. I go back up the steps, slam the red front door shut, and the house shouts back its echoed outrage. And I don't care.

*

The Witch is dragging me along a black corridor into darkness, her fingers pinching my skin, her breath loud and labored in my ear. And I've been shouting for too long; my voice is only a whisper. "No, no! I don't want to go!"

Belle and Mouse race towards me, take hold of my arms to pull me back into the light.

"Sail away with us," Belle cries. "Come with us!" Her boot heels scream against stone as the Witch pulls us along behind her.

Tears are streaming down Mouse's cheeks. "We have to go to Mirrorland! She can't get you there. You're safe in Mirrorland!"

And then El comes out of the darkness. Her face covered in paint, thick and careless as if spread by a knife. She grabs hold of the Witch, wraps an arm around her neck. Turns to me with bright fury in her gray-blue eyes. "RUN!"

It takes a few terrifying seconds to orient myself. I'm lying on my bed in the Clown Café. It's harder to shake the nightmare off, and I'm glad to be distracted by the sound of raised voices.

I get up, go downstairs on unsteady legs. DS Logan, DI Rafiq, and another younger woman are standing next to the kitchen table. Ross is pacing, pulling at his hair. When he sees me in the doorway, his reaction is one of furious relief.

"They're giving up, Cat! I told you, didn't I?" He barrels towards me, eyes wild. "I told you they'd fucking give up!" I see the moment he remembers that I'm the very opposite of his ally in this, and he stops, retreats, drops his hands to his sides.

"We're not giving up, Ross," Rafiq says, and to her credit, she does look like she means it. She glances at me. "The MRCC mission coordinator has called off the search. The official suspension will be announced tomorrow."

The gunslinger. I can feel some prickle of Ross's anger myself.

"It's been six days," Rafiq says.

"I don't care!" Ross explodes. His eyes are rolling and big veins stand out like ropes on both sides of his neck. His knuckles are so white they look nearly translucent. "You need to find her. You *need* to find her! I can't stand this!"

The young woman puts her hand on his shoulder, whispers something in his ear, and he bites his lip hard enough to draw blood, looks at the ceiling with shining wet eyes.

"I'm Shona Murray, the family liaison officer," she says to me, still squeezing Ross's shoulder. Her voice is high and squeaky like a child's. "It's really good to meet you finally." As if we're at a family wedding.

I turn to Rafiq. "You have to keep looking for her."

Ross has never been a great actor. Everything he thinks, feels, has always been writ large on his face, in his actions. He really is terrified that they're going to stop looking for El. He really is terrified that she'll never be found. And I realize now that I can't face the prospect of them never finding her either. Because it isn't just Ross's life that's stopped, it's mine too. She needs to be found, she deserves to be found. Even if it means I have to pledge false allegiance to that *something bad has happened*; a euphemism for *dead* that's almost as annoying as the fact that everyone seems so determined to believe that she is.

"Like I said," Rafiq says, "we've not given up. But we've only limited resources." Behind her, I see Logan wince, and like him a little better for it. "El can't be considered high-risk indefinitely, especially when the Coastguard . . ." She stops, shakes her head. A flustered DI Kate Rafiq is more unnerving than I might have expected.

I save her by saying the words myself. "Thinks she's dead."

She clears her throat. "We'll stay in touch with the MRCC. They'll contact us if they discover anything new." This time, she doesn't hesitate, even though we all know exactly what she means. "And we'll keep El's missing-person case open, review it periodically, resume active investigations the minute any new information comes to light."

Ross is right. They're giving up. I watch Rafiq pick up her black coat and black umbrella, think of her standing in the Throne Room and telling us, *We'll find her.*

"Right, well, we'll leave you to it. Shona'll stay as long as you need her to." Rafiq nods towards Shona, who's still hovering beside Ross like a bad smell, giving him doe eyes and oozing silent sympathy.

"Did you get any forensics off the card?" I say, as Rafiq tries to pass me in the doorway.

"No." Her expression is entirely impassive.

"I got another one today."

My scowl freezes as everyone looks at me.

Rafiq's mouth presses thin, the only outward indication that I've pissed her off. "Was I not clear about you getting in touch with us straightaway if you got any more?"

"I didn't think you'd care." And I know I'm being unfair. I know that my anger, my frustration, is massively displaced, but I can't help it. In America, I was watertight. Here, now, I'm leaking from just about every well-soldered joint.

"Where is it?"

I run upstairs, get the card from the Clown Café. Bring it back to Rafiq, who drops it into an evidence bag and then leaves without another word.

"Hey," Logan says, pulling me gently by the arm back into the hallway. "You okay?"

I'm so tired all of a sudden. I wonder what he would do if I just leaned my head against his big chest and stayed there.

"Yeah."

"Look, don't mind the boss." He smiles. "Her bark's worse than her bite, believe me." His hand is still on my arm, but his smile fades as he looks at me. "Is there something else?"

"No." I should tell him about the emails and the diary pages. But I know I won't. Unlike the cards, they aren't overtly threatening. That they *are* threatening is something that I can finally admit to myself. But I'm certainly not about to tell Logan—or anyone else—why. Not if I don't have to.

"You sure?"

I think of El's reply to my email: DON'T TELL THE POLICE. DON'T TELL ANYONE. YOU'RE IN DANGER. I CAN HELP YOU.

"I'm sure." I try to smile. "I'm just jumpy. Ever since I came back here I've felt like—I mean, I thought I might have seen someone or . . . I just, it feels like there's someone . . . watching me. Following me."

Logan's gaze sharpens. "You think someone's following you?"

I nod. "All the time."

He looks over my shoulder at the kitchen door, and then back at me. "On the afternoon of your sister's disappearance, neighbors reported seeing a suspicious person hanging around outside the house."

"Suspicious how?"

"Just the fact that they seemed to be loitering. And someone in the terrace across the road later saw them coming out the alleyway alongside the house before running off towards the Links."

"What did he look like?"

"Average build, anywhere between five-eight and -eleven, black jeans, boots. Wearing a dark parka, hood up. That's about it."

"There was a man yesterday," I say. "Just standing on the corner of Lochend Road, watching me."

Logan frowns. "Look, it's probably nothing, okay? But if you see him again, or if you're worried or concerned about anything— anyone—for any reason, just phone me straightaway. No matter what time it is."

"Okay."

"Don't approach them. Just phone."

"Okay, DS Logan. I won't. And I will."

He gives me a better smile as we reach the front door. He opens it and the hallway floods with bright light as he turns and runs his fingers through his daft hair. "It's just Logan. Craig, if you want. My mum named me after a bloody Proclaimer."

And then he steps out, closes the door, and the hallway returns to gloom. I go back to the kitchen, but something makes me stop at its closed door. On the other side, I can hear the chink of teaspoons against china, Ross's murmured thanks.

"If you need help in arranging anything, that's what I'm here for," Shona says. "I know you've got the help line and counseling numbers, but I've information about more practical things: organizing a private memorial or—"

"No." Ross's voice is sharp, hoarse.

"Okay, you're right. It's probably too early for that, but part of my job is to make sure that you're given all the practical help and information you need for when you do want it." She's stuttering a bit now, and I'm spitefully glad. A fucking memorial? Is she serious? El's been missing less than a week. "Legally, things have moved on a lot in the last few years, but it's still very difficult for the relatives of a missing person to organize their affairs."

"What do you mean?" Ross sounds a lot less indignant than he should.

The legs of a chair scrape against the tiled floor. "I'm not saying you should do it now, or that you're ready to do it now, but when a person has gone missing, and there's no body or a medical certificate to say that they have legally died, it's up to you to raise an action to satisfy a court that the missing person is presumed to be dead. If you're successful—and Ross, you probably don't want to hear this either, but you will be—the court will notify the registrar general and then the death can be registered. It used to be that you had to wait a minimum of seven years to register a missing person's death, but not anymore. I know you don't want to think about the practical side of all this, but you do need to prepare yourself. There will be an awful lot to sort out."

If she says "practical" one more time in her ridiculous voice, I think I might strangle her. I can't actually understand why Ross *isn't* strangling her.

I open the kitchen door with a little more force than necessary. Ross stands up, pulls both of his hands free of Shona's.

"Would you like some tea, Cat?" she asks, cheeks flushed.

"No tea," I say, but I'm not looking at her, I'm looking at Ross.

I make a long production of making myself coffee instead, and Shona gets ready to leave, with earnest promises to return tomorrow or the next day or whenever Ross needs her to.

"I'll see you out," I say, with a tight smile.

Inside the entrance hall, I put my hand on the night latch, and before I open the front door, I turn to face her. "She's not dead."

"What?" She has a scattering of light brown freckles across her nose. Her white-blond hair looks like it would snap in a stiff breeze. She's like a fucking pixie.

"She's not dead," I say again, and when I lean closer, my smile, I know, is El's: wide, cold, mocking. "Too bad for you."

CHAPTER 10

john.smith120594@gmail.com   9 April 2018 at 06:56

Re: HE KNOWS   Inbox

To: Me

CLUE 4. IT WAS THE BEST OF TIMES, IT WAS THE
WORST OF TIMES

Sent from my iPhone

★

john.smith120594@gmail.com   9 April 2018 at 07:02

Re: EL   Inbox

To: Me

I'M NOT IN TROUBLE. BUT YOU ARE

Sent from my iPhone

★

I find the diary page inside a battered copy of *A Tale of Two Cities*, on the shelf below El's self-portrait. It was her favorite book for a long time: the horror of it, the brutality; Madame Defarge and her knitting needles. She used to laugh at me for loving *Anne of Green Gables* instead.

October 12th, 1997: 11Y, 3M, 12D
Mum is always making us read or reading to us. She NEVER stops!

But at least now they're not baby stories or Shakespeare (YUKK). Now they're much more exciting—about wars and spies and murder! We just finished Rita Hayworth and Shawshank Redemption which is a stupid name but the book is the best!!! Its about a guy called Andy Dufrain whose in prison for murder but he didn't do it and he spends the next 27 YEARS! planning his escape. Its BRILLYANT!!! He has to use this tiny hammer to tunnel thru 4 feet of concrete and then he has to crawl thru a pipe full of SHIT!!! For 500 YARDS!!! IMMENSE/INSANE!!!!!!

The bit at the very end when his freind Red gets let out and he realises Andy has left him money and has set up a new life for him too is even more BRILLYANT! It made me cry which was SOOOOO embarassing but I don't care cos I LOVE it.

I LOVE MY MUM TOO
I LOVE CAT (sometimes!!! When she's not being a BITCH!!! Ha)

Mum never wavered in her belief that everything in life could be learned from books. By the time El and I were ten, she'd moved on from reading us fairy tales, to Shakespeare, T. S. Eliot, Dickens, Christie. Books piled up in that cupboard in the Princess Tower as we rattled through story after story: *The Tempest*, *The Count of Monte Cristo*, *Crooked House*, *Jane Eyre*, *The Man in the Iron Mask*.

By eleven, Mum had progressed to more contemporary novels: *The Hobbit*, *Papillon*, *Sophie's Choice*, *Slaughterhouse-Five*, *The Spy Who Came in from the Cold*. She started reading *Rita Hayworth and Shawshank Redemption* to us during the long, wet autumn of 1997. I can still see her sitting on the pantry's windowsill, ankles crossed, swinging her feet. Her voice, when she read to us, was never high and hectoring or fearful, it was slow and calm and steady. Less than a week after finishing it, Andy Dufresne had supplanted Madame Defarge, and El had turned Boomtown into the Shank. And less than a year after that, Mum was dead. And Mirrorland was no more.

I screw up the diary page inside my fist, watch the sky above Westeryk Road grow lighter. Today there are no *what ifs*. No shame or guilt or worry. Today, I'm angry. I offered El an olive branch, I offered her *help*, and all I got back was another clue, another page of her diary. It's so childish. Like she's trying to reboot me, restore old files she imagines are deleted. Does she really think I've forgotten our lives in this house? Choosing not to think of something is not the same as forgetting. The past is past. It's done and gone. I listened when Mum told me to *see the good instead of only the bad* because I saw how miserable seeing only the bad had made her. Since leaving this house—since running away from it—I've lived by that philosophy. And the closer those diary extracts get to September 4, 1998, the closer they get to the day—the night—that Mum and Grandpa died, that El and I ran, the more I'm glad I have. It's taken a lot for me to get to where I am, to shake off the weight of my first life in this house. And I won't let El manipulate me, for whatever reason, into picking it back up. Or into having to explain the sad and bad story of our childhood to someone else—and definitely not the police.

The tracker. I run back downstairs to the kitchen. Open the laptop, and get the password wrong twice before I can finally access my inbox. "Come on."

I click on the email, tick the small mail-tracker box. "Email opened once 1hr 14 mins ago." My heart is beating slow and heavy as the page starts to load. *"Come on."*

And then there it is:

John Smith 1hr 14 mins ago
EL
Location: Lothian, Scotland
City: Edinburgh
iPhone 7 secs, 1 view

I press the palm of my left hand against my cheek. My face is burning. Here. She's still here. I don't know what I expected. The Outer Hebrides? The Bahamas? But she's here. El is still here.

*

The graveyard is old, perched high on a bitterly cold hill. Ross and I have to pick our way through haphazard rows of eighteenth- and nineteenth-century graves: huge drunken stones chiseled into skulls and angels, vast gray slabs on stony stilts dressed in white and yellow lichen. The newer graves are far more modest and close together; most house only interred ashes.

It takes Ross a while to remember where the plot is, but when he does, I feel suddenly nervous. For a moment, I stand as still as the wind will allow, looking down at the black headstone, its ornate gold writing, so much like those cards left on the hessian mat. I wonder who put it there, who paid for it. Ignore the shiver that skates between my shoulder blades.

IN LOVING MEMORY OF
ROBERT JOHN FINLAY
AGED 72 YEARS

AND HIS DAUGHTER
NANCY FINLAY
AGED 36 YEARS
WHO BOTH DIED 4th SEPTEMBER 1998
GONE BUT NEVER FORGOTTEN

"You know they're called lairs?"

"What?"

"The graves." Ross nods down at the grass, mouth a grim line. I wonder if he regrets agreeing to bring me here. "Pretty appropriate."

I turn towards him. "Why did you always hate him so much?"

He gives me a sharp, almost suspicious look. And then he shakes his head, looks down at the neighboring gravestones instead. "Doesn't matter."

I think it does is on the tip of my tongue. But Grandpa was always grumpy bordering on mean, I can't pretend he wasn't. A flash of Mum standing at the kitchen table, dishing out stew as she described in a careful monotone the cleaning job she'd seen in the paper. Grandpa looking up from his plate. *Ye're better aff doin' whit ye're good at, hen.* Giving us a nod and a wink that made him look no less pissed off. *Lookin' efter the hoose and these fine wee lassies, eh?* And so, of course, she had. Grandpa never got the sharp end of her tongue. He never had to run around the house fleeing from imaginary fires or intruders or apocalypses.

I'm bending down to put the white roses that I picked from the garden into the grave vase when I realize it's already full. Pink gerberas. Mum's favorite. Strangely, I find this even more disconcerting than the fact that they're no more than a few days old.

"Who left them?"

Ross looks down. Shrugs.

"Don't you think that's weird? That someone would leave fresh flowers at their grave? I mean, who?" Even though I suspect I know exactly who.

I'm rewarded only with another unconcerned shrug. Ross seems different today. Lighter. Perhaps because he's finally given up on trying to carry both hope and grief around in the same bag and has plumped for the latter. I don't entirely blame him, and I still don't think for a moment that Vik is right about him, but his unwavering grief both irritates and unnerves me. As if he'd rather suffer it than entertain even the possibility that El has left him voluntarily. As if he'd rather believe she was dead. It's a nasty thought, I suppose, a snide one. That probably has more than a little to do with the memory of that stark look of horror on his face. And the long-fallowed fields that El's diary extracts are plowing through, churning up sour dirt.

"I saw spare vases by the main gates," he says. "I'll go get one."

As I watch him march away, I try to ignore my resentment, my regret. We haven't spoken about the kiss, haven't even mentioned it, but we can barely look each other in the eye, and our uneasy truce is just that: uneasy. Untrustworthy. I look down at the grave and I think about that I LOVE CAT, and perhaps inevitably, I think about the Rosemount.

I've never had the same difficulty remembering our second life as I do our first. My chest aches when I think of the Rosemount Care Home, a Victorian mansion that had once been a Catholic orphanage. The kind of cold, high-ceilinged, gargoyled monstrosity that makes you think about lunatic asylums and mass graves in the cellar.

The carers were nice enough, not kind exactly, but sympathetic to our plight inasmuch as they could be. No one in the Rosemount was ever of any real use to us, because we didn't allow them to be. We were twelve-year-old runaways and that was it, that was all we had sworn to tell anyone. Including that Old Salty Dog who found us at dawn, waiting patiently at the harborside for our pirate ship to arrive. It was probably the one promise we ever made to each other that we actually kept.

I cried more, but I suffered less, I can see that now. El stayed angry, defiant. Untouchable. She withdrew from everything and everyone, until I was the only one who kept trying to make her stop. Her elaborate plans for our future were furious, impervious: as soon as we turned eighteen we would leave Edinburgh and move abroad. She would be a portrait artist and I'd be a novelist, and we wouldn't need anyone. She had to have seen the lie in it, the fantasy. Because when we were alone in our room, she would talk incessantly, obsessively, *only* about Mirrorland and everything, everyone, in it as if they were what was real, what was important, what was unchanged. *I miss them*, she would say, over and over again like a mantra, like a wish while clicking ruby-red heels. I understood why, even then. Lies and secrets are hard, but pretending you don't care is harder. And I had a bad secret of my own back then. It wasn't Mum or Grandpa that I missed the most. It was Ross.

I hear him come back. His expression is still hard. Unreadable. "You okay?"

I nod, and he hunkers down to put the roses in the vase. When he stands up again, the atmosphere between us pulls thinner, even more tense. I want so badly to tell him about the tracker, but that would mean explaining the emails, why I haven't *told* him about the emails or the hidden diary pages, and everything between us still feels too raw, too fragile, too much like *this*. I don't have the courage.

I remember sitting next to him on a crate in the Three-Fingered-Joe Saloon. El had temporarily defected to the Indians, and was planning a surprise attack on Boomtown, and we were pretending not to be waiting for it. It must have been autumn or winter; the air was cold enough to fog the space between us. It had to have been close to the end of Boomtown and the beginning of the Shank, too, because it's one of my last memories of the saloon.

Ross had been quiet, almost pensive, until finally he turned to me, his gaze sharp, unblinking. "Tell me about The Island."

And I smiled. Glad that he was talking to me. Glad that he wanted something from me. Even though I knew it was only because El wasn't there to ask.

"It's called Santa Catalina, and it's in the Caribbean, and it's amazing. It's got beaches and lagoons and mangroves and palm trees. Captain Henry's going to take us there because it's his favorite place in the world. He built a fort there and a huge house, and the islanders have named streets and villages and even a big rock after him because they love him so much."

And Ross gave me that same sharp dark look. "Why doesn't he come back and do it, then? Your dad. Why doesn't he take you there?"

"I don't know." I stopped smiling. I stopped feeling glad. "Mum says he *will* come back. One day."

His eyes became even fiercer than before, the silver flecks inside them flashing, and I was suddenly afraid of him, of his anger, of what he was going to say. His lips turned thin. Mean. "Don't believe her. People lie, Cat. They lie all the time."

Perhaps that memory gives me courage, because I turn towards him now, put out my hand to stop him walking away.

"Are you going to tell me why you're pissed off with me?"

"I'm not pissed off with you." But he presses the heels of his palms against his eyelids.

"I would have told you about the second card, Ross. There just wasn't any time before—"

"You need to be honest with me, Cat. You need to tell me *everything*. We need to present a united front to the police, okay?" He grabs hold of my hand; his is icy cold. "I told you that Rafiq isn't taking the investigation seriously."

I don't think that's true, but then again, I don't think that a lot of things Ross believes are true. I look down at our hands. "Okay. I will. I'm sorry."

He exhales, long and low. Lets go of my fingers.

"Look," I say. "The other night—"

"Was a mistake," he says quickly, looking away.

I nod. Ignore that old melancholic ache.

"We were both tired, upset. That's all it was." A smile. "That and Laphroaig."

I try a smile of my own. It's probably as convincing.

"I didn't . . ." He clears his throat. "Cat. I want you to know that when I kissed you back it wasn't because I thought . . . it wasn't because you reminded me of El, or, you know, because I was imagining that you were El." He looks at me. "I don't want you to think that."

"I don't," I say. Because that, I have to allow him. Ross always saw us as separate. As different. He was one of the very few who ever did. That should make me feel better, but it doesn't.

*

We return to the house. And as soon as we reach the entrance hall, that oppressive weight drops back down onto our shoulders, goading us, cowing us, pushing us apart.

When I pick the envelope up, turn the **CATRIONA** away to open it, Ross leans against a crimson-red wall, a muscle working inside his cheek.

"What does it say?"

I look down at the **HE WILL HURT YOU TOO** in vivid red. Look up at the raw bruised skin around Ross's eyes.

I close the card, close the hallway door. "Just more of the same."

"Yeah," he says, turning away from me and towards the darkness of the hallway.

And I think of my nineteenth birthday. When El's fixed plans for the future—our future—were already supposed to have been well under way. And instead, I spent it inside a grubby dull waiting room with grubbier sofas and a plastic-framed seascape of rocks and sand and waves. And I said goodbye to it inside the stark white bright of a hospital side room. Looking at El looking at me. Swaddled in too-tight sheets, that bloodstained bandage pulling at the cannula in the back of her hand. Smiling that smile I've never been able to forget: tired and trembling, but filled with so much joy. So much hate. The croak of her voice, the laughter in it.

I win.

CHAPTER 11

john.smith120594@gmail.com   10 April 2018 at 15:36

Re: HE KNOWS   Inbox

To: Me

CLUE 5. WHERE THE CLOWNS HIDE

Sent from my iPhone

*

I get down on my knees on the Clown Café floor and lift up the bed's valance, wait for my eyes to adjust to the dark. I can see only one thing. Square and black. A terrible suspicion has me lunging for it, pulling it out into the light. I hear Mum's voice—high and furious—turning the rucksack upside down, scattering powder packs, tins of food, and a plastic bottle onto the bedroom floor. *These are off! This is empty! For God's sake, Catriona, why are you so useless? This is important! Will you never just do as you're bloody told, you stupid girl?* But it's not a black canvas rucksack. It's a lantern. Foggy windows of glass and sharp metal edges. An old candle burned to the bottom of its wick. A rusty hook. It's almost exactly the same as the lantern that hung from the stern of the *Satisfaction*. That *still* hangs from the stern of the *Satisfaction*. A lantern that three days ago made me shudder hard enough to make my bones crack. Taped to this one's metal frame is another diary page.

February 16th, 2004
Cat doesn't get it. She doesn't even try to get it. It's like she doesn't

*want to. She's an idiot. She thinks if she pretends something hasn't
happened then it hasn't happened. But if you forget something, you
might forget <u>Everything</u>. And that's just dumb. That's what makes
you an idiot. Sometimes I hate her for it. Sometimes I wish I didn't
have a sister at all. Sometimes I wish she would just disappear.*

I don't want to think about the El in the Rosemount anymore. I don't
want to think about *El* anymore. I hate that I can hear her voice: her
snide and mocking scorn. I hate that she can still reach me, hurt me.
Make me feel shame so big it's as if I'm the one disappearing.

I shove both the page and the lantern back under the bed, and
begin tearing around the Clown Café like a woman possessed, opening drawers and cupboards, looking under ornaments and books.
There are only so many rooms in this house, and El's treasure hunts
were endless: often, there could be three or more clues hidden in
every room. She always hated it when I did this—when I found clues
out of sequence—but I am sick of blindly dancing to her tune. I pull
hard on the dress-up cupboard door. When it won't budge, I pull
harder. It opens with a sticky protest. There are no face paints, wigs,
or jumpsuits. It's completely empty apart from the small square of
paper on its only shelf.

I feel suddenly afraid. The hair on the back of my neck stands up
stiff, like a long bony hand is inches away from falling heavy onto
my shoulder.

August 10th, 1998
Something's coming. Something's nearly here.
Sometimes I'm so scared I forget how to breathe. I forget that I can.

*The bells scare me all the time. It's what comes after the bells really
I know but it's the bells I think about the most. Sometimes I think I
hear them when I don't. Sometimes I dream them and wake up with
my hand on the door handle to run. Or shaking Cat hard enough to
make her teeth chatter. Sometimes I wake up downstairs and those
times scare me the most. What if one night the DEADLIGHTS
find me before I wake up? Once I woke up on the main deck of the*

Satisfaction. The wind was too loud and the port tacking sails were flapping like sheets hanging out to dry in the garden. And I know it was because I was trying to look for Dad. Because why does he never come back when <u>HE</u> always does? When ALL the bad ones always do? More often now. All the time.

I drop the page, slam the door shut, run to the bed, and pick up my laptop.

What do you want??? Please, El, just tell me what's going on.

The reply is immediate. I'M NOT EL. EL IS DEAD.

And still I can't resist. Even though I know—I *know*—that resisting is the only sane response left to me.

Then who the fuck are you?

This time, she makes me wait for maybe a minute.

I'M MOUSE.

*

"Let's go out," Ross says. "I'm sick to death of staring at these four walls."

And I can't say no, because I don't want to. I want to go just about anywhere as long as it's not here.

I take a long time getting ready. Too long. I put on one of my few expensive dresses, short and black, trimmed with blue silk thread. I pin up my hair, loose and high. I paint my nails the same red as my lips. And when I look in the mirror, I see El before I see me. And then convince myself I don't.

At the top of the stairs, I'm suddenly paralyzed by an awful sense of foreboding. It makes me want to run back to the Clown Café and stay there. Fingers push against my spine, my shoulder blades. *Stop being afraid of falling. Or you'll always be too afraid to fly.*

"You ready?" Ross calls from the kitchen. And I grip hold of the banister, heart thundering, until the vertigo, that old terrible urge to let go, to fall, vanishes to the same dark place as Mum's furious voice.

*

The restaurant is along a narrow close off Leith Street, its cobbles lit only by old Victorian lanterns. Ross puts his hand on the small of my back as he opens the door. Inside, it's busy without being noisy; low-beamed and cozy, with red-and-white checkered tablecloths and chocolate-dark walls.

A fat bearded man waves, makes his way over to us.

"Ross!" he says. "It's awfy good to see ye, my friend."

While he shakes Ross's hand, I'm treated to a scrutiny as uncertain as it is unsubtle.

"I heard there was still no news," he says, still looking at me, and the penny drops. He thinks I'm El, but at the same time he knows I'm not.

"No, not yet," Ross says. "Sorry, this is, em . . . Cat, El's twin sister. Cat, this is Michele. He also owns Favoloso in the Old Town."

Michele shakes his head. "Aye, it's a terrible thing . . . a terrible thing." His gaze slides back to me. "It's uncanny, hen, how much ye look like her."

"I'm sorry," Ross says again. "I know we haven't booked or anything, but I wondered . . ."

"Aye, of course, no worries. Come wi' me."

We weave around tables until we reach the rear of the restaurant. I can hear the muted clatter and chatter of the kitchen. Michele ushers us towards a corner booth. "I'm afraid it's a wee bit, em . . ."

It *is* a wee bit *em*. The booth chairs are high, and two long-stem candles flicker at each side of the table, a single red rose in a vase between them. There are no other tables anywhere near it. Clearly this is the designated *special romantic occasion* corner.

"It's fine," Ross says. "Thanks."

I take off my coat, and when Ross looks at me, I try not to enjoy the brief flare in his eyes.

He clears his throat, sits down. "You look great."

We order some antipasti and a Frascati that Michele recommends. His departure precipitates what seems like an endless procession of waiters to our table. It's around about the fifth—a teenage boy bearing a second basket of bread—that I realize this is just more scrutiny. I feel like a freak show curiosity.

"How many times have you and El come here?"

Ross stops pretending to be oblivious, rubs a hand over his face. "I'm sorry, Cat. I didn't think this would be weird, not even when I got here, you know? I'm really, really sorry. D'you want to go?"

"No. It's fine." Even though it isn't. But it's the situation that I'm really angry with, not him. It's El. The whole Mouse thing isn't just annoying, it's snide. Because she'd always really been my friend, not El's. The Mouse to my Cat. *My* creation. Her existence meant that I couldn't ever be at the very bottom of the pecking order; meant, too, that I could always be guaranteed kind company, a sympathetic hearing. And now El's hijacked even that. So why the hell should Ross and I feel like a sideshow? Why should we feel guilty? We haven't done anything wrong.

Our starters are delivered to the table by a waitress who tries so hard to avoid looking at us, she ends up nearly dropping Ross's plate into his lap. It makes me want to laugh, but I can see it just makes Ross even more tense. When she goes, he starts eating like it's his last meal. I want so much for him to relax. I wish I could take just a small part of his worry, his stress, his pain, and swap it for my anger. But I know he won't appreciate the effort, won't even want to listen to it, so all I can do is distract him.

"D'you remember the Rosemount?"

He stops, fork halfway to his mouth. "The Marshalsea Prison?"

"It wasn't that bad."

"It was, according to El."

"Not that she isn't prone to exaggeration." The wine has settled my nerves somewhat, stretched me less thin. "Remember the Shank in Mirrorland? Now, that *was* bad."

"Of course I remember." He looks at me a little too sharply. "Do you?"

"Of course."

El pretending to be Andy Dufresne, ordering me about: hide there, spy there, look out there. I think of the old gravel yard—replaced now by that flat paving in the back garden—the only part of Mirrorland that was ever outside. An exercise yard that El would insist she and I march around and around for endless, restless hours. Sometimes in the rain, sometimes until dark. Kicking up those silver and gray chuckies. The sound of their crunch and give under our prison boots, their powder chalky against the too-long drag of our prison clothes: Grandpa's old waxy fishing dungarees and jackets.

Inside the Shank, Ross was always the warder or the wing guard of Cellblock 5, built on top of the old wooden fruit crates that used to be Boomtown's boardwalk. I remember his stern glares of authority. The illicit thrill of his threats to lock us up and never let us go. We'd been fast approaching our teens by then; the Shank was the last bad gasp of Mirrorland, I suppose.

"I remember the Rosemount, but only vaguely," Ross says. He refills our glasses. "You'd both already done nearly six years' hard time when I saw you again."

I'm struck, then, by how easily, how vividly I can remember that day. Its colors, its smells. It was spring cold, coal-smoke sharp and white-pink with blossom. I was leaning against one of the pillars of the Scottish National Gallery, bored, chilly, waiting for El to come out. She could spend all day in an art gallery, from opening to closing, and even though we were barely speaking by then, I was still determined to at least try.

I saw Ross on the other side of Princes Street, coming out of a department store, carrying bags. Even now I can't describe how seeing him again made me feel. By 2004, the prospect of leaving the Rosemount loomed no longer as an opportunity, but a terrifying prospect. The carers kept talking to us about aging out as if we were a hundred and fifty instead of seventeen approaching eighteen. They also kept talking us through our options, enough that we knew we had very few. Ross was such a large part of our first life, already long abandoned and left for dead. So when I saw him—taller, bigger, just the same—that first initial bolt of joy and excitement was straightaway tempered with a sense of loss. Unease.

I didn't move, but he saw me anyway. My heart fluttered and

my stomach cramped as he crossed the road, started running. He stopped only when he got to within six feet of me, his breath fogging the space between us, his smile warm and big.

"Cat."

"Hi, Ross."

There were tears in his eyes before there were tears in mine. But I couldn't swear to who initiated first contact. One minute, Ross wasn't in my life anymore, and the next, his arms were tight around me and my face was pressed up against his chest. And he was all I could smell, breathe, feel.

"Where have you been? Are you okay?" The end of his nose was rosy red. His eyes shone. "I tried to find you. I tried to find both of you, but . . ."

"I'm sorry." Because we, of course, had always known where *he* was. That was part of the deal we'd made with each other at Granton Harbour—nothing from our first life could survive, no matter how much we might want it to.

His grin returned. "It's okay. I've found you now."

And then I know I was the one to hug him, because my face burned hot with working up the nerve to do it. To throw my hands around his neck, feel the broader span of his shoulders under my palms, feel the stranger *adult* scratch of his cheek against mine.

I didn't want El to come out of the gallery anymore. She would ruin this, I knew. But just as surely as if I'd conjured her, there she was.

Ross let go of me. "El?"

If it was a question, she didn't answer it. I was dreading the moment he stepped past me to her. The moment he touched her, kissed her, pulled her close. The moment when we resumed our old roles; where both of them forgot I even existed.

It didn't happen. When Ross moved forwards, El moved back. Only a few steps, but enough to make Ross pause. "El?"

"Why are you here?"

"I . . . I just saw Cat standing there, and . . ." I saw him swallow hard. His face was a study in hurt confusion.

I turned to look at El, and I could see her annoyance, her frustration with me. I balked at it, because it wasn't undeserved, but I also wanted to thumb my nose at it too. We were equal, we were separate. She wasn't the boss of me.

We stood awkwardly, none of us speaking. Eventually, El relented enough to kiss Ross on his cheek.

"We have to get back."

"To where?" Ross looked at me first, her second.

"Rosemount Care Home," I said, ignoring El's glare. "It's in Greenside. You could visit?"

"Come on," El said, grasping me by the elbow and hauling me down the steps to the gardens. "We have to go."

"Just ignore her," I said, privately both delighted and ashamed that I was delighted. "She's like this with everyone now." Because she was.

El didn't say a word until we were on the bus and halfway to the home, and then she turned to me, face flushed and furious. "We had a deal. This is our new life, and we don't need anyone else in it."

I couldn't understand why she was so upset, but I felt bad. It was her biggest display of emotion in years. "But it's *Ross*."

Her expression hardened, but her eyes were wet. "I don't care. We had a deal. And you broke it."

"It's weird," I say to Ross now. "The things I'm remembering. What happened then and . . . after." I'm in dangerous territory here, I know, but the wine and El's *She thinks if she pretends something hasn't happened then it hasn't happened* have made me feel reckless. Defensive. "The reason I left."

The candlelight flickers. Our eyes meet.

He drops his gaze first. "Maybe some things are better left forgotten."

"Maybe. Probably." And under the sudden hot flash of hurt, what I'm thinking is *definitely*. That was, after all, exactly the same philosophy that sent me running for America in the first place. But it's hard to turn off an engine that someone else has turned on, especially when they still have the keys.

"I'm thinking of hiring a marine investigator," Ross says. He glances at me. "You think it's a bad idea."

I drink my wine, more annoyed than I should be at the abrupt change in subject. "Why did El use that harbor?"

"What? You mean why did she moor her boat at Granton?"

"Yes."

He shrugs. "It's the nearest one. As far as I know it's the only one. There are no yacht clubs at Leith Docks. Why?"

"I just wondered, that's all. I don't know." I rub my fingers over my temples. "You really think it's an accident, don't you? What's happened to El. You don't think someone might have done something to her. You don't think she's done something to herself. You don't think she's run away."

He looks at me steadily. "Are those questions?"

I don't say anything. Press my lips together so that I can't.

"I want to know who sent those cards to El, who's sending them to you. But I don't think whoever it is has done anything to her. I'm just worried that . . . I'm worried the stress of the fucking things made *her* do something stupid." He leans forwards. "And I *don't* mean suicide. Yeah, she was depressed, she was a pain in the bloody arse, but she wasn't suicidal. I told you . . ." He must realize how loud he's being, how animated, because he looks around, lowers his voice. "She'd changed. She was different. Distant. Distracted." He sighs, closes his eyes. "So, yes. I think she went out on that bloody boat, and I think she had an accident."

I look at him, the shadows under his eyes, the tight hard lines of his frown. "You really think she's dead?"

He doesn't blink. "Yes. I really think she's dead."

"How were your starters?" Michele says through a smile that has frozen in its beginning, and we both lean away from each other like we've been electrocuted.

"Great, brilliant," we mutter, and he stops fake-smiling, takes away our plates without another word.

Ross looks at me, his expression resentful.

"Where else would she be, Cat? A Travelodge on the M6, living on *Game of Thrones* and room service? And *why*? Has your twin ESP, or whatever the fuck you think it is, told you that? *Why* would she do it?"

The first terrible thought that goes through my head is that Travelodges probably don't do room service. The second is that angry he looks good, better, less like he's drowning. The third is what I want to say but won't. *Because she's playing a game. Because she hates me. Maybe she hates you, too, I don't know. Maybe you're still too dumb to see her.*

"Christ," he says, shaking his head. "I know your mum did a number on you, but—"

"*What?*"

"She was textbook delusional disorder. Paranoid, grandiose, persecutory. She filled your heads with shit weird enough to confuse anyone, never mind two kids. Told you over and over that you were special, different, that you couldn't function without each other, until it was true. No wonder you had such a fucked-up relationship."

Have, I think, and my fingers tighten on the tablecloth. EL IS DEAD. I'M MOUSE. We *have* a fucked-up relationship. I nearly laugh, and then think of Mum instead, brushing our hair through long hard strokes: *You're growing up too fast.* As if we could stop it. As if the accusation wasn't entirely at odds with her apocalyptic dread; the adult books she read to us; the bravery she expected of us. The readiness. Those fingers always prodding at my spine, pushing against my shoulder blades. *Stop being afraid.*

Ross sighs, deflates. "Shit, I'm sorry. I'm sorry." He reaches across the table and squeezes my hand. Letting go only when another waiter walks past. "Can we just talk about something—anything—normal? Just for five minutes?"

I pour the last of the wine even though we're barely halfway through our meal. "I guess we can try."

CHAPTER 12

Four months nearly to the day after we'd bumped into Ross out-side the Scottish National Gallery, I woke up in our tiny room in the Rosemount, had breakfast, and snuck off to the communal shower block to get changed into my very best outfit of skinny jeans, Docs, and a Dutch army shirt tied in a knot at my waist. I got the bus to the Royal Botanic Gardens, where Ross was waiting for me by the big gates on Inverleith Row. He took my hand as we walked across the grass, and when we sat down we were both grinning, even though neither of us had spoken a word.

He stretched out on the grass and closed his eyes, and I took the opportunity to greedily watch him. His T-shirt was just the right side of too tight; he was growing muscles where before he'd only been skinny. His arms and face were tanned just like mine, after weeks of sitting in Holyrood Park and Princes Street Gardens, watching busk-ers and early summer tourists. El always came too: sullen, monosyl-labic. But this day, she was sick. This day, I had left her coughing and spluttering in her bed, and when I'd told her I was going to answer an ad for bar staff, I'd pretended that the heavy thickness in my chest was only phantom infection, sympathy pain.

Ross lit a cigarette, and I watched its smoke spiral. He seemed so changed, so grown-up. I knew he smoked weed, sometimes took pills. He talked about going clubbing and getting high, and it all seemed so unknown, so exciting. I knew I'd do anything—all of it—if he just asked me to.

When he laughed, I realized that I'd moved my scrutiny to his crotch instead, and the heat rushed into my face.

"Hey, it's okay," Ross said, pushing up onto his elbows. "I like it when you look."

I liked it when *he* looked. Even as a boy, he'd had this way of making me feel like the most important person in the world. And when he stopped looking, the least.

"I feel guilty," I said, and then instantly cursed myself for it.

"What for?"

But he knew what for. For lying to El when I never had before. About anything. For not telling her that Ross and I had been secretly texting for months. Or that sometimes I couldn't sleep for thinking about him, for wanting him for myself. For being glad—ecstatic— that she was sick enough that I could sneak out to see him on my own and she probably wouldn't even notice.

"She doesn't talk to you," Ross said. "She doesn't talk to anyone." And there was a hardness in his voice that I reveled in.

"She can't help it," I said magnanimously, trying not to notice that his hand was creeping closer to mine. "It's because she's stuck in the past. All she ever wants to talk about is Mirrorland, or Mum and Grandpa, and I don't. I want to live right now." I looked at him, at the intensity in his eyes, as if I were telling him the secrets of the universe, and suddenly I felt cripplingly shy, awkward. I stared down at the sun-bleached grass instead.

"Cat."

"I think that makes me a bitch."

"Cat."

He made me look at him in the best kind of way: by leaning close enough that I could smell his deodorant, his skin; by taking my face in his hands and turning it towards his.

"You're not a bitch."

And I knew it was going to happen then. Even before he leaned closer, dropped his gaze to my mouth, smoothed the hair from my cheeks. Before he made a sound, something low and inarticulate that flushed my face hot again, that turned my heartbeat into a drumbeat, and my insides heavy.

She doesn't want him anymore was what I kept telling myself. *She doesn't want anyone anymore.* And what I meant was *She doesn't want me.*

Then his lips met mine, his breath, his teeth, his tongue, and I stopped thinking about El altogether. My first kiss.

The taxi turns into Westeryk Road, and I turn to look at Ross. He's already looking at me. And I wonder if telepathy might not be exclusive to twins after all, because I'm pretty sure he's thinking about exactly the same things I am.

But as soon as the taxi drives off and we step up to the red door and close it behind us, the atmosphere between us changes. We go into the drawing room, loiter close to the door. Ross doesn't even take off his coat. This is what *normal* really is for us. Waiting with the gloom and ghosts and heavy silences.

"D'you want a drink?" Ross's question sounds oddly sullen, but I nod because I do. Maybe even more than I want to salvage our evening.

He mixes two vodka tonics at the Poirot. I watch him until I start to annoy myself, wander over to the window instead. Marie's house is in darkness. The road is empty, silent. I wonder if someone is watching us right now, and I step back, draw the big curtains shut.

Ross gives me my drink, and then hunkers down in front of the fire to light it, starts piling it with logs until the room is Christmas-warm and golden again. When he stands up, he turns to me with a better smile.

"Tell me how you've been."

"What?"

"I haven't asked. Not once since you got back, and I should have. So," he sits down on the recliner, "how have you been? What's your life in LA like?" He pauses. "Are you happy?"

He looks far too handsome in the flickering firelight. Even his unshaven jaw and the dark shadows under his eyes only make him look more appealing. I think of him angrily referring to himself as the wailing widower. I wonder if he knows that there are whole You-Tube pages dedicated to him.

"LA's good for me," I say, because I feel like I have to say something. "It doesn't sweat the small stuff. Or even a lot of the big stuff." I swallow a too-large mouthful of vodka tonic, because I want to tell him the truth. I want to tell him that sometimes I'm so unhappy it's like I can't breathe. El has a boat, a house, a vocation—a talent. Friends. A husband. I have a job I hate, writing ridiculous articles about spinach lattes, cheating spouses, and spiritual fucking Wi-Fi. And I date men I couldn't care less about; men who mostly act like they couldn't care less about me. I party too much. I drink too much. I spend too many hours sitting on the balcony of a condo I don't own—now, don't even *rent*—looking out at a vast blue sea and a vast blue sky, knowing that I'd rather be anywhere else and pretending I don't. I'm not living. I'm waiting. For something, anything, to happen. And worst of all, I've started to wonder whether this—all of this—is it.

I set down my drink. "I'm sorry, I need to go to the loo."

In the bathroom, I run the cold tap, splash water against my face. I look at myself in the mirror. I expect to look terrible, but I don't. I look vital, alive. I look like El.

What are you doing? What the fuck are you doing?

I'm pissed—somewhere quite far along from pleasantly so. I feel blurry and spaced out. But I know exactly what I'm doing. What I'm going to do.

We kept on seeing each other behind El's back. For months. We pretended she wouldn't care, knowing she would. Maybe we were trying to punish her for her wholesale rejection of us. I can see now that she was ill—depressed or worse—but even so, that isn't enough to dull the hurt, the anger. My excuses became less and less convincing, her withdrawal more and more acute. And I still didn't care. I wanted to hold on to everything she didn't.

"You fall in?" Ross yells from what sounds like the bottom of the stairs.

"I'll be right there," I shout back.

I look down at my dress. Think of my irrational jealousy towards Shona. My wide, mocking smile—*She's not dead. Too bad for you.* And then I start pulling the pins out of my hair, shaking it loose. I don't need to be El to stop being me.

"You okay?" Ross says, when I go back into the drawing room.

"I'm okay." I almost can't bear to look at him, at his frown, his eyes, the flicker of firelight between us. So ridiculous to feel like this, to still feel like this.

He stands up. "Are you sure? You—"

"Do you miss Mirrorland?"

He looks neither surprised nor pissed off at the question. Smiles all the way to his eyes. "I had the best times of my life there. I was sorry when it was gone."

"Have you been down there? After you bought the house?"

He nods. "It was pretty sad. The MacDonalds must have found the door in the pantry cupboard. They'd mostly cleared the alleyway up to the front garden, and pretty much left the washhouse to rot." He pauses. "I papered over the door; going down there upset El too much."

I change tack, as much to banish the returned furrow between his brows as to avoid telling him that I pulled that paper down. "God, do you remember the *Satisfaction*'s raids on the Spanish Main?"

"Much pillaging." His smile is so bittersweetly familiar. "That was my fault. I was a bit of a klepto."

"Your Treasure Trophies."

"Jesus, my Treasure Trophies. What a knob. You know, Mum found a whole load of the shit from our treasure chest in my wardrobe a few years after you'd gone. Including a complete set of Victorian sterling silver cutlery. Didn't ask me a thing about them. Just charity-shopped the lot."

I go towards him, and he stops smiling. His eyes widen as I get closer, and I take a breath, will myself to be brave, to keep going.

"I miss us," I whisper.

"Cat. What—"

I reach through the space between us, put my palms flat against his chest. "I miss us in Mirrorland the most."

"What are you doing?"

"I don't want to talk anymore," I say. When I stroke my fingers along his neck and jawline, they don't hesitate, don't shake.

He freezes, takes hold of them, backs away. "No. We can't do this."

There's a darkness around us, and I can feel it close in. The fire crackles. I can hear the grandfather clock tick, tick, ticking in the shadow of the hallway. And all around us the house groans and breathes and laughs.

I push myself hard against him, and even though I don't say it, I know it's in my eyes. *She isn't dead. She just left you. Like she left me.* I kiss his cheek, his jaw, his lips, run my tongue against the salt skin of his throat. I want him to give in. I want him to beg. I've always wanted him to beg.

But instead, he pushes me away again. Closes his eyes. Steps back.

I think of that look of horror, how quickly he scrambled to get away from me in this very room three nights ago. I hear the heavy turn and clunk of a dead bolt. The thunderous stamp of boots. *Something's coming. Something's nearly here.* And then I do start to shake. I put my hands on his face, his chest, smooth my palms over his shoulder blades, run my fingers through his hair.

"Cat, you have to stop," he says. But whether he knows it or not, he's already touching me; his fingers are gripping hold of my arms, keeping me where I already want to be. Already am. "Please."

I move my fingers down, down. Feel his hot fast breath, the glancing edge of his teeth against my neck as I press the heel of my palm against his crotch. His voice muffled against my skin. "God. Please. Please, Cat."

And as soon as I kiss him again, he gives in. The kiss is too wet, too hot, too clumsy, but it's what I need. Everything feels so raw, it almost hurts. We grab handfuls of each other, and it's just the same as it ever was. The same wonderful. The same rush. The same madness. He makes a sound, loud and almost distressed, and I think, *Yes.* Yes.

I suppose what we're doing is punishing El again, the only way we know how. But God, it doesn't feel that way. We stagger backwards. He kisses me like he doesn't need to breathe, and I kiss him back, and all of it—the noises we're making, the frenzied near panic of what we're doing: scratching, pinching, squeezing, biting—all of it feels good and clean and right in a way that nothing—and no one—else ever has. I lost my virginity to him in much the same way: pressed up against a chest of drawers in his bedroom; too fast, too desperate, the pain needy and raw, a spur to do more, feel more, take more. It was never ever enough.

He lifts me up onto the mahogany lowboy; its French polish is cold against my skin. We fumble with each other's clothes, making frustratingly little headway. He pulls me closer, presses himself harder against me, bites the space between my left shoulder and neck hard enough to make me cry out, to grab him back even harder. Every bit of me wants him, there is not an ounce of doubt or guilt in me. I think of El's *Sometimes I wish she would just disappear.* And how right now, right here, I'm not just glad that she has, I'm certain that all along she was the one that was supposed to.

When we finally manage to get rid of enough clothes that he can push against me, inside me, skin to skin, we both cry out, we both hold on, we both whisper *"Fuck"* into each other's mouth. And I stop thinking about El at all.

*

There was never a time when Mirrorland didn't feel real; when we couldn't feel the wind and rain and wonder of it, or smell the sea and smoke and sweat and blood of it. But sometimes, Mirrorland felt *very* real, and those were the times when we were clever or cruel or afraid.

One long hot Saturday afternoon, when the *Satisfaction* was between ports, El and I devised a game to pass the time. Ross would be put overboard into the open sea, and handfuls of sharp tacks would be thrown in with him. He'd have ten minutes to find and return every single one before we hauled anchor and left. He was reluctant, of course, but all Mirrorland rules set by either El or me had to be obeyed. And so he stood in the Caribbean Sea, some three hundred miles off the coast of Haiti, shoulders hunched and pretending not to flinch as we threw the tacks in after him.

He had to have known he couldn't do it. That the game was *supposed* to be impossible. But still, he tried. He got down on his hands and knees and searched every corner of the sea for those scattered tacks, collecting them in one hand, picking them up with the other—and only when there was one minute remaining did he start to panic.

"I can't do it! I don't have them all!"

"There are fifty," El said mildly. "How many do you have?"

"We'll stop the clock," I said. "While you count."

He had thirty-two.

"You better hurry up," El said.

When his time was up, and we got ready to sail away without him, he started to cry. "Don't! Please!"

I'd never seen Ross cry before, and seeing it didn't make me feel remorse, it made me feel powerful. It made me think of hiding in a box and sobbing into a tartan blanket.

"You can catch us up, stupid," El said, as if it was the most obvious thing in the world.

"NO! You can't leave me!"

That image is one of my most enduring of Mirrorland. El and I sailing away from a sobbing and inconsolable Ross on his knees in the Caribbean Sea, hands bloody and full of tacks. Calling out to us though we pretended not to hear him. "How will I know where you've gone?"

The alarm clock says 11:35. When I stretch, everything aches in a warm, lethargic way. Ross is still in bed with me. I can hear his slow breathing, feel the heat of him at my back. When I'm sure that he's still asleep, I turn around to look at him. He's lying half on his front, legs splayed under the covers. I've never gone to sleep with him before, and it feels strange, intimate, more of a transgression than fucking him did. At least we're in the Clown Café instead of their bedroom, *our* bedroom. I look at his thick hair, sticking up in all directions. His broad shoulders and back, his narrow hips, the curve and flat of his flank. And I still want to touch him, I still feel that itchy need to do more. I think the word *arsehole*, but it's lost much of its previous power. I do have guilt, and a sizable chunk of it, but when I poke around it, like the swollen gum around a bad tooth, it gets no bigger, no more painful.

She left him. She doesn't want him.

"Hey." His voice is muffled, still thick with sleep.

I snatch my hand back from his skin, but otherwise freeze, holding my breath.

He doesn't turn around, but gropes behind him for my hand. And for a horrible, punishing moment, I wonder if he thinks I'm El.

"I know it's you, Cat."

I sit up. Find myself looking at that framed photo on the bedside table. A young El and Ross grin back at me.

"Do you regret it?" I hate that my voice sounds so small. "Do you regret what we did?"

He sighs, and then sits up too, turns his head to look at me. "No."

But I realize that he's looking at that framed photo too. And I can see in his eyes that part of him does. Part of him *has* to. A big part.

"I don't want you to think that I don't love her," he says.

"I'm her sister" is just about the only thing I can think of to say. As far as culpability goes, genes probably trump vows.

We both jump at the sudden bell ring from downstairs, its echo winding up towards us. Ross gets up, pulls on a pair of jogging bottoms. I hear him move across the landing, the slap of his bare feet against the mosaic stair tiles. I stare at the bell pull set into the wall next to the dress-up cupboard. Think of all those bells lined up on the board in the kitchen like mismatched knives in a drawer.

I look back at the photo. And I can still hear her voice in the dark. After hours and hours of ugly silence. Hoarse and mean and full of the same gleaming fear as her eyes on the day she gave me the Black Spot. *How could you? You're supposed to be my fucking sister.*

*

By 2005, El and I had a bedsit in Gorgie. A predictably awful dump, though we were as grateful for it as shipwrecked sailors are for land. It belonged to the Rosemount, and was ours for exactly twelve months, while we sought alternative accommodation and the means to pay for it. We were both at college on scholarships, working whatever shitty jobs we could find. We still barely spoke, no closer at almost nineteen than we had been at almost eighteen. And I was still lying to her.

The care home was holding a reunion party that May Day bank holiday: a barbecue in its extensive grounds. El threw the invitation in the bin, but I rescued it, arranged to meet Ross at the rear fire exit. We probably thought we were being discreet and clever, but I doubt we actually were for even a minute. Ordinarily, we met at his mother's house—they'd moved from Westeryk to Fountainbridge by then—and we'd have fast and muffled sex in his small single bed, listening to the murmur of people downstairs. The opportunity that an empty Rosemount presented was too good to waste.

The long, high-ceilinged corridors were deserted. Ross held my hand as he led me along them, while I navigated from the rear in loud whispers. All the room keys hung on numbered hooks in the reception office, and I knew that the new occupants of the twin bedroom that El and I had shared were busy getting stoned behind a bush on the front lawn. But that probably wasn't all of it. I imagine that I wanted Ross there. To have him in my bed and not hers.

We had progressed past the urgent, desperate stage to slick and sweaty and loud, far beyond any shyness or inhibition, when she walked in on us. I saw her over Ross's shoulder in the very instant that he came, twitching and shuddering against me, moaning my name.

I froze, a twin statue of El, and a shame more potent, more powerful than even the love I felt for Ross grabbed hold of me, choked my breath.

Ross caught on soon enough. Pulled out and away from me, swaddling us both in blankets, his eyes close enough to mine that I could see my own reflection. He closed them before he turned slowly around.

"El," he said. "El."

She stared at us, all life, all color gone from her face, leaving only gray and slack horror. And my lips formed her name without letting out a sound.

"There was no one there," Ross says now, when he comes back. He stands by the bed, awkward, reluctant, and I can't think of anything to say to make him stay. Finally, he looks at me. His smile is flat, unhappy. He turns his back, sits on the edge of the bed, bows his head.

"I wish we'd never come back here. I fucking *hate* this place."

I don't say anything. Maybe if they'd never come back here, I wouldn't be here either.

"El was having an affair," he says, to the stripes on the wall. "I *think* she was having an affair."

"Why?" There are twin blurry pulses of pain inside my temples.

"I lied about us being okay. We weren't getting on. We were

barely speaking. For a long time." He shrugs his shoulders. "She had another phone."

And I can't help it. I think of those two words. Capitalized in a subject heading. Splashed bloody across the naked stone wall alongside the washhouse. HE KNOWS. I press my fingers against my temples.

"Did you know who it was?"

Ross shrugs. "Maybe. I don't know. There was this guy she sometimes talked about. Another artist. And I could just tell, you know? I mentioned him to Rafiq, but El never told me his name." He shakes his head. "Big red flag, right?"

When he finally turns around, his eyes aren't furious like I expected, but weary. "No doubt he was *sensitive, patient.* Listened endlessly to all of her problems." He tries to shrug his shoulders again, but they look too heavy. "*Nice* with a capital N. You know the fucking type."

I do.

But instead of telling him about Vik, I think about the mother who stole Ross from his father. I think of him bloody and sobbing, on his knees in the Caribbean Sea, watching us sail away. The sound he made the night I kissed him: low and keening, trapped like a howling wind inside a narrow space. *I don't know what to do. I don't know how to go on without her.*

And I crawl towards him, wrap my arms around his torso, and lay my cheek against his back, feel the slow, steady thump of his heart against his ribs. Reach my fingers inside his jogging bottoms, hear the sharp inhale of his breath as I close them around him, already hard.

She left him. She doesn't want him anymore. She took him from me.

It takes a long time, long enough that he starts to beg again, but I want so badly to keep him close, to keep him on the brink of still wanting me, still needing me, that I ignore his pleas until the very end.

And when it's over, I press my face against his skin and close my eyes.

"Don't regret this, Ross," I whisper to his heartbeat. "I won't let you."

CHAPTER 13

I always used to watch the news and wonder how people could carry on with their lives when they were stuck in limbo, but the answer now is obvious. It's just easier. Easier than giving up. Easier than stopping. Easier to just pretend that all is okay. Until it is.

The morning is cold, the sunlight through Colquhoun's of Westeryk's big windows blinding. I don't really want to go in, but we've completely run out of food, and Ross is still lying in my bed, his face relaxed in sleep. It's been two days. And three nights. And already, I've nearly forgotten what it's like to be anywhere else but with him.

I hesitate at the shop's door, my palm against its glass. Whenever I go out alone, the feeling—the physical sensation—of being watched is now so pervasive, so expected, that it almost feels normal. I allow myself one look: up and down the empty street from the Links to the corner of Lochend Road, and then I turn around, push through the door.

My heart sinks when I see Anna is the only cashier. I shop slowly, filling a basket with as much as I can possibly carry. When I finally have to approach the till, I realize that Anna's expression is just as wary. I set down my basket, and she clears her throat, makes an obvious effort to meet my gaze. "How are you?"

"I'm fine," I say.

She clears her throat again. "I've wanted to say I'm very sorry for what I said to you last week. I was upset about El, but I shouldn't have taken it out on you. It wasn't fair."

"Thank you," I say, even though I sense she doesn't completely mean it.

She sighs. "I was angry with you because she was alone. Because you weren't here when she needed you. And now . . . now that she's . . ." She shakes her head violently. *"Gone.* Here you are."

I bite down on my tongue, and it hurts. But I won't speak. I won't protest my innocence and El's guilt. It never does any good.

Anna doesn't say anything more until I'm handing over my money, and then she reaches out to close cool fingers around my wrist.

"El had them too."

"What?" I try to pull out of her grip, but it's surprisingly strong.

A nod to my arm and outstretched hand. The bruise is already a couple of days old and doesn't hurt at all, but it makes me think about the tiny chains of finger bruises all along my forearms; makes me flush when I remember how I got them. Pushed up against the Smeg fridge-freezer, Ross's breath moving hot along the inside of my thigh as he pinned my arms behind me: *Don't move, don't move.*

"Let go of me," I say, in a voice so cold I'm nearly impressed with myself.

But she doesn't. Instead she tightens her fingers, pulls me closer. Her expression softens, becomes almost beseeching. "I meant it when I said she wouldn't want you to be here, Cat. You should go."

I wrench my arm free. "I don't know what she told you," I say, rubbing my wrist, turning away. My face is burning. Two pensioners are eyeing us like we're opponents in a Wimbledon final. "I don't *want* to know what she told you. She lies, Anna. That's all she does. I'm fine. And *she's* fine."

I snatch up my bag and practically run out the door, desperate to escape into the cold fresh air. I barge headfirst into Marie. She's wearing a beautiful headscarf the same sapphire blue as the Smeg fridge-freezer, and my skin grows hotter, pricklier.

"There is news?" She looks panicked, out of breath. I wonder if she was watching me from her window and that's why she's here.

I slow my breathing, make myself calm down. "No. No news." Which isn't entirely true. I think of Rafiq and Logan's last visit, its poor prognosis. I think of all the wild sex I've been having with my missing sister's husband.

"I saw the police parked outside a few days ago." The scarred skin on her face is more visible today. It looks like a burn. Her frown deepens, and she steps forwards into my space. "She is my friend, Catriona."

I don't step back. "Were you the one who reported seeing someone suspicious outside the house?"

"What?"

"The police, they said a resident from your terrace reported seeing someone loitering outside the house on the day of El's disappearance. I just wondered if you'd seen anything?"

"*Non*," she says. "I didn't see anything." But something changes in her eyes.

"Did you know she was getting threatening cards?"

"*Oui*. She told us about them."

"Did she say she knew or suspected who they were from?"

"Why do you ask, Catriona?" She's suddenly very still. "You don't think whatever has happened to her is an accident?"

I glance back through the window at Anna. She's pretending not to look at us as she serves one of the pensioners.

"No." Which is the truth, inasmuch as I don't believe any of this is an accident at all.

"She was scared," Marie finally says. She follows my gaze to Anna, and then turns back to me. "She tried to hide it from us at first. But she was very scared."

I snort without meaning to, and Marie's expression tightens.

"I always thought, how sad and strange that *sœurs jumelles* should never speak. She said you hated her."

"*I* hated *her*? For fuck's sake—" But it's too late. Even if you stuff a jack back inside his box, everyone still knows what he looks like. And there are only so many times that I can bite my tongue, can bear blame for what she has done. "El hated me. And she kept on hating me until I left. Do you understand? This was my home too." And I don't know if I'm referring to the country, the city, or the house, or all three. Maybe even Mirrorland, or Ross, or what it was to be a sister, a Mirror Twin. "She took it away. *She* made *me* leave. It was her."

"Some of my friends come from places, countries, that are nothing like this one," Marie says, as if I haven't spoken at all. "And they have nothing. Sometimes—often—people are afraid of those who have nothing. Your sister wasn't."

I want to snort again, but don't. There's a hot weight inside my chest.

"On sunny days, she used to take my friends down to the Links or the sea, and she'd show them how to draw, how to paint." She refocuses on me again, and I know it's because she's comparing us. That's what people always do, as though character traits must be divvied up between us. "She'd show them how to be free."

I don't trust myself to reply. I'm angry. I feel wronged, persecuted, unbelieved. It's a feeling I haven't had for many, many years, and I've forgotten how much it hurts. I'm appalled to realize that I'm trembling.

"Maybe Ellice was right." The darkness comes back into Marie's eyes, like a shutter over a window. "She said you never listen. You never learn."

I bristle. The rage inside me physically hurts. "Ross said he didn't know you," I say. Too loud. Too defensive. "Her *very good friend*—and he said he didn't have a clue who you were."

She pulls her scarred fingers into fists. "He told me to stay away from her." The look she gives me is withering. "He *threatened* me."

When I say nothing, she shakes her head, turns on her heel, and marches back towards the road and her house. And then she stops. Looks back over her shoulder. "Ask him about that."

⋆

john.smith120594@gmail.com   13 April 2018 at 11:31

Re: HE KNOWS   Inbox

To: Me

CLUE 6. EL CAN STILL SEE YOU

Sent from my iPhone

⋆

I've stormed around most of the house, snatching up photos of El to look behind them, before I remember the self-portrait in the Princess Tower. I march to the white-painted cupboard and pull open its door. Try very hard not to waver when El glares back at me. As if she's Princess Iona now, kidnapped by a hag and trapped inside a tower; every year a little older, a little less hopeful.

I find the diary page taped to the wooden backing.

June 24th, 2005
He's mine if I want him. He's NOT hers. That's the way it was
and the way it is. I know why he did it, but that doesn't help. Every
time I think about them together it feels like a bag of rocks sitting on
my chest. I'm angry and I'm scared and I can't stop crying. It's like
thinking about Mirrorland and the Satisfaction and the Clowns and
remembering they're gone now. I can't ever go back.
But I CAN fix this. I CAN make everything go back to how it was
before. Cat'll hate me but I don't care. I'll be glad.

Because He CAN'T have her and She WON'T have him.

When I hear the bell ring I jump, nearly drop the page. I shove it into my pocket instead and go back downstairs.

There's no one at the door. When I go into the kitchen, I freeze inside its doorway, staring up at the bell board. One pendulum is still swinging, its five-pointed star like a metronome, a hypnotist's watch. Bedroom 3. I blink, and it isn't moving at all. Every bell stands silent and still.

I sense movement at the corner of my eye, and I whirl around—dizzy with dread, my nerves on a too-brittle edge. I see the blurry flash of someone outside the window, moving fast and quickly disappearing. I run for the scullery, wrench open the back door, and glimpse another **CATRIONA** card on the top step before sprinting down the rest of them. I stop on the paving stones, spin left, right. Listen. Nothing but the wind in the apple trees, the distant traffic on the other side of the house. The washhouse door is still chained and padlocked. I look around at the high, ivy-choked walls. There's no way someone could have climbed over them in the time it's taken me to get out here.

I turn warily towards the second alleyway on the other side of the house to Mirrorland. Its red door is open. I run the length of the alley and into the front garden, but there's nobody there. Even the gate has been latched shut.

I think about running into the street, but don't. Instead, I close and bolt the door, wander back to the garden and its walls. I look up at the house, big and wide and freezing bright. Casting a long shadow. I don't want to go back inside. I trudge back up the scullery steps only to pick up the envelope and pull shut the back door. Go back down through the orchard, my face turned towards the dappled sun, the rustling breeze. Ross will be able to see me, I realize, if he looks out of the Clown Café's window. But if he hasn't already come downstairs to see why I'm running around like a madwoman, then he's probably still asleep. We've both been doing a lot of that. It feels a little like hiding.

Old Fred creaks his welcome. I put the card under my arm and my palms against his rough bark, close my eyes so that I can't see DIG or our names carved inside a circle, and I think of all the times I sat or lay flat on his lowest branch, squinting up at the sky. How many times he gave me the same safe comfort as the loyal and timid Mouse. The kind of comfort that never needed you to be right or better, but was strong and warm and full of silent, reliable sympathy. When that only reminds me of El's I'M MOUSE, I step back from Old Fred and stand still for a moment, arms and fingers spread wide, tipping my head up until the sunlight burns warm and red behind my eyelids. On sunny days, El and I would stand like that for what felt like hours, holding hands for balance, laughing and mimicking Mum's high and reedy *Don't look! Don't look or you'll go blind!*

But I have to look. I open my eyes, and then I open the envelope. It's a landscape watercolor of a busy harbor beneath a sunny and cloudless sky. I shiver in the cold. I want to open it even less than all of the others.

HE WILL KILL YOU TOO

I close my eyes. Close the card. Think of the *He CAN'T have her and She WON'T have him* from today's diary page. A page that was written one week before our nineteenth birthday. One week before that grubby dull room with a plastic-framed seascape of rocks and sand and waves. One week before El did what she did to *fix this*. To *make everything go back to how it was before*.

I was working when Ross called me on July 1. Only my second shift in a bad West End pub called the White Star. And—it turned out—my last. By the time I got to the hospital, much of the initial panic was over. El's stomach had been pumped empty of acetaminophen, and she'd been sedated and rehydrated. Ross stood alongside her bed, gripping the hand that wasn't bandaged and bloody around a cannula. His hair was wild, the whole of him shook as if he had a chill, even though we both knew by then that she was going to be all right. He'd refused to leave her, to go sit in the grubby dull room on a grubby dull sofa as I had dutifully done. *He was hysterical*, one of the nurses whispered to me much later on, when the night had arrived and all other visitors had left. She squeezed my hand, pressed the palm of hers against her chest. *Oh, to be young and in love again!*

It was after he finally left to get some food from the canteen that El had opened her eyes and found mine, smiled that smile—so full of joy and hate. *I win.*

*

The day before El was discharged from the hospital, Ross met me at the Royal Botanic Gardens again. It was raining, and we stood under a big willow tree next to the wrought-iron gates. He held my hand as I cried, as I begged him. *Don't. Please.* He cupped my face in his hands, tried to catch my tears with his thumbs, his eyes nearly black with grief. *She left me a note, Cat. She said we'd broken her heart. She said she couldn't live with us or without me.*

Why do you have to be with her? I wanted to scream. *Why does it have to be* her?

But he just went on looking at me with his sad eyes and his stupid, knee-jerk shame. *I love you both*, he said, and that was when I knew that El *had* won—no matter how wretched he looked or how much he cried—guilt had finally managed to pry us apart. I'd lost him for good.

El has to be watching us. She has to be sending the cards. To get rid of me. But *why*? Because until she vanished, she *was* rid of me. All of it: the cards and clues and diary pages have only made me hate her more and him less. And I can admit to myself now that when I read LEAVE, the first thing I thought was *No*. And the second was *Come back and make me*. Because I should have fought back the first time. I should never have given up, run away, tried to forget. She's had my life for years. She's stolen it. While I've been what? A reflection in a mirror. A shadow on the ground, dark and flat and impermanent. Inconsequential.

The wind picks up, urges me back towards the house, and it's as I turn that I hear the shed door. It's not quite flush with its frame and makes a dull quick thud with every gust. Without knowing why, I go towards it, push it open. It takes a few seconds for my eyes to adjust to the dark inside. When they do, all I see are dusty, empty crates, some old newspapers and bags of compost. And then, a flash of bright blue.

I venture in reluctantly, picking my way through all the detritus. The blue is crammed right at the back of the shed, folded into an untidy cube. I lean down to touch it, and it feels like the same kind of material as the blow-up mattress El and I used to have in the bed-sit. Something stirs in my mind then, some bad conclusion that my subconscious has reached before the rest of me. I should leave this where it is. Whatever it is.

Instead, I haul it out from under all the rest of the crap, and hard enough that I nearly lose my balance. I try to straighten it out, pull it into whatever shape it's supposed to be. It's big, maybe as tall as I am. There's a large oval gap at its center, and inside it I find a carbon-fiber paddle folded into four pieces. The word *Gumotex* is printed along the length of the largest. And that's when I know for sure.

It's El's inflatable kayak.

131

CHAPTER 14

I have a terrible dream. El and I are running—and hard—the force of our sprint shudders up our legs, jars our knees and hips. Fear is a solid beating thing. Pushing down on our shoulders, snatching the breath out of our mouths.

Behind us is the Tooth Fairy, her heavy fast tread thundering over floorboards as we run into the Clown Café. Dicky Grock looks frightened instead of sad, his lips pressed thin as he ushers us inside the dress-up cupboard. Even Pogo looks worried, though his wide red smile remains frozen in place.

We crouch down in the dark. The Clowns close the cupboard door, the seams of their cloth feet scratching across the floor as they run to hide under the bed. Inside, we breathe stale cold air, hold on to each other hard enough to hurt. I can hear boots, heavy and erratic. I can smell blood.

The cupboard handle starts to rattle, to turn and turn, and then the cupboard is gone, the Clown Café is gone, and El and I are standing on the shoreline of a beach, the sea washing over our feet, the black silhouette of a pirate ship on the horizon. Bluebeard is standing over Grandpa on the sand, holding a long curved hook in one hand, a longer stovepipe in the other. Grandpa has half a head. *Dinnae worry, lassie.* He laughs. *Ah'm feelin' nae pain.*

Bluebeard grins at us with every one of his pointed black teeth. His face and chest and knuckles are covered with blood. He likes to hit. To hurt. His hair reaches down his back to swing heavily between his legs. His beard has bones in it. He winks, and then he brings the stovepipe up and around again, smashing what's left of Grandpa's skull, spraying arcs of crimson across the sky.

Mum grasps hold of our arms, pinches our skin. Her face is bloody,

132

eyes wild. *You hide from Bluebeard, because he's a monster. Because he'll catch you, and make you his wife, and then hang you on his hook until you die.* She shakes us, lets go long enough to point at the black ship. Nearer now, riding the incoming tide. *But you run from Blackbeard, because he's sly, because he lies. Because no matter where you go, he'll always be there, right behind you. And when he catches you, he'll throw you to the sharks.*

So we run. We run even though the sand is too deep and the tide is too high. Even though Blackbeard's ship is so much closer than it's ever been. Even though we can feel Bluebeard's snatching fingers, smell the rum on his breath.

Take me! Mum screams far behind us. *Take me instead!* But we know he won't.

And when the sun disappears in a loud and echoing thud, and we're swallowed up by the dark—thick and cold and full of horrors—we start to scream too.

And I wake up in the Clown Café, my hand clamped hard over my mouth. Ross still sleeping beside me.

★

john.smith120594@gmail.com   14 April 2018 at 12:01

Re: HE KNOWS   Inbox

To: Me

CLUE 7. EVERY BAD WITCH NEEDS A GOOD THRONE

Sent from my iPhone

★

I've looked under nearly every one of the chairs in the Throne Room before I remember that the only place I ever saw the Witch was the kitchen. And whenever she sat down, it was in Grandpa's chair at the head of the table.

I find two pages wedged inside the wooden frame of its seat.

4 August 1993 = 7+a wee bit!
THE WITCH was here tooday. AGAIN. Cat and Me hate her. She
is nasty she pinchies and sometimes she spits on us. Cat and me
are always thinking up ways to KILL HER—like drowning her
in the bath coz witchs cant stand water or skwishing her like the
WICKED WITCH OF THE EAST. Mouse says shes to scayerd but
shes always scayerd she is USELESS!!! Me and Cat arnt scayerd of
a nasty ugly old witch.

March 29th, 1997 = 10Y, 9M, 29D
THE WITCH was here again. She hates us and I don't know why. I
don't know why she comes if she hates us. She should be called THE
BITCH instead. Witches better watch out Grandpa says or they'll
cut themselves on their own tongues.

I can still see her face: sharp gray features pulled in tight together as
though something behind her mouth and nose were yanking hard
on a string. Narrow eyes, like the evil Madame Defarge, staring at
me as if I'm just about the worst thing anyone should have to look
at. Something else hides just behind that image and the memory of
You're a disgusting wee bitch! hissed thin into my cringing ear, but I
can't reach it, can't grab hold of it.

El and I always channeled our fears through Mouse. It made us feel
better. And braver. We would sit her down on the boardwalk or the
deck of the *Satisfaction*, and list all the ways we could do away with
the Witch—drowning her, poisoning her tea, creeping up behind her
with a Sioux war club or Pogo's bullhorn. *But she can't get into Mirrorland anyway,* El would say, with rare kindness. *Because it belongs to us.*

I'm blindsided by the clear and sudden memory of Mum and the
Witch standing inside the scullery doorway; the anger, the animosity
so thick between them that I flattened myself against the kitchen
door, stared transfixed through the crack between its hinges.

"Give me it back. It belongs to me."

I saw the necklace when the Witch leaned down to Mum; its oval
locket swung, catching the sun against its gold. "And now it belongs
to me."

134

I shrunk from that voice, but Mum didn't. The woman who cringed and fretted over all the bad things in the world; who made us pack emergency rations in backpacks hidden under our beds and subjected us to years of lessons and drills and grim fairy tales because there wasn't a thing that she wasn't afraid of, her life filled to the brim with certain doom, stepped up so close to the taller, bigger Witch that they were almost nose to nose. Mum's smile was as cold as black ice. "You always want what I have."

The Witch curled the necklace into her fist, thrust both inside the pocket of her long black dress. "And sometimes, I get it."

*

I stand in the middle of the kitchen for too many long moments, another slow headache pulsing hard behind my eyes. I don't even know if the Witch existed, I realize. If that conversation even ever happened. It's getting harder and harder, now that more memories are returning—the bad as well as the good—to pry apart what was real and what wasn't. Perhaps everyone's childhood memories are the same: part truth, part fantasy. But this house and our mother and her stories turned our imagination into a melting pot, a forge. A cauldron. And, I'm beginning to realize, I can trust nothing that came out of it.

I'm suddenly furious. I start opening and rifling through every single cupboard and drawer. I don't expect to find any more pages, not really, but like in the Clown Café, just the act of looking makes me feel more in control, helps penetrate this weird fog of inertia that seems to have taken hold of me and won't let go. El is manipulating me for her own inexplicable ends, just like she always has, and I can do nothing about it. Nothing but this.

The drawer under the counter is still the paperwork drawer: I shove aside dozens of bank statements and utility bills, until I notice an envelope addressed to Ross from a solicitor in Leith Walk postmarked two days ago. I pick it up, take out the papers inside. The first is a document entitled "The Presumption of Death (Scotland) Act 1977; Information Guide." And underneath, "Form G1 of initial writ." After SHERIFFDOM OF, Ross has written "Edinburgh" AT "27 Chambers Street." PURSUER, "Ross MacAuley" AGAINST

"Ellice MacAuley" DEFENDER. The only thing he hasn't done is sign it.

I'm still staring at it when I realize that Ross is standing inside the kitchen doorway. His face is white, but his jaw is set.

"I had to, Cat. The police advised me to contact a solicitor, and he told me it could take months to process or even get anywhere near the courts. It's just in—"

"The police?" I say, when I'm certain I can say anything. "Or Shona Murray?"

"For God's sake!" he explodes, and it looks like a relief. "She's the family liaison officer! It's her job!"

I want to punch him. I want to hurt him so badly, for a moment I wonder if I might, but instead I settle for shouting back just as loud. "She isn't dead!"

He gets so close to me I can smell the sourness of his fury, the hot rush of it through gritted teeth. "Then why are you *fucking her husband?*"

*

It's getting harder and harder to convince myself that El is only sneering. Plotting. Setting me up just to watch me fall. I know I'm overreaching, stretching my last bitter memories of her to their very limits. I feel trapped, under siege—and all these reminders of our first life here within these walls, these rooms, are making it harder and harder to shore up my defenses. There's a loosening inside me, and not of the good, clean kind. It makes me stand at the kitchen window, rubbing my fingers against those crooked nails as I stare at the wall alongside the washhouse and think of that first email exchange: HE KNOWS. THINGS HE DOESN'T WANT YOU TO KNOW. YOU'RE IN DANGER. I CAN HELP YOU.

Marie's *she was very scared.* Vik's *she was terrified of him.*

El isn't the one sending the cards. She's behind the treasure hunt, she's sending the emails—but she isn't sending the cards. I know it; most of me has always known it. I don't know who was in the garden yesterday, but it wasn't her. And the kayak in the shed. The Gumotex kayak that Logan said El used to get herself to and from her boat when no launch was available. Is it a spare? Or did El dump it here after using it to get off her boat? Did someone else?

Worry gies wee things big shadows, hen.

I take out my phone, find Vik's number.

Ross says you and El were having an affair. Is that true? Did he find out? Did he threaten you?

When Ross comes back from town bearing roses, a bottle of California red, and a heartfelt apology, Vik still hasn't replied. We drink as slowly as we can, sitting at the kitchen table and staring out at the garden, the afternoon rain battering against the windowpanes in a rhythm that's nearly hypnotic.

"Cat. Talk to me."

When I look up at Ross, his expression is open, concerned.

"I saw Marie again yesterday. In the shop." I swallow. "She said . . . she said that you threatened her, warned her to stay away from El."

Ross's brow furrows. "I told you, I don't know who the hell this Marie is." He takes out his phone. "But we should tell Rafiq about her. She sounds fucking unhinged. Maybe she's—"

"No, Ross, wait." I think of Marie's burned, scarred skin, the tears in her eyes. "Just—we don't need to do that. Not yet. Just . . . if she says anything to me again, I'll phone Rafiq. I promise."

He puts down his phone. When I can bring myself to look at him properly, I can see how tired he is, how unhappy, how lost. It stings the back of my throat, my eyes. I believe him, but how can I trust that belief? How can I trust myself? I loathe all this turmoil, this *emotion*, when I've been perfectly numb for years.

"Don't," he says, with a wince, before reaching out to touch my face. "I've no clue what I'm doing either. But this isn't grief, Cat. It isn't substitution." He swallows. "Not for me anyway."

"Or for me." But my stomach feels tight.

Ross clears his throat. "When El tried to . . . when she wrote me that suicide note . . . when I . . ." He looks away.

When you made your choice, I think. *When you chose her.*

"It was the worst mistake of my life, Cat. I felt so guilty and so shit-scared—it was my fault: what she did and what it did to you—

and when you left for America, it just seemed like the best thing was to let you go. I loved you. I *love* you. But how could I leave her and go running after you? What would she have done then?"

I close my eyes. The pain in his voice is raw, real. But even though he's telling me what I want to hear—all I've probably ever wanted to hear—there's a part of me that's still appalled by that mostly completed Presumption of Death form; by how quickly he has transferred his affections from one of us to the other, just like he did then. Whether or not El's having an affair with Vik. Whether or not she and Ross haven't been getting on for months or years. Whether or not thinking any of it makes me the worst kind of hypocrite.

When my phone beeps, I glance quickly at the screen. It's Vik.

No. To all of it. But are you ok? Want to meet?

I'm not angry with Ross. I'm not jealous of Shona on El's behalf, or because I think something is actually happening between her and Ross. I'm jealous, I'm *suspicious*, because it makes me feel better. It dilutes my own guilt.

I push my phone into my pocket, and Ross takes hold of my hands. "But what about you, Blondie? Do you love me too?"

I can't not look at him then. At his tired, beautiful face, so dear to me, so missed for so many years. I can't lie, or pretend my heart doesn't do a teenage skip at the old nickname.

"You know I love you. I always have."

He stands up, pulls me towards him, presses warm, slow kisses against my hair, my temple, my lips. We stay there for minutes, and I listen to the rain, to his heartbeat and his breath. And I try very hard not to think about anything else at all.

But eventually I have to. "There's something I need to tell you."

Ross pulls back, looks down at me. "Uh-oh."

When I don't answer, his expression changes. "Shall I go get us a proper drink?"

He lets me go, vanishes into the hallway, and I sit back down, listen to the clink of glass against the tiles of the bar.

"Here," he says, when he returns. "Vodka soda."

I take a sip, grimace, try to smile.

He sits down. Raises his eyebrows. "So . . . ?"

"I've been getting emails."

"What?" His surprise is nearly comical. Whatever he was expecting me to say, it clearly wasn't that.

"Emails. A lot of them. Since two days after I got here." I look down at the table. "They're clues. To pages from El's old diaries. You know how she always used to—"

"*What?*"

I flinch as his chair screeches backwards against the tiles.

"El's diaries? What the fuck?" He starts to pace, running his fingers back and forth through his hair. "What are they about?"

"Mostly when we lived here. El and I. About Mirrorland and—"

"Who are they from?" His voice is too high, his eyes suddenly furious. "For Christ's sake, El's gone missing, she was getting threats *before* she went missing, and now someone—they have El's *diaries* and they—" He stops, looks at me. "And you don't ever think to *tell* anyone about it? What's wrong with you, Cat?"

"Ross, stop. Stop! I'm going to tell the police *now*. That's why I'm telling you. Okay? And no one *has* the diaries. That's what I'm trying to tell you. They're here, they're hidden all over this house like a treasure hunt. The emails are the clues. It's El, Ross. It's El." I stand up. I'm horribly nervous, I realize. I need him to accept this. I need him to finally believe me. And I'm worried he won't. "When I told her I'd go to the police, she told me she was Mouse. Like the whole thing is just a joke to her. Like I'm a joke to her. So we can tell them, we can show Rafiq El's emails—"

"Mouse?" His arms drop down by his sides. His mouth has gone slack, his face gray. "*Mouse?*"

My nervousness grows frightened wings. "Yes. You must remember. You and me and El and Mouse and Annie and Belle in Boomtown? On the *Satisfaction*? In the—"

"Yeah, I remember Mouse. *Fucking Mouse.*" He says it in a way that sends a shiver the length of my spine. Too angry, too overly familiar.

"Ross—"

"She turned up maybe six months ago. Biggest mistake of my

139

life letting her back in this house. She was delusional. Completely obsessed with El. She started following us when—"

"Wait, what . . ." My breath is coming out in weird half gasps. "I don't—you're saying Mouse is real? An actual person? She isn't— you're saying she's an *actual person*?"

Ross's face changes. He looks at me with a dull kind of dislike, which might only be confusion. And when he finally opens his mouth to answer, I already know what he's going to say. "Of course she is, Cat."

CHAPTER 15

I don't know what to say. I don't know what to think. What to even *begin* to think. And so I just keep shaking my head over and over again. "But she lived in Mirrorland. Like . . . like Annie and Belle and Chief Red Cloud and Old Joe Johnson . . . Of course she did! Come on, Ross! Ross?" But I'm losing my certainty now, it's draining away through a hole I can't see, one I didn't make, and I'm fast filling up with panic instead. Mostly for what being wrong about this means for me. Worse, what it means—what it *could* mean—for El. "She was called *Mouse*, for God's sake!"

Instead of answering me, Ross marches from the room. I hear his boots stamping up the stairs. The rain is much heavier now; the whole kitchen has turned dark. My phone vibrates. It's Vik. I don't answer, look across at the two tiles in front of the Kitchener, the cracked line of grout that bisects them. Reach for the vodka and swallow all of it.

I don't think Ross is going to come back until he does. His face looks no less grim, and when he drops something onto the table in front of me, I jump. "El found it in the loft."

It's a photo album, vaguely familiar, opened to a page with only one photograph. El and me, standing at the kitchen table making lemon cakes. We're maybe eight, nine, wearing twin aprons and covered in flour. But I look at us for only a second, no more, because sitting on a chair, right on the edge of the shot, is a pale-faced, wide-eyed Mouse.

I realize that my fingers are pressed against my mouth only when I try to draw in a horrified breath. "My God." My body is too cold, my cheeks too hot. Shivers chase one another from the top of my scalp to the base of my spine. "God."

Ross sits down. "You really thought she didn't *exist?*"

I keep turning the pages of the album, my anxiety rising, afraid that I'll see her again. As if that matters. As if seeing her once isn't proof enough. The photos are few, each page containing one, sometimes two disparate shots. Some are black and white, some so old that the people in them are only silhouettes. Ghosts. I pause at an impossibly young Grandpa, just as impossibly handsome in a dark suit and bow tie, a blond woman sitting alongside him, formal and unsmiling. Mum's eyes. My grandmother.

And then, on the next page, a color portrait taken outside the house, in the front garden. Mum, aproned and uncomfortable, grimacing a smile. And standing taller next to her, in head-to-toe black—

"The Witch," Ross says, his mouth a grim line.

"The Witch." My voice is unsteady. "Who is she?"

Ross glances at me. He looks worried, concerned. "Your aunt? I don't know. She was Mouse's mum. Do you really remember none of this?"

I shake my head. "We didn't—don't—have any other family. I'd remember that. I'd know that."

Ross is quiet for too long, and then his reply is too careful. "You didn't remember Mouse either."

"I did!" I say, even though I know my defensiveness is ridiculous.

"A family friend, then?" Ross shrugs. "They were at the house often enough. We always had to be quieter when she was around; you were terrified of her."

All that venom and hate. Bared teeth and blood-filled gums. That oval locket glittering in her fist.

How could I remember every corner and code of Mirrorland, and yet twist my memories of two people enough that I thought them as imaginary as a monstrous Tooth Fairy or a sly, grinning Clown? And *why?* Because if I'm not crazy, then I've deliberately chosen to remember them that way. To misremember. Not even now that I know they existed is anything any clearer—they remain vague and indistinct, like smoke blown on an angry wind.

I KNOW THINGS. THINGS YOU'VE MADE YOURSELF FORGET.

142

I close the album, turn back to Ross.

"You said she'd—Mouse—that she'd come back?"

"'Round about mid-October last year." Ross folds his arms. "Ding-dong, the Witch was dead. Apparently." He stops, and I can see that he's trying to hide his anger, stamp it out. "I don't know how she knew we were here. I don't know why she waited until the Witch had died to come. She looked a complete mess. Worse than when we were kids. Said she wanted to get to know El again. And El was so happy about it at first, you know?" He looks at me. "Maybe she saw Mouse as a substitute for you, I dunno. Nothing El did in the last six months made much sense."

"What happened?"

He shrugs. "Like I said, Mouse was delusional. She needed help. She'd turn up at all hours of the day and night. Crying, inconsolable, and then the next minute lit up like a kid at Christmas. She hated me. Wanted El all to herself. One day—get this . . ." His anger wins, and he stands up, hands clenched as he paces. "She waited until I'd gone to work, and then turned up at the house with two one-way plane tickets to bloody Ibiza, of all places."

"Ross—"

He makes a visible effort to calm himself down. Sits, and takes two long, slow breaths.

"When El tried to get her to back off, she started following her, spying on her." He shrugs. "Us."

"You thought she was sending the cards."

"She was the first person we thought of when they started arriving. The police followed it up, found no evidence to prove it either way. But it did the trick because she left us alone, didn't come back. And we figured she'd turned all that crazy on someone else." His eyes go cold and hard; he looks suddenly like a stranger. "When we were kids, all she ever wanted to do was keep the three of us apart, turn us against one another. That's what she has to be doing now. It makes sense she'd have El's diaries, she probably stole them when she was here." He pauses. "You *really* don't remember her?"

What I remember is that the Mouse I knew wouldn't have said boo to a goose. She was timid and kind, most often submissive. A sponge for all our fears and weaknesses and secrets. A cabin girl, a powder monkey, a skivvy. Our favorite piñata. The Mouse I knew refused to fight pirates, refused to take sides, refused to choose punishment.

Ross is still shaking his head, still sporting that cold, hard expression that I've never seen before, when suddenly his shoulders slump. I see the pity in his eyes before the kindness or the love, and he reaches for my hands, grips them tightly enough to hurt. "El didn't send those emails. I'm sorry, Cat. Christ, I'm so sorry. But she's gone. She's just gone."

★

There's a squall coming in from Cuba. I can see the smoky gray clouds on the horizon: a tropical thunderstorm near the Bight of Bayamo.

The day grows darker as I scramble down from the crow's nest and run across the main deck. The *Satisfaction* is already listing hard to port, and the wind is picking up. I can feel hot splashes of rain against my face. When I look over at El, she's already fighting to hold the wheel steady.

"There's no time to get to Port Royal," I shout. "We won't make it!"

A scream, then a splash, and I've time to see a pirate slip over the port side and into the swirling, climbing sea as a wave washes high over the stern.

"Heave to?" El shouts. Her grin is big enough that I can see all her teeth.

And I'm grinning, too, as the bayamo rolls towards us. The wind gets higher, it slaps the rain against my face and into my eyes as I reef in the mainsail with Annie and Belle, my muscles shrieking, my heart thundering.

A sudden roar, and the *Satisfaction* begins to list.

"We can't turn downwind!" El yells, and I see her and Mouse clinging to the wheel, faces straining with effort.

And then Ross is sprinting along the half-deck towards the stern. Putting an arm around El and reaching for the wheel with the other. Shoving Mouse out of the way, hard enough that she lets go with a scream and is washed down towards the bow.

By the time the *Satisfaction* steadies and starts drifting downwind, the squall has blustered itself mostly out, and I stagger down towards the bow amid pirate cheers and backslaps. Mouse is curled up into a ball behind a lashed-down barrel, her short hair plastered to her skull, ugly sack dress sodden.

She looks up at me, her white face streaked with rain or tears. "I *hate* him."

And I don't turn around to look at Ross and El, but reach down to help Mouse back onto her feet instead, because part of me hates him too. Part of me hates them both.

Mouse doesn't let go of my hand. She looks at me, wipes her nose against her sleeve. "I wish I was like you."

And I believe that the wildness in her eyes, the envy, is for my benefit, because she exists at all only to make me feel better; to remind me that I'm worth something to someone. Because she is *my* friend. *My* creation.

I hold her hand and look out at the returning sun. "I wish I could stay in Mirrorland all the time," I say.

And Mouse gives me a slow, watery smile. "Me too."

*

I stare up into the darkness, fully awake. I should have remembered. I should have *known*. Part of me wants to laugh at the absurdity of it—of not remembering, not knowing that Mouse was as real as El or me. But I don't. Because I'm scared. Scared that I *didn't* know. And scared because there was never any explanation for those emails, other than El. Until now.

I get up without waking Ross, tiptoe downstairs with my laptop, sit at the table in the Throne Room.

I think of Ross's *Your aunt? A family friend?* She was Mouse's mum. And then the nightmare of only a few days ago comes rushing back to me. Sharpened. Changed.

The Witch is dragging Mouse along the hallway, into the entrance hall. Mouse is crying, *No, no! I don't want to go!*

And when Mum says, *You can surely stay a wee while longer?* the Witch stops dead. Shakes her head.

Mouse sobs louder, reaches her hands out to us—*I want to go to Mirrorland! Please, I don't want to go! I want to go back to Mirrorland!*—and we ignore our fear of the Witch and run forwards, take hold of Mouse's hands as we try to pull her back inside the hallway.

The Witch stops again. Turns and smiles an icy smile. And slaps Mouse hard across the face. Once. Twice. Until we let go. She stabs a long-nailed finger at Mouse's trembling, bowed head. Glares at El and me—now frozen into silence.

Obedience. This is what family is. The look she gives Mum is ugly with hate. *THIS is what it is to be a good daughter.*

A flood of light. A slamming door. And then darkness.

I blow out an unsteady breath. Fight the guilt and the fear growing inside me. I know that happened. And I know that I forgot it happened.

I open the laptop, google "national records for Scotland," and then type Mum's name and date of birth into the site's search parameters. When I filter to births in the Leith district only, Mum's is the only entry left. I delete her forename, change the date-of-birth range to five years either side of hers. Four new names are listed—Jennifer, Mary, two Margarets—but when I can't access any of their details, including exact dates of birth, without registering a subscription, I request and pay for all the certificates, including Mum's. After the confirmation email mentions a possible two-week wait, I open my email, start a new message to john.smith120594.

If you're really Mouse, meet me. I know you're in Edinburgh.

The reply comes right away.

NO. I DON'T TRUST YOU. NOT YET. AND I CERTAINLY DON'T TRUST HIM.

Tell me what you want. I need you to explain, to tell me what's going on.

I WANT YOU TO REMEMBER. I WANT YOU TO *WANT* TO REMEMBER. I'M TRYING TO HELP YOU. I'M TRYING TO SAVE YOUR LIFE. EL IS DEAD. HE KILLED HER.

And it's this last reply that convinces me my fears have to be unfounded. *Must* be. Mouse is real, I can accept that, but this last overdramatic cliff-hanger of a cliché is so much El, she is who I hear in my head as I read it. It's just a game. Just another of her merciless games. The desperate need for that to be true makes me furious again. And so I try to give her enough rope to hang herself.

Who killed her?

A lengthy pause, weighty enough to befit a drum-rolled reveal.

HER LYING HUSBAND.

CHAPTER 16

john.smith120594@gmail.com   15 April 2018 at 00:15

Re: HE KNOWS   Inbox

To: Me

CLUE 8. DON'T DRESS IT UP: EVERYONE IS AFRAID OF
CLOWNS

Sent from my iPhone

✶

The dress-up cupboard in the Clown Café. This is the clue to the
diary page I found five days ago after I discovered clue number five's
page under the bed. It's the diary page I found out of sequence
because I was sick of blindly dancing to El's tune. It's the diary page
that has frightened me the most.

I don't open the dress-up cupboard again. I don't want to read
the page again. But I'm shaking anyway. The hair on the back of my
neck is still standing up, pulling at my skin. Because I haven't forgotten what it said.

August 10th, 1998
Something's coming. Something's nearly here.
Sometimes I'm so scared I forget how to breathe. I forget that I can.

✶

El and I are running again. So fast and so hard we're tripping over our own feet. A loud metallic thud echoes up through the walls and the sun disappears. The bells ring in the dark. Too many to count. Too many to know which bells, which stars, which rooms.

Deadlights chase us, flash and judder across the walls as we try to run from boots and shouts and roars. Outlaws and prison guards, the Tooth Fairy and Madame Defarge, Bluebeard and Blackbeard. But we're so far from Mirrorland now, it's like a memory that isn't even a memory, just a place we've read about for so long that it feels as if we once lived there. Like a shire in Middle-Earth or a bloodied square in Paris. A prison in Maine or an island in the Caribbean.

And then we're crouching down inside the dress-up cupboard, fear pushing us lower, squeezing our fingers tighter, digging our nails deeper into each other's skin. Because the Clown Café can't protect us like Mirrorland does. It's just a place to hide.

We're pirates and our dad is the Pirate King, El whispers in my ear. In the cold, thick dark. *We'll be okay.*

But we won't be. I know we won't be. It's a lie.

And when the cupboard door handle starts to rattle, to turn and turn, I want to scream—I need to scream—because it feels like that's the only way to meet the blood and sweat and roar and rage and *wrong* that wants so badly to get in. I don't know what it is we've done. I don't know why they want to scare us, find us, hurt us. I don't know why they want us to die. To hang us on a hook until we rot.

We scream when the door splinters open. When the deadlight and that first terrible face loom into the space they've ripped wide. Black bones twisted inside a blue beard. Grinning pointed teeth. Rum and smoke. A wink and a roar. And the bells only shriek and shriek.

*

One bell is still shrieking—and far too loud. Too real. Not a hangover from my nightmare, but here and now.

I feel impossibly heavy, impossibly tired. I flop over onto my side like a beached whale and eye the alarm clock. One fifteen p.m. I've slept for thirteen hours. I'm not sure how that's even possible. I sit up slowly, blink gritty sore eyes.

Get up, I think. *That'll be a good start.*

But then I hear the bell again. Longer, more insistent. And I'm suddenly gripped by the worst sense of foreboding yet. The worst sense of doom. It keeps running through my head as I roll out of bed onto unsteady feet, casting about for yesterday's clothes, trying not to topple over as I struggle back into them. Trying not to think of my dream, or of *Something's coming. Something's nearly here.* Like a shrieking, jangling bell.

I go out onto the landing. I can hear Ross in the shower, so I go down the stairs, one solid step after another. At the bottom, the ringing starts again, but it's the knocking—loud and insistent—that finally wakes me up. I still hesitate at the front door, my breath shallow and too quick. But when the doorbell rings again, I pull back on the night latch, let in the bright cold outside.

It's DS Logan. And at the foot of the steps behind him is the white-blond pixie hair of Shona Murray.

"Hello, Catriona," he says, with no sign at all of any dimples or winks. Or even that he's capable of them. "We're sorry to disturb you. Can we come in?"

"Of course."

As they move past me into the entrance hall, I keep my eyes trained on the path, the gate, the yellowing hedges. I busy my mind with thinking this is when I'll tell them about the kayak. The emails and the diary pages. Even if they point a finger at Ross; even if they point another at September 1998 and the last day of our first life; the last day—night—of Mum's and Grandpa's lives. Even if those emails have told me to tell the police nothing. I'll do it anyway. Because, suddenly, I'm too afraid not to.

They wait for me in the hallway, and for a moment I have no idea where to take them. The Throne Room is too ridiculous, the kitchen too personal, the pantry entirely off limits. I decide the drawing room is the lesser of all evils, until I usher them inside it and catch both of them looking at the Poirot and Chippendale lowboy with something close to awe; remember the cold of French polish against my overheated skin.

"Would you like to sit down? Would you like something to drink? There's something I want to—"

"Cat," Logan says, and he puts his hand on my forearm. "Could you get Ross? Is he—"

"I'm here," Ross says. But he stops inside the doorway, his hand on the door as if he might be on the verge of slamming it shut in our faces. He's barefoot in old jeans and a Black Sabbath tour T-shirt, his wet hair flat on one side, spiked up like a toddler's on the other.

Logan lets go of my arm, clears his throat. "You might both want to sit down."

I choose the yellow brocade rocking chair next to the fire. Mum's chair. Straightaway it starts to rock, and I lurch forwards, plant my feet on the floor until it stops.

"What is it?" Ross says, in a voice that doesn't sound like his at all.

"Ross," Logan says. "Why don't you—"

"I'm fine as I am."

"All right." Logan clears his throat again, and in the horribly expectant silence that follows, I glance up to see Shona Murray plonk herself down on the chesterfield.

Logan's eyes flicker from Ross to me. "Yesterday, the MAIB . . ." He shakes his head. "The Marine Accident Investigation Branch were reporting on a commercial vessel incident in the Forth, when . . . when they discovered something else . . . without . . . it wasn't—"

"What *is* it?" Ross says again.

But I look only at Logan. *Craig, if you want. My mum named me after a bloody Proclaimer.* The grandfather clock's slow and metronomic ticking reverberates inside my skull, behind my dry tired eyes.

"They found the boat," he finally says. "They found *The Redemption*."

"Okay," I say. "How do they know—"

"It's got 'The Redemption' painted in fucking gold on both sides," Ross growls. But his voice is so hoarse now, it's hard to hear.

Logan looks at me. "They were using sonar, divers. The boat was in the deepwater channel, a few miles east of Inchkeith. We sent down our own divers and an underwater vehicle to confirm ID."

"Okay." I look across at the bottle-green fireplace, its carousel of pokers, shovels, and tongs. "Okay."

"We found evidence that it was scuttled."

"Sunk," I say.

Logan nods. He looks around at all the ridiculous chair options and elects to sink down onto his haunches instead, long arms dangling between his legs. "Deliberately sunk."

"How?" Ross asks.

Logan reaches into his pocket and takes out his tiny notebook, flips through its pages. "The transom drain plug had been removed. It's a small manual plug that's used in place of a bilge pump. Screwed into a hole in the stern of a boat while it's at sea and taken out on land to drain any water. The divers also found at least half a dozen holes in the hull, four and a half inches in diameter. Probably made with a hole saw. The bottle screws and retaining pins had been removed from the mast. Which basically means that it was taken down, collapsed. When the boat sank, the mast is what would have given its position away." His gaze refinds mine. "Visibility was poor on the third. East of Inchkeith, the boat would already have been hidden from Edinburgh and Burntisland. So, when she sank—when she was scuttled—as long as there was no floating debris, it could be assumed she would never be found."

"Okay." I can't see Logan anymore—he's just a crouching silhouette.

"It also looks like both the EPIRB and the GPS unit were destroyed, which explains why there was never any signal. And the life raft was still stowed in a locker on deck." A pause. "It looks like self-sabotage."

Self-sabotage? I think of that blue kayak in the shed. "Okay," I say.

"They found something else," Shona says. She gets up and moves closer to Logan in a small white-blond blur. Immediately, he stands up again, blocks her off, moves closer to where I'm sitting.

"The divers found something else," he says, slow and horribly careful. I can smell his deodorant, the sweeter chemical smell of whatever shit he uses on his ridiculous hair. "Inside the boat's cuddy."

"Okay." I realize that Ross is standing behind me, his arms reaching around my shoulders. I look down at the flex of his forearm muscles, the raised hairs and goose bumps on his skin.

Doom, I think. *Doom.*

"They found a body," Logan says. "A female."

Ross's arms tighten around me; his fingers dig into my collarbone.

Logan looks so pained, so wretched, I nearly get up to comfort him. "The Greenock Dive and Marine Unit recovered her this morning," he says. "I'm so sorry."

★

The windowpane is cold against the pads of my fingers. It vibrates every time a bus rattles past. I've been standing here for less than an hour, but it feels like days before DI Kate Rafiq's very shiny silver BMW parks in front of the house and she gets out. A few minutes later, I hear her come into the drawing room, but I don't turn around.

"Catriona, how're you holding up?"

I turn around. "It's not her."

Rafiq marches to the center of the room, indicates the chesterfield with the flat of her palm, nods once when I sit down on it. "We don't know anything for sure yet."

"You know it's her boat," Ross says. He sits on the footstool, nearly missing the edge of it and ending up on the floor instead. He looks like I do: shellshocked, slow, confused. Maybe he's not as resigned to El's fate as he thought.

"Aye. But at this stage, that's all. We don't know if the . . . deceased woman is Ellice. And while you should both prepare yourselves for that possibility, it's also important you don't leap to conclusions before we have any."

I don't see how managing both is even possible. "Have you seen her?"

She looks at neither of us when she nods. "I've come from the City Mortuary. It's why I wasn't able to be here earlier, I'm sorry." She clears her throat, indicates a tall, skinny man standing behind her. "Iain Patterson here is a forensic scientist," she says. "We want to be able to give you both an ID as soon as possible, all right?"

With his solemn frown, black suit, and big case, Iain Patterson looks like a cross between an undertaker and a Mormon. He nods at Ross, and then at me. Sets his case down and starts unzipping it.

"Ross," Rafiq says. "Would you mind maybe finding something of El's? A hairbrush maybe, or a used razor?"

He stays half-squatting on the footstool. "I already did that," he says, looking up at her. He sounds like a little boy. "Didn't I?"

"Aye, you did, that's right. We've already got her toothbrush. But two samples are always better than one. Shona, you want to give him a hand?"

Shona helps him up like he really is a child, and moves quickly into step alongside him, her hand hovering at his back as they leave the room.

Rafiq waits until the sound of their footsteps disappears before turning back to me. Her expression is either very grim or very pained, it's hard to tell which, but that look makes me feel claustrophobic all of a sudden. She's looking at me too hard, like she's hoping I'll trip up. I have no idea why.

"Catriona, would you give your consent to Iain here taking a DNA sample?"

When I don't immediately reply, she comes closer, lays a hand on my arm. Her nails are short and neat and white. "Initially, we'd only take reference samples from the missing person's belongings, rather than kinship samples from relatives, but in this case—"

"Because we're twins."

She nods. "Because you're identical twins, aye. You have exactly the same DNA. So, d'you give your consent?"

"Yes. Of course, yes." I look at her. At that expression. "Is . . . is there something else?"

Rafiq is quick to shake her head, force a smile, but I know there is. And I know, too, that whatever it is—whatever it is she thinks she knows, or thinks that *I* know—she isn't going to reveal it until she's ready to. My stomach clenches; the fog in my brain only gets thicker.

Rafiq nods at Iain Patterson, who gets up from his crouch after taking a plastic test tube out of his bag.

"Afternoon," he says with gusto. His voice is so low, it's more a vibration than a sound. He takes a long cotton bud out of the test tube. "Now, if you can just tip your head back a wee bit, and open your mouth wide, I'm going to take a quick swab of the inside of your cheek, okay? It won't take a jiffy."

He sounds entirely too cheerful for both his suit and the circumstances, but I nod, follow his instructions. As soon as he puts the cotton bud into my mouth, I have an urge to bite down on it hard, clamp my mouth shut.

"We may need to take a blood specimen from you at a later time," he says once he's withdrawn the bud and slid it back inside the test tube.

I'm shivering, I realize. I'm not sure when that started, but I don't seem able to stop.

"Here, Catriona, sit back down," Rafiq says, and her voice is no longer hard, but soft enough to make me want to cry. But I won't.

When we hear Ross and Shona coming back down the stairs, Rafiq looks relieved, buttons up her jacket.

"A DNA analysis can take anything between twenty-four and seventy-two hours," she says. "But obviously, we'll put a rush on this, okay?"

I nod. Ross nods too, while leaning heavily on the lowboy he fucked me against less than a week ago. I close my eyes, and when I finally manage to open them, Rafiq is giving me that hard probing look again.

"Try not to worry," she says. "Either way, it'll all be over soon."

*

After I close the door behind them, I stay in the hallway for a long time, standing inside that silver spear of sun from the fanlight window.

We're in this together, okay? Ross whispers in my ear. But, of course, when I whirl around to the hallway, he's not there. It's just another ghost.

CHAPTER 17

Time is so thick and slow, it's like I can feel it. Like I could reach down and push my hands inside it, watch it drain through my fingers. Ross and I move listlessly from room to room. We stay close together. Whenever we stop or sit, we touch knees or arms or fingers, and I can't bring myself to care about all the reasons why we shouldn't. He shakes; tremors rattle down through him and into me. We're sitting at the kitchen table when he finally lifts up his head. I realize that he's as angry as he is afraid.

"I don't want El to be dead, Cat."

"I know," I whisper.

"I never wanted her to be dead."

And I don't know if he means because of us, because of how quickly we've turned back towards each other, or because of how strong his grief has always seemed from the start, how certain. I reach for his fingers, weave mine between them. "I know, Ross."

Eventually, I have to be alone. I lock myself in the bathroom, blink at the face in the mirror, its eyes tired and just as afraid. I think of the last time I looked at this face and it wasn't a reflection. New Year's Day, 2006. Six months after El's *I win*. Six months before we would no longer be teenagers anymore. We met at Yellowcraigs. It was two buses and a mile-long walk from my house share in Niddrie. I had no idea where El had come from; didn't even know if she was still living in the city.

The beach was empty, the waves wild, wind vicious, the day sunny and cold. It was hard to look at her for long. I missed her and Ross so badly it was an angry, wretched ache; a stump that itched and tingled and couldn't forget what it felt like to be whole. She wouldn't let him talk to me, although he did and often, phoning me whenever he could—even if both of us could see that it was pointless, more painful than silence. I couldn't bear to hear about her, about them, about plans that didn't include me. I couldn't bear to hear his sadness, his guilt, his pleas for me to understand why. Why it had to be this way.

"You've lost too much weight."

I couldn't sleep. I saw too many doctors and took too many pills. I'd even flirted with the idea of suicide, and the only thing to stop me was the thought of how ridiculous I'd look if I failed, how pathetic. That then there would be nothing at all of mine that hadn't first belonged to El.

I kept looking at her in small snatches. Her skin was bright and her hair blonder. Her nails were red and long. I wondered when she'd stopped biting them.

"You need to eat."

I saw her glancing down at my ragged nails, the scabbed-over scratches and cuts on my hands that so often appeared without me knowing why or when. I flinched when she reached with her right hand to take my left. I looked back across the choppy waves, out towards the hazy dark line of the North Sea, and I swallowed, suddenly afraid.

"We're getting married," she said, and I kept on looking at the spindrift, the blinding flashes of sun. I could feel my hand tightening on hers, but she didn't wince, she didn't let go.

"You don't even want him. I know you don't. You're only taking him because I want him. Because I love him."

It was the first time I'd said it, I realized. To anyone but myself.

El turned to me then. "You're like a fucking puppy, you know that, Cat? The worse someone treats you, the more you try, the more you want them to like you. It's pathetic."

I blinked away the sting in my eyes. "I'll leave. I'll go to America." The college was running an all-expenses-paid internship program at the *Los Angeles Times*. There was already a list of volunteers a mile long. Before that day, I hadn't considered going even for a minute.

She looked briefly surprised, maybe even shocked, and then she looked away. "Good."

My fear, my hurt, I swallowed down with anger. "I'll never come back."

She turned to face me and her smile was wide. I wanted to shrink from the victory in that smile as much as the sudden bite of her fingers around my wrists, squeezing hard enough to leave bruises that would remind me of her words for weeks.

"That's not the threat you think it is, Cat. Because I hate you. Do you understand? I hate you. So, go. All I want is for you to be gone." The snarl did nothing to mask the hurt in her eyes, the fury. "To never have to think about you again."

And then she let me go. Walked away without once looking back.

There are many downsides to being an identical twin. Always knowing—seeing—what you look like when you smile, when you frown, when wrinkles start appearing around your eyes, like a mirror you always carry, sharp and heavy under your arm. Always being mistaken for someone else, just waiting for the moment you can interrupt, put them right, see the warm familiarity in their eyes disappear. Always being crammed into half a box, traits divvied up so that one must be outgoing, the other shy; one adventurous, one timid. Believing it yourself. Believing that when you're the one not picked, when you're the one kicked aside, it's never because of what you look like. It's because you're you. And not her.

But this is worse. This leaden, savage *knowing* that you aren't whole without each other. That you can never survive alone in the world. That you were never meant to. Thinking of her on that day hurts more than anything else ever has. Cheeks pink, eyes blinking tears that I hoped were for me, but knew were for the vicious wind. The squeeze of her fingers against mine, just like when we'd fight sleep under the ironwoods and banyans of the Kakadu Jungle, neither of us wanting to be the first to let go. How that was the last day, the last moment—even when she was being cruel—that I felt she might still love me. How she had been the first one to let go.

"I'd know." When I start to cry, it feels as frightening as watching the face in the mirror fall apart. I watch her cover her mouth with her hand. I watch her tears spill over white, blue-veined skin like twin waterfalls. I watch her shake her head as if that's enough, that's all that needs to be done. And then it will all stop.

I'd know.

*

john.smith120594@gmail.com   15 April 2018 at 21:15

Re: HE KNOWS   Inbox

To: Me

CLUE 9. LOOK UNDER YOUR MATTRESS

Sent from my iPhone

*

July 3rd, 1998
He's not real. Dad's not real.
I think I knew really but how could Mum LIE???
She was making me and Cat pack away our old costumes and
games and books into boxes to take downstairs to Mirrorland and
I found one of Grandpa's big encyclopeedias in her cupboard. So
I took it out and I opened it and on a page with the corner turned
down there was CAPTAIN HENRY MORGAN!!!!!!!

I was excited at first—coz the picture of him was exactly how Mum
had said—exactly like my painting in Mirrorland and there was all
this great stuff about him being a privateer (which I think is just
a posh disguise for a Pirate that works for the government. LIKE
MUM SAID TOO) He was even the LEUTENANT GOVERNOR
OF JAMAICA!!!

But then Cat saw when he was born. 1635!!!!!!

We couldn't beleive it. How could Mum lie to us? She always told
us he loved us and if we waited for him in Mirrorland he'd come
back. He'd take us to The Island. To Santa Catalina. And even tho
that sounds stupid now Mirrorland is magic. It's better than Narnia
or Oz or Neverland or Middle Earth. We can make things happen

there that never happen anywhere else. It's REAL. But it doesn't matter. Because she lied. He's not our dad. And when we told her we knew she cried—Mum NEVER cries!! She said she did it to make us happy. And then started going on and on about how she loves us so much blah blah BLAH

And Grandpa was so mean! Like we were stupid to beleive it anyway. Like it was our fault or something. He said she should have told us that our dad was a TOTAL FUCKING WASTER who left her as soon as she was pregnant. And when Cat asked Mum if our dad was a TOTAL FUCKING WASTER Mum just cried some more and left us with mean Grandpa.

I HATE them. I HATE THEM BOTH.

Look at the state ae them! They're allus tired. They never bloody sleep. Ye said yersel their school work's sufferin'. Ye've filled up their heids wi' so much bloody nonsense they spend aw their time in a dreamworld. And now ye've got 'em believin' their fuckin' father is a seventeenth-century pirate, for Christ's sake! They'll grow up slower than a week in the fuckin' jail, wumman!

I remember recoiling from that voice, from his lips flecked with spittle. So unlike the Grandpa I knew. As alien as a tear-streaked Mum telling us, *I'm sorry, I love you, I lied because I wanted you both to be happy.* Or a faceless father who was a total fucking waster.

The wind rattles the Clown Café window. It's grown so dark now all I can see is my own reflection. My phone vibrates. Vik again. When I don't answer, a text immediately appears on the screen. *I need to speak to you.* I shove my phone in a drawer, open my laptop, hit reply to that last message from john.smith120594. My fingers tremble, but not so much that I can't type.

They found a body. Tell me who it is. Please.

I close my stinging, salt-dry eyes. I am so, so tired. My heart is a slow, dull thud that I can feel in my chest and stomach.

No one answers me.

CHAPTER 18

They come back twenty-seven and a half hours after they left. All of them. I stand at the Princess Tower window and watch Rafiq's shiny silver BMW pull up behind Shona's pale blue Beetle—a convertible. Shona's wearing tight jeans and a thin silk shirt. Who living in Edinburgh wouldn't want a convertible and a thin silk shirt? I occupy myself with more petty observations as they open the gate, come up the path in slow single file. And when I run out of spite, I admire Logan's legs instead, the broad set of his shoulders, even his stupid hair.

Please, I think, when I hear the front door, the hallway door, the murmur of voices. *Please*, when Ross shouts my name from the bottom of the stairs—uncertain and thin—and instead of answering, I open the white cupboard and look at El's self-portrait, press the pads of my fingers against the angry brushstrokes of her skin. *Please*, when I go out onto the landing and grab hold of the banister, feel the world list and lurch. When I stop just short of the bottom, look down into the hallway at all those solemn, grim faces and the bell board inside the kitchen doorway: the curled black springs, the shiny bells, the star-shaped pendulums.

Please.

Rafiq clears her throat, looks at us both in turn. "I'm sorry, Ross. Catriona." She drops her head, her gaze. "It's definitely her. It's definitely El."

And that terrible day on Yellowcraigs doesn't hurt more than anything else after all.

★

I end up in Mirrorland. When I can see again, I'm on my knees on the stern deck of the *Satisfaction*, clutching the ship's lantern to my chest as I look out at the impatient white puffs of cloud and white frills of wave and Blackbeard, dark and stark and getting closer.

I don't cry, I can't cry, but every few minutes my whole body seizes with a kind of retching paralysis, where I can't breathe, can't see, can't think. In the lulls between, I cough and rock and choke down ragged breath after breath, but as swiftly as I start to recover it comes again.

I stumble from the *Satisfaction*, and up into the long empty alleyway. Stop halfway along the boundary wall, and think of El's Captain Henry Morgan, forever improved and never finished. Our seventeenth-century pirate king father.

It's not real. It's *not* real.

When I feel another seizure coming, I drop back onto my knees. What comfort I think I'll find in it, I don't know, but I start whispering, "We will not leave each other. Never so long as we live." Over and over again.

I hear a noise, see a shadow, feel my windpipe closing down tight to admit only thin sips of breath. I feel a rush of cold air, a shiver of dread. A line of white in the dark, throwing monstrous shadows against the walls. Deadlights. The echo of *RUN!* The high, long screaming panic of it, and then I'm scrambling to my feet too late, bolting away from the lurch and loom of a shadow that's no longer a shadow.

"Cat! Christ. Stop!"

Ross drops to his knees alongside me, grapples for a better hold of my flailing arms and legs. And I fight way past the point of needing or wanting to, because he's El's husband; he's belonged to her and she to him since he first dropped down from that skylight into Mirrorland—and somehow, that hasn't ever mattered to me until now. Somehow, I've managed to believe it isn't even true.

"Oh, God, please. Please. Leave me alone. *Please!*" While I grab hold of him hard enough to hurt us both, hang on to him like he's the only rock in a murderous black sea.

PART TWO

CHAPTER 19

john.smith120594@gmail.com 17 April 2018 at 05:50

Re: HE KNOWS Inbox

To: Me

CLUE 10. BEHIND THE BERLIN WALL

Sent from my iPhone

*

I'm in the Clown Café. Bluebeard and Blackbeard are here. They'll drag us out of the cupboard and carry us to Bedroom 3, and hang us on hooks until we're dead. And as we die, we'll scream in the dark like the sea, like dying pirates on a deck full of blood. And they'll throw our bodies to the sharks.

I'm in Mirrorland, sitting cross-legged on the gun deck of the *Satisfaction*, looking across at El. We're wearing matching tartan dresses over starchy white shirts. If it wasn't for Ross balancing on his haunches between us, it would be like we were both looking into a mirror. Like one of us wasn't really there. In his hand is a single sheet of paper covered in red and black pen. *THE PLAN.*

We're in this together, okay? Ross says. *The three of us. Together.*

And Annie winks solemnly at me from behind the ship's wheel. *Sometimes you have to be brave. Even when you're a grand wee coward.*

I'm in the kitchen, sitting at the table. Scrambled eggs on toast and porridge that's too hot to eat. A bird is trapped inside the old chimney flue. I can hear it scratching and flapping. My hand is shaking. I miss my mouth and Mum's goes thin. *Don't slitter, Catriona.*

Grandpa sits with his bad leg up on the spare chair, throws back his head to laugh, but his hands tremble, and worse than mine. He looks at El next to the door, her fingers on its handle. *Ye're bein' a stander, lassie. Sit the shit doon.* And El looks at me. Her smile is terrible. I pretend I can't see it. *Can I have some tea?*

The pantry's black velveteen curtain was the Berlin Wall. El was always Alec Leamas, the heroic spy who came in from the cold, while I'd always be on the other side with the Clowns—the cruel George Smiley and his Circus—leading Alec to his doom. I find the diary page pushed inside the curtain's hem.

September 4th, 1998
Today at breakfast everyone pretended everything was Normal.
Even me really I suppose, even tho it's not, even tho I'm just about
as scared as I've ever been my Whole Life.
And Mum and Grandpa and Cat were all like pass me the salt and pour
me some tea and hurry up it's time for school. And I'm like how can
you be Normal? Didn't you Hear? Didn't you See? Aren't you Scared?
HE'LL COME BACK.

But I didn't say any of that either so maybe we were all thinking it
in our heads and none of us could say it out loud. In case He did.
Come Back I mean.
So after breakfast I pulled Cat behind the Berlin Wall and I put my
hand over her mouth and I whispered in her ear "IT HAS TO BE
TONIGHT"!!
Because It Does. No matter what she says. No matter how scared we
are. It's THE PLAN. It's what we agreed.

I'm behind the curtain in the pantry, struggling to breathe through El's clammy hand and the dusty dark. The ghosts whisper and thump around us. *It has to be tonight.*

No, I think. *NO.*

Yes, says El. I feel her smile under my fingers as if we've swapped places—I've become her and she's become me. And when I let her go and pull back the curtain, every wall in the hallway and kitchen is painted ugly wet crimson. I hear an owl hoot: high and long. I hear boots, I hear *RUN!* I hear rings. The noise is deafening. The wooden board shudders, every one of its bells shaking left and right, star-shaped pendulums flashing in the gloom, the dark. I see the moon.

Wake up! El screams in my voice. Our voice. *Wake the fuck up.*

*

I fall off the stool onto the pantry floor. My arms and legs feel too heavy. My stomach is empty, queasy. My head aches, aches, aches. Is this what grief feels like? Or guilt? Is this what it feels like when half of you is gone? When half of you is dead?

I pick up my phone, press reply. The screen stays blurry no matter how many times I blink.

Answer me. Meet me. Explain. Or leave me the fuck alone.

Ross is standing by the kitchen window, looking out at a back garden distorted by rain. It pounds against the roof and the flue cap, the guttering. He turns around when he hears me. Last night, I insisted that we both sleep alone, and spent the entirety of it longing for his breath on my neck and his arm across my belly and his legs tangled between mine. Today, I can't even look at him.

"The tea's stewed," he says, picking up the pot. It shakes in his hands, enough that the lid starts to rattle. "I'll make some more."

I take it from him. "It's okay." I fill a mug and sit down. Take too large a swallow. *Don't slitter, Catriona.*

"Cat." Ross sits down next to me. His fingers are warm against mine. I try to tell myself their touch doesn't help, doesn't straightaway soothe a hollow place deep inside my chest. "Please don't shut me out."

I take back my hands, press them between my knees instead. "I need to see her."

Ross almost recoils. "What? Why? The DNA—"

"You're the one who said she wasn't suicidal," I say. Because just about the only thing still holding me together is that stubborn and enduring *I'd know.* That I would have felt the moment she died, the moment she drowned, the moment she left. That those hopeless, help-less, horrifying seizures of yesterday were only shock, only shame.

"Maybe she didn't mean to do it." He takes hold of my hands again, pulls them in hard against his breastbone. I can feel the too-fast thud-thud of his heart. "Maybe it *was* an accident. Maybe she just wanted me to notice she was in pain." His eyes are wet with unshed tears. And when I take back my hands again, he stands up, turns away from me.

I look down at the two tiles in front of the Kitchener. That cracked line of grout stained dark. My smile feels tight, like my lips might split and bleed. "Years ago, I read about this tribe. It was in one of Grandpa's encyclopedias. And it . . . it was one of those lucky tribes that had managed to avoid the rest of us for centuries. In South America somewhere, I don't know."

"Cat—"

"If a member of this tribe did something wrong, got caught doing something wrong, or even just thought they'd done something—anything, you know, from telling a lie to committing a murder—this tribe, this entire tribe, would take them into the center of their village, and they would form this circle around them, so tight they couldn't escape, couldn't hide. And then they would tell that person everything that was good about them. Every good thing they'd ever done. Every good thing they'd ever been. Over and over. And they wouldn't stop. Not until that person heard them. Believed them."

My voice breaks. My eyes burn with tears I refuse to cry. My hands twitch to hold his. My body aches to lie down. To feel his hard, warm, sure weight against me, inside me. And all of me wants to look in a mirror and see only El. To stand on a freezing cold beach and say this is where I'll stay. To never allow her to let go of my hand. No matter how much it hurts. No matter how many times she pushes me away.

CHAPTER 20

Marie stands on the doorstep inside a swath of bright morning light. She's holding a huge bunch of calla lilies, and tears are running down her cheeks.

"*Je suis désolée. C'est affreux. Je suis tellement désolée.*"

I take the flowers—their antiseptic smell waters my eyes and stings my nose. "Thank you, Marie."

She takes out a beautifully embroidered handkerchief and dabs at her skin. "I knew . . . I knew she had to be . . . *mais* . . ."

"Sorry—I'd invite you in, but I'm just about to go out."

She blinks at my denim jacket. Today, I can't even look at the gray cashmere coat hanging on the stand behind me.

"Is Ross here?"

"No." I'm pretty sure she knows he isn't here. That she waited until he'd left for Colquhoun's before deciding to come over.

She leans close to me, her eyes suddenly sharp and dry. "Did you ask him? About what he said to me? How he threatened me?"

"Marie—"

"You are in danger." Her fingers close around my wrist. "*Tu comprends?*"

"Marie! Stop." I snatch my hand back.

She shakes her head, takes a phone out of her pocket, and then thrusts it at me. "*Regardez.* Look what he says to me one week before Ellice disappears. Look!"

Stay away from her. Stay away or you'll regret it.

It's Ross's number. I think. But I shove the phone back towards her, start trying to close the door. "I can't do this now. I have to—"

"You must! You're in danger!" She pushes back. Tries to grip hold of me again. *"S'il te plaît!"*

I'm glad of the fury that burns suddenly through me, laying waste to everything else. I drop the flowers and wrench the door wide, pushing Marie aside as I step out and slam it shut behind me.

"Catriona—"

I battle to lock the door as her hands continue to touch me, pull at me. I want to scream. I want to run away from all of this, and never look back.

"Catriona. Listen to me! You—"

"I'm going to the *morgue!*" My shout sounds, even to my own ears, more like a scream. Marie closes her mouth and steps back, drops her hands to her sides.

I can feel other eyes on me as I run down the steps and through the gate, along the road towards the number 49 bus that's pulling in to the stop. But I don't slow, don't turn around. Don't look back.

*

The City Mortuary is an ugly concrete block sandwiched between beautiful Victorian terraces. Logan is leaning against a set of double doors next to a big metal-shuttered garage. When he sees me, he straightens up, and his smile is solemn, fleeting. I fight the threat of another choking seizure by biting down hard on my bottom lip and pushing my fingernails deep into the fattest part of my palms.

"Hi, Cat."

A sign on the wall alongside him says EDINBURGH CITY MORTUARY. It's a very grand, gold-colored plaque, polished enough that I can see my face in it. I blink hard, look up at the sky instead. It's white and heavy with the threat of spring snow.

"You're bleeding."

I feel the heel of Logan's palm against my cheek, the rough warmth of his thumb against my skin. I turn my head and pull my lip between my teeth.

"I'm okay."

He nods. Drops his hands down by his sides. "Okay."

"Logan." Rafiq is standing inside the double doors. Just looking at

170

her sleek ponytail and intense stare transports me back to the house. *I'm sorry, Catriona. It's definitely her. It's definitely El.* "You're needed back at the station."

He doesn't argue, but there's some defiance in the way he steps closer to me, briefly squeezes my hand. "Take care, okay? You've got my number."

Rafiq holds the doors open, nods at me as I pass her. The waiting room is a soft magnolia. It's very warm and very empty.

"Sit down a minute," she says. "Are you absolutely sure you want to do this?"

I nod. Even though I'm not.

She sighs. "Would it help if I showed you the DNA report?"

I don't know what she means by *help*. Although I do know that I want to see it enough to nod again.

She takes out her phone and hands it to me.

<u>DNA ISOLATION TEST</u>
<u>Reference Samples:</u>
ID 1551204: Soft-bristle toothbrush belonging to Ellice MacAuley (dob 01/07/86) [Collected 04/04/18]
ID 1551205: Wide-barrel hairbrush belonging to Ellice MacAuley (dob 01/07/86) [Collected 15/04/18]

<u>Kinship Sample:</u>
ID 1551206: Buccal swab from identical twin sibling, Catriona Morgan [HID1551_201] (dob 01/07/86) [Collected 15/04/18]

<u>Jane Doe [HID1551_200] Samples:</u>
Partial facial and upper body saponification; DNA extracted from femoral bone marrow

DNA isolation was carried out separately for all samples. Genetic characteristics were determined by the following PCR single-locus-technology analysis.
Results were confirmed by retesting original samples.

All laboratory analyses and interpretations follow the recommendations of the DNA commission of the International Society for Forensic Genetics, ISFG.

Conclusion:
Based upon our analysis and the biostatistical evaluation of its results, it is practically proven that Jane Doe [HID1551_200] is >99.9999% Ellice MacAuley (dob 01/07/86), of 36 Westeryk Road, Leith. And that Catriona Morgan [HID1551_201] (dob 01/07/86) is 99.9999% the living identical sibling of the deceased.

Expert Witness:
Dr Iain Patterson MB ChB, BMSc (Hons), FRCPath, MFFLM
Head Forensic Pathologist
North Lothian CID

I read it twice, three times, until my eyes go blurry. When I give back the phone, my hand is shaking.

"I want a copy of that," I try to say with some authority, but my voice is shaking too. White noise rushes through my ears as if I'm underwater.

"Of course," Rafiq says.

"I still want to see her."

"I really think that would be a bad idea. It won't help. If anything—"

"I have to." I make myself look at Rafiq. Her brow is wrinkled, her mouth thin, her eyes full of concern. "Please."

She finally nods. "But afterwards, I have to ask you some questions, Catriona. Okay? It's important."

I barely hear her over the beating of my heart or the roaring in my ears.

*

Rafiq takes me through another door: VISITOR FACILITIES. As if we're in a stately home. In the corridor beyond, more doors: INTER-

VIEW ROOMS, COUNSELING ROOMS. I follow on behind Rafiq. I don't speak. I don't think.

We pass a door labeled BIER ROOM, but before I can ask her what a bier is, Rafiq opens the door alongside it. VIEWING ROOM. And my mouth clamps shut.

Everything inside it is soft focus, unobtrusive, warm. Noninstitutional. The lights are low, and the acoustics somehow muted. I realize that what I've been imagining ever since Logan's *The Greenock Dive and Marine Unit recovered her this morning* is one of those sterile white-tiled rooms with metal storage drawers and steel tables with big plugholes, like something out of *CSI* or *Silent Witness*.

When Rafiq asks me to sit down, her voice has lost all of its sharp edges too. The armchair is beige and cushioned. There are watercolor landscapes hanging on the walls, reminding me of that hospital waiting room of nearly thirteen years ago, its plastic-framed seascape of rocks and sand and waves. I look everywhere but at the big blue-curtained window on the wall opposite.

The knock makes me jump. The door opens, and I spring up, grateful to stop sitting, to stop trying not to look.

"Catriona," says Rafiq. "This is Dr. Claire MacDuff."

Dr. Claire MacDuff is about mid-fifties, and five feet if she's lucky. Her sandy hair is short but thick, her glasses green-rimmed, her smile solicitous. She's wearing jeans and a sweater, which is the thing I find most disconcerting of all. I'd been expecting scrubs, shower cap, gloves, gumboots, the works.

I accept her offered hand, and halfway through a very vigorous shake, she tells me, "Hello. I was the lead doctor on your sister's postmortem."

"Oh," I say, swallowing the ridiculous *great* that wants to follow it.

She finally lets me go. "I understand why you're here, but I'm afraid that I've recommended no relatives view the body in this case. As SIO, DI Rafiq was also in attendance at the PM, and so is aware of the reasons for my objections." She holds up a palm before I can speak. "However. She has also explained the circumstances, and I'm not unsympathetic. But you'll hear me out before I agree to anything, okay?"

"Okay."

"Ordinarily, when we find a body in the Forth, it's because decomposition gases bring it up to the surface after a few days. But your sister was *in* the Forth for thirteen days. That means that in addition to normal decomposition, the body has been subjected to many other changes and traumas. It's important that you know that, and it's important that you know *what* before I'm happy for you to see her, okay?"

For the first time since phoning Logan, it occurs to me that what I'm about to see might be just about the worst thing I've ever seen in my life. Even though I've been shaking since I woke up—since probably before I woke up—I suddenly go still.

"When a body has been in water for some time, it can undergo a natural preservation process known as saponification. This process forms something called adipocere, which means that much of Ellice's body tissue has become waxy, brittle, and deformed." She looks at me. "Think of a well-used candle or soap on a rope."

"Aye, okay." Rafiq bristles, laying the flat of her hand between my shoulder blades. "Is it necessary for you to be quite so—"

"She needs to know what she's asking for," says Dr. MacDuff. She turns her steady gaze back to me. "The head, more specifically, the face, is always the most disfigured part of a submerged body. It's why we almost always rely on DNA for ID. Ellice's lips, ears, nose, and larynx have been colonized and partially eaten away by comestible marine predators. There has been significant damage."

I have no clue what comestible marine predators are, though I'm not about to ask. "Okay."

"Cat," Rafiq says, now rubbing slow shallow circles across my back. Her eyes are so black I can't see their pupils. There are two deep lines between her eyebrows. "Are you hearing this? Seeing her isn't going to help. She'll not be recognizable as your sister anymore. I'd strongly advise—*we'd* both strongly advise—that you don't do this."

I step away from her, and out of reach of her hands, her concerned gaze. I preferred it when she was a cold and efficient robot who called me Catriona; I can't bear this strange kindness.

"I want to see her."

"Okay," Dr. MacDuff says. "If you wait here, I'll have the technicians move her from the bier room."

I wait until she's gone to take in an unsteady breath.

"Cat—"

"I'm sure," I say, and wish that my voice wasn't wavering.

Rafiq squeezes my shoulder, moves towards the curtain. A small green light comes on in a switch panel close to the door.

I'm holding my breath. And even when I realize it, I can't stop. I can't let it go and breathe in another. Shivers are trickling down from my scalp, pressing my shoulder blades together, cricking my neck. My bottom lip throbs when I bite down on it again, and I taste old blood, new blood. "I'm *sure*."

Rafiq's nod is short. She pulls back the curtain, exposing the well-lit room beyond in slow increments. I close my eyes. Open them.

I need to *know*. That's all there is.

And then. There *it* is.

It has no hair. Its scalp is completely bald. Shiny, creamy, and rippled thick—and the first thing I do think of is a well-used altar candle, its wax melted and remelted into asymmetric waves. Its nose is just a hole, a black maze of sinus passages. It has no eyelids. No eyes. Its teeth are fixed in a lipless grin. Beneath its waxy gray neck and a blue drape, I can just about see the thick black closing stitches of Dr. MacDuff's Y incision at the wide end of each collarbone. I try to imagine the body underneath the drape, so still and flat on top of the gurney. I stop.

When I back away from the window, Rafiq is there to help turn me towards the door, and this time I don't resent those hands against my back. My legs give way as soon as I reach the corridor, and when she pulls me close, when she comes down to the tiled floor with me, I don't resent her strange kindness anymore either. I reach for it instead, just as hard as I reach for her, and I let all that silvery horror and shame spill out of me in sobs and cries and retches against her neat black suit jacket.

*

"Here you are."

I take the mug from Rafiq's hands. The tea is too hot, too sugary, but I drink it anyway. Her office is cold. I can barely remember the car journey from the mortuary to the police station. I feel sick and my head is pounding. My eyes are so swollen I can hardly see.

"Are you sure you don't want to see someone? A doctor, or—"

"How did she die? I didn't ask how she died."

Rafiq looks at me, shows me the flat palms of her hands. "We can't be sure. Not enough to satisfy the procurator fiscal anyway. The most obvious CODs would be drowning or hypothermia. But . . . there wasn't enough intact lung or circulatory tissue to confirm either."

Comestible marine predators, I think, and I see that black maze of sinus passages, those deep eyeless holes.

"What we do know is that El had very high levels of diazepam, fluoxetine, and oxycodone in her bone marrow."

I think of those pill bottles behind the bathroom mirror. "Enough to kill her?"

"We can't be sure of that either. The time that toxins are deposited in bones can't be accurately calculated, and samples measured in bone marrow are generally found to be higher than those in blood specimens." She leans forwards. "Oxycodone is an opioid, commonly used for severe pain. Stronger than morphine. Her GP never prescribed them. Do you know if your sister had a history of drug abuse? Recreational drug use?"

"What? No. Of course not." I can no more imagine El taking opioids than Valium. She didn't even like to drink. Could never risk letting go of control for even a moment. I look down at Rafiq's desk, at a photo of a grinning man in scrubs. "Is *that* what killed her, then?"

"It's probable that they contributed to her death, one way or another."

I think of standing on cold wet stone. Looking out at the eastern breakwater wall and the volcanic rise of the Binn behind stony studs of houses. At the white-frilled waves of high tide and the distant flat of the North Sea. And thinking that this place—the place we once ran to—was the place El had disappeared from. But she hadn't. She'd been right there, all that time, under the howling wind and rain and all those gray waves, down in the thick black murk of the deepwater channel.

"When will you be bringing the boat up?" I manage. "For forensics or whatever. Because someone removed that drain plug and drilled holes in the hull. They took down the mast. They—"

"They also disabled the onboard toilet," Rafiq says. And not in the manner of somebody who's on my side. "So that it would let water in instead of flushing it out."

I look at the heavy white day through the window: the city's gothic and steel towers, its distant green hills. My skin itches and shivers. I inhale as if I'm getting ready to hold my breath, dive underwater.

"El didn't kill herself. She *wouldn't*."

"Well, you say that, and I can understand you needing to believe it, but in 2005, she—"

"For fuck's sake, I already told you that she never tried to kill herself back then! She did it to piss me off, to get Ross's attention, to make me leave. It wasn't—she took just enough acetaminophen to have to go to hospital and have it pumped out of her, that's the—" I stop. Will myself calm. "Ross doesn't think she killed herself either," I say, even though I suspect that might no longer be true. "We won't leave this alone. If that's what you want, neither of us is going to do it. This isn't her fault. Someone else did this to her. I know it."

Rafiq doesn't remind me that I also knew El wasn't dead, but the look she gives me says she's thinking it.

"Listen," she says. "Neither the Marine Accident Investigation Branch nor the Scottish Environment Protection Agency will fund a recovery of *The Redemption*. It's not a commercial vessel, and we already know *how*—"

"So you're just going to leave it down there to rot?"

"Sometimes, CID will get an amount granted by the government to fund further investigation in certain cases of murder. But this is not one of those."

The finality in her voice makes me want to punch something. "But what about the cards? Someone was threatening her. And I've had more! I've kept them. There's a kayak in the shed! And I've also been getting—"

Rafiq shakes her head, holds up a hand. "I don't think that the cards are connected to what's happened to El. We investigated them, followed up on every suggestion Ross and El gave us, but the cards never explicitly threatened El's life—or yours. If anything, Ross was the target, and we've already investigated *him* too. They weren't getting on. Maybe El was seeing someone. Maybe he was. People always love to meddle, to interfere in dramas that have nothing to do with them."

I feel numb, frustrated, backed into a corner. For days, I've been emailing El, I've been angry with El. And all the time, it really was Mouse. And if Ross is right, and the cards are from her, too, then I should tell Rafiq. I should show her the emails. Because even if they've already investigated her, Mouse *is* involved. She's been telling me that she knows what's going on from the very start. I KNOW THINGS. THINGS HE DOESN'T WANT YOU TO KNOW. EL IS DEAD. I CAN HELP YOU. I think about Ross's text on Marie's phone. *Stay away from her. Stay away or you'll regret it.*

"Catriona." Rafiq reaches her hands across the table. "Listen to me, okay? El's previous suicide attempt, her depression and the drugs she was taking at the time of her disappearance, the leaving behind of her wallet, her phone, her passport, *The Redemption* not being found anywhere near where she'd told the boatman she was going—all of these things point to either accident or suicide. And you'll not want to accept this either, but we'll probably never know for sure which." She lays a small hand over mine. "I'm sorry. I truly am."

I feel dizzy. My head throbs. I don't know what to say. What to do. If I tell Rafiq about the emails, I have to tell her about Mirrorland, El's diary. I have to tell her what happened on September 4, 1998. And I can't.

I want to get up, I want to run. I want to keep on setting fires no matter how brutally efficient Rafiq is at putting them out. Because if I don't, all I'm left with is this leaden savage knowing, this terrible emptiness that's bigger, deeper than everything else. Than being more special than a hundred thousand other children, rare like owlet-nightjars or California condors. Than lying sick in bed and still being able to fly, to feel the fast, cold air against my skin, the tickling scratch of leaves and branches, the terror of falling, the agony of landing, the wonder of knowing. Than being half of a whole, never alone; days, hours, minutes away from being fused into something new, like sand and limestone into glass. I don't want to be left with only savage emptiness. I don't want to realize that nothing before it was true. That we were never special at all. That El died and I didn't feel it. That I can survive alone in the world after all.

I'm crying again, I realize. Crying and choking and crouching on the floor, clinging to the legs of my chair like a toddler.

Anna was right. I've done all of this wrong. I've let El down. Worse, I've betrayed her in every way. I stole from her, hated her, disbelieved her, deserted her, over and over again. I thought only the worst of her for years, when I was the coward. I was the one who ran away. And now I can't even get justice for her. I can't even say sorry.

*

Rafiq doesn't try to calm me down. She stays with me until my grief runs out of fuel, and then she helps me back up onto my chair, produces a bottle of whisky from her desk drawer.

I gulp down one measure, and she pours me another. Every few seconds, tired tremors shake through me like aftershocks.

"She always said she wanted to be cremated," I whisper.

"It'll be a wee while yet before you can start making arrangements," Rafiq says. "The procurator fiscal has to see our report and the postmortem report and make his own ruling before the body can be released to the next of kin. And if El did want to be cremated, the PF has to sign off on that as well, I'm afraid."

"But why? If it was an *accident*, or if she *killed herself* like you say she did, why do you—"

"Because no matter what we might think or know, all evidence must still be collected, reported upon, and ruled upon in exactly the same way, in every single case, without prejudice." She looks me square in the eye. "Besides, there have been some complications in this particular case. Some anomalies, uncertainties."

I sit up straight. "What anomalies? Why didn't you tell me about them earlier?"

And I recognize far too late the return of that speculative look. The sharp scrutiny in her too-dark eyes.

"These days, we can ID a body in a variety of ways, but we always follow the same checklist: personal effects, distinguishing marks, visual ID, dental records, DNA." She holds my gaze. "In El's case, like Dr. MacDuff said, there was significant trauma and decomposition, so distinguishing marks and visual ID weren't possible."

Just like in the viewing room, I suddenly can't let go my breath, can't breathe in another.

"And I know this is a traumatic time for you, I understand that. But what you want is what I want. For El's body to be released, for her case to be correctly and properly closed. Which is why these . . . anomalies need to be addressed." She blinks. "Explained."

I don't speak. Don't breathe out. Don't breathe in.

Rafiq leans forwards until we're nearly touching. "Do you remember I said there were questions I had to ask you, Catriona?"

I don't nod, even though I do remember. And even though I know now what those questions will be. What has been behind all those sidelong stares and pregnant pauses, as if she always thought I knew something she didn't, as if she was waiting for me to trip up, to give it away. She was right. And I think I just have.

"After the forensic divers went down to collect any personal effects," Rafiq says, "we moved on to El's dental records. What do you think we found, Catriona?"

I swallow.

"We found no dental records for El at all." Rafiq's smile is small, humorless. "So I had Logan run a more detailed case history on her while we started DNA investigations. Just the basics: birthplace, parents, schools. And what d'you think we found then, Catriona?" Her voice is still kind, but her words are steely.

I manage to shake my head.

"Nothing. We found nothing."

I close my eyes.

"Because before September the fifth, 1998, it's as if El—and you—never existed at all."

CHAPTER 21

El and I are sitting cross-legged on the bed in the Clown Café. El, in shiny pantaloons held up by spotty braces. Me, in tartan dungarees, an orange wig. My face is painted to match Dicky Grock's sad eyes and sad mouth. El is white-faced and red-lipped, grinning like the terrifying Pogo.

We're sitting at a plastic table in a fifties American diner. Drinking black coffee and eating fried doughnuts. Pogo sits next to us, while Dicky Grock mans the deep fryer. A jukebox plays "Teddy Bear," "Love Me Tender," "Blue Moon of Kentucky." I whisper to El, *When can we leave? When can we go?* Because we're not really Clowns and they might know it, they might work it out. Because Clowns are clever, Clowns are scary, Clowns are a species entirely separate from people. Clowns *hate* people. Everyone knows that. But El's big red grin says, *Not yet, not yet.* Because she's more scared of the Tooth Fairy, and everyone knows that the Tooth Fairy is terrified of Clowns.

But Bluebeard isn't.

*

The café is busy, hot, too noisy. Chatter and the constant scrape of chairs, the grind of coffee beans and the loud hissing of steam. I look out a big window running wet with condensation, watch the bob of umbrellas and bundled-up bodies fast-marching along the streets outside.

"Snow in bloody April," Rafiq says as she sits down, pushes a huge cappuccino and a three-pack of bourbons towards me.

I warm my hands around the cup. On a table behind us, a child starts to yell and a baby starts to scream.

"Try and eat the biscuits," Rafiq says.

Nausea sits inside my stomach like a stone. Another baby starts to wail.

"Never wanted kids," Rafiq says, rolling her eyes. "Apart from a very weird day in 2006. One wee tick-tock, and then my clock stopped for good, thank God."

When I still don't speak, still don't look at her, she sets down her cup, clasps her hands tightly.

"Look. It's not my intention to cause you any more grief, but this needs to be sorted." She pauses. "Instead of a birth certificate, or a hospital report, or even one of those wee hand-and-feet prints, the first actual document we have for either of you is the police report of one PC Andrew Davidson dated the fifth of September, 1998, stating that you were runaways found by a Mr. Peter Stewart, sixty-six, of 10 Muirdyke Place. And when Logan and I took a closer look at that report, d'you know what was even more bizarre?"

The heat from the coffee cup burns my skin.

"Mr. Peter Stewart found you at Granton Harbour."

My fingers tingle, as if they can still feel El's heat, the tight grip of her hand. I shiver from the bone-cold North Sea wind trapped inside the firth's gullet, whipping up waves, rattling masts and buoys. And instead of a white sky heavy with snow, I see a red dawn creeping over the breakwater like a bruise. Like blood, sour and dark and sly.

"When you're both twelve years old, you appear—*poof!*—out of nowhere at Granton Harbour. You refuse to say why you're there, where you've come from, anything but your names. Not one person ever reports you missing, comes looking for you, although you've both got injuries indicative of physical assault. Your names don't exist on any register of any sort. *You* don't exist."

She pauses again, leans back in her chair. Waits. I say nothing, do nothing, look back out the window at the worsening snow.

"So, what happened then? Social services take you into care, ask you no questions, just give you new lives?"

They asked plenty of questions. We just never answered. And when it became obvious that we wouldn't be adopted, they helped us apply and register our names, our new lives, as long as it took, as hard as it was. Mum had always told us our surname was Morgan.

After the pirate king who'd abandoned us. The father we had never known. I watch fat flakes of snow disappear into the wet sidewalk.

"Okay, Cat. Then start with this. Why did El have no dental records?"

I close my eyes. Pretend I'm not shivering. Shuddering. "She had a phobia about dentists."

"Okay."

"She was always meticulous about cleaning, hygiene, all of that. Mum made sure we both were. And when we were in the Rosemount, El always refused to go to the dentist." I swallow. "I guess that didn't change."

"Why?"

One of the wailing babies passes by our table, its arms and legs fighting to escape a sling, its mother grim-faced.

"Mum would pull our teeth. You know, like parents do." I chance a quick look at Rafiq, but her expression is blank. "If a tooth was loose, she'd tie one end of a piece of string around it and the other around a door handle, and then slam the door shut. That usually worked. And if it wasn't loose enough, she'd just pull it out with pliers."

Rafiq frowns. "Your baby teeth."

I don't know if it's a question. "Mostly. And once or twice, when we were older. If we got a bad cavity or an abscess."

"Jesus," Rafiq says.

"Parents do that. Sometimes."

"No, they don't, Cat."

I remember El screaming and screaming. Me banging on the locked bathroom door, feeling the fear, the pain, the helplessness. I remember what it was like to have a mouth full of blood. To be spitting it out for days. I remember the silvery, shivery dread of hearing the squeak of the kitchen cupboard where the bent-nose pliers lived.

"Mum was scared of clowns." I try to laugh, but it comes out as a choking cough. "She was scared of a lot of things, but she was *terrified* of them. I think there's a word for that; I've never looked it up, but she had it. So El got the idea that if one of us had a toothache, we'd dress up as clowns so Mum couldn't . . . you know, do anything. Grandpa bought us the costumes, thought it was just fun. He always said Mum was too afraid of everything, that she'd pass it on to us." I only realize I'm twisting my fingers back and forth when one of them makes a loud crack. "We'd paint a clown on the bathroom mirror as a warning, and then dress up and hide in the spare room—we called it the Clown Café—and stay there. For days sometimes. Till we got too hungry or thirsty, or bored. And Mum would never come in."

"Jesus," Rafiq says again.

"It wasn't her fault." I think of her pinched unsmiling face. Her endless stories and lessons and warnings. "She just . . . worried. She just wanted us to be safe. They both did—her and Grandpa. Why do you want to know all this?"

"Why did they not just take you to a dentist? What happened if you got sick?"

I remember lying in bed and wondering if you could die from the flu. El's black-and-blue ankle after falling out of Old Fred. How when it healed it left a knobbly bump. Separating us a little more. "We got better."

"But they never took you to a doctor, right? They couldn't. Just like they couldn't take you to a dentist. Because your births were never registered. What about school?"

"We were home-schooled. Mum was a great teacher." I think of the pantry and its walls of messy orange and yellow daffodils, the wooden desk that looked out across the exercise yard and the orchard beyond. *The Tempest, The Count of Monte Cristo, Jane Eyre, Crooked House.* I think of lying in the Princess Tower as she told us about Snow-white and Rose-red; Bluebeard, Blackbeard, and the pirate king.

"They kept you prisoner?"

"No. No!" But I think of those long crooked nails driven into every windowsill; the turn of the red door's dead bolt. And I start to get up, the back legs of my chair scraping noisily along the floor.

Rafiq grasps my wrists, pulls me back down.

"Were you ever allowed outside?"

"Yes. We played in the back garden all—"

"Outside the garden?"

"No. But that—"

"Did you ever see or talk to anyone but your mum and grandpa?"

"Yes!" I say, and the first person I think of is not Ross, not even Mouse, but the Witch: tall and skinny and full of black fury.

"Who?" The quick flash of Rafiq's eyes is the only indication that she isn't as calm as she wants me to think she is, and that frightens me suddenly. Revives my dread. I know exactly what name she's expecting me to say.

I start shaking my head, start trying to get up again, but not even my legs will obey me anymore.

"Where was your house, Cat?"

I still can't seem to move, to get up. My teeth are chattering.

"Cat. It's *okay*. Try to relax." Rafiq lays her palms flat on the table between us. Takes a long breath. "Okay. Here's what I think. Most of it's what I know. But some of it's what I think."

I say nothing. Look at nothing.

"Back in September 1998, I was a lowly shit-for-brains PC, working in the East End of Glasgow. Not much happened there back then, same as in Leith, I suppose: drugs and drunks. But after Logan and I read that PC's report from the fifth of September, someone in my team who was working in Leith at that time remembered something. On the morning of the fifth of September, he remembers an anonymous 999 call was made by a young male, directing officers to an address on Westeryk Road. Less than three miles from Granton Harbour. And when the police went to 36 Westeryk Road and eventually broke in, d'you know what they found?"

I say nothing. Look at nothing.

"They found two bodies. One male, one female. A murder-suicide it was reckoned." She looks at me, looks for a response. And I go on trying my hardest not to give it to her. "So I wondered about that anonymous caller, that young male. Had Logan run a check on everyone doorstepped or interviewed in relation to the case. And imagine our surprise when whose name should come up but one Ross MacAuley, living right next door at number 38." She stops, softens the sharp voice she probably uses in interrogation rooms.

"That's what I know, Catriona. So, do you want to tell me what it is that I think?"

I shake my head.

"I only want to clear things up, that's all. It was nearly twenty years ago. You were both just kids. Kids who, as far as I can see, had a pretty frightening upbringing." She looks at me as if she expects me to object. "Seems like the police did investigate the possibility that you had come from 36 Westeryk Road that night. Because in that first report from Granton Harbour, Mr. Peter Stewart insisted that one of the girls had been wearing a sweater covered with blood. Now, PC Davidson also reported that Mr. Peter Stewart was *drunk as a skunk*. And no bloody clothing was ever subsequently found. Nor did a search of number 36 find any evidence that anyone other than the victims—much less two children—had been living at the address. So it stayed what it was: the moving mystery of two identical twin girls exhibiting signs of abuse, who appeared from nowhere and belonged to no one.

"But now, a young woman—an identical twin—who lived at the very same address of that murder-suicide, has been found dead after leaving that very same harbor. So maybe I'm just a wee bit ahead of the curve. Because, you know, the first rule of being a detective, apart from the fact you can no longer be a shit-for-brains, is that coincidences do happen—but they don't come in multipacks."

I try to breathe, but I can't. I try to speak, but it's even more impossible. I have no idea what to say.

Rafiq takes pity on me, leans back in her chair again, gives me a good smile. "I don't think you're guilty of anything, Cat, that's not what this is. But I need to be able to tell the story the way it was. Because someone else *will* ferret all of this out. And when they do, I need to be able to head them off. To explain it, draw a line under it. So, please. Tell me. Do you know the names of the two people who were found dead at 36 Westeryk Road?"

I can't stay still. I can't settle my thoughts on anything at all. I want to run. I want to hide. I want everything to stop. I want to tell her. "You must already know their names. Why do—"

"You know why. Because I think you were there—you and El

both. Because I think that was where you lived. Because I think you witnessed what happened the night they died. And that's why you ran. Because I need to know that these things are true. I need you to tell me. Do you know who they were?"

"Yes." I whisper it. I can hear children crying, babies wailing, hot-water hissing, chair legs scraping, my heart beating. I can smell damp coats and umbrellas. Coffee and doughnuts. I can see the snow, the dull white sky, the slick wet sidewalks, the bundled-up bodies rushing past the window. I can see Rafiq's small bright eyes. The warmth that has always been behind their dark scrutiny. She reaches for my clenched fists, wraps them tightly inside her own.

"Tell me their names, Cat."

I swallow. I look at her and look at her until I can't see anything else.

"Nancy Finlay and Robert Finlay," I whisper, but the names still sound too loud.

"Your mum and your grandpa?"

No, I think. The Tooth Fairy and Bluebeard.

CHAPTER 22

The house is as empty as it ever gets. It echoes with silence, is thick with threat, with memory. I stand inside the hallway and look around at its closed doors, the grandfather clock, the telephone table, the dark curlicue of staircase, the spill of green and gold light across mosaic tiles, the dusty black curtain hiding the pantry and the entrance to Mirrorland. I look around at all the mounted plates: finches, swallows, robins perching on leafy branches, bare branches, snowy branches. I hear Mum's voice: *There's a bird called a glorious golden curre, and she's the cleverest of all birds. Because whenever she spreads her big golden wings and flies away, where she lands is where her next life begins as if the one before it had never happened at all. All she knows, all she remembers, is who she is now. Like a caterpillar turning into a butterfly. Don't be like me. Be like her. Never be too afraid to fly.*

I have to lean against the hallway wall. All this time, I've pretended that twelve years ago I flew away; that twelve years ago my life began again. But it was a lie. I've gone nowhere at all, because I never forgot who I was, who I had been, and the memories that I took with me were only one half of a whole. Their goodness, their fairy tale, has turned sad and sour inside me, has haunted me far more than this house and its ghosts. And what loosened and broke free inside me on the day I walked back through its big red door might have been sharp with brittle edges and warm with deep dark chasms, but it wasn't fear, or dread, or expectation. It was relief.

And I owe it the truth.

One truth is I need a drink. I don't want one, I need one.

There's a half-full bottle of cheap vodka sitting on the kitchen table next to an empty tumbler and a note.

Cat, I'll be back soon. I just need some time alone. We both probably do. I'm sorry I couldn't go to see her with you. I love you xxx

I sit, pour the vodka.

Another truth is that I thought—I absolutely believed—that El was still alive even after the body was found. That it was someone else. That she had escaped the boat, the firth. That the blue Gumotex kayak in the shed had been left there by her. That it wasn't my hate or my hurt that needed it to be true—that it was just the truth. Some people find strength in courage, fortitude, hope. Ross was right: I have always found mine in denial.

Another truth. Grandpa was the worst and best person I've ever known. I shake my head. A half-truth. I drink some more, look across at the bell board and its bells, its faded calligraphy. I think of I WANT YOU TO REMEMBER. I WANT YOU TO *WANT* TO REMEMBER. I don't want to. But I will. Because the ways in which I betrayed El—by lying, sneaking, hating, leaving—they were only symptoms and never the disease. I betrayed her first and last by denying, by pretending, by forgetting.

There's an arsehole on every boat. And if there's no, it's prob'ly you.

Grandpa was vast sideburns and the smell of pipe tobacco, a loud laugh, grinning still-white teeth, and shrieking hearing aids that didn't work. An Old Salty Dog. A salve for Mum's indiscriminate terrors. A grandpa who liked the sun and orange Tic Tacs; who would spend whole summers making daisy chains in the back garden and forts under the stairs. Who could always be relied upon for comfort: a wink, a grin, a pat of our hands. *Ye're a long time dead, lassie. Nothin' else ever worth greetin' over.*

But Bluebeard. Bluebeard was a tyrant. Bluebeard liked the night and dark rum. He told us that he hung his oldest friend, Irvine, from a hook just so he could be the one to let him go, to let him drown—for freedom, for money, for a house full of gloom and ghosts. And he hammered long nails into its windows—windows with small, thick panes and hardwood Georgian bars—so that everything in it would always belong only to him. Bluebeard ranted and raved and chased our mother through hallways and rooms with a stovepipe. Called us nasty wee bitches and shook the house with what he wanted to do, what he promised to do. Because Bluebeard loved to hate, loved to be feared, needed always to be everyone's *worst fuckin' nightmare.*

I stop. Look at those tiles in front of the Kitchener. I can't think about Rafiq's *murder-suicide*, not yet. But I can make myself remember how it was before. Not *that* night. Not even every night, but enough of them. And more and more. Until it was the quiet—the respite—that we stopped expecting.

I remember the heavy clunk and turn of the red door's dead bolt just like the jail cells in the Shank. Over and over, echoing with the quality of habit. Because a wise sailor never leaves port on a Friday. He goes down to the Mission instead, drinks rum on dry land. And every time he did, every time he closed and locked the big red door against the light and the outside, Mum would send us into the entrance hall to listen for the bells. She'd go around the house and into every room, pulling on every bell pull, ringing every bell. And we'd write down which rooms they belonged to in pencil, so she could check them, rub them out, begin the test again the next Friday. Because it was never a game, never a telepathy test. It was so she could always warn us exactly where Bluebeard was. When he came back.

And then the long hours of running up the stairs, down the stairs, along hallways, across corridors, under tables and beds, into cupboards, into Mirrorland. El and I whispering and laughing; our hearts beating fast and well because these were only Mum's drills, they weren't real. Never fire drills, intruder drills, nuclear war drills either. *Run faster! He's coming!* They were Bluebeard drills.

After dark, El and I would lie in our bed, holding hands and fighting sleep. Some nights there would be nothing, and we'd wake up to light and birdsong. But if a bell rang loud and long in the darkness, we'd get up quickly, already dressed, ears straining for the next. The kitchen was easiest to recognize because it had no bell of its own; Mum used the pull in the drawing room instead, ringing its bell twice and short. If we heard that, we always had more time, because the kitchen was where his rum stores were. We'd creep down the stairs, slower and slower as we neared the bottom. Mum would always try to shut the door of whatever room they were in; we'd hear her voice high and wild like the Throne Room bell, like a laughing stranger, and we'd rush around the oak banister and the Berlin Wall, past the orange and yellow daffodils, and up into the cupboard. We'd find our flashlights and shine their light onto the blues and yellows and greens of The Island as we drew back the bolts and crept down into the dark. Into Mirrorland. On those nights, we'd always turn east to the wide decks and tall sails of the *Satisfaction*. And we'd wait for Captain Henry to come to our rescue while we battled frigates and brigantines, our ears ringing with the screams of splintering wood and dying men, the bellows of cannon and musketoons, the roar of the squall.

But some nights—more and more nights—we were what Blue-beard wanted. Instead of Mum. Some nights, the bells rang too many and too quickly. Some nights, he'd turn out all the lights—with a loud metallic thud of the fuse-box master switch—so that his deadlight was all we could see, jagged as it searched for us, roared for us, caught us. Some nights, it was the stovepipe; some nights, his big-buckled belt; more nights, his fists. And those nights were the nights that Mum didn't only have to warn us but save us. Those were the nights we had to pretend never happened. Bluebeard demanded it. Mum demanded it. Mirrorland demanded it.

I'm shaking. I'm freezing cold. I remember crouching inside the dress-up cupboard in the Clown Café. Terrified. Because the Clown Café was only for hiding. It couldn't protect us like Mirrorland could. I remember the thunder of boots on the stairs, the landing. Scream-ing at the ripped-open door, at the deadlight and Grandpa's grin-ning teeth inside it. The smell of pipe tobacco and rum. The fist that grabbed me by the hair. The fist that squeezed El's arm enough that I heard—felt—her bones groan. *I'm goin' tae kill ye this time, the both ae ye. Nasty wee ungrateful bitches.* A sly look, cold and flat. *Or maybe it's time ye start earnin' yer keep.*

And I remember Mum's voice, shrill and high, *No! You can't. They're just children! Take me instead. Please.* El and I holding on to each other and crying; hoping, *praying* that he would, the back of the cupboard rough against our clothes, our skin, as we pushed against it, feet scrabbling for purchase, for any way to keep hiding, to disappear.

In the thick, awful quiet, I hear the front door open. I get up fast, furious, desperate to do anything to escape all this truth at once like an avalanche, a terrible landslide, a towering wave—high and wide and freezing bright. I run through the hallway, wrench open the hallway door, see the card on the hessian mat with my name capitalized across it, and then I'm barging through the front door, throwing myself down the steps.

Marie freezes, her hand on the metal gate, her horror so great it manages to make her look ugly, childlike. She recovers more quickly than I do, slamming the gate shut and running across the road towards the Gingerbread Coop.

I don't give myself time to reason, to stop, because that's what I always do. Another truth. Marie's already closing her door, but I ram into it, gritting my teeth and pushing. She cries out, the door gives way, and I stumble in.

She backs down a short hall and into the kitchen. Leans against a counter, breathing heavily. But when she looks up at me, her eyes are defiant. She glances at the big steel-handled knife in the block next to her. And then she looks back at me.

I should probably be afraid of her, but I'm not. "Why have you been leaving those cards?"

She presses her lips together. I make myself walk towards her.

"*Why* have you been leaving those cards?"

Marie folds her arms. "Because I didn't want Ross to hurt you. Either of you."

She sighs, sits heavily down on a chair. The sadness that comes into her eyes infuriates me. "Sit down, Catriona," she says. "Sit down, and I'll tell you."

But I don't. I'm done doing what people tell me to do.

"*D'accord.*" She sighs again. Squares her shoulders. "My name isn't Marie Bernard. I'm not from Paris. In the nineties, I paid a lot of money to come here from the Democratic Republic of Congo." She looks at me. "I loved my country. Very much. Its motto is 'Justice,

Paix, Travail.' I worked very hard for my life here, and once I had it, I finally found peace. So all that was left was justice."

"Justice?"

"I help people. Women." She stares down at her scarred hands. "Anna saw El's bruises. We saw the changes in her character, her habits. The fear in her eyes. How much her husband always needed to be in control."

"And that—*that*—was enough to tell you Ross was abusing her? Do you realize how—"

"*Non.*" She pushes up the sleeves of her shirt, exposing crisscrossing scars that carry on past both elbows. Pulls wide its neck where the skin beneath her collarbone is mottled and raised like the burn on her face. "What I left behind in the Congo told me." Her gaze sharpens. "Tells me."

"He *isn't* abusing me." But those sickening scars have doused my outrage.

She smiles. "That's what she said at first too."

I shake my head. "How many times have you done this?"

Her chin goes up. "Many."

"You terrorize the terrorized. That's how you *help*?"

Marie's smile turns pitying. I want to smack it off her face. "After a while, it's all they understand. As much as I wish it wasn't so."

"El never knew, did she? That it was you?"

Marie shifts in her chair, for the first time looks uncomfortable. "She was frightened of him."

"I don't believe you."

"She was going to run, and I was going to help her. But then she changed her mind. Said she couldn't. Wouldn't tell me why."

"Marie. I *don't* fucking believe you."

Her mouth flattens and she folds her arms. "You saw his text. I just wanted her to be safe."

"It didn't work, though, did it? Your genius plan. So why the hell did you think the same threats would work on me?"

She smiles again. It's a bad smile, maybe even a mad smile. It pulls taut her scarred skin. Turns her eyes sly. "The cards weren't for you."

"What?"

"They were for *him*. I wanted Ross to know that someone knew. That he'd killed her. That he'd probably kill you."

I remember Rafiq's *the cards never explicitly threatened El's life—or yours. If anything, Ross was the target.*

"Do you know how *insane* that—"

"Abuse fears only exposure." She shrugs. When she gets up and starts coming towards me, I back up the hall towards the open door.

"Have you done anything else?"

"*Que veux-tu—*"

"Have you been following me? Watching me? Have you done anything, do you know anything—*anything*—else?"

The look she gives me is confused. "*Non*. What—"

"I don't believe you."

Her expression clears. "I lied only about my name and where I came from. Never once have I lied to you about anything else."

I recoil as she reaches towards me, and only barely resist slapping her hand away. "He is *not* abusing me."

She drops her hands to her sides. "Yet."

"I'm sorry for whatever happened to you." My voice wavers, and I turn around, step back down onto the path. If I don't get away from her, I know I'm going to say something I'll regret. "But you're the one who needs help, Marie. Leave me alone. Leave us alone. Or I'll tell the police what you've done. And that's *not* a threat. That's a promise."

I march back across the road and into the house, stopping only to pick up the card before slamming shut the front door. I can already see what's written in bold black through the thin envelope.

GOOD LUCK

CHAPTER 23

I go into the kitchen and shove the card down to the bottom of the bin. I try to calm down, force myself to sit. I look at the bottle of vodka, at Ross's note. Okay. Since I was facing things, I'd face this. I pour out two measures of vodka, drink one of them.

Logically, it doesn't make sense. He loved her. Why would he hurt her? If El *was* having an affair, he could have just left her. Ross has a good job, more money than she did. He never wanted to live in this house, this *mausoleum*, anyway.

And *if* he was abusive and controlling—

I drain the last of the vodka as I suffer through a montage of Ross touching me and kissing me, the warm slide of his skin, the warm welcome in his eyes. The bruises I dismiss out of hand. They were sex. Good sex. *Great* sex. And while I don't like to think of him having the same kind of sex with El, the fact is that people like what they like. It's in his nature to be passionate. It's just the way he is. The way he has always been. I think of his grief and then his fury when the Coastguard gave up on the search. His sobs and desperation. *What am I going to do without her?*

If he was abusive and controlling, why didn't El just leave him? This time I'm rewarded with a flash of Grandpa's grinning, snarling face, but I dismiss that too. El was always stronger than me. She didn't forgive, she didn't forget. If Ross was hurting her, she would have left him. And if Marie is right, if Vik is right, if Mouse is right, and Ross is exactly what they say he is, he would have killed her in passion, in anger, like any other violent husband. He wouldn't have orchestrated some elaborate plot to sink her and her boat in the Firth of Forth. And how would—*could*—he have done that anyway? Rafiq confirmed that Ross was in London when El went missing. And

195

when she left Granton Harbour she was alone. How could Ross, witnessed by no one, reach her, overpower her, sink her boat, and get back to shore, all while he was supposed to have been somewhere else? Apart from anything else, he can't swim, is afraid of the water.

But.

There's the Gumotex kayak in the shed. And someone who had orchestrated some elaborate plot to sink his wife and her boat in the Firth of Forth *would* say that he can't swim, is afraid of the water. I think of that Presumption of Death application. Of Ross insisting he didn't know who Marie was.

I think of forgetting Mouse. Forgetting all the bad that has happened in this house. The lengths Mouse is going to in order to make me remember. I need to email her again. I need to *make* her meet me this time, no matter what. Because I can't trust what I believe or think I know anymore.

I pour more vodka. Because it's Ross himself who's the biggest, reddest flag. When I ignore those old familiar stabs of jealousy every time I think about the HOT GRIEF-STRICKEN HUSBAND who screamed into the sea, I have to admit to myself that it's pretty hard to reconcile him with the man who's been in my bed for the past week, whispering into my ear, my skin, my heart, how much he wants me, needs me, loves me. Guilt, or even remorse, could probably look a lot like grief.

I put down the vodka. It hasn't helped one bit. *I tried to drown my sorrows. But the bastards learned how to swim.* My head feels heavier, thicker, my body achier. I stand up, holding on to the table for balance.

For God's sake, Catriona, why are you so useless? But I'm not useless. Or helpless. For weeks, I've been trying to look like El, think like El, *be* like El because I don't want to be me. I know that. But it's not the me that came back to this house that I'm scared of. It's the me that lived *in* this house. The me that was always afraid. Of falling, of running, of flying. Of facing the truth.

So I go up the stairs, hanging on tight to the banister. And I only hesitate outside the Kakadu Jungle for a moment. I don't know when Ross is going to come back. I push open the door to our old bedroom. The biggest shock is that it doesn't look the same. There are no wooden shutters, no rain-forest wallpaper, no golden yellow bedspread. Instead of the old oak armoire and dressing table, there's an antique writing bureau and chair, a white chintz wardrobe. The room is magnolia, the carpet lush. This is the only room in the whole house that has been entirely erased and redrawn.

I go to the bureau and its many drawers, start rifling through them. I've no idea what I'm looking for, but all I find are empty notebooks and postcards, paper clips, business envelopes, dozens of pens.

I regret the vodka again when I turn too quickly, and the floor starts to list, enough that I have to grab hold of a bedpost to stay on my feet. My mind is sticky, too slow. I look at the double bed, blindsided suddenly by a far too vivid image of Ross and El together. When I glimpse the leather satchel leaning against the legs of a bedside table, I reach for it quickly, glad of the distraction as I try to open its stiff buckles. Inside, there are loose papers and a thick plastic binder. "Southwark University" is printed along the length of its spine in gold lettering below a blue-and-red crest. Bingo.

THE PSYCHOLOGY OF PSYCHOPHARMACOLOGY
THEME: PSYCHOACTIVE DRUGS: GOOD VS BAD MEDICINE;
THE EFFICACY OF THERAPIES VS SAFE RATIOS
April 2nd, 9 a.m.–April 3rd, 4 p.m., 2018
Southwark University, St James Road, London

I thumb through the conference timetable, extracts of papers to be presented, Ross's name on the list of attendees. I remember his *By the time I got back, she'd already been missing for at least five hours*, and skip to the Contacts page. The first listed is the phone number and email for a Professor Catherine Ward, head of Pharmacy and Pharmacology.

I sit down on the bed, take out my phone, go online, create a new email address. When DI Kate Rafiq isn't accepted as a username, I give her a middle initial of M. I've no idea how to spoof an email address, and I'm too keyed up and too drunk to try to find out. I'm just going to have to hope that Professor Catherine Ward doesn't stop to wonder why a detective inspector from Police Scotland would be using Gmail. If—when—I get found out, I don't care. If this breaks a law, I don't care. I need to know. Something. Anything. My email is short: a follow-up to original inquiries seeking confirmation of Ross's attendance and movements. As soon as I've sent it, I wish I hadn't.

And then I start a new email to john.smith120594.

Mouse, I know El's dead. I'm sorry I didn't believe you. Please meet me. Please.

I stand up and put the folder back, this time swaying only a little. I return to the landing. The house is still uncharacteristically quiet. The hairs on my forearms and the back of my neck prickle and itch against my skin as I look towards the dark mouth of that corridor between the Clown Café and the Princess Tower. Towards the matte-black door at its end. Bedroom 3. Bluebeard's Room. The pull of it is like my childhood vertigo: the dizzying paralysis of waiting to fall. *Wanting* to fall. And when my phone suddenly starts vibrating against my leg, I cry out—high and long—fumble it out of my pocket and answer without looking, such is my sudden and absolute terror of being alone.

"Cat! Thank God you've finally answered."

"What do you want, Vik?" My voice is unsteady, but I've already begun to feel foolish.

"I . . ." There's a pause. A long one. "I heard about El, and I—"

"It's okay," I say. "Thank you. I—"

"No. You don't understand . . ." The signal breaks up, hisses and roars. ". . . something I have to tell you . . . I didn't know . . ." His words are swallowed up by the nearing wail of a siren, the honk of a horn.

"Vik, I can't hear you. Where are you?"

"Where are *you*?"

I stand inside that swath of gold light from Westeryk Road, and turn in a lethargic, dizzy circle. "I'm upstairs."

"Cat, listen to . . ." His voice cuts out, comes back louder. ". . . have to leave."

"Why?" I've stopped moving, but the walls are still turning, turning.

". . . can't tell you. I'm sorry. I'm so . . . but you have to believe me."

"*Why?*" My stomach squeezes, and I wonder—with distant concern—if I might be about to throw up.

"Cat . . ." Some shouting; the roar of another passing car. Maybe bigger. A van. ". . . hear me? You *have* to get out of that house."

And then he's gone. And I'm alone with the silence. Alone with the glass globe that hangs from the ceiling rose, the closed doors, the gold light, that narrow dark corridor. Alone with the house.

I shake my head. My voice is steady, calm. "Where else would I go?"

It feels physical, the sudden wrench back into Mirrorland: less of a pull than a yank. Hard and sharp and real. And painful, because my throat is hoarse from screaming, and I'm on my knees in the dark, the storm tossing us from main deck to gun deck, roaring its rage, choking El's breath.

No.

Grandpa was on his knees. He shoved me away hard enough that I banged my head on the deck and saw stars, but I could still see El's bulging red face, his hands tight around her neck, the sweat running off his nose. I could still hear Mum screaming, *Leave them alone!* Hoarse now, too, because it was the night after the Clown Café and Bluebeard's Room, it was the last night of Mirrorland. The last night of our first life.

And when I try to yank myself away, to yank myself *back*—Mum lets out a scream and moves through me like a ghost. She stands behind Grandpa, her good arm raised up over her head, in her hand the *Satisfaction*'s stern lantern. And when Grandpa turns, looks at her with a wink and a grin—*Put it doon, lassie*—she doesn't. She brings that lantern down on the crown of his head instead. Again and again. Until the sound is no longer hard and short and white, but soft and long and copper-dark.

"God."

I'm on my hands and knees at the top of the stairs. My breath is hot and quick as if I've been running. Cold sweat slides down my spine.

When I hear the hallway door creak open, snick closed, I stand up too fast—the world spins and briefly staggers before righting itself again.

"Cat?" Ross shouts. "You up there?"

I swallow, reach for the banister. I no longer feel drunk. I feel sick, feverish, and horribly sober. Horribly awake. The vertigo comes again, and I ignore it. I can't let it belong to me. Any more than that sound. That wet, soft, *long* sound.

Ross is waiting for me at the bottom of the stairs. I step down into the hallway, and he moves forwards without warning, pulls me close. "Hey, Blondie." And when I have no choice but to let him in, to breathe him in, I feel all that heavy slowness, that brittle dread and uncertainty fall away. I hate myself for it, I'm afraid of myself for it, but it happens anyway.

He squeezes for a moment too tight, and then pulls back, his palm warm against my cheek. He's been crying again, his eyes are bloodshot. His skin is damp. His hair has been tangled by the wind.

"I've been walking," he says. "Just walking. 'Round and 'round. For hours."

I swallow past the lump in my throat. Everything Marie and Vik said, everything I thought, suspected, tried to do my best to drown in vodka, all of it turns to dust when he's standing in front of me, looking at me the way that no one else ever has. Even though he knows. He's always known about everything that has happened in this house. And still, he looks at me in exactly the same way. The same *good* way.

I can't believe he hurt El. The *police* don't even believe it.

And I feel so much guilt and so much grief. Guilt at wanting him, having him, doubting him. Guilt at everything I've done in pursuit of all three. Grief for two children abused and terrorized until they couldn't recognize it. For that melted, shiny, eaten thing under a blue surgical drape in Edinburgh City Mortuary. For the sister who used to hold my hand as we fell asleep; who always shared the same pain and the same nightmares, and the same wretched hope. For my poor, tortured, fucked-up Mum. On her knees next to Grandpa's body. The cruel twist of her mouth, the black of her eyes, cold and calm and full of fury.

"Are you okay?" Ross says. He shakes his head. "Shit, that's a stupid—"

"It's been a very bad day," I say. Because it has. When I think about sitting at the kitchen table and telling him about a lost tribe in South America, it feels like it happened weeks ago.

"I'm sorry I didn't . . ." He blinks. "Was it—I mean, I know it was, but, I thought maybe . . ." There's hope in his eyes. A hope that could surely never be faked.

"It was El. It was . . ." I've reached out to grip hold of his forearms. I know I must be hurting him, but he doesn't even wince. "She was—"

"It's okay, I'm sorry. I'm sorry." And the tears that run off his cheeks, his chin, are as real and as terrible as mine. I don't know who grabs hold of who first. Which of us starts the kiss, which of us starts to pull at whose clothes, which of us demands and which of us yields. He pushes inside me as I lie on the stairs, and I look up at the high coved ceiling and the green-gold light as I let him, as I hold him, as I feel him, the stairs cold and hard against my skin and my bones.

And I come so hard that I scream. I forget.

Because where else *would* I go?

He's all I have left.

CHAPTER 24

I speed-walk past Colquhoun's, but before I'm even a few yards beyond it, I hear the door bang open and Anna's "Wait!"

I stop, turn around. Though I don't want to.

Anna is already crying; big ugly sobs that get in the way of what she's trying to say. "It's so terrible. I can't believe it. I can't believe she's dead. I'm sorry. I'm so sorry."

When she pulls me into a fierce hug, I hug her back in the hope that will be enough. I can't deal with other people right now—not their sympathy, their grief, their *need*. Finally, she lets me go, and I step back. She sniffs hard, takes two big breaths as she wipes her cheeks. Smears a long black line of mascara from her left eye to her temple.

"When I heard yesterday, I couldn't even think," she says, lowering her voice and fixing me with the hard stare I better recognize. "But now . . . now I know that I have to go to the police."

"Anna—"

"No, listen. I do. I have to tell them that she was scared. I have to tell them about the bruises. Marie said El wanted to leave Ross." She raises her palms when I start to interrupt. "And that's when husbands murder their wives, isn't it? When they're about to—"

"Anna! I can't deal with—"

She grabs me hard by the elbows. "But you have to! I should have pressed her more, should have helped her more." Her grip tightens. "She'd want me to help you, Cat. You need to get away. You need to—"

I step backwards, dig my nails into her fingers until she lets go.

"You do what you have to, Anna," I say. My voice is unsteady. My legs tingle with the panicky urge to just start running. Instead, I turn around and make myself walk away. "I can't talk now."

And I ignore her shouts and that urge to run, until both have gone.

*

The Links is completely deserted. But here, I feel eyes on me; my skin crawls with the familiar certainty of being followed, *examined*. I turn back once, look around the flat, empty parkland. No Anna. No one at all.

I pull up my hood and keep going. Past the same trees fighting the same bitter wind as on that freezing dawn morning all those years ago: sycamores and elms hiding tormented ghosts swollen black with plague. Past the same brownstone tenements and terraces where the murderers of children lived and lurked. And watched.

All those obstacles, those booby traps Grandpa laid so that we would never want to leave 36 Westeryk Road. He'd overegged it, I suppose, as abusers do; by the time we'd crossed over the Links, we were as tired of being afraid as we were of running. And we knew by then that he was a liar. 36 Westeryk Road was just as frightening, as dangerous, as anywhere else. But we loved him still, even against all of that fear and lying, the hot copper stink of blood on our skin. Because then, as now, it was still so easy to separate Grandpa from Bluebeard. So necessary. Far harder and more painful to push them together, to accept that the biggest nightmare from my childhood was once my very favorite person after El. There's grief for that, too, now as then—as if I've lost him twice. As if he never existed at all.

I glance back towards the road before turning onto Lochinvar Drive and heading down towards the yacht club. I have to squeeze around a few more boats on raised blocks to get close to the water. The wind coming off the Forth is as cold as ever, but it's low; the jostle and rattle of the moored sailboats seems muted, faraway. I stand still at last. Breathe in, breathe out.

I look down at the stone slip and then up beyond Granton's breakwater wall, northeast towards the small squat islet of Inchkeith, the yellow smudge of its lighthouse barely visible. The dark water beyond it. *The deepwater channel*. I look and I look, and I'm nearly glad when the clouds drop lower over Burntisland, and the rain starts bucketing down, hard and fast enough to drum at my aching skull and obscure my view.

My phone beeps. It's a text from Ross.

Have to check in with work, then I'll pick up something for dinner. Any requests? x

I don't reply. Even though there's nothing wrong with what he's said. He has a job. We have to eat. We haven't died. Which doesn't stop me flinching when the phone beeps again.

john.smith120594@gmail.com   18 April 2018 at 14:55

Re: HE KNOWS   Inbox

To: Me

YOU'RE RUNNING OUT OF TIME.
<u>REMEMBER WHAT HAPPENED ON THE 4TH OF SEP-
TEMBER.</u>
THEN YOU'LL UNDERSTAND.
YOU'LL KNOW WHAT YOU HAVE TO DO.

Sent from my iPhone

I won't know. I *don't* know. I've remembered everything—every last horrible fucking thing—and I still haven't a clue what it is I'm supposed to understand. To do.

No more riddles, Mouse. This isn't a game. This isn't Mirrorland. Tell me what you know. Meet me. Tell me. Or leave me alone.

I send my reply, turn back for the road. The rain is getting worse. The sky has become so dark it's as if dusk has arrived. I struggle to negotiate my way around the boats in the yard. Their hulls are jagged with rust and barnacles. They smell of the sea, of the things that lived and died in it. I shiver. And when I hear something too close behind me, I whirl around, the knuckles of my hand smacking loudly against the nearest boat. I go down hard and fast, dizzy and sliding against the slick concrete, ending up spread-eagled on my back. I turn my head, straining to hear anything over the rain—and then, through that narrow space under the raised hull, I see boots. Leather with steel-cap toes. And above them, jeans.

I scramble backwards, struggling for purchase on the slick ground. By the time I manage to get back onto my feet, I'm breathing too hard, too *loud*. But I don't run. I want to run—I always want to run—but instead, I inch around the boat, and then launch myself into its black shadow. And when I come up against movement, solidity, I punch and I kick and I shout. And I scream.

Hands reach for me, and I scratch at them, punch them away. A greater weight pushes against me, but it isn't as angry, as desperate, as prepared to fight dirty. I stab with my nails, kick up my knee again and again and again.

"Stop! *Stop*."

Vik lurches into the little remaining light, holding up his palms.

"You!" I shout, and the loud outraged fury in my voice—the authority—hides the relief.

"Cat, please. Stop!" The last he shouts as I come towards him again. He's soaked to the skin, his jacket plastered against his torso, rain dripping into his eyes and off his chin. He looks wretched.

I stop. It takes about all the energy I have left, but I do. We stand staring at each other in the shadows and the rain, both breathing hard and too fast.

"How long have you been following me?"

"Cat, I—"

"How long, Vik?" I shout. Because now that all the rage inside me has finally escaped, not even the promise of an explanation—of any possible end to all this *not knowing*—is enough to call it back.

He looks down at the ground. "Since you came back from America."

"How the fuck did you know I *was* back?" I ask—before it occurs to me that the question I should be asking is *Why?* And then a sudden suspicion turns me in a new direction. "Do you know Mouse? Is she—are you—"

But although Vik is already shaking his head no, the weariness in it, his lack of confusion as to who Mouse is, only makes my suspicion more certain. "You know her. You *know* her! You're both—"

"Cat. I need to—"

"Wait. Is Marie in on whatever the hell this is too? Is that what your bloody phone call yesterday was about? *You have to get out of that house.* Are all of you—"

Vik steps forwards. "There's something I need to tell you."

"Then *tell* me."

I can hear him swallow, even over the hammering rain. And then he looks at me without blinking. "I'm Mouse."

"What?"

His gaze slides away. "I'm sorry. I'm Mouse. At least, I've been pretending to be her. I'm the one who's been sending you those emails."

I step back, shake my head. "I don't—I don't understand. *Why?*"

"Because El asked me to," he says.

"Show me your phone." I'm still shaking my head. I can't seem to stop. "Show me your phone, Vik. Now."

He reaches into his jeans pocket, brings out an iPhone, and keys in its passcode before reluctantly handing it over.

I open his inbox with trembling fingers, smearing rain across the screen. And right at the top:

Cat Morgan
No more riddles, Mouse. This isn't a game. This isn't Mirrorland.

"Oh, God."

He lets out a long sigh. "She said it was to keep you safe. She said if something happened to her, you'd come back and . . . when I agreed, I thought she was being paranoid, I didn't believe anything would happen. I knew she was scared of Ross, but I never thought . . ." He stops, closes his eyes. "And when she went missing, I felt like—I felt like I had to do what she'd asked. And now—*now*—she's dead, and I—"

"Are you trying to tell me that in the event of El's death—in the event of her being murdered by the big bad brute of a husband she just couldn't bring herself to leave—she asked you to start stalking and threatening me? To keep me safe. From him. Is that what you're saying?" It's better to stay angry. Better not to think or feel anything else.

"I *never* threatened you."

"*Were* you having an affair?" Because I can't think of any other reason on earth why he would do any of this.

"I loved her." And there is such affection, such adoration in his eyes that I want to punch him again.

"Is that a yes?"

"I already told you, no. Nothing ever happened."

"What *exactly* did she ask you to do?"

"To follow you, make sure you were okay. To email you messages that she'd already sent me before she . . . disappeared. To send them in a specific order at specific times." He clears his throat. "To answer any of your questions with the same replies. That El was dead. That I was Mouse. That I couldn't meet you. That you had to remember what happened on the fourth of September. I didn't—don't—know what any of it means. I promise you."

"Right. So you don't know what she wanted me to remember? What the fuck she wanted me to do?"

He shakes his head, miserable again. "She just kept on saying it was about the end of your first life. She kept saying, *He knows*."

A chill works its way down my spine, but I refuse to feel it. I hear the rattle of the Clown Café door, the dress-up cupboard. The rusty scream of the *Satisfaction*'s lantern. A sound no longer hard and short and white, but soft and long and copper-dark.

"Why?"

Vik blinks at me. "Why what?"

"Why did he kill her?"

"Because she wanted to leave. She'd planned to leave."

"Then why didn't she just *leave*? Why didn't she go to the police?"

"I don't know. I wish she had."

"Why the hell didn't *you* go to the police?"

"I did! After she went missing, I phoned them. Told them about her being scared of him, being scared he was going to do something to her. I told them—"

"No. The police haven't mentioned you, Vik. *I* only know you exist because apparently you've been following me around for two weeks!"

"I didn't give them my name. I didn't want—"

"What?" I spread my hands wide across the space between us. "To be *involved*?"

"You don't understand. El made me promise not to contact the police at all. She said she was afraid Ross might come after me. I couldn't have given a shit about that, but I was afraid that . . . I'm engaged. And I—"

"You're engaged."

He looks at me, and not even the defiant square of his shoulders or clench of his jaw can hide the shame in his eyes. "El made me *promise*, Cat."

"Right." I can't look at him anymore; I look at the rusty wet hull, its peeling paint instead. "What about Mouse? Does she know about all of this? Is she involved?"

"I don't even know who she is," Vik says, subdued now. "El said that pretending to be her would help you remember."

"What about Marie? D'you know her?"

"No. I swear."

"Have you been in the house?" And I'm not only thinking of the diary pages, the lantern, the pirate code taped to Mirrorland's ceiling, but the kayak in the shed, the whispers in my ear, the feeling that I am never alone inside 36 Westeryk Road.

"Of course not. What—"

"Did you leave pink gerberas at Mum's grave?"

"Yes. El—"

"Asked you to." When he only looks more miserable, my flagging anger revives. "Just over a week ago, you stood here and comforted me. You made me feel better. I liked you. You *cried*."

"Cat, I—"

"And when I told you that I didn't think El was dead because she'd been sending me emails, you stood there shaking your head and didn't say a word. Not a fucking word! And now you expect me to believe a single thing you say?"

"Don't you get it?" He looks frustrated now, as if he suspects he's failing. "She *knew* this would happen—all of it! She knew he'd kill her, and he did. She knew you'd come back, and you did. She knew what questions you'd ask. She knew the police would think it was an accident." He looks at me. "I'm telling you the truth, Cat. You *have* to believe me."

But I don't. Vik loved El, I can see that. I can see, too, that his devastation is just as real, and maybe his conviction, but I can see something else too. In his eyes, his body language. I'm good at pretending. Better than Vik is. And I can recognize another liar with my eyes closed. This isn't just guilt or some kind of warped obligation. He wanted to follow me, to spy on me, because then El isn't dead. She's still in the messages he sends, and she's in me—her eyes, her face, her voice; that mirror I always carry under my arm. I'm his last remaining link to her.

How? How is it possible that she can still be manipulating all of us like this? Me, Vik, Ross. The police. And without any of us having the first clue why.

"I'm going to the police today," Vik says, staring down at his boots. "Make a proper statement this time, tell them everything El told me. I should never have—"

"Are there any more?"

"What?"

"Are there any more messages that you haven't sent me yet?"

"No."

"Vik."

His shoulders sag. "One more, that's all."

"Show me."

Vik reaches for his phone. And for the first time since confronting and punching him in the chest, I can feel the rain streaming down my face, running off my nose and chin and fingers, drumming hard against my skull. I can hear it: tinny and quick against metal masts and frames, duller and slower against concrete, asphalt, wood. Loudest of all against the firth: deep and sharp and resonant, like an old memory, a forgotten fear, a *yank*—hard and sharp and real.

"Here," he says, handing the phone back, and when I take it, I stare at him long enough that he has to meet my gaze.

"Don't go to the police yet, Vik. Not yet. If needs be, we'll go together. But I need you to let me do this first. You owe me that."

When he nods, slow and uncertain, I take a long, deep breath. Okay, El. *One more, that's all.* And then we're done.

john.smith120594@gmail.com   Drafts

Re: HE KNOWS

To: Cat Morgan

CLUE 11. THE ONLY PLACE OUTSIDE MIRRORLAND WHERE YOU WERE EVER RED INSTEAD OF WHITE.

Sent from my iPhone

CHAPTER 25

I stand on the paving in the back garden. I'm soaked to the skin. But my head no longer pounds or pulses. I feel more clear and awake than I have in a long time. I pace in circles a few times before realizing what I'm doing: kicking up silver and gray chuckies, pulling up old waxy fishing dungarees. Marching around the exercise yard behind El's Andy Dufresne. The only time I was Red instead of White.

I go to the first ugly concrete plinth, look inside its urn. Empty. When I try to shift it, it doesn't budge. The second is empty, too, but it moves when I push—enough that I have to grab hold of it before it topples to the ground. Underneath, there's an envelope inside a ziplocked freezer bag. I pick it up, push the urn back into place, and climb the stairs to the scullery. In the kitchen, I pour myself a vodka I probably shouldn't have and sit at the table. I should go to the Clown Café, in case Ross comes back, but I can't wait even the length of time it would take me to climb the stairs. Because of the word written across the envelope in El's heavy scrawl.

SNOW-WHITE

I take it out of the bag, rip the envelope open. It's only one piece of paper: narrow-lined and thin.

Dear Cat,
    I'll say it and then it's said. Maybe I should start with I'm sorry. Or How are you? Or What has your life been like for the past twelve years? But you have to still know me well enough that what's first on my mind is what's last too. So I have to just say it. And then it's said.

211

He's going to kill me. If you're reading this, he already has. I'm already dead.

If you're thinking good riddance, I guess I can't blame you. If you're thinking serves you right, I guess I deserve that too. I hated you once. I don't blame you for hating me back. And if you're thinking liar, then all I have is this letter to convince you I'm telling the truth.

It started out as love—or what I thought love was. You know what he was like, you can't have forgotten that. The intensity of it—of him—how good it could feel when he turned his light onto you. And then all that passion and angst became suffocation, jealousy, control. All men are pirates, remember? Good Prince Charmings don't exist. He made me feel so small. I'd thank him for looking after me. I'd thank him for his scorn and then his rage. The first time he hit me, he cried for a week. The second, less than a day. By the third, I was the one saying sorry to him. I used to wonder what it was he'd seen in me, but now I think I know. He knew what Bluebeard had done to me. He knew I was weaker than you. He knew I would be a goner for him from the start.

A few years after we were married, he heard about the auction for the house. Our house. I begged him not to, but he bought it anyway. Anything to lock me up inside this prison again. He had me describe every detail of every room. And everything bought, everything put back in place, made my prison smaller, more secure.

You loved Grandpa the most. You loved Mum's stories the most. Your imagination was always better than mine—when you didn't want something to be true, you just pretended it hadn't happened. I think that's why you forgot the end of our first life, and why you never tried to remember it. I used to think it was for the best.

I could just tell you, right here, what happened the night Grandpa and Mum died. I could tell you and I could promise that it's the truth, and maybe you'd believe it, maybe you'd even remember it. But I don't think you would. It doesn't take a psychologist to know that all those unconscious fantasies you've created—embedded—are so much stronger than what they've repressed. And the only way I can think of to destroy all of them is to give you back what was real, piece by piece, clue by clue. Until you're forced to remember all of the truth for yourself. Because it's the only way you'll believe it.

I know you'll be angry about the treasure hunt. I hid the diary pages and wrote the clues. And a friend—a good friend, who I know, after I'm gone, will respect my wishes—is emailing them to you. I'm sorry for the subterfuge. I'm sorry I had him pretend to be Mouse. She turned up to the house last year out of the blue. And instead of being her friend, instead of being happy that she was back, I saw only how mad it would make Ross, how badly he'd take it out on me. Because I'm a coward. And maybe it was cowardly to pretend to be Mouse in the emails too, but I thought it would help. I thought you wouldn't listen to me, but you might listen to her. I'm sorry if the emails or my diary have frightened you. But I guess I want you to be frightened. I want you to remember what happened the night Mum and Grandpa died. I want you to remember what Ross did.

I've left something for you in the Silver Cross. That and this letter are all I've got left to give you. You have to believe them. You have to believe me. I don't know what he's going to do, but I know it won't look like murder. Because he was born to be a pirate.

I think about you all the time. Please don't think I don't. When you left, I cried every day, every night, for weeks. And he'd hold me and tell me it was okay. It was okay because at least we had each other. It suits him for you and me to be apart. It always has. I wanted to reach out to you so many times. But I didn't. Because I knew you were better off without us. Because I knew he'd take away what freedoms he'd allowed me to have if I did. I have my painting, some voluntary work, some friends. I have my boat. He agreed to buy it before he realized that it would be my best escape from him. That's why I called it "The Redemption." If you've found this, then you must remember. How much I loved that story. Any escape is better than none.

I can't ask you to trust me, because I know you don't. I can't ask you to believe me, because I know you won't. I regret every day what I did to us. I should never have given him control. Not in our first life, and certainly never in our second. Remember HE KNOWS. Remember THE PLAN. The Silver Cross. X MARKS THE SPOT. Remember them and you'll remember the rest. You'll know the truth. You'll know him. You'll believe me. You'll be safe.

I'm sorry.
All my love,
Rose-red x

I read the letter again. And again. Run my fingers over El's pen strokes. It's her handwriting, her voice, I know it, I know her, but at the same time it feels false. Too careful, too scripted. *If you're reading this I'm already dead*; El would once have rolled her eyes in dismissive scorn at something like that. Because surely what she's saying is madness. I try to imagine Ross hitting her, and I can't. It's like trying to imagine him hitting me. It *can't* be true.

But it was Ross who told me El had wanted to come back here, had wanted the house to look exactly the same as it always had. And I realize now how ridiculous *that* sounds. How false. Why would she want to come back here to our prison of twelve years? To this place of death and dread and darkness?

But. If I believe that El really was afraid of Ross and is only trying to protect me, why *wouldn't* she have told me what she thought I'd forgotten—whatever it is that he's supposed to have done? Because everything that I repressed I now remember. Those memories are *not* false. They can't be. I remember everything that happened in our first life, including the night Mum ended it by smashing Grandpa's skull with the *Satisfaction*'s stern lantern. What else is there?

My head pounds. Silver Cross. I know I should know what that is—I know I *know* what that is—but I can't think. I can't remember.

I finish the vodka. Stand up. Because El was right about one thing at least. A thing that makes me feel cold and afraid and uncertain. She thought she was going to die. And now she's dead.

★

I stand at the entrance to that narrow corridor leading to Bedroom 3, fumbling for a light switch I can't find. I force myself to walk into the darkness, arms outstretched. Cringe when my fingers hit against the panels of the door at the corridor's end. Hesitate inside the memory of *Don't go in! We can't ever go in!* This is the only room I've never been inside, not even as a child. Mum made sure of that; made sure that El and I were so afraid of it we'd pass by the corridor without ever looking. I think of her screams. The echo of this door's slam. Grandpa was afraid of it too—sometimes I saw him standing inside the doorway to the Donkshop, staring across the landing at this corridor, and all of him would be shaking, his mouth slack, eyes blank. Would El have hidden something in Bluebeard's Room? Would she have *come* in here? I don't know. But I know I have to look.

When I touch the handle, I realize I'm muttering hard and fast under my breath, "He only comes out at night, he only comes out at night." I make myself stop. All of Bluebeard's wives ended up hanging on hooks rusted red with blood, except for the last. And what saved her was ignoring her fear long enough to look, to unlock the only door he told her never to open. And so I turn that handle. Push open that dusty dark door. And go inside.

Bluebeard's Room has no windows. I knew this on some level because its exterior wall is Mirrorland's alleyway, but still, it catches me unawares. The darkness. I find the light switch. Turn it on before I venture inside.

The air feels coldly heavy, smells of old paint. In one corner is a battered leather armchair, a standard lamp. Everything else is hidden under drawsheets. I look at every wall, every shadow, as if I still expect to see the corpses of Bluebeard's wives. Or hear Mum's shrieks echoing and thrashing their way through the floorboards to the pantry and cupboard and ocean below.

Focus.

I step farther into the room, start pulling off sheets, coughing out dust. Under the second sheet is a big wooden box. I stop. My heart stutters. Not a box. Our treasure chest on the *Satisfaction*. Bound with bands of black leather and a padlock gold with rust.

I kneel. The padlock hangs open. I take hold of the lid and lift it up, cringing at the loud squeak of its hinges.

It's full of old sheets. I start taking them out, piling them on the floor. When my fingers hit against something hard, I instantly snatch them back.

Come on.

I reach back in, take out the last sheet.

There are two objects. One large, one small. The large: a blue-handled drill with a hollow cylinder attached. The small: a round steel handle at one end, a black rubber screw plug at the other.

I rock back on my heels. Press my clammy fingers to my face. El didn't put these things here. She didn't put them in this awful room for me to find. Because I know instinctively what they are.

I think of Logan's face, the careful tone of his voice. *We found evidence it was scuttled. Deliberately sunk.*

I look back down at the hole saw. The transom drain plug.

They're Treasure Trophies.

★

The stairs are in darkness. The only light comes from the red milky Victorian lamp in the hallway. I feel my way down the staircase, the banister cold under my palm. The house continues to sleep, loud and old; its clanking, creaking veins like a hidden map of black roads and copper wires, like secrets locked behind doors and inside cupboards, oceans, midnight worlds of fire and fury and fun.

I pass the kitchen, look at my face in the mirror above the telephone table. I open the door to the drawing room. Finally let go of my breath.

The room is warm, golden. The big floor-to-ceiling curtains have been closed against the rain and the night, and the fire is feeding noisily on a pile of shaved logs, dancing against the bottle-green tiles. There are clusters of tea lights on side tables and along the length of the Poirot, reflecting gold and silver in mirrors and polished wood, so that it looks like every Christmas Eve. All that's missing is the eight-foot Fraser fir, twinkling white and shedding its needles, making the whole room smell like a winter forest.

Unconscious fantasies. I think of the words until they blur inside my head. Until all I can see is Bluebeard chasing us with his deadlight. His blood coughing out of his ruined skull, seeping black into the *Satisfaction*'s gun deck.

Ross gets up from the chesterfield, smiles cautiously.

"Are you okay?"

"Yes."

His eyes dart quick around the room. "Say if this is too much."

"No. No, it's fine." But I can't seem to come any farther into the room. I can't seem to make myself *do* anything.

"Are you sure you're okay?" The deep frown line between Ross's brows is back. I want to press the pad of my thumb against it, smooth it flat.

"Yes." I make myself move towards the couch, towards him.

"Sit, please," he says, briefly reaching out to squeeze my cold hand before moving past me to the bar.

I sit. Watch him. The silhouette of his narrow waist and broad shoulders in the flickering, twinkling light, the thick curl of his hair against his neck. My fingers move to the pocket of my jeans, where El's letter sits inside its ziplocked bag. Its presence both comforts and terrifies me. I see the sherries sitting on the turquoise tiles of the Poirot. Gold inside carved crystal. Two instead of four. El really did tell him everything.

"Aperitif," Ross says, setting them down on a candlelit coffee table, reminding me of that *special romantic occasion* corner in the Italian restaurant. When he sits next to me, I can feel the heat of him against my thigh. I can smell the piney, musky familiarity of him. I can hear my heartbeat, heavy and too loud.

"Cheers," he says, and solemnly enough that I finally drop my frozen smile. The low, long ringing of our glasses outlives my sherry. I feel its wonderful burn all the way to my stomach. I should ask him about his day, I know. What happened when he went into work. How he's feeling, coping. I'm doing a very poor impression of normal. Ross thinks so too. He reaches for my chilly fingers, wraps them inside his own.

"It'll be okay, Cat," he whispers. "At least we have each other."

And I close my eyes against the warm press of his lips against my temple.

CHAPTER 26

I sit at the kitchen table, while Ross stands in front of Mum's Kitchener. The rain batters against the window; the wind howls, trapped inside the garden's high stone walls. The kitchen is hot and wet, yet still somehow cold. I'm shivering.

I pick up the Shiraz that Ross poured for me. Put it back down without drinking. The smell of minced beef turns my stomach. My head aches, feels thick and boggy, and I'm too jumpy, too nervy. Every few minutes, my heart skips one beat and then overcompensates with too many. Maybe it's grief, shock: too many ground-shifting tremors in too short a space of time. El dying. Marie's confession. Vik's "Mouse." El's letter. Everything that's ever happened in this house. I need to ask Ross about what I found in Bluebeard's Room. I need to ask him about Marie and that text. About what Vik said. And I really need to ask him about everything that El has accused him of. But I can't.

Ross sets a lid over the chili pot and comes back to the table, sits close enough to me that I can see those silver flecks inside his irises.

"There's something I need to talk to you about. Jesus, you're freezing."

I look down at my hands inside his. I hadn't even felt him take them.

"I'm okay," I say, but he starts to rub my fingers, blows warm breath against my palms.

"I know it probably isn't the right time to say this, but . . . I'm going to sell up."

"What?"

"As soon as I can, I mean." His voice is gentle, like I'm a skittish horse. "It'll be a while. El didn't have a will, and then there's all that registering-the-death stuff." When I try to take back my hands, he only holds them tighter. I wonder how he knows that El didn't have a will. "I know how this all sounds, Cat. I know how hard it is. I know . . ." He falters, bites down on his lip.

"It's okay." It's ridiculous how much I still want—need—to comfort him. Smooth away that line between his eyes, rub my thumbs against his skin, its dark, tired shadows.

"Stay with me."

"What?"

He stares at me so closely, so minutely, I can't bring myself to even blink. "Stay with me. *Be* with me. I know it's not the right time for this either, but I love you, Cat. Not the same way that I loved El. Different, it's different." He closes his eyes as if he's in pain. "Better."

I don't know what to say. I don't know what to feel.

"I know we'll be judged. But, Cat, I'll put up with it if you will. We can stay here until the house is sold. Or we can leave, go somewhere, anywhere else. It's up to you. Everything is up to you. I love you. I need you." He lets go of my hands to cup my face, stroke my cheek. His fingers are shaking, his eyes are shining. "And El loved us both. She'd want us to be happy."

I don't know if the drain plug is *the* drain plug. And the hole saw could just be a hole saw. I need to go to Logan and Rafiq. Show them everything. Let them run traces, forensic tests. Because it's *Ross*. And neither my shame nor my grief can erase the memory of El's cleverness, her sometimes casual cruelty. She was right: I don't trust her. I haven't trusted her for a very long time. She is still pulling our strings. The letter could be just another lie. Like the emails from "Mouse."

Because someone *has* lied to me. They can't both be telling the truth. Some large part of my life, its conviction, is false. A parallel universe where a person I love is a monster. Where a mirror's reflection lies. I remember El's *She thinks if she pretends something hasn't happened then it hasn't happened*. I don't want that to be true anymore. I'm confused, uncertain. Most of all, I'm scared. Because when I was twelve, I ran away from Mum and Grandpa and this house. And when I was nineteen, I ran away from El and Ross and my heartbreak. But I'm not running away this time. I'm not going anywhere until I find out the truth.

I close my eyes, and instantly the room is colder, brighter. I smell overcooked eggs and burnt toast. Hear the frenzied panic of flapping wings. *Don't slitter, Catriona.* Mum's hunched back, arm trapped against her torso inside a tea-towel sling, a fist-sized bald spot close to her crown, the raw pink nakedness of it. The horror in Grandpa's loud and familiar laugh. *Ye're bein' a stander, lassie. Sit the shit doon.* Silvery, shivery dread. Something coming closer. Something nearly here.

I open my eyes. Ross is looking at me with a mixture of concern and impatience.

"Where did you go?"

I shake my head, pick up the wine. Swallow, and then shudder. "I've been thinking about the past. About this house. About Grandpa."

Ross sits up straighter.

"About what he used to do. The drinking, the violence."

"There's no point dwelling on the past. It's not important anymore." His fingers trace my cheekbones, and his smile is tentative. "That's why we need to sell up, leave. It's why we—"

"But I'd boxed it all away, Ross! So much of it. What happened here. What happened to us. Don't you think *that's* important?"

"Your fucking grandpa was decades ago, Cat! *This* is important." He takes hold of my hands again. "*We* are important. I don't see why—"

I pull away and stand up. My chair screeches against the tiled floor, its back legs wobbling, sliding, until Ross lunges towards me to catch it. I cringe, and far too obviously—the incredulous hurt that flashes across his face makes me look away.

"Because what if I'm wrong? What if there's something else— something worse—and I can't remember it? What if I've pretended it didn't happen?" I'm shaking, still standing, but little of the fog in my head has lifted. Ross looks confused, angry. But of course, he can't understand, because I'm talking about fantasy versus the truth. The answers to the terrible questions that I still can't bring myself to ask him.

But it has to be tonight.

El's bloodshot eyes. Her terrible smile behind the Berlin Wall. *It has to be tonight.*

Ross is shaking me, his fingers squeezed tight around my upper arms.

"Cat! Can you hear me? Are you okay?"

"Stop! I'm okay. I'm okay."

He doesn't let me go. "Jesus, are you sure? I thought you were having a fit or something."

Maybe I *should* stop. Cram everything I've kept packed away for so long back inside that box. Except that there's just too much of it. I can see now that choosing not to face anything that scares you—including the worst of your past—is not normal, and it strikes me as even stranger that I haven't thought so until now.

Mum pulling out the black rucksack from under my bed, tossing out-of-date tins of food onto the floor. *For God's sake, Catriona, why are you so* useless? *This is* important! Rapping her knuckles on the flat of our desk, stoking that ever-present hum of dread, of doom. Look, listen. *Learn.* The pantry walls of orange and yellow daffodils, and the high steady sound of her reading voice. A Tale of Two Cities, Papillon, The Man in the Iron Mask, The Spy Who Came in from the Cold, The Count of Monte Cristo, Rita Hayworth and Shawshank Redemption.

Don't be like me. Never be too afraid to fly.

"Oh my God." I sit down with a thump. I press my hand against my mouth. When I pick up the wine, my fingers tremble so much I can't drink. My stomach clenches.

"Cat, what the hell's going on? Should I call someone?"

Not Survival Packs. Not English lessons. Not fairy stories or make-believe. Paranoia, cruelty, or delusion. Not even just trying to survive living in the same house as a monster.

Ross stares at me. "*What?*"

All of it the same thing. The same *PLAN. It has to be tonight.* That last night of our first life. That last stripe of gold light across the hallway carpet, that last clunk and turn of the dead bolt on Friday. Silence, darkness, and then running down the stairs, rucksacks rattling, dragging at our shoulders. Mum buttoning up our coats over our sweaters, face pinched and raw and alive, her left cheek dark and swollen, eye little more than a black-purple slit. Holding us too tight with her only working arm. *Are you ready?*

"God." My voice is flat. Something halfway between hope and horror is trying to claw its way up my throat towards it. We never ran away from this house. We never ran away from what had happened in this house. We were always supposed to be going. *That* had been THE PLAN. "It was about escape. It was *always* about escape."

"Cat—"

I look at Ross. The hairs along both of his forearms are standing up straight, like his spine; it's as if his whole body is at attention. "That was it, wasn't it? The night they died? September the fourth? We were escaping. El and I. And you and Mum knew. You and Mum were helping. That was THE PLAN. Wasn't it? For us to escape him. Here. For us never to come back."

Ross sags. Turns his hands palm upwards to curl his fingers around my wrists. "Of course it was."

I hear a sound. Above the batter of the rain and the rattle of the wind. Eerie, long and low, like the hoot of an owl.

We stood in this kitchen, just a few feet from this table, moonlight streaming across the floor. Uncertain, impatient, frazzled by nerves, dazzled by excitement, terrified by Mum's furious urgency. Even then we didn't know what was happening. Any of it. We had no concept at all of what escape meant.

An owl hoot. A heartbeat in which I looked at El and she looked at me. Mum's frown. That slow slide of suspicion reserved only for us.

"Someone's helping us," El said.

Someone we can trust, I wanted to say, but didn't. Because Mum believed handsome Prince Charmings were sly. Never ever to be trusted. Because Ross had always been our secret from the very start.

"The owl hoot means *Danger*, Mum! It means *Run!*"

And so we did.

"You were the lookout," I say.

Ross has gone pale. He glances out at the black wet night—so different from the eerie moon-bright calm of September 4, 1998—and then he stands up. His shoulders are rigid. I can see the veins in his neck, the tic inside his jaw. He won't look at me at all.

"I tell you that I love you. That I want to live with you, be with you. I expected you to want to talk about El. And all you actually want to talk about is *this* house and your fucking loony grandpa." He marches towards the door. "I'm going upstairs. When I come back, we're going to have a normal fucking conversation, all right?"

And then he's gone. His footsteps stomping their way up the stairs.

A rumble of thunder makes me jump. The window frame rattles, lifts, and thumps back down. My thigh starts to vibrate, and when I realize it's my phone, my shaking fingers struggle to reach it. By the time I do, the caller has hung up. I don't recognize the number, but there's a text. *Phone me when you get this. Rafiq.* And when I listen to the voice mail, she says exactly the same thing, but the tense, terse order of it alarms me. She sounds like a DI Kate Rafiq I haven't met yet. She sounds worried. Maybe even afraid.

I should call her back. But I feel so close to the edge of something. And I've already looked down. I *want* to fall. *It* has *to be tonight.*

There's an unread email in my inbox. From ProfessorCatherine Ward@southwarkuni.com. The kitchen light flickers as it downloads, and I stare at the buffering symbol, trying to ignore my hammering heart, my slow muzzy thoughts.

Dear DI Kate Rafiq,

Many thanks for your email. I've only just returned from a three-week Arctic cruise, but when I heard about your investigation, I had already resolved to contact you even before receiving your email. My colleagues (through no fault of their own, I hasten to add) were incorrect when they told you that Dr. Ross MacAuley did not leave the conference until it finished at 4 p.m. on April 3rd. He did, in fact, leave on the evening of the 2nd. Specifically, at 5:45 p.m.

I am certain of the time because my Bergen flight had been brought forward due to predicted bad weather—I had only a few hours' notice to leave the university, pack, and get to Gatwick. I saw Dr. MacAuley loading his suitcase into his car and driving out of the car park exit. I know Dr. MacAuley by sight;

last year, he presented a paper at the BPS Symposium held in Glasgow.

Many apologies that this account should come so late in your investigation. I saw on the news that the missing woman had tragically been found, but that her death was not thought to be suspicious. It is my hope then, that my omission so late in the day matters little, although I am, of course, available should you need me to be. My personal and office contacts are below.

Kind regards,

Catherine Ward

She's right, of course. It doesn't matter. It doesn't mean anything. Another rumble of thunder rattles the window frame. I swallow. It means he lied. To me. To the police. It's exactly why I emailed her in the first place. It's exactly what I worried she might say. It's exactly what I *expected* her to say.

Lightning turns the kitchen white and bright like a flare, and I blink. Imagine that I see something in the garden, something wrong, something out of place, before the window returns to darkness. The house groans, restless and awake. I can hear Ross moving around upstairs; old floorboards creaking as if in warning.

I stand up. Stumble against the table, suddenly light-headed enough to see black dancing spots. My head rolls forwards, too heavy, and the accompanying dizziness is bad enough that I grab for my chair. When it falls, the crash it makes is muted, as if I'm underwater. Only when I bang my hip hard against the table do my ears recalibrate with simultaneous pops, and the sounds of the weather and the house roar back in. I set my palms on the table, steady my breathing, lean against the wood until enough of its solidity transfers to me.

I look across at the Shiraz. It's red like old blood in the dull flickering light. It occurs to me that I've felt like this, strange and slow and leaden, for many, many days. I think of all those twelve-hour sleeps. All the drinks that Ross has made me while standing in front of the Poirot. The bottle of vodka on the kitchen table. The tea he always makes fresh because the pot is stewed. El's tox screen after she died. All those pills. *It's probable that they contributed to her death, one way or another.* PSYCHOACTIVE DRUGS: THE EFFICACY OF THERAPIES VS. SAFE RATIOS.

I stagger over to the sink, pour out the wine, and then drink straight from the tap, tepid swallow after swallow until my stomach feels hard and full, and my head clearer. Another flash of lightning, the rumble of thunder this time scant seconds behind. I look back at the window. The thick hardwood Georgian bars and panes too small for even a child to fit through. The long, crooked nails set into its sill. Ross's *I didn't mind them too much. Thought they would help keep El safe when I wasn't here.* And El's *everything bought, everything put back in place, made my prison smaller, more secure.* Maybe they aren't the same nails Grandpa hammered into the old scarred wood after all.

I look at those tiles in front of Mum's Kitchener and, for the first time, I see the blood running fast and dark between them, pooling in the cracks of grout.

The floorboards creak overhead. *Danger. Run.*

I do. The rest I'll think about later. Including whether or not running is a mistake. I sprint through the hallway, ignoring the warning rattle of the bird plates. In the entrance hall, I snatch a quick glance back at the staircase. Another flash lights up the empty hallway, the stained-glass window. I run for the front door.

It's locked.

I waste stupid moments pulling back on the night latch over and over again, but I know it's useless. I know there's only one dead bolt key.

I run back through the hallway, casting another look up to where the stairwell curves into darkness before I race back into the kitchen, ease shut its door.

Run.

I sprint across the tiles, into the icy scullery. I can't find the light switch, but another flash of lightning exposes my worst remaining fear. The mortice key is gone. When I turn the handle, the door to the back garden is locked too.

There's nowhere left to go. I need to calm down. Ross will be back soon. I need to *think.* And then I need to act.

I go into the kitchen. Right my fallen chair. Take out my phone and return Rafiq's call.

"I'm in the house," I say, when it goes to voice mail. And I've no time to say anything more before thunder breaks over the house in an explosive roar, my signal cuts off, and the garden reappears in a frozen white sheet of light.

The orchard, the ugly plinths and paving, the washhouse and its slate roof, its chained door. And there, on the naked expanse of wall alongside, standing out in stark relief against it, like an over-exposed photo flash: high and wide and blood-red. Loud enough to be a shout. A scream.

El *did* scream as she stared out the window, her finger pointing. I saw her reflection against the dark glass, her mouth a horrified O. The moonlight made silver shadows of the apple trees, the exercise yard, the high prison walls. And the words painted in an ugly red warning.

HE KNOWS

The horror of them froze me still.

Until I heard the dead bolt. Turning over with a clunk, heavy and loud. Just like the jail cells in the Shank.

The lights go out in another bellow of thunder, and I scream, drop my phone with a clatter. I'm on my hands and knees on the floor, frantically scrabbling around, when the lights flicker back on with a low humming buzz.

"Cat?"

I freeze. My phone is under the table. I lunge for it, scramble to my feet.

"You okay?"

Creak, creak, pause. He's at the top of the stairs.

"Yeah." My voice cracks on the word.

Another creak, a longer pause. "I'll get the flashlight just in case we're in for a power cut, and then I'll be back down." Creak. "Don't go anywhere." He sounds too cheerful; the smile in his voice has teeth. Especially after our argument. Especially after what I said, and what he didn't. Especially after my scream.

The bell ring stops me in my panicked tracks. Low and heavy, ponderous. I look up at the bell board, at the violently swinging bell. Thin, tinny, F sharp or G flat. *Bathroom* is nearly obscured behind the frantic star-shaped pendulum. I look up at the ceiling. Why the fuck would Ross be pulling the bell pull in the bathroom? I look at my reflection in the kitchen window, the dark shadows of my face distorted by the rain. *It isn't him.*

This time, when the lights brown out and then flicker before turning the kitchen back into black, I don't scream. Nor when thunder shakes the house from ceiling to floor and the garden lights up white again. I expect the words to be gone. I want them to be gone, because then I'm just crazy, a person so determined to forever run away that she invents more fantasies than she can ever possibly examine or refute. But there they still are, in the second before the garden turns back to darkness, and the kitchen to light. The words, the facts. The writing on the wall.

HE KNOWS

Mum did scream when she heard the dead bolt. Seizing El with her good arm, and me with her bad, she pulled us away from the window, pushed us back into the hallway. We didn't want to go. Mum shoved us towards the pantry, the Berlin Wall. *Get to Mirrorland now.* Her lopsided, black-bruised face so determined, her nails scratching, feet kicking—she was never afraid to hurt us. A glance over her shoulder like a bird about to peck, about to fly. *I'll stop him. But you have to be quick. It's time. It has to be tonight. You have to go NOW. RUN!*

There are two bells ringing together now, discordant and frenzied, their stars swinging drunkenly, the bell board shuddering, shedding dust. Bedrooms 4 and 5. The Princess Tower and the Donkshop. Ringing together, because both are opposite each other at the end of the landing. Then Bedroom 3: low and long inside their fading echo. *He's coming back.* I stumble out of the kitchen as the lights flicker again, as the bells change again. Bedrooms 1 and 2. The Kakadu Jungle and the Clown Café. *He's at the top of the stairs.* I run for the pantry, tear back the curtain. Because it doesn't matter if those blood-red words are only repressed memory. It doesn't matter if the ringing bells are real or only in my head. It doesn't matter that there hasn't been a Mum or a Bluebeard or a drill in nearly twenty years. They are a warning. A warning that I have to obey. Because even more than fantasies or creaking old floorboards, those bells have always been this house's best alarm system. And Mirrorland has always been its sanctuary.

In the wake of another roar of thunder, I hear Ross's shout. I don't look out the window as I run for the cupboard, lift up its latch, drag the stool over, climb up inside. The lights flicker, and I turn on my phone's flashlight, close the cupboard door behind me. The light throws deep shadows; they advance and retreat as I reach up to slide back the two heavy bolts. I don't know what I'm doing, but I can't stop it, I don't even want to. For just once I have to trust myself. I open the door to Mirrorland, step down onto the wooden staircase. Freeze when I hear another bell, twice and short. Ross is in the kitchen. He shouts again, closer this time. A jangling, nervy bell. A moment's silence, and then another. Both muffled, but still my old muscle memory wins out. *Drawing Room. Dining Room.* He's running out of places to look.

I close the door, but that's all I can do. Ross knows it's here. And he knows that just like the cupboard door, there are no locks on its inside, nothing to wedge up against it. Vertigo has me groping for a hand that isn't there, and I stop, breathe through it. I move into the dark, stepping down onto the next step and the next, and all I let myself think of is Ross swinging up through the skylight in the washhouse roof like a chimpanzee. Escaping into the day. I whisper the words I thought in this very place eleven days ago. *I'm no longer a child.* This time, I won't be too afraid of climbing, of falling.

The rucksacks were too bulky. They dragged and scraped against the staircase walls. El's hand held mine, too tight, too hot, our flashlight dancing angry spikes. Grandpa roared above us. Mum's protests soon turned into screams. And when an almighty crash shook the walls, El pulled me down faster. *Come on, come on. Quick.*

A high, polite tinkle like an old-fashioned clothes shop door. The

Pantry. It has to be—the only bell I've never heard, not once. Because Grandpa never came into the pantry. He thought it was a narrow, cold schoolroom. Up until that last night, he didn't even know Mirrorland existed; didn't know there was a way into the washhouse that wasn't padlocked or chained. I look up and over my shoulder, but only for a second—the darkness is too thick and the steps too steep. And Ross will be behind me soon enough anyway.

CHAPTER 27

I reach the bottom of the steps, and flail around for the bulb's dangling cord, pull down hard when I find it. This time, the light is neither immediate nor strong. It flickers, browns, settles on a muted butter glow.

When El pulled down on that same cord, flooding Mirrorland in cold silver, I dropped my rucksack, cringed from an overhead bang loud enough to vibrate the wooden rafters. *What do we do now?* And I hardly cared that it was the wail of a child, or that El thought so too, pushing me towards the border between the Shank and the *Satisfaction*. *What Mum said. Come on!*

Now I run along the alleyway to the washhouse, wrench open its door, shine my light up towards the ribs of its roof, searching for the skylight. All I can see are deep-braced shadows and old cobwebs.

Please, please.

I see it. Not a skylight. But a square of pale new wood. It's gone. The skylight is gone.

I whirl my light around the icy space. It stutters over that stern lantern and its hook screwed into the eastern wall. It's not the same lantern, of course. I know that now. The lantern that caved in Grandpa's skull must be sitting in an evidence locker somewhere. But just like the lantern under the Clown Café bed, it frightens me. Reminds me that I'm not okay. I'm not safe.

I run back into the alleyway; my light stalls this time over the bricked-up wall at its end. I'm trapped. I feel sick and afraid. My head pounds and my stomach twists with poison. I suppose I expected to know what to do once I got here. Perhaps I expected Mirrorland to tell me. Instead, it's more of a prison now than it ever was.

I stumble into the wide three-wheeled pram as I fight off another wave of dizziness. My light catches the white faded label in the corner of its cover in the instant that I remember it. *Silver Cross*.

My fingers are unsteady as I pull back the hood. Lying across a moldy pillow is a blank postcard with a tack hole in its corner. I pick it up, turn it over. Recognize Ross's handwriting. And then the butter-yellow light goes dark with that familiar metallic thud. And he bangs through the entrance to Mirrorland.

He comes down fast, too fast for me to do anything but hide. I hunker against the wall beneath the staircase, wince against the thunder of his boots as he shouts my name. He sees me straightaway, although I can't see him. His face is obscured by a hurricane lantern. In place of a candle stub, a kerosene flame dances and splutters.

"What the hell are you doing down here?" His voice sounds normal, bemused. "Didn't you hear me shouting?"

I blink against the too-bright light. "Why did you turn the power off?"

"I didn't. The power's out everywhere." He holds the lantern higher. "Come on, it's freezing. Let's—"

"Did you board up the skylight?"

The kerosene hisses. I can hear the steady drip drip of the washhouse's guttering.

"I took it out," Ross says. His voice is lower, less bemused. "Anyone could have used it to get into the house. You could open it from the outside, remember?"

I swallow. Take a long, deep breath. "I know you came back from your conference on the second, not the third." I know, too, that this is terminally stupid. If Ross is guilty, confronting him down here in this dark and forgotten space is lunacy. Even if it seems like the only place I'd ever have the courage.

A pause. And then low, too steady: "You've been checking up on me?"

He's still little more than a silhouette. Every time I close my eyes, all I can see is the imprint of the lamp's gold flame. But I can smell him. And I can *feel* him.

"I left early because El *begged* me to come home, said she was scared, she needed me. She was so unstable by then, I was worried she'd do something stupid." The shadow of his shrug leaps across the wall. "There were no flights available, so I drove. But I didn't go back to the house in the end. I couldn't face it. I couldn't face *her*." He makes a sound somewhere between a laugh and a snort. "I didn't do anything to El, Cat."

"Then why lie to the police?"

"I panicked. They always go for the husband, and I knew—even then—that she was gone. That my leaving the conference early would look bad. I mean, for fuck's sake"—that half-snort, half-laugh again—"even you don't believe me."

He puts down the lantern. When he moves nearer, I make myself be still. I can see him now: hollowed cheekbones and wild hair. *Ross.*

"Why are all the doors locked?"

"*What?*"

"Why did you lock the front and back doors?"

"Because when I came back from town today, I found two reporters standing in the front garden and peering into the drawing room." He throws up his hands. "I'll unlock them again if that's what you want." A long pause. "Did you come down here to *escape*?" He makes it sound like the craziest thing he's ever heard. "Through the *skylight*?" He takes two steps back, runs his fingers through his hair. "Jesus, Cat. Are you scared of me?"

"The fourth of September. You were there. You said you'd help us. You helped us." This time it's not a roar of too-close thunder that makes me jump, it's a snapped crack of lightning directly over the house. I imagine its icy white fingers chasing through the webs and wires and hidden spaces to the ground under our feet.

Ross sat between us on the deck of the *Satisfaction* when El first told him all of it. How Mum had said that every bad night from now on would be just like that night Grandpa found us in the Clown Café's cupboard. And beat us so hard that she'd lost her voice screaming at him to stop. Because hurting Mum was no longer enough for Bluebeard. Because we'd grown up too fast despite Mum's insistence that we shouldn't. We couldn't hide anymore. She couldn't save us anymore. And so we had to escape. We had to come up with *THE PLAN*.

"Cat!"

I shake my head. Press my palms hard against the cold stone at my back. Remember that tester pot of red paint in the shoebox.

"You painted 'HE KNOWS' on the wall that night. Didn't you?"

Ross gives an annoyed sigh. "Fine, we're doing this, then. Yes. You know I did. That was part of the *plan*. I was the fucking *lookout*. I saw him coming back from the Mission, and the first thing I thought of was all those tins of red paint in the washhouse. I had to warn you, Cat. *That* was the *fucking plan*. What—"

"You could always get into the garden, couldn't you?"

"What?"

"I remember now. I used to think—afterwards—that it was like you were a superhero that night. That your love for us—for me—had somehow *flown* you over the wall or down from the washhouse roof and into our garden to save us." I make an ugly sound in the back of my throat.

He frowns, his jaw working. "So I could get down into the garden from the roof. What does it matter?"

"It matters because it's another lie. You told us you could only ever reach us through the skylight—because you wanted to be able to drop right into our lives, our world, whenever you wanted." I look at the narrow planes of his face, the shadows that smooth flat whenever he smiles. *Don't tell your mum about me. She'll ruin it.* "You wanted to be our secret."

"Cat." He grabs my arms without warning, and when I wrench them backwards, he only holds on tighter. His eyes are furious. "Why are you down here in the cold and dark, banging on about a night twenty years ago? I know the last few days have—"

"He never came back early from the Mission," I say. "Not ever."

Ross lets go of my arms. "He did that night."

"Why? He *never ever* came back early. How did *he know*? Did you tell him?"

"Are you—are you serious? First, you all but accuse me of killing my wife, then of locking you in this fucking house, and now . . . what? You think I was once in cahoots with your crazy grandpa?"

"No. No." Because, of course, that makes no sense. No sense

at all. My head is pounding, my mind is racing as fast as my heart. Faster.

I try to push past him, and my light jumps drunkenly across the boundary wall on the opposite side of the alleyway. I see an X drawn in black marker on a brick half a foot from the ground, and sink to my knees, press my fingers against it. I think of El's letter: *X MARKS THE SPOT*. It was here. El's life-size painting of the pirate Captain Henry Morgan, The Island's blues and yellows and greens behind him. It was here.

Mum knew that there was a bolted door in the alleyway of next door's house—Ross's house—a door with no lock that led to a front garden with no gate. She knew, too, that I could no more climb up a ladder to the skylight than climb back down over the washhouse's roof and the boundary wall. She'd never been able to cure my terror of heights, of falling—neither through kindness nor cruelty. And El and I had to escape together—because we would not leave each other. Never so long as we lived. But what Mum knew the most—what Mirrorland had shown her, had shown us—was that there was *always* another way. A way through. A way out. And in the end, that way out was this snecked-rubble boundary wall between two alleyways.

Andy Dufresne took twenty-seven years to tunnel out of Shawshank Prison. Mum said we had only weeks, but could afford to be no less careful, no less meticulous. We never questioned her. Never complained. El took to *THE PLAN* like a duck to water, if only to follow in the footsteps of her hero. And I did what I have always done. I followed her.

We didn't use a rock hammer, but a heavy claw hammer that made our shoulders ring and ache. Sometimes, when we stopped and leaned heavily against the cool stone of Mirrorland, we could hear Mum's calm and steady voice filtering down from the pantry above as she pretended to read to us, to teach us what we'd already learned.

We hid the growing hole in the garden wall behind Captain Henry's painting, and we hid our excavations in cardboard boxes and the umbrella bases on the *Satisfaction*. When they became too full, Mum sewed cloth bags inside the legs of our prison-gear clothes. Andy

Dufresne had called them cheaters: long, narrow sacks that could be opened by pulling on lengths of string in his pockets, scattering the evidence of his excavations all over the Shawshank's exercise yard. And so we would pack our own cheaters with stones and powdered brick, and traipse slowly through the kitchen and the scullery—if we were unlucky, past Grandpa's rolling eyes, his *Aff tae join the chain gang again, bloody wee mentalists*—and then down the scullery steps to our exercise yard. Where we would march around and around, kicking up the silver and gray chuckies, while pulling on the strings in our dungaree pockets and scattering our secrets, just like Andy Dufresne. Over and over, day after day, because Mum was too afraid for half measures. Because Grandpa might not have known about Mirrorland, and he might have been deaf as a post, but he wasn't stupid. And the whole house was his domain.

"Cat, will you talk to me? What the hell is going on?"

I ripped Captain Henry away from the wall, and momentarily balked at the dark hole through to the alleyway on the other side. El pinched my arm, pushed me down. *We have to go!* The cold ground scraped against my knees as I turned, reached for my rucksack. And then that terrible thud of the fuse-box master switch, and the light-bulb winked out, leaving a darkness darker than anything. When the door to Mirrorland crashed open, El whimpered. When the stairs started shaking, shouting, Mum screamed. And when I started push-ing into the hole, I knew there wouldn't be enough time. Not for both of us.

A roar like hot wind, like thunder, like ironwoods and banyans torn out of the earth, a landslide of mud and stone. *Where the fuck d'ye think ye're goin'?* His fists, his feet, a breath before each punch or kick landed. For once I didn't feel it, any of it. El screamed, she grasped hold of my coat before she was jerked back into space. And for a second—just one pure second—I kept on going without her, kept pushing into our escape, the edges of it rough and jagged, catching on my hair, my hands, my coat.

But after that second there was no air, no night, no autumn smells of woodsmoke or rotten leaves. No freedom. No *hole*. My fingers scrabbled in the dirt and the debris, but something on the other side of the wall was blocking the way. Something cold and hard and impossibly heavy. My mind imagined an African elephant in iron chain-mail armor, a tank with gun turrets and stenciled black numbers. *You cannot pass.*

And then I was hauled back into Mirrorland, my head smashed hard against stone. A curse, a loud and booming laugh. Mum lying prone and unmoving on the ground, a thread of light washing cold silver across her hair and bloody temple.

A deadlight. Because Bluebeard had finally caught us.

"What was it?" My voice is a dull, flat monotone. "A grit box? A garden waste bin?"

"What?"

I close my eyes. They sting, even though they're bone dry. I push against the wall as I stand up, and I make myself look at Ross, keep looking at him. "You blocked our escape into your alleyway. You pushed something up against the hole, so we couldn't get out."

"What?" His horror is palpable. "No! Of course I didn't." He moves forwards. His gaze locks onto mine. "I was—I am—on your side. Always. I hated that old fucker. I *helped* you. I'd never hurt you."

"Did you hurt El?"

"No."

"Did you kill her?"

His fingers dig into my arms. "No! For fuck's sake, I loved—I love—both of you!"

I take a breath. "You're lying about that night. I know you are. The hole was blocked from your side, Ross. Yours. And if you're lying about that, then you're—"

"This is El talking. Or this house. This fucking house." He stops, lets go of my arms. "Look. It's been a shitty few days, a shitty few weeks. Come back upstairs, and I promise we'll talk. Just—"

"I'm not going anywhere." Because here is where I get to remember, here is where I get to be whole again. And I'm not scared enough of Ross to sabotage that. Not yet.

He holds his palms up. "All right. Then stay here. I'll go upstairs, I'll unlock the doors. And then I'll bring us down something to drink and we can talk right here, okay? If that's what you want."

I don't answer. Outside, the storm seems to be waning; the roars and cracks are getting farther and farther apart, the drum of rain is no longer hard and echoless.

Ross moves closer. He's smiling with his teeth, his eyes. He kisses my cheek, and his skin is smooth. I think of the *Bathroom* bell—F sharp or G flat. He shaved for me. I shiver.

He leaves me the hurricane lamp, his shadow passing over its light before I hear the resumed creak of the staircase.

I take the phone out of my pocket. No signal. And no reply from Rafiq. This should freak me out every bit as much as Ross's promise to return with something to drink; as still being trapped down here—and, for that matter, up there—but it doesn't. Panic tries to return, but it's only an itch, a dull suggestion. I feel eerily calm, removed from the present. Perhaps because at least half of me got left behind in this place twenty years ago. When I press my cold fingers against my cheek, I can still feel the ghost of Ross's touch.

Annie winks solemnly at me inside the washhouse door, standing tall in her high buckled boots, alligator-skin belt, and cowhide jacket with buttons made from whalebone. *Sometimes you have to be brave. Even when you're a grand wee coward.*

I take the postcard out of my waistband. Turn it over.

EL,

God, thank you, baby. I've missed you so fucking much. You don't know how long I've waited for you to get back in touch. It's been like dying, you know? I don't know if you do. I don't know if you could ever love me half as much as I love you. Your letter was pretty cold, but I understand why—I was just GLAD to get it!! I understand why you didn't want anything to do with me that day outside the National Gallery. I understand how much he fucked you up. You're wrong, but it's not your fault.

Meet me—just you and me. No Cat this time. I heard the Rosemount is having a May Day party next week, and I know you're invited (YEAH, I'm your stalker, what can I say? I fucking LOVE you).

Just text me your old room no. I'll meet you there. 2 p.m. Just do this for me, meet me this once, and if after that you don't want to ever see me again, I'll leave you alone. I promise. Even though it'll break my heart to do it.

Please come, baby. Come so I can show you just how much I need you. Want you.

I love you, Blondie. You know I do.

All my love forever and always, Ross xxx

(P.S. DON'T tell Cat. She'll ruin it.)

My laughter is just the wrong side of hysterical. I think of El's face over Ross's naked shoulder. Her gray, slack horror, her furious reproach. When the staircase door bangs open again, and Ross starts creaking his way back down, my laugh turns into a more alarming giggle.

Doom, I think. *Fucking doom.*

CHAPTER 28

Six months after I moved to LA, still shell-shocked and alone, but certain that I'd done the right thing—the brave thing—I met a man whose crooked smile so badly reminded me of Ross that I ended up having sex with him less than an hour after we met. In the staff car park of a seedy late-night bar. So frantically, so *desperately*, that it shocked even me. Afterwards, I stalked him around Venice Beach for weeks, mindless with hope. And when he let me down gently— probably more gently than I deserved—I sobbed in his arms and begged him for just one more night. One more night when I could feel. When I could pretend. And El had thought she was the weak one; the one who'd been a goner for him from the start.

Ross steps back down into the lantern's pool of light. He smiles his smile and holds out a glass of red wine. *Stay with me. Be with me. I love you. Not the same way that I loved El. Different. Better.* I accept the wine, feign a small sip.

HE KILLED HER

HE WILL KILL YOU TOO

One postcard doesn't make that true. Any more than my weakness or Ross being a manipulative bastard makes him a murderer. Annie snorts in the darkness. A sudden bellow of thunder makes me start. In its aftermath, the silence is broken only by the return of torrential rain, a jarring flash of white-silver through the washhouse's window. My hand presses against my breastbone and the erratic thump of my heart. Nothing has passed. Nothing is over. I've only been hiding inside the brief eye of the storm.

But what about you, Blondie? Do you love me too?

I take out the postcard.

Ross blinks. "What's that?"

239

I move incrementally closer to him as if he's a wild animal; hold out the postcard until he takes it from me and I can retreat again. I watch him read, a muscle working in his jaw, the frown line deepening between his eyes.

"Why do you have this?"

"It was here."

"*Here?*" He looks at me. "This isn't true. You can't believe it."

I put the wineglass on the ground. "It's your handwriting."

"All right." He screws up the postcard in his fist. "*All right.* I wanted her to find out about us. That's why I wrote it. Why I set it up. I was sick of lying. I wanted her to know how much we wanted each other. And I know how bad that sounds, I know how bad it *was*, believe me." He drops the postcard, breaches the space between us, and inside the next roll of thunder, takes hold of my hands, presses his lips quick and warm against mine, and looks at me with such sincerity and sorrow that I almost forget why we're here.

"But then she tried to kill herself. Because of what I'd done. She begged me. She told me I was the only man she could ever love. That she would destroy all of us before she'd ever let you have me." He strokes his fingers up and down my skin. "She wasn't in her right mind, Cat, she needed help. And I already felt so guilty. You know I did."

"I know you did."

"She blackmailed me, that's all. You're the one I always wanted."

There's no point in me asking him about El's letter or "Mouse's" accusations. His text on Marie's phone. Every answer will be the same. *She's crazy. Delusional. She needs help.*

When I move away from him, from the relentless stroke of his fingers, he steps between me and the staircase.

"What are you doing?"

"I'm leaving."

"No." He folds his arms. I make myself walk towards him.

"Let me past."

He grabs for me, pulls me against him, pushes his cold hands up under my T-shirt, licks and kisses my neck.

"Ross. Let me past."

His hands move around to my bra, his thumbs pressing hard against my nipples, teeth grazing the underside of my jaw just enough to hurt.

"Let me go!"

But of course, he won't. That's not what he does.

I have a sudden sharp memory of El and me sitting inside our cells in the Shank. Ross, the wing guard, looking in at us through chicken-wire mesh. Brown eyes, warm smile. *I'll let you out. I'll let both of you out, but only if you promise never to run away. If you promise to stay with me forever.*

The minute I retreat backwards, he lunges for me again. When I slam my knee up into his crotch, he grunts, eyes widening in shock. He lets go just long enough for me to dodge around him and up onto the first step. His shout is almost a wheezed cough; I feel the heavy topple of him against the stairs, and I start sprinting upwards, my body and mind suddenly—finally—awake.

He catches me on the second-from-last step, his fingers closing tight around my ankle like the clichéd kind of monster I'm beginning to think he is. I kick out, but his fingers only wind tighter, higher, digging into the muscles of my calf. My palm slaps echoless against the door out of Mirrorland before Ross turns me around and drags me back down alongside him, the stairs' hard edges scraping my bones, banging hard enough against the back of my head that I see brief black spots.

After Grandpa dragged us away from the wall, from our escape, he let us go long enough that we tried to run. He caught El on the stairs. By the time she stopped screaming, my eyes were blurred with blood and panic. I reached down for her hand and it was gone. Bluebeard's deadlight shone its thin silver thread against the staircase ceiling. I could hear grunts and mutters over a wet dreadful choking.

Ross's sweat is sour. I struggle to get out from under him. Furious tears sting inside my eyes. I can't breathe.

I'm here. And her voice isn't an echo, it's as hot and urgent against my ear as Ross's curses against my face.

I screamed when I climbed down close enough to the bottom of the stairs to see Grandpa's hands around El's neck, her mouth half open, eyes wide white. Our slingshots and war clubs were shut inside the armoire, but I punched him like a cowboy and kicked at him like a Sioux. Screamed at the impotent horror of seeing El's bloodshot eyes fix onto mine and knowing Mum was right: I hadn't practiced enough. I wasn't strong enough. I couldn't stop him.

I look up. Stop struggling against Ross and go limp when I see that piece of white card fixed to the ceiling with black electrical tape.

SNOW-WHITE SAID: "WE WILL NOT LEAVE EACH OTHER."
ROSE-RED ANSWERED: "NEVER SO LONG AS WE LIVE."

The silence is thick and urgent. Even the storm retreats.

"She's here."

"Who's here?" Ross sounds uncertain, maybe even afraid.

"What are you doing, Ross?" I muster as ordinary a voice as I can—no small feat under the circumstances.

He looks down at me, draws his bottom lip between his teeth. That familiar furrow between his eyes returns, and he plants his hands against a step somewhere above me, takes away his weight with slow reluctance. He turns, backs up a few steps towards the pantry. Stares down at me, and then up at the ceiling. That furrow drives deeper. He doesn't know it's our pirate code. He doesn't know we *had* a pirate code. And he certainly doesn't know that it means *Trust me. Trust me and no one else.* Even when you don't want to.

The rain rattles against the wooden roof, and I think of the door behind Ross and the cold dark wet outside with a longing worse than thirst. "You sabotaged our escape. You blocked our way out and then you warned him, you helped him. And then you pretended you didn't. You pretended to warn us, to help us instead."

"No. No." He scrambles back down towards me, banging his knuckles against the wall hard enough to make me wince, though it hardly gives him pause at all. "Baby, you're wrong. This is wrong." He looks at me, cups my face between his hands. And this is worse, so much worse than him coming after me like a movie monster, suffocating the breath and fight out of me. His thumbs stroke my cheekbones, my tears. "Please, Blondie. I love you. You know I do."

I always remembered a good grandpa and a bad mum. But I always remembered, too, a mean, cantankerous bully and a mother that stroked our hair and told us that more than a hundred thousand other children had to be born before a mum got to have children as special as us. But this—only this—is why I never wanted to remember what truly happened in this house. Not because I couldn't bear the truth about my bad grandpa and my good mum, but because I couldn't bear the truth about my Prince Charming. Easier to cover dirt and dark and dread with gold and twinkling, glittering lights, the smell of burning wood and winter forest, the feel of his hands on me, all the same as it ever was. The same wonderful. The same rush. The same madness. El was right: if she'd told me the truth about Ross, I never would have believed her. Because I've been pretending—*lying*—to myself ever since I ran from this house.

El was already going limp before I remembered the shank in my pocket. I took it out—two razor blades parcel-taped to half a toothbrush—and it didn't seem like it would be enough until I jammed it into Grandpa's neck and he gave a high female scream. He reared back and pulled it out, and I gave precious seconds away to the horror of waiting for El to start breathing again. And then Grandpa was on me, teeth snapping open and shut like he wanted to bite, blood pulsing out of his neck, thick and dark. I pushed him, and he slipped an elbow in his own blood, giving me space enough to scramble down the last few steps. El was still clutching at her throat, and as we ran back into Mirrorland, I realized that it wasn't her screams that were echoing around the narrow space, deafening and frightening. It was mine.

"It was you, it was always you," Ross says. Pleads. "I always wanted you. And she ruined it. *She* did."

"*She's* here," I say again. Because I know it's true. The house has helped me, Mirrorland has helped me; it seems like the most natural thing in the world that El should help me too. Not the El that has festered and grown inside my heart and my dreams. But my sister. My friend. The smell of her, the smile of her, the thoughts of her, running parallel to mine. It's as if my whole world has changed from mono to stereo, 2D to 3. And it's the first time I've felt it in so long—

that I've even realized it was as missing as she was—I want to sob, I want to say sorry, I want to plead for her forgiveness.

"Stop saying that!" In the dim light, Ross's expression is furious, but his eyes flicker up and around as if trying to find her.

I step back down onto the stony slabs of Mirrorland, let go of the banister. I'm already stronger, braver. "Just tell the fucking truth." Because the truth is the only way out of this place for either of us.

He stays silent for a very long time. Comes out from the shadow of the staircase. His jaw is no longer tight, and his eyes are warm, full of the love I always longed for. His hair is too long, his shaved skin looks pink and vulnerable; I want to rub the back of my fingers against it. This is Ross.

"You were going to leave. You were going to leave and never come back." He moves towards me. Reaches out his hands in supplication. "I would never have seen you again. I would have lost you. Just like Dad lost me."

My breath stops at the moment the rain does. The silence is suddenly absolute.

"He killed himself. Five years after Mum took me away. Hung himself from the ceiling light in my old bedroom." Ross's smile is terrible. His hands shake. There is less than three feet of space remaining between us. "And I loved you so much. What would have happened to you? No one would look after you like I could. No one."

I swallow. I don't know who the *you* is in his mind. Maybe there, El and I were always fused together like sand and limestone. When he comes one last step closer, El's musky perfume waters my eyes, and her whisper is loud in my ear.

RUN.

I do.

We ran east into the washhouse, Grandpa thundering behind us. The stone gave way to wood as we ran across the deck of the *Satisfaction*, the shriek of its boards spiking my terror. He was too close, too close. *Ye're goin' naewhere, ye wee bitches.*

I run towards the stern and the barely faded specter of Blackbeard's ship. Towards the small red-framed window. I frantically search for something, anything, I can use to break it, until I realize that its glass panels are even smaller than those inside the house.

"You can't leave."

"Ross, please."

"I've never told anyone about my dad before, Cat. Not even El."

"Ross. You're scaring me. I won't leave. I promise. Just let's—" When he keeps on coming, stepping back is as automatic as breathing. "Please don't—"

"I won't hurt you." He looks affronted, wounded, but still he keeps coming, still the passion in his eyes is wild and dark. But I don't think it's love anymore. Here, after all, is where we first sailed away from him. Left him on his knees in the Caribbean Sea. Left him bloody and sobbing and calling out to us, while we pretended not to hear him.

Grandpa slammed El against the wall above the stern. I howled, launched myself at him, but his elbow thrust backwards into the softness of my belly, winding me enough that I couldn't get up. He grinned until all I could see was teeth. And the blood around his neck like a scarf, soaking into his shirt. *Dinnae worry, lassie.* He laughed. *Ah'm feelin' nae pain.* And then he punched me in the side of my head so hard that my legs collapsed.

"Ross, no. Stop." I cringe from him, batting his hands away, and I've time enough to wonder if this was what it was like for El. If this is what happened when she tried to leave him too. Until I remember what happened to her instead.

"I'm not going to hurt you." He reaches out again, catches my hands and squeezes them tight inside his, tight enough that my bones crack. "I won't ever hurt you." I wonder if he knows he's nodding his head.

I can't stop struggling, but he's too strong and I'm too weak. He holds both of my wrists one-handed; the other he moves up along my shoulder, my collarbone, softly enough to make me shudder. There's another kind of shining madness in his eyes now. A war between taking what he really wants and settling for what he's always had instead. His hand slides up the side of my neck, his fingers tracing the skin under my ear, tighter, then tighter still, his thumb suddenly pressing down hard enough against my windpipe that I let out too much air in a gasp. And that madness shines brighter.

When I came to, Grandpa was choking El again. Her eyes were rolled back, her face was purple, her fingers blindly grasped at the air. I staggered towards them, but it was too hard. I couldn't save her. I wasn't enough. That was it. That was all.

"I won't hurt you. I won't hurt you," Ross mutters in a horrifyingly reassuring voice, the veins in his neck getting fat with the exertion of choking me tighter. I slide down the wall, rough and cold against my back.

"I didn't kill her," he says. In that same calm voice, sweat dripping off his nose. "I didn't."

But he did. Just like he's going to kill me.

My head feels heavy, full. El's liquid gasps are mine. My sight begins to shrink and curl black around its edges.

And then El grips hold of my hand. Hard enough to hurt, to punish. *Deadlight*, she says. Screams. *Deadlight*.

I lurched across the deck, scrabbling for purchase as if we really were pitching and rolling against a Caribbean storm. I ignored Grandpa's desperate grunts of exertion, made myself look only at the stern. The lantern. Hanging on a rusty hook over the hull. Grandpa turned to see me lift it high up over my head. His frown was startled, then almost tender. A wink. A grin. *Put it doon, lassie.*

I almost did. And so automatically I hardly registered I was doing it, until I saw Mum crawling along the deck towards us, blood running into her eyes. Her hoarse, rasping cries as Grandpa turned dismissively back to the job in hand: *Leave them alone! They're just children!*

I open my eyes. *No*. Tell the fucking truth.

Leave them alone! They're your children!

Ross makes a sound like a sob in the back of his throat, and I feel his fingers loosen around my neck, feel the air rushing back into my lungs. But it doesn't matter. I know he won't stop. One way or another. He won't ever *ever* stop.

As I scramble backwards, grab on to the lantern hook to pull myself back to my feet, I hear all of the bells at once. High and discordant, low and long—loud enough to tremble eardrums and shake stone.

Your children. That horrifying truth of what we were. Not cowboys or Indians or Clowns or pirates. Or prisoners. Our grandfather's children.

My fingers shook against the lantern; its hinges squeaked. I looked down at El's lifeless body. The back of Grandpa's head, his hunched and working shoulders.

And I bring the lantern—*my* deadlight—down on top of Ross's skull. Just as hard as I brought it down on Grandpa's. With the same black fury and icy horror. Again and again, until all the strength left in me has run out through my fingers. Until the sound is no longer hard and short and white, but soft and long and copper-dark.

*

It takes me a long time to climb the stairs out of Mirrorland, but once I have, I find that I can't leave. Instead, I sit down on the top step, lean against the door. I think about phoning Rafiq, but don't. I look down into the shadows of the Shank, the turn of the corner east towards the *Satisfaction*.

Mum didn't speak again for a long while. She was angry. Then, I imagined, at us; now, I imagine, at herself. At how badly her plan had gone awry. She looked at Grandpa for a long while too before dropping down to her knees. At first, I thought to touch him, to wail, to mourn, but instead, she pushed him onto his side like he was a sack of potatoes. When she let him go, a gasp of air pushed out of him, and either I or El shrieked.

"He's dead," Mum said. And then she stood, knees cracking. Looked around at our painted walls and the long cells of the Shank with a pained kind of anger. "We can't leave him here. Help me get him up the stairs."

It took at least half an hour. By the time we managed to drag him into the kitchen, exhaustion had burned away our shock.

"Go upstairs," Mum said. "Get together what's left of your clothes, your books. And then go back down to Mirrorland, lock it all in the armoire with everything else."

She'd already had us pack and store most of our meager belongings in the armoire weeks before she first told us about THE PLAN. Just another game. Another drill we never questioned.

When we went back down to Mirrorland, numb and silent, our arms full, Mum was pulling apart the Shank, stacking the old boardwalk planks against the boundary wall. Our claw hammer was at her feet.

"I need to cover up the door in the cupboard," she said. She frowned, looked at us both in turn. "No one can ever know you were here. Do you understand?"

We nodded, even though we didn't. Even though we'd barely thought of anything that might happen beyond escaping through a hole in a wall, a door with no lock, and a front garden with no gate.

When Mum had dragged the last of the wood up into the pantry, she put her hands on her hips, nodded back towards the cupboard.

"Close the door to Mirrorland." The look she gave both of us was fierce in her bruised and bloodied face. "And bolt it shut."

We did. And then followed her back into the kitchen. She sat down at the table. There was a key in the center of it. Grandpa's key.

"It's for the front door. I want you to do what we planned. Go as quickly as you can."

"But now you can come too," El whispered.

"I told you. I have to sort this out, that's my job. It was always going to be my job."

She sighed, stood up, took hold of the tea-towel sling that now hung only around her neck, and began scrubbing hard at the cuts on our faces and the blood under our nails with her usual brutal efficiency. We knew better than to complain, never mind cry, even though the pain soon swallowed up our fear. My head throbbed in the places where Grandpa had punched it or slammed it against the ground; it ached inside as if my brain had grown too big for my skull. El was struggling to swallow now; her eyes were full of tears. Both of us couldn't stop staring at Grandpa's body slumped next to the Kitchener; his blood running fast and dark across two tiles, pooling inside the grout between them.

"El. There's a tartan scarf on the coat stand. Wind it 'round your neck and don't take it off. And there's a powder compact in the drawer of the telephone table. Take that with you and cover the worst of each other's bruises and cuts."

We stood, stock still and silent, throbbing with pain, the remnants of horror, the beginnings of regret.

"What are you waiting for?"

"Is Grandpa . . ." I looked at his face, the dark red blood still coughing out of his ruined skull. "Is Grandpa our *dad*?"

Her lips thinned, eyes narrowed. "Only follow the route on the treasure map. Go nowhere else. Only the harbor, only the warehouse. There's always someone there, so you'll be all right."

"Mum," El whispered. "Was Grandpa—"

I winced when Mum grabbed for my right hand and El's left.

"You must always hold on to each other's hand. Because?"

"We will not leave each other," I said.

"Never so long as we live," El whispered, pushing her cold hand into mine.

"Rely on no one else. Trust no one else. All you will ever have is each other."

We nodded, tried not to swallow, to blink, to cry.

"Remember, you're the eldest, Ellice, the poison taster. Be brave, be bold, look after your sister." Mum's hands were trembling; the blood at her temple had begun to run freely again. "Remember, Catriona, don't be like me. Be brave. Always see the good instead of only the bad."

And I nodded, thought of the shrieking, squawking Kakadu Jungle, all the nights El and I had run through the darkness and the lightning, the roaring wind and towering water, the shadows crouching, bristling with rage and sharp teeth. This would be no different, I thought, even as I knew it would be.

Mum stayed on her knees, and though nothing about her softened, tears ran down her lopsided face, soaked into the bloodied collar of her blouse. "Never forget how special you are. How special you have been."

And then she let go of our hands, closed her eyes. "Go now."

When I opened my mouth to object, El squeezed my hand tighter.

"Go."

When we didn't, Mum's eyes snapped open black, her hands uncurled to show their nails, her mouth flattened into a thin, cruel line. *"Run!"*

It wasn't how she'd wanted—planned—to do any of it, I suppose. No long goodbye, no *I love you*—nothing beyond the awful, practical now. She knew we would obey because, in many ways, we were more afraid of her than of anyone else. El and I had been numbed by a lifetime of her anger, her disapproval and disappointment, but perhaps she had been too. That was how she'd protected us, safeguarded us against even the smallest part of what she'd had a longer lifetime to suffer. Her love was cruel; she built us mercilessly piecemeal.

El and I only discovered a week later that she'd killed herself, in a news headline on the TV in the Rosemount's common room. A murder-suicide, probable history of domestic violence, a screen-crawling help-line number. She'd swallowed all of Grandpa's heart pills and then lain down right next to him on the kitchen floor.

The last picture I have in my head of Mum is her kneeling on those tiles, blocking our view of Grandpa's body. The fierceness of her jaw, the raw pink nakedness of that fist-sized bald spot close to her crown. And the last thing I remember that she said—shouted in echoes that shook against the thick walls and high ceilings as we ran towards the blood-red entrance hall—was no less terrible or kind.

Don't ever come back.

But we did. Both of us. Because we didn't keep our promises. We relied on someone else. We trusted someone else. We left each other. We forgot.

I open my eyes. They sting, my head aches, my throat throbs. I run my fingers across the smooth wood of the door, and though they leave trails of Ross's blood in their wake, they're steadier than they've been in weeks. I can remember Mum's treasure map of black roads and green spaces now. Long blue water and a volcano. Its X drawn in the space between breakwater walls, alongside a huge wooden warehouse and a vast rusty crane. Where we believed we'd find a pirate ship to take us to The Island. Where Mum believed we'd find a second life worthy enough that we could forget our first.

I lean back against the wall, look up at the ceiling. The rain sounds like hail, hard and echoless. El has gone. Everyone has gone. And that's when I finally start to cry. I curl up small enough that I can wrap my arms around myself as I sob. As all my grief, my regret, my horror, and my shame spills out of me and into the heavy dark corners of Mirrorland, leaving me nothing but empty.

CHAPTER 29

Logan finds me first. Though his shake is gentle, I come awake with a scream. Just as well then that I have no voice. He's inside the cupboard, crouched down over the threshold into Mirrorland. His hair is soaking wet, plastered to his skull. He doesn't touch me again, for which I'm grateful, but his expression is not one of a detective sergeant. I'm even more grateful for that.

"Cat. Are you all right? Can you get up?"

The answer is probably yes, but I don't really want to. I feel bone-weary. Maybe now that the adrenaline has worn off, whatever was in the Shiraz is kicking in again.

Light floods the cupboard as Rafiq pulls back the door, elbows Logan aside. I wonder if they had to break down the big red front door to get in. I hope so.

"Catriona?" She gives me a long assessing stare, head to toe. Never once stops looking like a detective inspector. And I find that I'm most grateful of all for that. "Where's Ross?"

I swallow. It hurts even more than I expect it to. "Are you here to arrest him?"

She points at my neck. "He do that to you?"

I nod.

"Where is he?"

I look down into the darkness of the staircase.

"All right, we need to get you out of here, and then we can go take care of Ross. Logan, take her to the front room, get a uniform to sit with her."

But I've no intention at all of limping quietly away. When I manage to stand, I don't take Logan's arm; instead I start stepping back down into Mirrorland.

"Shit, stop her, Logan!"

He tries to. It's too awkward in the confined space, and he's too focused on not hurting me. Evading him is easy, until he stops trying to manhandle me and takes my hand instead.

"Okay. You can come down with us. But we go first. All right?"

I hear Rafiq's tut, but she doesn't object.

I press myself up against the wall, let them both shuffle down past me. It's something of a relief. I don't know what we're going to find at the bottom.

"What the hell *is* this place?" Rafiq mutters, as we go down through the gloom towards the gold circle of Ross's hurricane lantern. She momentarily stops, turns to me. "Is this where—"

I nod once, quickly, and her expression sharpens.

At the bottom, Logan picks up the lantern.

"Left." My voice is whisper-thin.

We pass the armoire, the Silver Cross pram. Our feet sink down into the floorboards of the washhouse. My heart is beating faster, but only a little. I don't know what I want to find. I don't know whether I want Ross to be alive or dead.

The lanternlight swings left, finds him. He's crawled from the stern—as far as the gun deck and El's chalk scrawls of *Rum and Water Stores HERE!!*—but he isn't moving now. And then he flinches against the light, moans loud enough to kick-start my heart again. He looks up, tries to rise. His left eye is completely shut, the wound above it scabbed over with blood.

Rafiq turns back around to me. "You do that to him?"

I nod.

"What's going on?"

I recoil from his voice, I can't help it. He still sounds like Ross, and I don't see how that's possible.

Rafiq moves around Logan, drops down to her haunches. "Can you stand?"

Ross looks up at her with his one good eye. "I think so."

"We'll get those head wounds seen to down at the Royal," Rafiq says. "Logan, give us a hand."

I stand there on deck as they both haul him to his feet. He sways for a few seconds, leans heavily against the washhouse wall of sea and sky. He looks at me.

"What . . . what's going on? Cat?"

Rafiq takes one short step away from him. "Ross MacAuley, I am arresting you on suspicion of common-law assault to injury. You're not obliged to say anything, but anything you do say can and will be used against you. Do you understand?"

Ross's mouth opens and closes twice. He shakes his head. "I haven't done anything." He pushes off the wall, and only Logan's grip on his arm keeps him from lurching towards me. "Cat, tell them! Nothing's happened. It was just a disagreement and it got out of hand, that's all. I haven't done anything!"

I touch my still-burning throat out of little more than reflex, and he inhales sharply, as if he's only just noticed the marks there. He looks horrified. I wonder if he's as practiced in forgetting what he doesn't want to remember as I am.

"I think you have, Ross. In fact, I think you've been pretty busy." There's something quite dangerous about Rafiq down here. Her crust is much thinner. She's angry, but more than that, she's excited. "We were coming here today to detain you for wasting police time and hindering an investigation. We believe the statement you gave us regarding your whereabouts on the day of your wife's disappearance is false."

Ross says nothing.

"I've had a very interesting conversation with a Professor Catherine Ward." Rafiq gives me a sidelong look. "She wanted to follow up on her reply to an email I apparently sent her."

"I don't know who that is," Ross says, but the confusion in his voice has been replaced by caution.

"Well, she knows who *you* are. Has made, in fact, a statement to the effect that she witnessed you loading your suitcase into your car and leaving Southwark University twenty-two hours before you said you did."

"No, I—"

"We're currently checking ANPR cameras and CCTV footage, so we *will* track the timeline of your journey all the way back here,

Ross." She folds her arms. "We also got a warrant to check your phone records on the third; lucky for us, your phone was switched on when PC Thompson phoned at eighteen thirty to tell you about your wife's disappearance. And where do you think your phone company's cell-site dump placed you?"

"I was just driving." Ross looks worried. He's no longer leaning against either Logan or the wall. "I was just fucking driving!" He points a finger at me. "I told her that. Ask her!"

"I don't need to ask anyone. I already know you were in Edinburgh."

"She phoned me—El phoned *me*! *She* asked me to come back."

"So, why did you not tell PC Thompson—"

Logan steps between them. "He's got a head injury, boss."

"And, like I said," Rafiq says, never taking her eyes off Ross, "we'll be getting that seen to down at the Royal."

"I don't know!" Ross shouts. "We were having problems, I told you that. I just needed time to think. I had no time to bloody think! I just parked somewhere after driving through the night and slept in the car. That's all! I knew it would look bad, I . . . maybe I panicked. I don't know. I don't—"

"There *was* one phone call logged to you at seventeen thirty on the second, but it wasn't from El. It was from an insurance company based in Newhaven. And when Logan here gave them a ring, they told him it was likely a courtesy callback because you'd completed an online quote inquiry the previous day. And can you imagine our surprise when we found out what kind of insurance it is they specialize in?"

Ross's face is gray. His whole body is vibrating, and even now, my throat swollen and throbbing, my stomach clenched tight with something like hate, it takes far too much effort not to go to him.

"Accidental or negligence-based marine insurance," Rafiq says. Her eyes shine. "Bit of a coincidence, wouldn't you say? That why you didn't take it out in the end? Thought even us plods might find that a wee bit too suspicious the day before your wife disappears in her boat?"

"This is wrong," Ross says. "You're fucking wrong."

Rafiq shakes her head. "D'you remember that anonymous phone call I questioned you about two days after El went missing? Well, yesterday, two people actually came forward to make official statements alleging that you were hurting El—"

"What? Who?"

"I can't tell you that," Rafiq says. But I think of Anna's determined grief, the long black line of mascara from her left eye to her temple. And Marie's dismissive smile when I threatened to report her if she didn't leave us alone.

Rafiq pauses, then reaches into her pocket. "We've also got a second warrant to search this house." Her voice drops, softens. "So I'll ask you just once more, Ross. Do you know what happened to your wife?"

"Boss," Logan says, "we can't do this, not until he gets seen by a doc. You know that." And then closer, under his breath: "We can't fuck this up now."

"He knows," I say. As loud as I can, even though it hurts. It hurts more to look at Ross, but I do that too. Because now, surely, even he can see the writing on the wall. Red and stark and bloody. "He knows. Because he killed her."

"No!"

Rafiq turns, cocks an eyebrow at me. "Do you have any proof of that?"

"The kayak in the shed. And I found a chest inside Blue—inside the bedroom at the end of the corridor upstairs." I swallow before I remember it's a bad idea—the pain is momentarily so bad it eclipses everything else, even the burn of Ross's horrified gaze. I raise my head, look back at him without faltering. "I found your Treasure Trophies."

"Cat." Rafiq turns me towards her.

"I think it's a drain plug," I say. Sorrow washes through me, leaving me emptier still. "And a hole saw."

Ross makes a sound somewhere between a shout and a moan, and I close my eyes as Rafiq thunders back up the stairs.

"What are you doing, Cat?" His voice is broken, as hoarse as mine. "How can you—"

"Ross, I'd advise you to stop talking." Logan's expression is pained. "For your own sake."

Rain drums against wood. Pain is everywhere now, not just in my throat, and I have to numb myself against it: the fear, the horror, the regrets that are growing—too fast for me to think of anything else. *Think of El. Not him. Think of El.*

When Rafiq comes back, I've stopped shaking. She marches over to me, ignores both Ross and Logan.

"Is there anything else?"

I can hear the flat, echoless rhythm of police boots against mosaic tiles. The groan of the landing, the scream of a dusty black door. I stand on the *Satisfaction* and look up into the dark of Mirrorland's alleyway, my thin sips of breath getting thinner as I think of us battling storms and brigantines. Looking up, always up. Towards the screams of splintering wood and dying men, the bellows of cannon and musketoons, the roar of the squall.

I reach into my jeans pocket for the letter El wrote to me, hold it out to Rafiq.

She pulls some latex gloves out of her coat. Opens the letter, reads it, takes a sharp inhalation of breath. And when someone shouts down from the summit of Mirrorland, "They've found them, ma'am," something a lot more savage than relief lights up her face.

Ross makes a sound that's half gasp, half moan.

"Don't look at him, look at me," Rafiq snaps. But her eyes are shining, shining. "Is there *anything* else?"

"He's been drugging me." My voice is less than a whisper now. I point towards the glass of wine on the corridor floor. "I think he drugged El too."

"No!" Ross shouts. When I look around, I see that Logan's actively having to restrain him now. "She's lying!"

But I don't cringe from him anymore. Not even from his shouts, his curses. I hear the spin and click of handcuffs. Logan's grunts of effort as he tries to drag Ross back towards the Shank.

"It wasn't me! I didn't kill her! I loved her. Tell them, Cat. Tell them, you lying bitch! It wasn't me. I didn't do anything! I loved her! I loved you!" His eyes trap mine one last time. *"I let go!"*

My fingers press hard against my throat, so that the pain is all I can feel or see or hear. And when I open my eyes again, Ross is gone.

"It'll be okay," Rafiq says, and her voice is kind. She pulls my fingers from my throat. The arm she puts around me is still and sure and comforting.

"I know," I whisper. Because in Mirrorland, anything— everything—is possible. In Mirrorland, you are safe. Fear is never to be feared, horror is only make-believe, and escape is inside every bone and vein and breath and brick. And all it asks for in return is one thing. Only ever one thing. That you have to be brave.

And so, for the first time in a long time, I am.

CHAPTER 30

I arrive early. Sit behind the wheel of Vik's beat-up Golf, watch the car park fill up through a windscreen obscured by rain. My eyes are gritty, sore through lack of sleep and a new kind of merciless grief that sits heavy and strange on my chest. I can't get rid of it. I can't pretend it's not there. It's taken everything that was sustaining me, keeping me alive throughout the trial and the two months since—my anger, my pain, my need for revenge and justice and closure. And it's eroded all of it down to nothing. A once-towering cliff ground into powder and washed out to sea.

The prison looks modern, sleek, not at all what I'd been imagining. The slit-windows and dark guard towers of Shawshank maybe. Instead, it's smooth and curved and no more than two stories high, matte-beige sandstone and big windows, HMP SHOTTS in gray glossy relief over the revolving entrance door.

I feel nervous, scared, sick to my stomach, but more clearheaded than I have in a long time. It's been two weeks since I last had a drink. Every morning throughout September, I used vodka to fortify myself for another day of *HM Advocate vs. MacAuley* in Court 9 of the High Court of Justiciary. Invariably, I'd end up drinking behind closed curtains instead, but some days my resolve would win. And every one of those days—reporters, cameras, stares, whispers, intimate details, *Ross*—would be followed by long, numb spaces of nothing. Familiar fantasies kept me company in the darkness, and I would become convinced that the trial was just another dream, another place inside the cold stone walls of Mirrorland.

I was drunk on the day the jury of seven women and eight men finally came back with a verdict. The sticky-hot Court 9 hummed and thrummed; my stomach squeezed, my hands shook. I hid close to the back of the court, but, just like all the journalists and rubber-neckers on Parliament Square, Ross saw me straightaway. He looked tired, so thin. And I loathed the ache in me, the echo of longing.

I barely heard the jury find him guilty by majority verdict of the common-law murder of El. But I did hear him cry out—once, long and loud; the back of his voice broke on it—before the courtroom erupted into chaos and Rafiq appeared to pull me away from gawking faces and shouted questions.

I close my eyes. I don't know if I can face this. If I can face him. I think of that terrible cry again. Try to use it to make me feel brave, strong, *better*. But I'm no good at lying to myself anymore. I've lost the ability.

I take the letter out of my pocket again. Battered and crumpled because I can't leave it alone. "CAT" printed in El's handwriting across its envelope. It came two months after Ross's conviction. Two days after Vik texted me asking for my new address. I'd used my dwindling savings to pay the deposit and first month's rent on a cheap bedsit on the edge of Leith, because every new day of square lawns and apple trees, of gray ashlar bricks and Georgian bar windows, copper bells, red doors, and gold light, had become a torture—one that I'd started to crave, to need, to look forward to. Like a toxic love affair. Or a fantasy world of monsters and ghosts. When I first closed the bedsit's door and sat down on its sagging bed, I cried with relief.

I take the letter out of the envelope, pick up the smaller piece of paper inside before it can fall onto my lap, look down at the *Dear Cat* and *All my love, El*, and all the dreadful words in between. When I first opened it, there was a scrawled note too. *She told me not to read it. So I don't know if it will help or make things a hundred times worse. Vik.*

April 3rd

Dear Cat,

This is the last letter I'm going to write to you. I should have written it before now, but I didn't know how. And now I can't put it off any longer.

I've lied to you. More times than I can count. More times than I

should have. But you need to know that it was for you: everything I
kept from you, every lie I told you, every time I said trust me, this is
the truth now—and it never was.

Trust me. This is the truth now.

I look out at the cars, the people, the blurred beige and gray, open
the glove box and push the letter inside. This new grief might be
heavy and cruel, but this new sense of responsibility is worse, heavier; a dread no longer silvery but black and thick like cooling tar. I
used to think that people whose lives were stuck in limbo carried on
only because it was easier. Easier than giving up. Easier than stopping. But now I know it's because there's no alternative, no escape.
That the tide will come, and all you can do is stay afloat. And wait
for it to turn.

I fold up the smaller piece of paper and push it into my jeans
pocket. Open the car door and get out. Face those smooth stone
walls and high windows.

Because I can't put it off any longer either.

*

I try not to look at the receptionist who checks my ID, or at my
unsteady hands as I put my phone and bag inside a locker, or at the
guard as I walk through the metal detector and consent to a rub-
down search. The secure waiting area is upstairs, and I sit down,
keep my eyes trained on the neutral carpet. Maybe no one knows
who I am anyway, or who I'm here to see.

Ross's sentencing was big news. It was televised. I watched it
alone, in the dark, while reporters banged on my door. The judge's
voice reminded me of Mum's: high and hectoring, inviting neither
opinion nor dissent.

Mr. Ross Iain MacAuley, a jury has found you guilty by majority ver-
dict of the callous murder of your wife, Ellice MacAuley. After subjecting
her to months, perhaps years, of physical and mental abuse, you decided
and then planned, motivated in part perhaps by the realization that she
was intending to leave you, to murder her and pass it off as an accident
at sea. I find that showed significant premeditation and cold-headedness.

*I also find that you believed you would profit financially from her death.
You pled not guilty. You have shown no remorse. Against these aggravating
factors, I find little in the way of mitigation. Therefore, I feel I must pass a
sentence of life imprisonment, with a punishment part of fifteen years for
the murder of Ellice MacAuley, and three years for attempting to defeat the
ends of justice.*

The reporters have stopped hounding me now. The trial, the conviction, have already been all but forgotten. And Rafiq was wrong.
No one has made any connection between us and the two twelve-
year-old girls found at Granton Harbour in 1998. And no one has
mentioned the murder-suicide at 36 Westeryk Road, except as maca-
bre coincidence.

I catch the eye of an old man with yellow whiskers, and when he
grins, I look away. The intermittent bang of vending machines turns
my headache into a dull throb.

A guard opens a door, beckons us all with a half-arsed finger.
"Twelve," he says to me as I pass him inside the doorway. I find the
table, sit down, clasp my fingers together. I don't want to see him. I
never wanted to have to see him again. And yet.

The prisoners file in. I feel Ross before I see him: a trickle of
cold against my spine, a flutter in my heart. He stops next to the
table, long enough that I have to look up. He looks great. His hair is
short. His eyes are no longer bloodshot, the skin beneath them clear.
On the day he took the stand, the flesh beneath his cheekbones was
sunken, dark with stubble. He was charming, passionate, credible.
He cried. Though I'd felt his stare throughout most of the trial, that
day he never glanced in my direction once.

"Hello, Cat," he says, and his smile is warm, unsure. "It's good to
see you. I didn't think I would." The last is a question, but I refuse to
answer it, not yet. I need to be in control of this whole conversation;
I can't let any bit of him in until I've made my choice.

He sits down, keeps his smile. When he stretches out his legs, I
cross mine at the ankles under the seat of my chair. But when he
clears his throat, I make myself look at him. If I can't do that, I'm
screwed before I've even started.

"Why are you here?" His gaze is too intense. Peat-brown eyes flecked with silver.

I close mine, and they sting. Because I've been grieving for him too, I can't pretend I haven't. "I don't know yet."

He leans closer. Close enough that I can smell him. "I want—I need—you to know how sorry I am about what happened that night . . ." He swallows, and his throat clicks. "I'm so sorry that I hurt you, Cat. I've thought about it every day, and I don't blame you for what you said at the trial, I don't blame you for anything. I promise you I don't."

Because I am the main reason he's here. I am why there was so *little in the way of mitigation*. I was the Crown's best witness, and the most damning part of my testimony was not what I'd found or heard, not even the oxycodone and diazepam that they found in my wineglass and my blood—but the fact that Ross and I had been having sex. I endured the telling of that truth, even the snide cross-examination of it by Ross's QC and then the wider, snider world, because it was so damning. So much of the prosecution's case was circumstantial: El's letter, Ross's false statements, the physical finds, the mobile phone data, camera footage, even the turning up of a will that Ross knew nothing about, in which El left everything of hers to only me. None of it perhaps would have been enough. But her husband—her charming, handsome, grief-stricken husband; YouTube's *wailing widower*—shagging her twin sister within days of her disappearance carried a deliciously scandalous weight that would not be moved. Even as I was testifying, I could see the jury members bristling.

"That last night in Mirrorland, I want you to know that I would never . . . I would never have—everything just got out of hand, and you wouldn't listen." He shakes his head hard. "But I let go, Cat. I let go. You know I—"

"I don't want to talk about that."

He purses his lips, furrows his brow. "But I need you to believe that I wouldn't—"

"You wouldn't have killed me." It's an effort to keep my voice steady, neutral, because I'm not sure that's true. But I believe he believes it. He believes that there was never a shining madness in his eyes, nor fat pulsing veins in his neck as he choked mine tighter. We only ever believe what we want—what we need—to believe.

He smiles. There's a dried spot of blood under his chin, and I find myself wondering if he shaved for me again. But this time I don't shiver. I don't hate him anymore. I've worked hard at not hating him. Perhaps too hard.

Under the table, I pinch my skin. "It's kind of ironic." My voice is too high, too loud. "Me visiting you in prison, instead of the other way around."

Ross flushes, and although his smile endures, it's insecure, uncertain, hides its teeth. Should he laugh? Is it a joke? Is it a joke he's supposed to laugh at? I've never been disposed to studying his reactions before, but now it's as if every thought process is lit up in neon above his head. I wonder if he's always had to pretend to be human, if it's always been this obviously hard.

It suddenly occurs to me that the prison might be listening in on our conversation. Is that allowed? The possibility makes my heart beat too fast again; cool sweat slides between my shoulder blades. Ross looks at me, and I reach for my calm, my anger, because it doesn't matter. Nothing matters but the choice I'm here to make.

I lower my voice, soften my tone, look into his eyes as if I want to. "There are some things I need to ask. Things I need to know. And I need you to tell me the truth."

Ross casts his gaze quick around the room. "I've told the truth, Cat."

"Then it should be easy."

He blinks. "And then can we start over?"

"I don't know what happens next yet."

"Okay." Another smile. When he sees me hesitate, he leans even closer. "I didn't kill her. I swear it, Cat. I didn't kill El."

"That's not what I want to know."

He can't hide his surprise, his relief.

"Why did you drug us?"

When he immediately shakes his head, I stand up fast, start moving away from the table.

"Wait. Wait!" His shout is loud enough to attract the attention of the prison guard closest to us, tall and bored and chewing gum. Ross shows him the palm of his hand and drops his head down, stares at the table between us. "Please, Cat. Sit down. I'll tell you the truth."

I sit down.

When Ross finally looks up again, his eyes are blurry. "Because I wanted you to stay. I always want you to stay."

"You didn't think we'd stay *without* being drugged?"

"I know it was wrong, weak. But when Mum left—when she just woke up one day and decided to take me and leave Dad, it shocked me. That someone could do that and never look back." He closes his eyes tight like a child. "And then, after he killed himself, it *terrified* me."

He reaches his hands across the table. His nails are ragged. "When El was—when she got depressed . . . I got scared. I didn't know what to do. I thought she might try to hurt herself again. I just wanted to look after her, to help her, that was all." He leans closer. "And with you . . . I was so scared of losing you again—I could feel it happening. Because when you went to America, Cat"—he swallows—"you never once looked back. Not once. But I'm—"

"Why did you want me?"

"What?" The confusion is back. His hands are reaching for me again, though I don't think he knows it. "Because I love you. I've always loved you. You know that." He holds my gaze, until I feel something inside me giving way. *This is Ross*, it says. But straightaway, I harden against it. The reflex and the longing.

"Then why did you choose El instead of me? Why was it always her?"

For a moment, he's silent, but the neon over his head is still flashing panic, uncertainty. *What does she want me to say?*

"Was it because you wanted her more? Or because you loved her more? Or maybe because she needed you more than I did? Or you needed her?" I force myself to relax. "Just tell me the truth, Ross, that's all. Not what you think I want you to say, or what you think is the right thing to say. Just the truth. That's all I want."

The brightness that comes into his eyes then has all the confidence of someone who's sure their answer will be all three: what I want, what is right, and the truth. He beams all that brightness onto me. "I didn't love her more than you, you know I didn't. I did love her, but with you it's always been different. Easier. Better." His smile is sad, eager. "I chose El because you're right, she needed me more than you did. I couldn't leave her. I *couldn't*."

I let out a long, slow breath. "That's what I thought you'd say."

He hears something in my voice, some remnant of anger that I'm no longer trying so hard to hide. He withdraws his hands, his smile disappears. It hasn't worked, his perfect answer, and he knows it.

"Cat, this is beginning to feel a bit like an interrogation, and I've just about had enough of them. I told you I didn't kill El. I would never have killed El. But if that's what all these bloody questions are leading up to, I'll tell you again. I didn't do it."

I don't answer him, barely manage to look at him. But a part of me—the good little girl who has never been able to learn that love can't ever be trusted, still—*still*—wants to comfort him, wants to press the pad of my thumb against that deep frown line between his eyes and smooth it flat.

Emboldened, he sits up taller. "I mean, think about it, Cat. You must have. If I'd wanted to kill her, if I'd organized it all down to the most minute detail like that fucking oily lawyer said, why would I screw up my alibi so badly? Why would I have let a witness see me leave? Why would I have left my phone on? And why the fuck would I have left all that so-called evidence lying around the house? That Treasure Trophy stuff was juvenile crap, and you know it. He twisted it, just like he twisted us." He's angry now and can't help directing some of it at me. "And you let him. You helped him."

"Maybe I believed him."

"You didn't!" He bangs his fists on the table, making me jump, and the prison guard looks over. Ross lifts up his palm again, drops his head, but when he looks back up at me, his gaze is anything but submissive. "Why would I do it, Cat? Why the fuck would I have done any of it?"

I think of that terrible day under the willow tree when he cupped my face in his hands, tried to catch my tears with his thumbs, his eyes full of grief as I begged him *Don't, please*. I think of him barefoot, in old jeans and a Black Sabbath tour T-shirt. His messy hair, his dear and familiar face. The filthy, wonderful words he always whispered against my skin: the promises, the kindnesses, the hope. The fierceness with which he held me, touched me, kissed me. As if nothing else mattered. As if there was no one left in the world but him and me. How much I wanted that to be true.

And I think of a child who chose to believe in superheroes and fairy-tale villains rather than in anything real. Anything sharp enough to wound, to cause scars that she'd be unable to forget. To unsee.

"You did it because, one day, we might have sailed away from you again," I say. "Because you couldn't trust us to stay. Better to be sure. Better to make us. So you lied and you manipulated, and you drugged and you plotted, and you divided to rule. Because you're a coward." I think of the Shank. *I'll let both of you out, but only if you promise never to run away. If you promise to stay with me forever.* "Because stealing someone else's air is how you breathe." *Stay with me. Be with me. I love you. I need you. El would want us to be happy.*

I look down at the plastic tabletop, its stains and scratches. "You chose El because you thought she was weaker than me." I think of her lying in that hospital bed, dark-ringed eyes in a talc-white face, that tired and trembling smile. But I can't. I can't. If I think about that, I'll unravel completely. "And you're so good at it, Ross. You can make someone believe that your want is *their* want, their idea, their betrayal. And afterwards, when you banish them into exile, you can make them believe that was their fault too."

"I don't know what the fuck you're talking about."

I haven't heard this voice before. Low, snide, sharp. I wonder if it's the one he was born with.

"Mum was the only one who saw you, who knew you for what you were. And she never even met you. She tried to warn us, but she'd brought us up in a dark and exciting world, full of pirates and witches and red poisoned apples. It was why we wanted a sly and handsome Prince Charming who couldn't ever be trusted in the first place."

I watch his face change. All his rage twisting and boiling under his handsome, careful mask. And it bolsters my resolve. I prefer him angry. "Except that was never what you were, was it? It was never *who* you were. Are."

"What the fuck are you—"

"You're Blackbeard."

Mum pinching our skin, pointing at that black ship always on the horizon. *You hide from Bluebeard, because he's a monster. Because he'll catch you, and make you his wife, and then hang you on his hook until you die. But you run from Blackbeard, because he's sly, because he lies. Because no matter where you go, he'll always be there, right behind you. And when he catches you, he'll throw you to the sharks.*

His eyes darken, his mouth curves up into a sneer that's pretending to be kind. All that boiling rage is calm now; I'm not worth its trouble. "Cat, I think maybe you need to see someone. The last few months have been—"

"I've made a choice, Ross." I look at him, commit every line and color and shadow of him to memory; everything on the surface and everything beneath. *This* is Ross. This is what I'll remember if ever I think of him again.

"*What the fuck* are you talking about?"

"I wasn't sure what my choice would be, but now I am." I reach into my pocket, take out the small piece of paper. I allow myself just one more second's hesitation before I put the Black Spot on the table and push it towards Ross. "I choose *Punishment.*"

He reaches out a hand, and then snatches it back. His face is a study in baffled anguish.

"Cat, I don't know what's going on. I don't know what you mean." He looks down at the Black Spot. A single tear splashes against the underside of his wrist. I flatly ignore the clench in my belly. "I don't know what *this* means."

I stand up, put my palms flat against the tabletop, lean as close as I can bear to. "It means give it up, Ross. I can see you."

When he looks at me, I recoil from his expression, stumble against my bolted-down chair.

"You're witches," he says, and his smile is pure Ross: crooked

268

and sexy, slow and intimate. Left canine overlapping his front incisor. "Both of you. Crazy, fucked-up witches. You've ruined my life."

The last gasp of doubt drains out of me. I smile, and it's easier than I ever imagined it would be. "You just chose the wrong victims," I say. "That's all."

And then I start to walk away from him, towards the waiting room.

"No!" Ross shouts, standing up and lunging for me, squeezing my arm tightly inside his fingers. Hard enough that I know I'll have to see their black imprint for days. "You can't leave me. You don't get to leave me!"

Everyone is looking at us. The tall guard is striding towards us, followed by at least two others, even though I'm not afraid, I'm not trying to struggle, I'm not trying to get away. I look hard at Ross, and something in him deflates. His face goes slack, his eyes turn wet and pleading. "You can't leave. You can't leave me. I didn't do it, Cat. Please! I didn't kill her."

He tugs at my arm, pulls me closer. And until that tall guard and his colleagues get too close, I let him. Everyone is still looking at us. I keep looking only at him. *I loved you so much.* But I don't dare think it for more than a moment, because he's taken enough of me already.

"I didn't kill her, Cat!"

I close my eyes. Briefly press my lips against his ear. "I know."

And then I do leave him. Raging and screaming and sobbing in my wake. I don't look back. I close the door behind me. I leave him hanging on his hook to rot.

Outside, the rain has stopped and the sun, low and blurred, turns glass sparkling and the prison golden. I stand in the middle of the car park with my arms and fingers spread wide, head tipped up to the sky. And then I close my eyes and let the world burn warm and red.

I looked, El, I think. *And I didn't go blind.*

CHAPTER 31

April 3rd

Dear Cat,

This is the last letter I'm going to write to you. I should have written it before now, but I didn't know how. And now I can't put it off any longer.

I've lied to you. More times than I can count. More times than I should have. But you need to know that it was for you: everything I kept from you, every lie I told you, every time I said trust me, this is the truth now—and it never was.

Trust me. This is the truth now.

<u>Here is the why:</u>

Do you remember what upset me the most the day we found that encyclopedia entry about Captain Henry Morgan? It was that Mum had lied to us, and for so long. I don't think I ever fully trusted her again. I stopped believing in her. I stopped believing in us. All because of one lie.

Do you remember what upset you the most? It wasn't that Mum had lied to us, or even that he wasn't our dad. It was the fact that he liked to torture people by tightening bands around their head until their eyes popped out. Because that wasn't how a pirate king behaved—a father, a hero, a man. And so you instantly forgot it. You withdraw from what you can't bear to be true and you believe the lie. And when you stopped talking to me—when you refused to ever talk about that last horrible night in Mirrorland—I withdrew from you, because the truth was <u>all</u> I could see. It felt like a slow-spreading disease, one that I couldn't bear to pass on to you. I didn't <u>want</u> you to remember.

But then Ross came back. Long before that day outside the National Gallery. For months, he followed me, harassed me, begged for forgiveness. I hated him. I hated him so much for that night. But he was all that was left of Mirrorland and he knew it. That day outside the gallery? It was to show me that if he couldn't get to me, he could get to you instead. And that May Day in the Rosemount was him proving it.

So I had to make him believe that he wanted me more. I had to make him think that I needed him more. I faked my suicide attempt—you always knew it, but he didn't. To him, it was the ultimate proof of loyalty. And maybe it was. Because I've tried to tell myself that I did it for you. To protect you from a monster just like you protected me. But I don't think that was the whole truth. Not then. Because I still loved him.

So maybe our marriage was my punishment. My sentence. I didn't lie to you about that. One day he'd be raging and cruel, the next so loving it was like agony. I'd get these cards, threatening me, telling me to leave—I guess he did it just to mess with my mind. Like the drugs he put in my food and drink. He hides them in his bedside table. And every day, I wake up craving them so much, I can't think straight. They're chains. Just like those "freedoms" that I told you he's allowed me to have. He succeeded, in the end, in chasing off Mouse after she came back. And when he thought I might be having an affair with my friend Vik, he threatened to find out who he was and kill him. He stopped letting me do any voluntary work. Threatened to stop letting me paint, if I ever contacted either of them again. To take away my boat. He even papered over the door to Mirrorland. And I let him do all of those things. Until I wanted to die for real.

He found me, of course. Made me vomit all the pills back up, made me walk around that fucking house until I could see and hear and cry again. And that was when he told me that he was still in touch with you. That if I ever tried to leave him again, he would do everything to you that he had done to me. And I remembered that encyclopedia entry about Captain Henry Morgan. I knew that you'd try to survive by pretending what was happening wasn't happening. By pretending your prison wasn't a prison and your jailer wasn't a monster. Until the day that you died. And so, of all the whys, that's the real one. I'm not noble, I'm not brave. He just finally made a mistake. He gave me no possibility at all of parole.

Here is the how:

I like to plan, remember? Just like Andy Dufresne. So, here is THE PLAN No. 2.

Phase I: It was Vik who unwittingly gave me the idea for using The Redemption. He works for Lothian Marine Insurance, specializing in accident or negligence claims for recreational vessels. He told me all sorts of stories of deliberate sabotage—and how they were discovered. Yesterday evening, I visited him at his huge open-plan office, and while he was making coffee, I went to an empty desk on the other side of the building to call Ross and beg him to come back from London. I'd already made an online query in his name from our home computer, requesting a callback. The call should never be traced back to me through Vik because he's just a very small cog in a very big wheel; Lothian Marine Insurance employs thousands of people— and anyway, no one other than Ross even knows we're friends, and he doesn't know Vik's name. I have a second phone, a pay-as-you-go that I use to talk to friends without Ross knowing. And I've made Vik swear never to go to the police, no matter what happens to me. When LMI call back Ross for real, he'll hang up before they get to the end of their first sentence; he hates cold calling. So he will have no alibi. And a husband speaking to a marine insurance company the day before his wife is lost at sea is perhaps unlucky, but more likely guilty.

I bought a drain plug with cash a few weeks ago. Exactly the same as the one I already have. I bought two hole saws. I've drilled some holes with the first in the underside of the cuddy that will hopefully go unnoticed because I need that saw to be forensically traced back to the boat. I've left that and the new drain plug in the house, in Bluebeard's Room, and my kayak in the shed, where I hope the police will eventually find them.

When the time comes, I'll take the original drain plug out, toss it into the firth. It shouldn't ever be discovered, because it takes a while for a boat to sink only from the lack of that. I'll sail to the deepwater channel, take down the mast, disable the EPIRB and GPS. The hole saw is more of a risk. The boat will sink fast after I've used it for real, but I'll just have to throw it overboard as far as I can and hope that The Redemption drifts far enough that the hole saw is never found.

Phase II: One good thing about Ross: he's predictable. A few weeks before I had anything close to resembling even a Phase I, I found the note he left me all those years ago, setting me up to catch you both in the Rosemount. It was in his wallet, of all places—I guess he still likes his trophies. Finding it was a gift. Because I couldn't be sure that he'd get the blame for my death, that he'd even be suspected of it. I could be sure that you'd come back. That he'd get to you, try to keep you. Unless I could get to you first. Both of us have to escape—that's the deal I've made with myself. That's the whole point of THE PLAN No. 2.

For weeks now, I've been acting like the abused wife I am, instead of hiding it. It's surprisingly liberating. And it's surprising too, how comforting it is to know that friends really are friends, that all they want to do is help. (By the way, if you've met her, I'm sorry about Anna, she can be loyal to a fault. But if you need her, she'll be on your side.)

I know how Ross works. I know the what, the why, the when, the how of everything that he'll say and do to you. I've even given Vik a timetable for the email clues I've asked him to send you as Mouse. Please believe me, if I could spare you any of this, I would. But there's no other way. And I think you'll work all of it out just like you're supposed to. I think you'll remember. I think you'll stop believing the lie. I think you'll believe me. I think you'll be believed. I think you'll be the one who finds him guilty, and then the world will follow. I think you'd avenge me before you'd ever think of saving yourself. That is my hope. That is my plan. That is what keeps me sane.

Because today I'm going to die. I can say that now, I can think it, and most of the fear has gone. Maybe that's because I'm more like Red than Andy now: institutionalized, beyond redemption. But I'm not brave enough to drown. It would look worse for Ross if I did, but every time I think of it I see that poison taster, choking on a black and boiling pearl, and I know I can't do it. I've been stockpiling my antidepressants. And there are the pills in Ross's bedside drawer. I have to hope that they'll be enough. I have to hope that this time the plan is foolproof; this time we both get out and stay out. Maybe you think suicide is a pretty fucked-up way to do it. I don't. I might have been faking it last time, but it worked. You escaped. All I want, to paraphrase Stephen King, is for you to get busy living while I get busy dying. Or, if that's too flip for you, maybe this is better. Think of a snowy day in the pantry. Mum sitting on the windowsill and reading Sydney Carton's last words before he was taken down to La Place de la Révolution. "It is a far, far better thing that I do, than I have ever done." Because it is. It makes me happy, at peace for the first time in years.

There's just one thing that doesn't. In doing all this, planning all this, I haven't given you a choice. We've never had many choices. No one ever thought to allow us any. This letter is your choice. It proves what I planned, what I did. You could show it to the police, or Ross's lawyer—because even if everything has gone to plan, I know he'll appeal; he'll never give up.

Maybe you still don't trust or believe a single word I say. But I hope you've remembered the truth anyway. I hope the house, the clues, the treasure hunt, the diary have worked, have forced you to face what really happened that last night of our first life in a way that I couldn't have by only telling you—that the person who was lying to you was you. Because I want you to choose what happens next. The Black Spot is yours. It's up to you what you do with it. Don't think about me. And never think that whatever choice you make is the wrong one.

Maybe I'm not so different from Mum after all. She told me once that a white lie was just a lie that hadn't got dirty yet, and I guess that's true—I guess I'm pretty dirty now. But that doesn't matter. Nothing matters except this: once upon a time, you saved my life. Now I'm saving yours. That's it. That's all.

Please. Don't stop believing in me.

All my love,

El xxx

CHAPTER 32

I take El to Lochend Cemetery to visit Mum. Set her down next to the headstone. Her urn is a great ugly thing: stern ceramic curlicues and brown flowers. It's become my security blanket.

I replace my white roses with a fresh bunch of red ones, look down at the grass, the headstone, the ornate gold writing. *GONE BUT NEVER FORGOTTEN.* And although I'm trying very hard these days not to forget anything at all, here I make an exception. I don't look at his name, I don't think of his face. I don't think of him lying next to Mum in the dark until they're both dust and earth and old stories.

I remember thinking that El loved *A Tale of Two Cities* because of its horror, its cruelty; Madame Defarge and her knitting needles. I remember standing in the sunlight of the back garden and thinking: *She's had my life for years. She's stolen it.* And being furious instead of grateful. Horrified. I don't deserve any of it. Mum's sacrifice, El's sacrifice. All their terrible years of suffering, while I wallowed in self-pity and wilful ignorance; a reflection in a mirror, a shadow on the ground, dark and flat and impermanent.

*

I hold a memorial. Put a notice in the paper. Plant a tree for El in public gardens close to Granton Harbour and the wide Forth. I make a terrible and stumbling speech mostly to people I don't know, who afterwards give me a half-arsed clap. I notice Marie standing maybe twenty yards away, but she moves no closer. And when I look again a few minutes later, she's gone.

Some people come back to the pub, but few stay beyond the complimentary drinks and sandwiches. Within a couple of hours, there's only Vik and Anna left. We talk about El, and it's less awkward than I imagined. By unspoken agreement, Vik and I don't talk about what she had him do. We don't talk about Ross or the trial. We talk about the El that we knew, the El that we miss. I stick to Diet Coke because I'd just about kill for a vodka. And when Rafiq pushes open the pub door with Logan in tow, I'm relaxed enough to be glad.

"That was a good speech, Cat," Rafiq says.

"You were there?"

Rafiq smiles. "Polis always loiter at the back like a bad smell."

"Double scotch is it, boss?" Logan mutters. And I realize, with a ridiculous pang, that he's shaved off his daft hair.

"Naw," she says, giving him the stink eye. "Double Talisker." She looks at us. "Anyone else? He's paying."

After Logan stomps off to the bar, Rafiq moves closer to the table, leans against the back of an empty chair.

"We'll just be staying for the one," she says. "If you don't mind, that is?"

"You're more than welcome." And I'm surprised to realize that I mean it. I'm surprised to realize that I miss her. Whenever I think of Rafiq now, it's not as a detective inspector but as the woman who got down on the floor and held me while I cried for my dead sister, rubbed slow warm circles across my back; the woman who never believed Ross and never believed me, and never gave up until she got an answer, an end. She knows there's more to it—of course she does—and maybe she knows that the answer she has is not even the true one. But I'm pretty certain she believes it's the right one.

I go to the bar to help Logan, and his smile is contagious, warming my stomach better than vodka.

"Hi."

"Hi."

"You shaved off your hair."

His smile turns sheepish. "Boss said I looked like a center forward for Chelsea, so . . ." He rubs his palm self-consciously against the nape of his neck.

"It looks good. Suits you."

"Yeah?"

I smile again. Am rewarded with a flash of teeth and dimples.

"So," he says. "What's next? Will you be going back to America?"

I look away from him and out at the gray rainy day, the slick cobbles, gothic spires, and sandstone tenements. "I don't know yet."

Logan stares hard at a point between my neck and shoulder. I can feel the heat rising in my cheeks, but Anna saves us both with a loud tut as she starts thumping the drinks onto a tray.

"There," she says, pushing it towards Logan. "Now maybe you can take them over *there*."

In the end, the five of us stay until it gets dark, until the pub starts filling up, getting noisy. Rafiq and Logan leave first. Rafiq holds out her hand, squeezes mine hard and quick.

"Take care of yourself, Cat."

"I will. Thank you. For everything you did."

She gives me one last long look. And then she nods, starts moving towards the door. "Logan, I'll wait in the car. Don't take half an hour."

He grins at me. "I've had better wingmen."

Someone jostles us closer, and I reach my arms up around his neck to hug him. "Goodbye, Logan."

He squeezes me, presses his face briefly against my neck. "Craig."

"I kind of prefer Logan," I say. "I've got a bit of a thing for super-heroes."

He draws back, gives a solemn nod. "I get that a lot."

"Thank you for every—"

"You don't have to say that. To either of us. We were just doing our job."

I smile, kiss him on the cheek. "I want to say thank you anyway."

He holds my gaze just long enough that I wish I'd said something more. "You've got my number, Cat. You know where I am."

And then he, too, is gone, leaving me feeling less bereft than wistful. I do, after all, know where he is. Where he will be.

In some ways, saying my goodbyes to Anna and Vik is easier. Anna gives me a quick hard hug, a kiss on each cheek, and a "Look after yourself" that has the tone of an order.

I look at Vik, his smile sad though it still crinkles the skin around his eyes. "I'm sorry for—"

"It doesn't matter anymore." And I hug him, squeeze his hand.

"I loved her so much," he says.

"I know. She knew too, Vik."

He blinks, looks away. I think not seeing me will be good for him; I know it's never me he sees.

When I leave the pub, I'm alone. But I'm not afraid when someone steps out of the shadows, blocking my way. Maybe because there's so little left to be afraid of now. Or because I've already guessed who it will be.

"Hello, Marie."

An oncoming car flashes gold against her skin, her eyes. "How are you, Catriona?"

"You could have come to the pub, you know."

"I didn't know if I would be welcome." Her smile is flat. Fleeting. She wouldn't have been, but what's the point in saying so now? "El would have wanted you to be there."

Her gloved fingers twine together, restless. "I didn't help her, but I helped you, didn't I?" She squints against the glare of another car. "I saved you. Didn't I?"

I look at her beautiful scarf, her leather gloves, immaculate makeup. All those terrible scars she thinks are hidden. I move forwards, take both of her hands in mine, and nod. Because in a strange way, she did. She woke me up. She made me remember what it was to be afraid. To be terrorized.

Her smile is brilliant. Her fingers strong as they grip mine back. "Be happy, *cherie*. *Vis ta vie*. For her."

She spins on her heels and I smell Chanel. And then she is gone.

*

I go back to the house alone. I don't really want to leave El in my crappy bedsit, but she deserves a return to this house even less.

The flat lawns of 36 Westeryk Road are littered with fag butts, empty juice bottles, and Greggs bags. I climb the stone steps up to the big red front door. The house has been locked up for months. When the solicitor first handed over the huge bunch of keys, I sat with them heavy in my lap for a long time, just looking at them, remembering *Run!*, the darkness and the thunder, my fingers pulling on the night latch again and again. Now I select the dead bolt key with steady fingers, listen to its heavy clunk as it turns, the sun warm against the back of my neck. I push open the door, step up into the entrance hall. The smell—old wood and old age—is tempered now with an air of abandonment, neglect, and the relief I feel belies my steadiness. There's an envelope addressed to me from National Records of Scotland lying on the mat. I pick it up, put it into my pocket.

Arcs of green and gold light crisscross the parquet, the banister, the grandfather clock. But I don't look up at the stained-glass window. I don't go upstairs. The solicitor suggested taking inventory, but I care about none of it. I've instructed him to sell the house and everything in it as soon as he can. I'm pretty sure that Ross will agree. What is the point, after all, in a prison without prisoners?

I'm here for me. For whatever it is I left behind. Because I still can't move on. I still don't deserve what El did, what Mum did; I still can't find a way to live with myself. I know that I need to shake it: this martyred despondency, this fucking ingratitude. I know the longer I don't, the more I'm letting El down. But it still doesn't feel right—it feels horribly, horribly wrong—and I don't know why.

I walk through the staircase's shadow, pull open the heavy black curtain. Dust makes me sneeze, allows me to reach the other end of the pantry without having to look or linger. I step up into the cupboard, slide back the bolts, turn on my light, and step down into Mirrorland for the last time.

The sun breaks white through the cracks in the roof. I smell the damp wood and musty air, feel the hairs rise up from my skin and scalp, hear the echoes of our whispers, giggles, screams. At the bottom, I turn left without looking right, keep going until I'm in the washhouse. Someone has cleaned up Ross's blood; the *Satisfaction* no longer has a gun deck or rum store. I walk to the main deck and sit, cross my legs, look up at the green ocean and white frills of waves, at the blue sky and white puffs of clouds. The Jolly Roger with its painted skull and crossbones. The hulking specter of Blackbeard's ship beyond the empty lantern hook.

I don't know how long I stay there. Long enough for those cracks of white to dim, leaving me in darkness except for the fading day through the washhouse's window. I don't know who or what I think of, but by the time I come back, I'm stiff, sore, lighter.

I get up, massage the feeling back into my legs and arms. Take down the Jolly Roger and fold it into a square. Run my fingers over the chalk and stone of the washhouse walls as I leave. At the bottom of the staircase, I look once more around Mirrorland: its countries and its borders, its bricks and its wood, its cobwebs and its shadows. And then I climb the stairs.

Close the door to Mirrorland. And bolt it shut.

I start a coal fire in Mum's Kitchener, and when the flames are hot and high, I hold my hands over them until the heat spreads through me. I open the NRS envelope, pull out Mum's birth certificate, and the four others I requested all those months ago: Jennifer, Mary, two Margarets. Under *Father's name* for Mary Finlay, it says Robert John Finlay; *Occupation*, Fisherman. And under *Date of Birth*: Third of March, 1962, at 14:32. I look at Mum's certificate. Nancy Finlay was born on the Third of March, 1962, at 14:54.

I sit down at the kitchen table. Twins. Mum and the Witch had been twins. Not Mirror Twins like El and me. Not even identical twins. Because Mum was as light as the Witch was dark; as small as the Witch was tall. But still twins nonetheless. I think of the hate in the Witch's eyes—the hate for her own sister—and another wave of shame threatens to dissolve the small amount of peace that saying goodbye to Mirrorland has given me.

I look across at the bell board. And then out the window. Bright sunlight instead of blood-red colors the high garden wall. I will never know if the bells rang or if HE KNOWS really was painted on the wall that last night with Ross. I will never know if El whispered *RUN!* hot against my skin. But it doesn't matter. Mirrorland existed because we believed in it. It was real to us. And that's how it saved us.

I stand up. Go over to the Kitchener. Drop the birth certificates into the grate, one by one. Including the Witch's. Without Mouse's father's name, I can't trace Mouse through her anyway. I can only hope that one day, no matter how damaged she is, Mouse will come to find me like she came to find El.

I look down at Mum's birth certificate, rub my thumb over her name. When I first came back to this house, I remember feeling like my life in Venice Beach—its safety and certainty—already felt lost to me, just a glossy photograph of a place I visited a long time ago. But it was never real. Not even its boardwalk of clowns and mystics and magic. I never believed in it. And that's why it never saved me.

I let go of Mum's certificate, watch its edges curl gold and black. Watch it disappear. And I think, *You can leave now*. Because I know she's still here too. In all these years, none of us have ever really escaped this house. Or that moment of catastrophe, preserved like a body trapped under pumice and ash.

And then I reach into my jeans pocket, take out El's last letter. Read it through one more time before tossing it and the Jolly Roger into the fire. I make a sound as they catch and go up in flames: the excited, scared yip of a child. And I look across at that naked stretch of garden wall one last time. I hope he knows. I hope he knows that neither El nor I are here anymore. That we will never ever come back. Because his Donkshop was never this house's heart, its engine room. That was always Mirrorland. And now it's gone.

I put out the fire, close up the grate, and it feels a little like turning off the ventilator of a patient who has already died. In its wake, the house returns to a tomblike silence. I leave it in peace.

I pause again only once I'm standing outside. I glance one last time into the gloom—red and gold, black and white—before reaching up to pull the big front door shut for good.

And maybe as it closes I hear the muted protest of bell clappers inside copper and tin; the impatient shudder of wires and veins inside hollow walls; the whisper of worlds behind doors, inside cupboards, beneath still blue skies and oceans of green.

I don't care if I do.

And that's when I know why I came back. Why I had to say goodbye.

So that I would no longer be afraid to fly.

CHAPTER 33

I buy a seat for El on the plane. An indulgence maybe, and one that earns me a few strange looks, but it's one I can afford after booking a late Christmas Eve flight from Heathrow. Besides, El squirreled away more money from her art sales than anyone had realized, so it only seemed fair. I didn't want her to be in the hold or an overhead locker—anywhere but right beside me as we finally flew over the ocean to The Island.

I had to transfer her ashes from the ugly great urn to a cardboard box with pink-painted flowers and a viewing window. Already, I'm dreading the moment I have to literally let go of her, but I'm more afraid about what happens after I have. Carrying her around with me has begun to feel as natural as feeling her pain when she's not there.

Halfway across the North Atlantic, I finally fall asleep. I dream of The Island—of Captain Henry's Santa Catalina—its beaches and lagoons and palm trees painted in El's thick brushstrokes. I dream of Captain Henry finally standing at the wheel of the *Satisfaction*, and El and I at its bowsprit, as turquoise Caribbean waves bear us ever closer to The Island's shores. I wake up feeling uneasy, maybe even afraid. Outside my window it's dark as tar. I can see the white plains and black shadows of my reflection, the dark hollows of my eyes staring back at me.

"A wise sailor never leaves port on a Friday," I whisper.

I hear El's voice, clear as a bell. *It's Saturday now, you idiot.*

And when I look at my watch, I see that she's right. It's Christmas Day.

So I look back out the window and I think of a pink dawn sky. El gripping my hand tight as we watch the sea and wait.

And I smile, lay my fingers over the box's lid. "We're finally doing it, El. We're finally going."

*

I'm feeling less enthusiastic after a nearly ten-hour layover in Bogotá, followed by a two-hour flight to San Andrés, and another to Providencia. It's night again by the time I manage to escape El Embrujo airport. The taxi driver keeps up a friendly commentary that I'm in no shape to appreciate as he rattles along empty streets, lit only by the lights of cottages and cabanas, the occasional hotel. I can't see the sea, but I can smell it: far stronger and cleaner than in Leith.

When he finally stops with an abrupt squealing of brakes, I'm so glad to have arrived, I could kiss him. Until he's pulled my suitcase out of the trunk, and both it and I are standing in the middle of another empty road.

"Where's the hotel?"

He grins, flashing gappy teeth. "On Santa Catalina."

"I know that."

"Santa Catalina is a different island from Providencia."

"Yes, I know that too," I say, now very close to panic. "But they're supposed to be joined."

"They are," he says, pointing over my shoulder.

When I turn to look, I realize that what I thought was a boardwalk lined with benches and bright lanterns is actually a footbridge. A very long footbridge.

The taxi driver takes pity on me, pats my shoulder gently. "It's okay, okay. It's only one hundred yards, and then you are on Santa Catalina. The hotel is only past the fort, not far. Okay?"

The bridge is beautiful. Painted blue, green, yellow, and orange, it jostles and bobs against floating rafts. Not even in Mirrorland would either of us have imagined we'd ever have to *walk* to The Island, guided by swinging lanterns. The thought manages to make me smile.

When I finally reach the other side, there is a tree of high wooden signs, and my heart lifts when I read the first two: "Morgan's Fort,"

"Morgan's Head." I walk along the water's edge towards the only lights. I can hear the sea, see the shadows of boats. The lights coalesce, revealing the hotel in increments, but I'm certain that I've arrived only when I see its small recessed entrance lit up gold. Just before I turn off the walkway, I see another wooden sign, faded and warped with age. "Welcome to Santa Catalina," it says. "Pirates will be Hanged and Protestants will be Burned." And I smile again. This time so wide, my lips hurt.

*

The hotel is basic, clean, wonderful. But after I've got into my room, I find that my tiredness has vanished. I don't want to sleep, to risk dreaming about another place, another time. I want to be *here, now*.

I leave El on my bedside table and go back out onto the walkway, wander until I see more lights. I stop. The bar they belong to is called the Henry Morgan. Set into its wall is the encyclopedia's picture— El's picture—our pirate king, bearded and long-haired and unsmiling. I go around the entrance, onto staggered tiers of decking and palm trees strung with fairy lights. It's deserted, so I go down to the bottom deck, sit as close to the water's edge as I can get. The warm wind smells of seaweed and smoke and cooking fish. A low-hanging line of lanterns swings between my table and the other side of the decking like a golden shield.

A waitress in a T-shirt emblazoned with the same Henry Morgan portrait comes out of the bar with a smile, and hands me the cocktail list. She looks young, maybe still in her teens, her black hair braided short, makeup glittery. I probably look like I've been dragged through a hedge backwards.

"I thought it would be busier."

She shakes her head. "Christmas is a time for family." And I find that I don't care if her smile is one of pity or disapproval.

"I saw a sign for Morgan's Head back at the bridge. How far is it?"

"Not far," she says. "You can walk there. It is very beautiful."

I smile, glance back down at the menu. "Can I have your special rum punch, please?"

After she leaves, a group of tourists arrive, loud and celebratory.

A second waitress herds them quickly towards the other, darker side of the deck, and I'm glad. My own sense of well-being still feels too fragile, as if it's held together only by the promised magic of this place. Captain Henry Morgan's place.

I turn my face towards the wind, breathe in the smell of the Caribbean. I'm here. We're here. Inside El's painting. Tomorrow morning, I'll wake up to blues and yellows and greens. A far better resting place than a windy graveyard of lairs or a dark prison of make-believe. This is the place where I will finally be able to let her go.

*

I see the cocktail long before the waiter carrying it. The thing is huge: a tall glass that is more of a jug, silver straws and umbrellas, and worst of all, fizzing sparklers. I know it has to be my special rum punch; my heart sinks as it gets closer and louder. The tourists cheer its passage, tapering off only when they clock its solitary recipient.

The waiter is grinning when he sets it down. Sparks bounce off the table.

"Thank you," I mutter. "It's a bit . . ."

"It's our special," he says, with an apologetic laugh, as finally the sparklers dim and grow silent. I blink in the sudden return to darkness, realize he hasn't moved. Am I supposed to tip him? I surreptitiously root around in my jeans pocket for change. "I'm sorry, I don't . . ."

He smiles again. He's incredibly good-looking, the sort of good-looking that always makes me feel nervous, inadequate. His teeth are very white. I start to wonder if I have some airline food in my own.

"You are very beautiful."

"Oh." My face gets hot again. I laugh, take a big sip of the rum punch, and it's strong enough to make my eyes water. "Thank you."

"You are only visiting?"

I nod.

"I came here from Cameroon five years ago," he says, with another grin. "Also only to visit."

I've never been to Africa. I've never truly *been* anywhere. Now, if

285

I wanted to, I could fly across the world to the Kakadu Jungle. "I've come from Edinburgh." I smile. "I'm *definitely* only here for a week."

"Well," he says, "it is very good to meet you. You are very welcome."

He turns away from my table, and I watch him walk towards the other, busier side of the deck. I'm still smiling, the rum warming my belly, tingling down the length of my legs, as he approaches the loud tourist table, claps one of them on the back. His laugh is deep, booming. I watch the second waitress's dark swinging rope of hair as she picks up an empty cocktail glass, and when he comes up alongside her, his hand going around her waist, I allow myself one last look back, one last fantasy. *If I could, I'd take your place, El, and you could have mine. You could have hers. You could have everything you never thought you deserved.*

But then I see the waitress stiffen. And his grip on her waist tighten. Something dark and cold extinguishes the rum's glow, my new sense of hope. I peer into the shadows between us, but I can't see her expression, only her stillness, the rigid set of her spine, her shoulders. Is she afraid of him? Does she long to escape? But then she turns towards him, and in the light from that low swinging line of golden lanterns, her smile is wide and dazzling.

I stand up. I feel dizzy, drunk. I start walking across the thick creaking boards of the bar, so much like the deck of a boat that it feels as if I'm on the ocean, riding the swells of a North Atlantic storm. Shouting into the wind, *Come about! Heave to! All hands hoay!*, even though I know I'm not saying anything at all.

When I start to fall, she doesn't try to catch me. Instead, she runs forwards and falls with me, wraps her arms around my back as our knees smack loudly against the wood. She squeezes me hard enough that I cry out, though I'm crying already: great paralyzing sobs that steal my voice, my sense. She kisses me, strokes my hair, whispers "Shhh" to me as if I'm a child, one who has just woken up from a nightmare.

I remember how much I used to hate always looking into my own eyes, seeing my own smile, my own frown, my own imperfections. Like a mirror I always carried, sharp and heavy under my arm.

To always be a reflection; half of a whole. Fused together like sand and limestone into glass.

Now my fingers shake as they touch her face. And my eyes blur with tears.

"I knew you'd come," El says.

CHAPTER 34

I sleep like the dead.

I wake up to bright light and birdsong. Despite a hangover, jet lag, and more emotions than I can process, I know immediately where I am, what has happened, who I'm with. I'm in El's bedroom. Above me, the ceiling fan turns and hums through slow rotations. I sit up when I realize I'm alone. Last night we slept together, just like we used to in the Kakadu Jungle, on our sides and holding hands.

I get dressed, go into the narrow hallway. The apartment is basic, bright, small. Nothing at all like 36 Westeryk Road. El is in the tiny kitchen, her new dark hair gathered into a loose bun.

"Samuel bought some food," she says. "Coconut bread and mangoes."

"The guy from the bar?" It comes out wrong, belligerent. Last night, El and I couldn't stop grinning at each other. Every so often, one of us would break off just to laugh. Or cry. We were like children, I suppose, for whom the wonder of finding a dearly loved lost thing eclipsed all else. Today, I don't know what I feel.

"He's a friend. There are more good men than bad." Her smile is tired. "Took me a while to realize that."

I find that I can't look at her, which is ridiculous. She touches my shoulder, and when I flinch, she sighs.

"Go out onto the balcony. I'll bring us some coffee. And then you can ask me anything you want to."

The balcony is small, the table and chairs plastic. I sit, look out at all those blues and yellows and greens. No rocky coastline here after all, but a long, sandy bay and a pier surrounded by wooden fishing boats. I can hear the rattle of mooring rings, the creak of straining hawsers, and I fix my gaze on a boat painted red and pastel blue, bobbing low between waves.

When El comes out with the coffee, I do look at her. It's still so new, so strange to be able to do that, to know that it *is* her. It's been so long. Far longer than just these months that she's been gone. It's been years. Lifetimes.

She sits down. Sighs. "I needed Ross to believe I was dead. I needed you to believe that he'd killed me. I needed him to let you go. And then I needed you to let him go." A long pause. "So I lied."

"But why couldn't you just *tell* me? Why didn't you *ever* trust me?" It's what has hurt the most.

"God, it wasn't you I didn't trust, it was him!" She takes hold of my hands. "I wanted to tell you, of course I did. I wanted to tell you everything. But I had to save your life like you saved mine. And I knew you wouldn't believe me. *Couldn't* believe me."

Because believing hurts. No one has ever lied or hidden the truth from me better than I have.

"After the trial," I say, "why didn't you get in touch then? Let me know you were alive? What did you think I would do? Tell the police? Choose him over you?"

"I thought you would forgive him. That's what you do." She looks out to sea, blinks to hide the tears I've already seen in her eyes. "I'm counting on it."

But I can't. "You wasted years of your life in an abusive relationship. You wasted years of our lives—*our* lives, El—because our crazy father chose to choke you first instead of me? You made me think that you were *dead!*"

"I'm the eldest, Cat," she says, as if it's the most logical explanation in the world. "I'm the poison taster. I'm *supposed* to look after you."

"Jesus Christ." I get a sudden flash of Mum: the meanness of her frown, the pinch of her fingers; cold eyes and a sharp, hard voice. And I'm as close as I've ever been to admitting that a part of me has always hated her—even now, even knowing what she did for us.

"I need to know why. I need to know *how*."

Her smile is pure El: half-defiant, half-sorrowful. "Then ask me."

"How did you get here?"

It's a question with a thousand answers, I realize, but she only nods. "After I . . . scuttled *The Redemption*, I kayaked to Fisherrow. It's an old harbor in Musselburgh, mostly disused now. No one saw me."

"You were the person in the parka, weren't you? Seen hanging around the house that day? Coming out of the alleyway?"

She nods again. "I dumped the kayak in the shed. And I'd hidden a Survival Pack under the bed in the Clown Café. Just like we used to. It had been there for months. Money, clothes. There was a neighbor, a friend. We both once volunteered at a charity for immigrant families. I told her about Ross, and she gave me a false passport and papers. Before I decided that I couldn't run."

Because of me.

"Marie," I say.

El's surprise makes her look better, lighter. "You know her?"

"Ross didn't send you those cards," I say. "It was her. She sent them to me too."

"God." El's shoulders slump. "Poor Marie."

I feel angry again, and I don't know why. El sees it, visibly squares her shoulders.

"I got the express to Heathrow. I was so scared. I didn't know what to do, where to go—I just needed to get away. I ended up buying a ticket to Mexico because it was the next flight leaving for another continent. But I was so afraid that Ross was going to find me. I kept thinking, any minute, he's going to appear, he's going to walk right through those airport doors. And find me." She half laughs, half sobs. "And the only thing that kept me sane was wondering if Andy Dufresne had been just as scared. When he was crawling through that tunnel, that pipe, those five hundred yards of shit; when he was so close to being out, to being free, after all those weeks and months and years of being so far."

Instantly, my anger dilutes, mixed with all that new relief and happiness; the sheer joy of knowing that she's here. The luxury of being angry with her.

"I came here maybe a month after Mexico. I'd gone south to

Costa Rica because I was still too scared to stop running, and then there it was on a map in a bar. Santa Catalina." Her smile is fleeting. "And I thought, is that why I bought that ticket to Mexico? So that I could come here? So that I could stop running?"

I close my eyes. I'm aware that I'm doing what I always do—circling around the pain so that I don't have to feel it. So that I can pretend it doesn't even exist. And El is doing what she always did—she's letting me. I think of that pink cardboard box at the hotel, and my heart picks up in a hard and heavy drumbeat that even I can't ignore. I breathe in, out. Look at that red-and-blue boat. "Tell me what happened, El."

She says nothing until I turn back towards her, meet her gaze.

"What I told you about my life with Ross was true. I couldn't leave him. I couldn't kill him. I mean, I thought about it . . ." She pauses. "But if there was even the slightest chance I'd hesitate or fuck it up, what would he do? What would he do to me? What would he do to you?" She shrugs. "I'd given up, I suppose. I just didn't care anymore."

"What changed?"

El takes in a long breath. "Mouse."

"Mouse?"

"You remember how she always was? Needy." She closes her eyes. "Vulnerable."

"Because of the Witch," I say, thinking of her standing in front of the gate onto Westeryk Road, tall and cold like a waxwork. "Mum's twin."

El looks at me, surprised again. Nods. "When Mouse came back into my life, when she just turned up to the house about six months before the Plan, I didn't recognize her at first. She said the Witch had just died. And so now she was free. Free to come back. I don't know if she tracked me down to the house, or just expected me to be there. You think our childhoods were bad—the Witch beat Mouse, starved her, hid her away. Her whole life, she made Mouse small until that's all she was. I used to think I knew what that felt like. But until Ross, I had no idea. Because you and I—through all of it, all of the abuse and the isolation—we had each other. We had Mum. We felt love.

We were never alone. So I felt guilty. We were pretty shitty to her too, remember?"

I think of the Witch dragging Mouse along the hallway. *No, no! I don't want to go!* The hard, echoless clap of those slaps against her face. The Witch's smile as we let Mouse go. The way she stood inside that flood of light from the open door: head bowed and trembling like a dog.

"Ross hated her," El says. "Hated anyone who might take any part of me away from him. So I let him think that I wanted her gone too—I let him think that she *was* gone—but I'd still phone her on that second phone. I'd still manage to sneak the odd hour away to meet her while he was at work. And we'd tell each other all about our horrible lives. It didn't help. In the end, nothing helped. In the end, nothing mattered." She closes her eyes. "Because I'd just had enough."

"You never planned to escape, did you?" I reach for my anger again, but it's gone. "That last letter wasn't a lie. You were going to kill yourself. Just like Mum did. That really was the Plan."

"I was just so tired, Cat," she says with an almost wistful smile. "So . . . *sad.*"

"Tell me." I look back out at the boat, the pier, the sea.

"April the third was a beautiful morning." Her voice softens, goes faraway. "The Forth has its own microclimate, you know. That day, it was like a bright gold corridor between all the dark clouds over the land. Seals followed me out to the shipping lane, gannets were wheeling around the sails and mast like they thought I was a fishing boat. I could see the flat nothing of the North Sea. I was ready." She stops. A tear runs into the corner of her lips. "But then it all went wrong."

"How?"

She swallows. Her smile is anguished. "Mouse."

A familiar dread stirs in my stomach. "How—"

"I'm sorry," she says, standing abruptly, disappearing into the apartment. "I'll be back in a minute."

She comes back in less than a minute, holding two tumblers in one hand, a plastic bottle filled with red-gold liquid in the other.

"Bushi rum," she says, pouring two big measures, handing one to me. Her hand shakes. "Local and lethal."

I drink. It burns all the way down.

"She phoned me. When I was on *The Redemption*. She asked me where I was." El's voice is so quiet, I have to strain to hear her. "I told her I was out on the boat, and I tried to sound normal, but she could tell something was up. She said if I didn't talk to her, meet her, she would go to the house, find Ross. I'd already told her too much. About how he was. About what he'd done to me. I shouldn't have, I should have known how dangerous that was. Mouse wasn't always small—you must remember how possessive she could be? How impulsive?"

I think of the marshal's office. Her hands on her hips. The shine of her teeth, like the Cheshire Cat in *Alice's Adventures in Wonderland*. *Do you want me to help you?*

"She thought that I was escaping. Running away again, like we did as kids. She was so *angry*." El shakes her head. "The Witch wasn't the only reason she'd stayed away from us for years. Mouse had been angry with us for a long, long time."

Please, I don't want to go! I want to go back to Mirrorland! Her hands reaching out to us as the Witch dragged her through the entrance hall, towards the door. I press my fingers against my eyelids. "We took Mirrorland away from her."

"And we left her alone." El sighs, bows her head. "I knew Ross had to be back from London. I worried what would happen, what he might do, what *she* might do, if she went back to the house without me. I was only about an hour out, less than." She takes a long swallow of rum from the bottle. "I couldn't abandon her again. No matter what it cost me." She looks at me. "So. I picked her up from Fisherrow."

A dreadful certainty beats hard inside my chest now, and I find that I can't speak.

El lets me off the hook again, takes my hands and gives me a small smile. "I told her all of it. All of the Plan: Ross, the pills, the boat. I don't know why. Maybe because, deep down, I wanted someone to stop me. And I was glad she'd forced my hand. I think the moment I answered that phone, I ran right out of courage." Her smile is terrible. "I scuttled myself."

When I still say nothing, El squeezes my hands harder.

"Even after I told her, I was shaky, panicky. I guess I was still coming down from adrenaline, cortisol, I don't know, whatever it is your body thinks you need when you're about to kill yourself." She shivers. "But I promised her it was over. That I wouldn't do it, that I'd go back to Ross. I talked and talked at her like she was our cabin girl again. Our skivvy. Our comfort blanket. Like she wasn't a person. A person who had suffered. A person who only ever wanted to belong, to be needed. To *help*." El shivers again. "I didn't stop. Not until I was done. Not until I'd taken as much comfort and sympathy as she had to give. And then I left her alone in the cuddy. While I went back up top, kept sailing for a bit longer, until I felt ready to go back to the harbor." She closes her eyes. "I was relieved. That's the ugly truth of it. Of me. I was relieved. I'd tried. I'd failed. And now I could go back home.

"It was too quiet when I went back down about an hour later. I knew something was wrong. Mouse was lying on her back on the seats. And she was . . . she was just gray. She was this awful gray. And I just knew. Even before I saw the bag on the floor. The diazepam and the fluoxetine, Ross's fucking pills. My suicide kit. I tried bringing her back, but she was already going cold." She shakes her head, and when she looks at me again, it's with that familiar mix of sorrow and defiance. "I saw it then. My chance. I could sail back to Granton, face Ross—all the questions and consequences of Mouse being dead, of me being on the boat when I'd begged him to come back from London. Or I really could escape. Him. All of it. Everything at once."

I think of that body on a gurney. The white of its skin, the black of the closing stitches at the ends of its collarbone. Its terrible face.

El's fingers tremble against mine as she swallows hard. "I decided to substitute Mouse for me."

"But I don't understand," I say. It's a lie. I want to get up, I want to run. I don't want to listen. But El won't let go of my hands, my wrists. "I don't—"

"There always had to be a body," she says, and she's actively pushing me down now, as if she knows if she lets up for a moment, I'll escape.

"If one wasn't found, I knew Ross would never give up, he'd never stop looking. And maybe he'd never be found guilty. It was why I'd decided I had to kill myself. But as soon as I realized I didn't have to die, I didn't want to. I could go back to the house, replace the drain plug and hole saw in Bluebeard's Room with the real ones, so that the forensics would match without any margin of doubt. I could get my Survival Pack. And I could escape. *Really* escape." She looks at me, suddenly fierce. "But I didn't want it to happen like that. I didn't want her to die."

"I don't understand," I say again, now twisting my wrists so hard, so frantically, that a bone cracks loud enough to make both of us wince. But El doesn't let go. Instead, she only moves closer until we're inches apart; until I have no option but to meet her hard gaze.

"Yes, you do. And you have to face that this time, Cat. You have to know the truth and believe it. Accept it. Even if you don't want to." She lets me go. "You have to say it."

I breathe in. Out. Think of that body on the gurney again. That DNA isolation test on Rafiq's phone. "She's our sister." I stare down at the purple crescent-shaped welts on my skin. "Mouse is our identical sister."

El takes my face in her hands, smooths cool fingers against my brow, my temples. There are tears in her eyes, but she's smiling. Nodding. "Do you remember how special we were?" she says. "More than one hundred thousand other children had to be born before a mum got to have children as special as us?"

I nod. Close my eyes.

"The odds of giving birth to Mirror Twins are about one in twelve hundred births. For a fraternal twin like Mum, the odds drop to one in seventy." El lets out a long breath. "It's not that rare at all."

I think of Mouse curled up into a ball behind a lashed-down barrel in the bow of the *Satisfaction*, her chalk-white face streaked with tears. And my selfish, *stupid* belief that the envy in her eyes was only to make me feel better—to let me know that I was worth something to someone. Even if that someone wasn't real. *I wish I was like you.*

"The Witch told Mouse just before she died." El's face is so pale. "That we were identical triplets. That her grandpa was her father, and our mother was her mother."

"But *how?*" I think of Mouse's raw pale skin and cropped dark hair, her bony smallness. I can still feel my denial like a palpable lump under my skin. "She didn't even look like us. She was—"

"Mouse said the Witch cut off her hair, dyed it black, barely fed her. And remember how often she'd plaster herself in our clown face paints? To try to look like us. Like Belle. To stop looking like herself." The glance that El gives me is almost angry, even though tears track down her cheeks. "We never saw it because we believed what we were told to believe. Just like we always did. But maybe Mum wanted us to know that we were so much more special than we thought, than she'd told us we were, and so she mixed the truth with fantasy. Just like she always did."

"The odds of us being identical triplets," I whisper. "That was the one in a hundred thousand."

El nods. "Probably less," she says, and her voice is small. Her smile smaller. "If twins already run in the family, and your grandfather is your father."

"But *why?* Why would Mum just let the Witch take her? Why would the Witch even want—"

"Mouse said that the Witch would sleepwalk. Would have night terrors. Mouse would wake up, find her outside on her knees, alone in the cold and the dark, begging to be let back in. No one ever wanted the Witch. No one loved her. No one wanted to make her his wife, and then hang her on his hook until she died. She was never picked. She never belonged. When Gran died, Grandpa kicked the Witch out of the house with nothing. Only allowed her to visit in exchange for her silence. Mouse thought the Witch took her because she needed to have something—to take something—from Mum, from Grandpa. She thought that the Witch needed someone else to know what it felt like. To never be loved, to never belong."

Her long-nailed finger pointing at the trembling, head-bowed Mouse. *THIS is what it is to be a good daughter.*

An oval locket swinging from her fist, catching the sun in gold sparks. Mum's smile as cold as ice. *You always want what I have.* The Witch thrusting the necklace inside the pocket of her long black dress. *And sometimes, I get it.*

El looks at me. "But I think Mouse was wrong. The Witch paid for that big ugly headstone, you know. Paid to have them both buried together." Her eyes flash. "Her whole life, she just wanted *everyone* to suffer more than she did."

I think of those birth certificates. Third of March, 1962, 14:32 and 14:54.

"The Witch was the eldest," I whisper. I'm shaking: minute tremors that make me want to shudder. "She should have been the poison taster."

The enormity of it all hits me then. What Mum must have gone through. Why, every year on the date of Gran's death, she would shut herself in her bedroom and not come out again until the next day. All that horror and suffering, and the injustice of being the one blamed for suffering it. The lies she must have told herself. I wonder if she even remembered by the end that Mouse had once belonged to her.

"Mum just wanted us to be safe," El says. "Maybe she convinced herself Mouse *would* be safer. Maybe she was."

It's a lie. Because Mum never taught Mouse how to survive. How to hide, how to run. How to feel joy in the dark or fearless in a storm. But I can't think about that. I can't think about Mouse being all alone, while I couldn't even bring myself to believe that she was real.

"Did Ross know?"

El shakes her head. "He always thought Mouse was a family friend or a cousin. She still looked the same as when we were kids; nothing at all like us. *I* didn't know. Not until that day on the boat. Mouse told me she was our sister after I told her about my plan to frame Ross for my death." A pained smile. "You show me yours, and I'll show you mine."

"Oh, God." I stand up. Almost stagger. Warm wind blows against my face. I close my eyes. Remember running along the boardwalk and into the marshal's office, the Black Spot crushed inside my hand. Mouse's eyes, big and black and round. *Don't be scared. I'll help you, Cat. I'll save you.* The happy hope in her wide smile. The old baggy dress painted with clumsy red roses to match the pinafores El and I wore. *You can be me. And I'll be you.* "She did it for you, didn't she? Mouse took those pills for you. Because you were going to go back to Ross."

El covers her face with her hands. "I didn't believe that she was our sister. Not then. Not when she told me." She hunches over and starts to sob. "She just kept pulling at me, smiling at me, telling me all she wanted to do was help. All she ever wanted was for me to trust her, to love her like a sister. You know, you must remember, how suffocating it was: her need, her desperation. And so I didn't believe her. I *couldn't.*"

I go down on my knees, grip hold of her hands before they can do any more damage. Already there are bloody scratches on her cheeks and chin to match those on my wrists.

"She left a note," she whispers. "Just her name. The one Mum gave her." El's whole body is vibrating like a tuning fork. "That was when I knew she'd been telling the truth."

"What was her name?"

El's laugh sounds broken. "Iona."

The fairy princess who was stolen from her mother by an evil hag. Who cut off her wings and imprisoned her in a tower so high that no one even knew she was there.

El's sobs get louder, harder. I can hardly make out her words. "I left her alone after she told me. She listened to me while I talked and talked at her like she wasn't a person, and I never once listened to her. When I went back up on deck, the last thing I said to her was *Leave me alone. I want you to leave me alone.*"

"El. El." I lean closer. "You didn't know."

She pushes me away. Staggers back onto her feet. "What if I did? What if I did believe her? What if I told her everything, and then left her down there alone with my drugs, knowing that—"

I stand up. "You didn't believe her. Not when you went back up on deck. You were relieved, remember? Relieved that it was all over. It wasn't your fault."

When she just goes on shaking her head, I grab her, force her to look at me again. "None of it was your fault. What Mum always said about the eldest having to look after the youngest, she was wrong. Just because her elder sister never protected her, you've had to sacrifice your whole fucking life for mine."

"Wasn't such a great sacrifice," she says, and her smile is terrible, her gaze unfocused. "I loved him. I always wanted him, right from the very start. I always used to think I was so good, so brave. But lying and manipulating, *planning*, it's like breathing for me now. Maybe I *am* bad. Maybe there is something wrong with me. Because it *was* my fault. I should have died and Mouse—"

"I'm a drunk," I say. "I'm selfish. I'm disloyal. I'm a coward who has never faced anything. I wanted Ross, and I didn't care when it hurt you. I hated you, and I never ever suspected that you didn't hate me. And that night—that last fucking night—I would have kept going. If Ross hadn't blocked up the hole, I would have left you behind, I would have left you with Grandpa, just like the Witch did to Mum, and I wouldn't have looked back. I *didn't* look back."

El tugs on my arm. "That's bullshit. You're nothing like her. You're nothing like *them*. None of it was your fault—" She stops. Her gaze suddenly sharpens, her fingers loosen. She sits back down with a choked laugh. "I suppose you think that was clever."

"It *wasn't* your fault, El." And I smile, even though it's the very last thing I feel like doing. I sit down, move my chair close enough to hers that we can look at each other as if we're looking in a mirror. Her eyes are red, her skin white. I think of her lying in that hospital bed. I think of all Mum's stories, all her lessons. *Shawshank, A Tale of Two Cities, The Count of Monte Cristo, Papillon, The Man in the Iron Mask, The Spy Who Came in from the Cold*, all those Agatha Christies. I'd only ever understood escape in them, but El had seen subterfuge. Imitation. Opportunity. Sacrifice. Rescue. That a white lie was just a lie that hadn't got dirty yet.

And she would have come back. If I hadn't escaped Ross too, she would have sacrificed her freedom, her new life. I know that absolutely.

I remember that hidden tribe in South America. How they would form a circle so tight around someone that they couldn't escape. I clasp El's hands. I make her look at me. And then I tell her about every good thing that she has ever done. Every good thing that she has ever been. Over and over. Until finally she sees me. Hears me. Believes me.

*

And then—then—I cry for Iona. I cry for the sister that neither of us even had the chance to love. To need. To save. I cry for the moment she sat beside me in Chief Red Cloud's teepee, eyes big and blue and full of the best kind of sympathy.

It'll be okay, Cat. I love you.

I cry for that melted, shiny thing on a metal gurney. A bald rippled scalp, deep eyeless holes, teeth fixed into a lipless grin.

And most of all, I cry for Mouse. The little smiling girl with the chalk-white face and ruby-red lips who once told me, *If you're quiet and small and scared in the dark, no one will ever see you.* Because no one ever had.

EPILOGUE

The day after Boxing Day we get up before dawn and make our way along the walkway in silence. The wind is low and the sea is calm. The lights of houses and boats slowly vanish until only the occasional streetlight remains, reflecting gold against the water. We climb, and duckboards take us through dark close mangroves, until finally we break into fresh air. And light. The dawn is coming: a thin bright line on the horizon, bathing the sea silver. A distant cockerel crows once, twice. I can smell flowers, something sweet like lilac.

We walk along a track, skirt around rocky outcrops and leaning trees. When we turn a corner, the wind blows hard against us, pushing my hair away from my face, cooling the sweat on my neck.

"Oh my God."

El turns to me, smiles. Looks at the huge shadow of rock sitting on a ledge above the water. "Morgan's Head."

I follow her as she steps down through a path overgrown with ferns and bushes bright with red and yellow flowers, grasping the bark of palm trees as the way grows steeper.

"The lagoon's just down here," she says over her shoulder, as we reach the vast craggy crown of Morgan's Head.

I fight the ridiculous urge to say hello. Flatten my palms against the stone instead.

El smiles again. "I did that too, the first time."

And then I see the lagoon. It's beautiful: shallow blue-green water, turning darker as it gets closer to the rocks and reefs at its mouth. Surrounded on all other sides by high cliffs of stone beneath dense green thickets. At the bottom, we step straight down into the water, cool and shallow, sandy underfoot.

"It's beautiful, El."

"I've come down here every day since I got here," she says. "It was exactly how I always imagined it would be."

For a few moments, we stand in silence and the sea, look out to the silver-gray horizon turning gold. It's so unimaginably quiet. Peaceful.

I turn to the rucksack slung over El's shoulders, take out the cardboard box with pink-painted flowers. We both look down at it, and then at each other. It's the first time we've all been together since we were children.

"I wish—" My voice catches.

"Me too," El says, and her voice is as close to breaking. She presses her palm against my knuckles, against the box.

I open it, and we each take a handful of ashes and throw them out over the clear blue water. Watch as they catch the low wind, fan and float and fall, settle like spindrift across the waves, disappear. By the time the box is empty, the sky has lightened and the air is warmer.

"Goodbye, Iona," El says.

And I know she hears the whispered echo of my "Sorry" in the same moment that I hear hers.

We're quiet for a long time, until finally El packs away the empty box, clears her throat. "What will you do now?"

I don't reply. I know what she's asking. I think of the vast blue sky and sea of Venice Beach; the gothic spires and cobbles of Edinburgh. The wind tickles my hair against my neck, my bare shoulders.

"There's no such bird as a glorious golden curre, you know." El looks out at the horizon. I hear Mum's reading voice, low and steady and comforting. *Whenever she spreads her big golden wings and flies away, where she lands is where her next life begins as if the one before it had never happened at all.*

"*Curre* is Latin for *run!*"

I turn to look at the press of El's lips, the set of her jaw, as she tries not to ask me again what I'm going to do, where I'm going to go.

"*Anne of Green Gables* was never my favorite book," I say. "It was always *Papillon*."

"What?"

"It didn't matter how many times he was caught and imprisoned—in penal colonies or camps, asylums or prisons or islands—he never ever stopped trying to escape. In a sailboat. With a pirate."

"I miss *The Redemption*," El says, and her voice is uncertain. Uncertain of me.

Four minutes. Four minutes and God knows how many generations of pain and lies and suffering have always separated us. But she still knows me better than anyone else in the whole world. Not because we were once almost fused together like sand and limestone—we never were—but because we will always be bound together by something much stronger.

Mirrorland *was* magic. It taught us how to fight. To hide. To dream. It taught us how to escape long before we broke through its wall or its world. I look back out to sea, where the sun has begun pushing up over the horizon, turning the sky and sea a bloody and beautiful red. X marks this spot. A rough coastline of rocks and beach, an interior of forest and flatland. A tropical paradise instead of a snowy wonderland. The end of Mirrorland's treasure hunt.

And so I turn to look at El. Reach across the space between us to take her hand.

"We can buy another *Redemption*," I say. "Sail the Caribbean together."

And at her sob, I close my eyes, remember for the last time the give of the soft, creaking wood as I shifted my weight from left foot to right under the ocean swell, the cool touch of a twenty-knot southeasterly against my face, the excited shouts of our crew and the ringing screams of splintering wood and dying men, the bellows of cannon and musketoons. How safe we had always felt, no matter how terrifying the battle. No matter how loud the roar of the squall. No matter who looked back at us from the mirror.

We will not leave each other, I think. *Never so long as we live.*

I squeeze El's hand tighter, hear the long-ago echo of her chattering teeth as we looked out towards the harbor and the blood-bright promise of the firth and the dawn. And I wish Mum could see us. I wish she could know that all of it had been worth it in the end. All the suffering, all the horror, all that dark and wonderful magic. That we made it to The Island. That we're together. All three of us. We will always be together.

And even though I haven't said anything at all, El looks at me and smiles wide, the rising sun turning her face golden.

"She knows."

*

And that was the day our third life began.

ACKNOWLEDGMENTS

So many people make a book. Probably more than I know about or am able to mention here, but to whom I am immeasurably grateful nonetheless.

I owe many thanks to everyone at Scribner. Most especially, Valerie Steiker, for going to bat for *Mirrorland* in the first place and for being a terrific editor. Thanks also to Nan Graham, Kara Watson, Colin Harrison, Roz Lippel, Brian Belfiglio, Brianna Yamashita, Ashley Gilliam, Kate Lloyd, and Clare Maurer for all their brilliant efforts in bringing *Mirrorland* to as many readers as possible. To Jaya Miceli and Erich Hobbing for great design and artwork. And thanks also to Sally Howe, Dan Cuddy, and especially, John McGhee, for catching all my mistakes before anyone else could see them! It has been a pleasure to work with you all.

Huge thanks must also go to my US agent, Allison Hunter at Janklow & Nesbit and my UK agent, Hellie Ogden at Janklow & Nesbit UK. I can never say thank you enough for your tremendous support, enthusiasm, and fantastic advice.

I am also indebted to Detective Constable Robbie West, as well as Steph Miller and Dougie MacLeod, for their invaluable advice regarding Scottish criminal law, sheriff and High Court protocols, and police procedure. An extra special thank you must go to James Loosemore. Your endless patience, advice, and attention to detail was and is very much appreciated. Any and all inaccuracies are entirely mine.

Thanks, too, to forensic biologist Steph Fox, for advice regarding forensics and crime scene processing. *Forensics: The Anatomy of Crime*, by the brilliant Val McDermid, was also an invaluable resource. Dr. Boris Cyrulnik is a French psychiatrist and ethologist, who has spent years studying childhood trauma and experience. His book *Resilience* was a fascinating and, again, invaluable resource when writing *Mirrorland*.

A big thank you to Richard Leask for teaching me the basics of sailing and sailboats. Even more helpfully, all the ways in which I could sink one.

Thank you to the two very talented writers, Nina Allan and Priya Sharma, whose wonderful support and friendship over the years (and, of course, early readings!) has meant more to me than they can ever know.

And also to Stephen King, a man whom I've never met, but who will remain forever my first writer crush. Whose fantastic memoir, *On Writing*, was the push I needed to get my first short story published back in the mid-2000s, and one of the reasons I kept writing even when it seemed impossible; when the rejections were piled so high I could have filled a room with them. His books taught me that stories can take you anywhere and everywhere. And that they're the best escape there is.

Thank you to my godmother, Susan McEwan, for always believing in me even if I didn't.

Thank you to Mum and Dad, for too many things to mention. Mostly for instilling in me the kind of resilience and discipline required to keep going no matter how hard it gets or hopeless it looks. (The teenage me is spinning in her grave).

Thank you to my husband, Iain, for all the love, support, and patience required to be married to me. For never saying no to any adventure, no matter how mad or selfish.

And to my sister, Lorna, to whom I have dedicated this book. Thank you for never once rolling your eyes when I turned up to yet another holiday with yet another A4 binder of pages for you to read. Thank you for always reading them. And thank you, most of all, for being the very best friend a sister could ever have.

And last but absolutely not least, thank you to every reader of this story, of all stories. This book would never have become a book without you.

MIRRORLAND

Carole Johnstone

This reading group guide for *Mirrorland* includes an introduction, discussion questions, and ideas for enhancing your book club. The suggested questions are intended to help your reading group find new and interesting angles and topics for your discussion. We hope that these ideas will enrich your conversation and increase your enjoyment of the book.

Introduction

Cat lives in Los Angeles, far away from 36 Westeryk Road, the imposing gothic house in Edinburgh where she and her estranged twin sister, El, grew up. As girls, they invented Mirrorland, a dark, imaginary place under the pantry stairs, full of pirates, witches, and clowns. These days, Cat rarely thinks about their childhood home, or the fact that El now lives there with her husband, Ross.

But when El mysteriously disappears after going out on her sailboat, Cat is forced to return to 36 Westeryk Road, which has scarcely changed in twenty years. The grand old house is still full of shadowy corners, and at every turn Cat finds herself stumbling on long-held secrets and terrifying ghosts from the past. Because someone—El?—has left Cat clues in almost every room: a treasure hunt that leads right back to Mirrorland, where she knows the truth lies crouched and waiting . . .

A twisty, dark, and brilliantly crafted thriller about love and betrayal, redemption and revenge, *Mirrorland* is a propulsive, page-turning debut about the power of imagination and the price of freedom.

Topics & Questions for Discussion

1. In the prologue, we meet twin sisters Cat and El, who've run to the harbor at night to join a pirate ship. How do we begin to sense that this is more than a childish lark? What about the dynamic between the girls? What can you tell about their relationship?

2. Describe your first impression of 36 Westeryk Road. Why is Cat unnerved to see the same furniture from when she was a child? How do the features of the house—the echoing bell pulls, the fantastically named bedrooms—create a particular atmosphere? Is there a moment that frightened you caused by something in the house?

3. When Cat first returns to Mirrorland, she says, "As the creak of that old wood settles and suffocates, I wonder if my nervous excitement is merely the ghost of the child I once was" (page 46). Why did Cat and El create Mirrorland? What were they trying to find there?

4. The girls' mother, Nancy, explains to her daughters that they are mirror twins. How does this shape their sense of self? How do they seem the same, and how are they different, physically and psychologically?

5. Loving and fierce, Nancy is a complicated figure throughout the course of the novel, a woman who's always thinking one step ahead and yet sleeps in a frilly room called the Princess Tower. How did your initial impression of her change as more of the girls' childhood was revealed?

6. On page 77, we meet many of the characters of Mirrorland: "El and Ross were sitting cross-legged in the Captain's Quarters. In

the stern stood Annie, Mouse, Belle, and Old Joe Johnson, the barkeep of the Three-Fingered-Joe Saloon. The Clown representative, to my dismay, was not Dicky Grock, but Pogo." How did you imagine these characters visually? Did you feel they were there to harm or help?

7. How do Ross's experiences as a young boy affect how he behaves with Cat and El? Why do you think he became a psychologist? How did the way you felt about Ross change throughout the book?

8. On page 107, Cat says about Mouse, "Because she'd always really been my friend, not El's. The Mouse to my Cat. My creation." As the character of Mouse evolves, how does Cat's perception of Mouse shift? What do you make of Mouse in the end?

9. At first, we see El from almost entirely Cat's perspective. Does Cat seem like a reliable narrator? How does El's voice make itself heard?

10. "But this house and our mother and her stories turned our imagination into a melting pot, a forge. A cauldron. And, I'm beginning to realize, I can trust nothing that came out of it," Cat observes about their childhood (page 135). As the treasure hunt clues force Cat to confront buried truths and secrets, were you surprised by how much was revealed and how successfully she'd managed to live a lie for so long? Did it make you question any of your own memories?

11. Rafiq is determined to solve the mystery of El's disappearance; Cat is determined to solve the mystery of their past. How did the narrative balance those two quests? When did they start to overlap?

12. *Mirrorland* offers several twists and turns. As a reader, which one was the most shocking to you? Which developments did you expect, and which ones took you by complete surprise?

Enhance Your Book Club

1. *Mirrorland* is in some ways a novel of escape. Read Stephen King's novella *Rita Hayworth and Shawshank Redemption* or Alexandre Dumas's *The Count of Monte Cristo* and compare and contrast their escape narratives. Why were these stories so inspiring to Cat and El? Why do you think the author chose quotes from these two works for *Mirrorland*'s epigraph?

2. *Mirrorland* features a grand old house with such a strong, haunting presence that it almost becomes a character in the story. Compare and contrast 36 Westeryk Road with the house in *Rebecca* or *The Haunting of Hill House* or *The Witch Elm* or another film or novel of your choosing featuring a spooky, atmospheric house.

3. Much of *Mirrorland* is devoted to the idea of how children use imaginative play to understand mature, adult situations. Were there concepts or situations that you created myths or misunderstandings around when you were young and that you had to revisit when you grew older?